TOMORROW I SHALL WALK TO
THE SECRET GARDEN

What is it that compells me? I can only say that I have a sense of new beginnings. Is it just the spring? Or do I perhaps hope, somewhere in the dried depths of my soul, that Colin's Magic may work again if I go back there?

Hidden away behind walls of deep red brick, the only entrance concealed by thickets of ivy, it truly was a secret place. Sensing that the poignancy of the contrast between what ought to have been and what is would be too painful, I have only been there once in all these years. *I'm going to live forever and ever and ever,* Colin said, the first time Dickon and I pushed his wheeled-chair through the doorway. . . .

Now that you've read *Return to the Secret Garden*,
return to the original classic of wonder and enchantment . . .

THE
SECRET
GARDEN

Francis Hodgson Burnett

"When Mary Lennox was sent to Misselthwaite manor to live with her
uncle, everybody said she was the most disagreeable-looking child ever
seen." So begins one of the best-loved stories in the world. The tale
of a lonely girl, orphaned and sent to a Yorkshire mansion at the edge
of a vast lonely moor, is a story that touches on the feelings of children
eveywhere. *The Secret Garden* opens the door not only into a real
hidden garden, but into the innermost places of the heart. It has left
generations of readers with warm, lifelong memories of its very special
charms. **With an afterward by Faith McNulty.**   (525817—$3.95)

"**A blend of power, beauty, vivid interest and honest goodness.
Yes, if this is magic, it is good magic.**"
—*New York Times*

Return to the
Secret Garden

Susan Moody

Previously published as
Misselthwaite

A SIGNET BOOK

SIGNET
Published by the Penguin Group
Penguin Putnam Inc., 375 Hudson Street,
New York, New York 10014, U.S.A.
Penguin Books Ltd, 27 Wrights Lane,
London W8 5TZ, England
Penguin Books Australia Ltd, Ringwood,
Victoria, Australia
Penguin Books Canada Ltd, 10 Alcorn Avenue,
Toronto, Ontario, Canada M4V 3B2
Penguin Books (N.Z.) Ltd, 182–190 Wairau Road,
Auckland 10, New Zealand

Penguin Books Ltd, Registered Offices:
Harmondsworth, Middlesex, England

Published by Signet, an imprint of Dutton Signet,
a member of Penguin Putnam Inc.
Previously published in Great Britain by BCA, by arrangement with Hodder
and Stoughton, under the title *Misselthwaite*.

First Signet Printing, February, 1998
10 9 8 7 6 5 4 3 2 1

 REGISTERED TRADEMARK—MARCA REGISTRADA

Printed in the United States of America

PUBLISHER'S NOTE
This is a work of fiction. Names, characters, places, and incidents either are
the product of the author's imagination or are used fictitiously, and any resemblance to actual persons, living or dead, events, or locales is entirely
coincidental.

BOOKS ARE AVAILABLE AT QUANTITY DISCOUNTS WHEN USED TO PROMOTE
PRODUCTS OR SERVICES. FOR INFORMATION PLEASE WRITE TO PREMIUM MAR-
KETING DIVISION, PENGUIN PUTNAM INC., 375 HUDSON STREET, NEW YORK, NEW
YORK 10014.

In memory of my mother,
Kym Horwood,
who first led me to the Secret Garden,
and
with grateful thanks to
Frances Hodgson Burnett,
who created it

MARY

Uncertainty is the worst of diseases. Now that I know, my heart is easier than it has been for many days. And lighter.

Freedom. At last. The words float into my mind. It is not so much that I am weary of living, nor am I eager to die. But since leaving is inevitable, I have always hoped that mine would be quick.

Pulling open the long windows, I step out on to the terrace. Winter, dying, rushes to meet me. Despite the chill, the buds below me have pushed out of the dull earth between the low box hedges of the parterre, are swelling along the branches of the lilacs which sit against the walls. Tentative almond blossom trembles on black branches. I think that tomorrow, I shall walk to the secret garden, although this afternoon, the wind is acidly cold, gnawing at my face, and in the distance, trees churn. Beyond lie the moors.

I never grow tired of them. Green shading to brown, becoming gradually purple-gray. Now that spring is at last upon us, they are golden with gorse. When the sky changes, they change too. Shadows scud across them. The grass ripples like the surface of a lake. Sometimes they seem close enough to touch; at other times they float like distant islands. For most of my life they have remained a constant when so much else has proved inconstant, fickle. Not least myself. I think of my lost loves and wonder how I could have acted differently, given who I was, given the forces which shaped me.

My thoughts are melancholy. I wish I believed in God. In an afterlife, where we three might meet again. But I do not. As Richard used to say, this could be as good as it is going to get. The trouble is that without them, it can never be good enough.

The wind comes at me again, carrying snow on its bitter breath. This may be my last winter. I want to let it swirl and live around me. I want to embrace it, rejoicing in the cold. I want to be embraced. Instead, tamely, I step back inside and close the door. As I twist the brass catch, the ring on my finger taps against the windowpanes. It is loose now, where once it was tight. Made of three kinds of gold: rose and white and yellow, the three intertwined into a single strand, indivisible. As *we* were.

Somewhere deep within the house there are the servants, and soon Norah will bring me tea, pale oolong in a silver pot, two thin biscuits, one of the delicate oriental cups. Norah is as much a part of this house as I am. Should I tell her what the doctor predicts for me, when she comes with the tray? Or shall I leave it for a while? I do not wish to be fussed over. I do not want to see tears, for tears there will undoubtedly be. Norah is a sentimental creature, quite belying the image of dourness which attaches to people from this part of the world. If I tell, she will not alter her routines. As always, she will set down the tray beside me, then plump the cushions, pull the curtains snug, switch on lamps to make the room comfortable against the cold which clamors at the windows. But each action will no longer be itself, it will have become a symbol of all that will so soon cease to be, heavied with anticipated grief.

It is possible, of course, that she already knows. Up here, in this isolated spot, it is impossible to live privately, to keep one's business to oneself. There is little else to do except to speculate on one's fellows, and while I do not generally mind this, since no one has so far managed to penetrate further into my privacy than I am prepared to allow, nonetheless, if it is possible, I myself should like to choose the moment when she learns about my condition.

Norah arrives. I am relieved to see her. Introspection leads too easily into self-pity. From her expression, I deduce that she does not yet know of the sentence which has been passed on me. And as she pulls at the curtains, shutting out the darkening afternoon, as she reaches beneath lampshades to turn on lights, I decide that today is not the time to tell her. Leaning back in my armchair, I close my eyes, tired.

"Miss Mary!" she exclaims suddenly, the old-fashioned address which she has never been able to throw off. Childish voices jeer in my mind: *Mistress Mary, quite contrary,* and opening my eyes again, I see her looking up at me over her shoulder as light from the oriental lamp on the side table illumines my face.

"What is it?"

"You look right poorly."

"Nonsense, woman."

"Best have a nap before dinner."

"Don't fuss at me, Norah. You know how I hate it."

She hovers about me, a big comfortable woman, my servant, if that is not too emotive a word in these egalitarian times, and my would-be friend. Why do I say would-be? Not from any perception of class or social position. It is simply my nature to be closed against friendship, and I am unlikely now to change. Norah reminds me of the Holman Hunt painting I saw once in Oxford: *The Light of the World.* She stands at my door, the lantern of kindness in her hand, knocking at my heart for entrance. Often I think that I would let her in, were it not for those others. They were my friends and I want, I need, no one else.

"But you're shivering, Miss Mary."

"That's because I had the windows open."

"What? In this cold?"

I almost tell her, then. Almost explain about the wish to submerge myself in winter, the *notion* of winter, because it is possibly the last I shall see. Instead, I say crossly: "The room was so stuffy, Norah. Is the chimney smoking?"

She stares at me shrewdly, knowing as well as I that the chimneys at Misselthwaite do not smoke, that like everything else here, they are maintained and looked after, regularly cleaned, just as the carpets are swept, the lusters on the chandelier are washed, the furniture polished, the fabrics dry-cleaned, the leather tops of the library tables kept supple, even though this whole big house is occupied by one elderly lady and the people paid to look after her. "Don't be daft," she says, robustly but her voice has changed and I know that in a minute she will begin to ask questions I shall find it difficult to evade.

"Tomorrow, I intend to go round the gardens," I say, commandingly, heading her off.

"You'll not see much, then," she says, placing the fragile cup beside my chair, adding a slice of lemon as sheer as an insect's wing.

"Nonetheless, I need to know how they're coming along." And, if I am not too tired, inspect the public gardens. Despite the persistent chill of winter, spring is already here and they must be readied for display. Three times a year, they are thrown open to the public, for charitable purposes. It is important that things are right. For an extra fee, people may visit part of the house. It always astonishes me, the avidity with which they are prepared to pay in order to examine the domestic trivia of other lives, even though the picture painted by such details as they are permitted to see is not a true one. When I first arrived here, I was told that there were a hundred rooms. This is, in fact, not so, but the house is large and, in former years, was entirely occupied by Cravens and their attendant households. Gradually, as the line of descent grew thinner, as families of fourteen gave way to four or three or even, in the final years, one, the house began to be closed up, bit by bit. When I was a child here, my guardian-uncle used rooms in the West Wing for himself while we were kept to the East Wing. Even so, there was space enough for a substantial household. But in recent years, my husband and I used little more than half a dozen rooms. This sitting room, of course, and a couple of bedrooms. The library. The dining room, and the large drawing room, for such formal occasions as there were. And the parlor on the other side of the wing, where, if I am up early enough, I like to sit and enjoy the morning sun.

The gardens are kept up, of course. Once they have paid, people are allowed to wander through the grounds as they please, apart from certain clearly defined areas. One of these is the walled garden full of roses which we used to call the secret garden.

"It's mostly brown earth and dead leaves out there at

the moment," Norah says. "Besides, even if there's blossom and new leaves, the wind's like to tear your face off, if you aren't careful."

"I must take a look at the Great Palm House," I say. "According to Allerton, part of the roof needs some work, and he can't do anything until I've seen it." The Great Palm House is one of the main attractions of the Misselthwaite gardens, a huge trefoil of glass and cast-iron, filled with a jungle of plants and exotic flowers.

"I suppose you'll be shinning up ladders, wanting to fix it yourself," she answers, lifting the hinged lid of the silver teapot and fiercely adding water. I remember Richard, home on leave, saying that Norah was good at being fierce.

At the thought of him, a sudden gush of pain washes over me, molten as lava, so radical that I almost swoon. It is not a physical pain but an emotional one. I am seized with the wish that things were other than they are. For Colin's sake, if not for my own, I so much wanted the line to carry on, things to continue as they always have. "Don't be ridiculous, Norah." I speak sharply, for I can see that she does indeed suspect something.

"What did the doctor say?" she asks, and I am touched by the concern in her voice.

"What he has said for the past ten years." I affect ennui. Yes, he has told me yet again that I cannot fight the ageing process. But this afternoon, he added more.

"Those tests," says Norah.

"What about them?"

"Didn't he tell you what the results were? I thought that was why you drove yourself all the way to Thwaite, on a freezing winter's day, in spite of me wanting to get him out here."

"Dr. Craven is a busy man. And I went for my usual checkups, Norah. That is all." I hope I have achieved the right tone of slight concern. Anything less, and she, who knows me so well, will be aware that I am keeping something back. Anything more, and she will call upon that extensive network of friends and relations which keeps her supplied with the most up-to-date information, despite the fact that we live five miles from the nearest habitation, ten from the nearest metropolis.

I use the word ironically: Middleburn is our market town, but hardly a center of activity and excitement, though there is a cinema, and a glorious old theater, one of the last of the provincial playhouses left in the country, gilded and swagged in red velvet, with clouds and cupids and simpering naked ladies painted on the ceiling.

"You think I don't know," she grumbles, leaning over to poke the fire so that she does not have to face me.

"Don't know what?" It is obvious that she knows nothing. Had she done so, she would have been more direct.

"That you're not well."

"I'm as well as I've ever been," I say and in one way, it is true.

"You ought to be taking it quietly. Especially now."

She is right, of course. Last month, my husband was buried in the Misselthwaite chapel. He would have been pleased at the number of his parliamentary colleagues from both sides of the House who made the long journey from London, even though a memorial service will be held later, in Westminster Abbey. It was not a shock, nor unexpected: he had been ill for many months. Nonetheless, now that he, too, has gone, I am overwhelmed by mental exhaustion.

Sometime soon, I must make a decision about whether to stay here at Misselthwaite, or to hand it on to the heir and his family. There is no need for me to go: the will makes sure of that. Nor do I wish to. Yet is it fair of me to stay? I think I should feel like a usurper. If only Richard were here . . . but such thoughts are a weakness, and I have always tried to ignore them.

I love this room. Little has changed since I first entered it, as a child of ten. The covers have been refurbished, the walls painted, but essentially, it is as I saw it for the first time, ushered into the presence of my guardian. A scrawny yellow thing I was, too. Sallow-faced, liverish, my spirit as deformed as his body. Both of us, though we did not know it then, grieving. Both of us lost.

Above the gray-veined marble mantel hangs the picture of the plain, stiff child who reminded me so much of myself. She captured my imagination from the first time I saw her. The green of her brocade dress matches the green feathers of the parrot who clings to her finger; she has Colin's eyes. Today, the green seems brighter, the gray of her eyes more intense. As does the gloss of the polished oak table in the window embrasure, the glimmer of light through the teardrops which hang from the glass lampshades, the pink of the roses which spatter the linen covers of the armchairs. The inlaid boxes, the bronze statues, the hummingbird under its dome, all seem to have become more intensely themselves. Is it only the prospect of my approaching death which imbues them with this marvelous accentuation, this enhancement of sensation, so that wood and bronze are transmuted into feeling, color and light grow concrete?

In the window bay is the Irish Chippendale card table which belonged to my guardian's paternal grandmother. On it stands a large box of ebony, intricately carved, inlaid with mother-of-pearl and ivory. I never knew whether it had belonged to my father or my mother, whether it was a gift from one to another and therefore imbued with some sense of their relationship, or whether it was simply an object they possessed, one among many, without personal significance. But it had come with me to England as part of my baggage and, because I had so little connection with them, I gave it a history of its own. A present from him to her, I liked to think, seen and coveted as they strolled together through some Indian bazaar. Perhaps her eye had lighted on it and she had expressed a wish that it were hers. Or perhaps he had noted it among a hundred other objects of brass and wood and silk and, without mentioning it to her, had gone back for it later, in order to present it to her on her birthday. She would have been dressed all in floating white, a fringed parasol on her shoulder, her face smiling beneath a wide hat. And he would have been wearing the regimental dress, the tight trousers and red jacket with brass buttons, his handsome features bright with his love.

She was beautiful. I know this not merely from photographs and portraits, but because I was so frequently told when I was a child, generally with the implication that I myself did not resemble her in the least. Also, I remember how much I used to enjoy looking at her. Standing at the doorway of her bedroom as she dressed

to go out, her thin, floaty dresses full of lace, her white
arms lifting, the graceful curve of them, the glitter of the
bracelets which slid down them when she patted the
thick curly folds of her beautiful hair. It did not worry
me to be unfavorably compared with her. I have never
been vain, and at first it seemed perfectly right and fitting that I should be plain, just as it added to my valua-
tion of myself to be the daughter of a beautiful mother.
Later, when I might have minded, too many people
made it clear that, in fact, I was not as plain in their
eyes as I perceived myself to be. I believe, from other
things told to me, that she was a silly frivolous creature,
more interested in clothes and parties and flirtations
than she was in her child, but though I passionately re-
sented this at one time, I now understand that we all
have some purpose in life. Perhaps my mother's was
simply to please others by her charm and beauty. And
what is wrong with that?

That pretty, pretty woman—I remember someone saying that to Barney as they walked through the cholera-
devastated bungalow toward the nursery where I had
been left alone. He was in love with her, of course. So
many of the officers were.

But I hate this looking back. One of the indignities of
being old is that the present never seems as good as the
past. What is unforgivable is the way the old insist on
saying so. Even with so short a time left to me, I intend
to look forward, I must go on expecting things to
burgeon.

The ebony box. A hundred times have I held its contents; indulged in a thousand memories over the long
years. It houses the usual paraphernalia of recollection.
Among these are faded photographs. Letters. A bird's
nest with a single egg cupped in the smooth interior. A
string of cheap blue beads. Yellowed newspaper cuttings.
A diamond ring. Keys. A faded flower. Three tarnished
medals on a strip of rainbowed grosgrain. A delicate
bracelet of thin gold chain, made for a baby's wrist. And
diaries, though not mine, for I have never seen the sense
in writing down what has already passed. I have read
them often and each time I am moved to tears as I see
myself on those pages, the self I used to be. Such hurt
I inflicted. Such unnecessary pain. If only we could go

back, re-knead the dough of the past, form it into different shapes.

More than anything, I would like to have told them how much I loved them. Not in the throes of passion, where such exclamations are part of the whole experience and therefore have no real existence of their own. But soberly, standing with one of them on the terrace, watching the cloud-shadows move across the moors, or walking with the other beneath the big trees in the park, watching as he whistled to the birds. Giving the words their due significance because they came out of nowhere, unprecipitated by the touch of beloved skin. *I love you.* Would saying it have made any difference?

They knew. They must have known. But it would give me such satisfaction to be able to remember that, if only once, I had said those words I was never able then to articulate. *I love you.* From my current vantage point, they seem to me, now, to be the most necessary words one human being can say to another. Love was there, inside me. Sometimes it was almost released. For a while, indeed, it flourished, in the springtime when the three of us first came together. But with the frosts, the winters of tragedy, it withered again. Sometimes I envisage my heart as a dried-up seed pod, dead within my breast, waiting for rain. It is too late: there can be no rain for me now.

For years the days have simply passed and I have done no more than survive them. Nor do I regret my lack of purpose, of action. Nothing before, or since, has ever meant as much to me as those two did, separately or together. Not marriage or children, not love or money or war. Richard, of course, I adored. But I have come to see that he was the symbol, merely, of a happiness I did not deserve. As for Misselthwaite, I have done my duty, and done it because I wished to. But without them, it has become an egg without salt, a dish without savor. Sometimes the sadness of things overwhelms me. My heart pains me so. I feel that if I could reach inside my breast, I could pull it out, as thin and pale as the biscuits Norah brings me each afternoon, and snap it in two.

The loneliness I feel is my punishment, I imagine, for the lack of consideration I showed them. There is noth-

ing I can do now except endure it for as long as I
have to.

Since my husband came home to die, I have had difficulty sleeping. Night after night, I come down to this
room, to be among my familiar things. Touching them,
my fingertips are passionate: I long to draw back into
myself the emotions these objects once possessed. Love,
laughter, happiness. In my old age, I had hoped to have
laughter nearby. I had hoped to have someone to love,
someone who would love me. It is always assumed that
passion dies as the years pass, but this is a fallacy. Urgency may fade, but never the fire in the blood. To die
unloved strikes me, now, as a terrible fate. Norah loves
me, in her own way, I know that. But it is not the same.
I had love, and I chased it away. Not just once. I had
laughter and through pigheadedness, through stupidity,
through my own damned bloody-mindedness, I chose to
let it go. I want another chance.

I can hear the wind on the moors. Wuthering, Martha—Dickon's sister—used to call it. A lonely sound
when the heart is lonely too. It grumbles in the chimney,
and the flames stagger momentarily, as though pounded
by invisible fists. Smoke billows outward from beneath
the marble mantel and curls slowly up and around the
objects which sit upon it: the china spill-holder, the framed
photographs, the carved ivory elephants, the heart-
shaped Victorian pin cushion, the candlesticks. It drifts
higher, briefly obscuring the face of the child with the
parrot on her finger. Who was she? Nobody is sure,
though family tradition has it that she was Lady Caroline
Leighton, painted to mark the occasion of her betrothal
to Edward Craven, who later perished on Bodmin Moor.
I prefer not to know. When I first came to this house as
a child, first saw this portrait, I hoped I might find the
parrot still in residence, for I had read somewhere that
parrots can live for centuries. I was to be disappointed
but later, up in the attics, I came across trunkfuls of
clothes which had belonged to Craven ladies, and wondered if the wide-brimmed hat trimmed with green
feathers was all that remained of poor Polly. I wore the
hat once, at a party in London.

The wind sweeps around the house. It prowls, impatient at the shutters, dangerous among the chimneys. Such force. So strong can it be up here, that when I was smaller it was possible sometimes to lean back on it and be upheld. I have climbed the fells about here and felt it huge against my body, almost believed it capable of lifting me and carrying me off. Somewhere in the house a door bangs. Norah? I hope not. If she realizes I am down here, instead of asleep in bed, she will interrupt me. She will fuss. I feel that I cannot waste time in sleeping. I want to remember, to relive, to return to that time when the three of us were still together. Not because I believe those times to have necessarily been better than the times are today, but because, for me, I was most alive then, and there was so much promise in the air. Until I deliberately chose to extinguish it.

This room has become my envelope. Gradually, over the years, I have added my favorite pieces to its original furniture. Nothing which would change it from what it had been on my first visit, but enough to suggest that here, almost, is the living history of the child I once was, the woman I later became, the dessicated husk I have grown into. My favorite books line the shelves. The frame which holds my embroidery, not yet discarded for my eyesight has remained keen, leans against the arm of the sofa. In the rolltop desk are paper knives I was given twenty or thirty years ago, when books arrived from the bookseller with their pages still uncut. Who, today, can imagine the pleasure which lay in slitting those thick edges, the heightened anticipation bestowed by the enforced pause at the bottom of each page. Colin used to cut all the pages before he started to read, but I never could do that. In the desk, too, is the shagreen cigarette box he bought me in Paris and the fountain pen I have used all my life to sign my letters. The paintings I like best hang from the picture rail. In the pigeonholes of the desk is my correspondence, both sent and received, and my ancient typewriter.

Most of the major events of my life have taken place here. Starting with that first momentous one, when my uncle-guardian asked if I would like anything, expecting a conventional answer of dolls or books or toys, and I, swallowing hard, quavered out a request for the only thing I really wanted. "Might I have a bit of earth?" I asked, for already, by then, the blossoming of Mary Lennox had begun.

Might I have a bit of earth? He was startled, as well he might be. A queer knobbly sort of child I was, and no doubt he found it difficult to encompass me.

The clock on the mantel—a black marble object with doric columns, liturgical numbers and solemn filigreed hands—strikes three. Three in the morning. It seems, at the same time, so late and so early. I remember other nights when I have sat up like this, here in this house. I think of poor Barney. It was not so long ago that I read his obituary in *The Times*. Amazing that he should, after all, have lasted so long. Would I ever have gone back to India, if it had not been for the coincidence of his presence here, in the hospital? And if I had not, would it have made any difference?

I think of the little girl. Even after all these years, the memory aches, yet she was much too small for me to have established any kind of relationship with her. It was a lack in me of which I was always aware. Until Richard. My son . . .

No use. No use hankering for what might have been. It is far too late now. I have made my own bed and now I must lie in it. Nonetheless, I look over at the desk, at the typewriter, at my pen in its special alabaster tray, at paper and envelopes, lying there on the leather top, asking, almost pleading to be written upon. If only I knew where to write.

Is it too late?

The ebony box calls me to open it yet again, to take out my souvenirs. To remember. I do not want to do this. Partly because it will be painful, partly because I have done it so often in the past. The only way to escape the straitjacket of age is to continue to look forward. To make the heart anticipate, however strongly the brain tries to insist that there is nothing except a dwindling future to wait for. I hold my hands toward the flames and the ring on my finger grows suddenly warm, then startlingly hot, a band of fire.

"I don't want to live . . ." I begin, aloud, then stop, abruptly. The curse of loneliness, this, the not remembering whether the others you want to talk to are with you or absent. If there were a choice, I would vote for euthanasia. Who cares, now, about the life Mary Lennox has lived, or will grieve when she departs it? Oh, Norah will, of course. And maybe one or two others. But the ones I *want* to grieve will not be there. "Will you come to my funeral?" we used to ask each other. "Will you be sure to be there? Do you *promise?*"

That was Colin. He was always keen on promises, not realizing that promises can be—all too frequently are— broken. I did not break my promise to him. I was there.

Who will come to mine?

One of the portraits in the library shows an Elizabethan Craven. He wears black doublet and hose, velvet slashed with silver. His expression is melancholy. A skull stands upon the table against which he is leaning. A lighted candle, almost consumed, is set in a pewter stick, next to an hourglass where the sand has almost run out. He is the same Craven who kept a coffin beside the marital bed. Such morbidity. I do not need reminders of that sort. Death has always walked beside me. I have no fear.

Tomorrow, I shall walk to the secret garden.

What is it that compels me? I can only say that I have a sense of new beginnings. Is it just the spring? Or do I perhaps hope, somewhere in the dried depths of my soul, that Colin's Magic may work again if I go back there?

Hidden away behind walls of deep red brick, the only entrance concealed by thickets of ivy, it truly was a secret place. Sensing that the poignancy of the contrast between what ought to have been and what is would be too painful, I have only been there once in all these years. *I'm going to live forever and ever and ever,* Colin said, the first time we pushed his wheeled-chair through the doorway. Even thinking about it makes my heart unexpectedly race. I press a hand to my breast and long, so deeply, for everything to be different. The last time we three were together was in the secret garden, ten— no, twelve (is it already so long?) years ago. And today there are no little Marys, no Colins and Dickons, to bring it back to life.

We always kept it wild, clematis and honeysuckle twining together, lavender bushes unclipped, lilacs shoot-

ing off wherever they wished to go, buzzing with bees.
The gray stone urns were filled and overflowing. The
smell of clove pinks filled the air, and the sweet scent
of gorse from the moors. I was always happy there—
until the day when Dickon came walking toward me between the apple trees and, seeing his face, I understood
that I could never be happy again.

Ah well. Happiness is supposed to be ephemeral, is it
not? Would I have made more effort to retain it while
it was mine, if I had known how little of it I was to
have? Or would I just as wilfully have thrown it away,
as I threw so many precious things away? Except for
those in the ebony box.

I touch the inlaid ivory which decorates the top. An
elephant, set in a circle of leaves. There is a howdah on
its back and a turbanned rajah sits inside, spear at the
ready. Around it are geometric patterns of mother-of-
pearl. I cannot resist it. Prevaricating, I carefully roll
back the tambour lid of the desk and take a cigarette
from the green leather box. A bad habit. One I took up
after the Great War—though there was singularly little
that was great about it—and have never shaken off.
Have, indeed, never wanted to.

The ebony box waits. I lift the lid. I breathe in the
shadowy scent of the sandalwood with which the box is
lined and see my mother again, in her white frothy
dresses. The bird's nest sits plump in my hand. Even
after all these years, the moss woven in among the twigs
is still green. These objects are like a hair shirt, endlessly
abrasive. Why do I not throw them away, accept that
the past is past, that it cannot be changed? While I save
them like this, shut away inside the box, I cannot forget
all that has gone before. I cannot cease to ask forgiveness of those who are not here to bestow it. Perhaps the
very fact that I have *not* thrown away these objects
whose only worth is in their connection with what no
longer is, implies that I need to keep on doing so. An
endless cycle of remorse. I pick up the blue beads. I
wind them around my wrist. There are blotches on my
hands, now, and a small purplish bruise beneath the skin.
I touch the tiny crumpled note, the awkward writing
which time has almost erased: *I will cum bak.* Dickon's
first letter to me. But he will not come back. Not now.

Again I speak aloud. "Do you remember . . . ?" I say.
But I am alone still and there is no one left to share my
memories. I am buried in this room. Entombed. I have
conferred upon myself a living death. For a moment I
am ready to weep, though I despise such weaknesses
and try to prevent myself from giving way to them.

From the oak press I take a glass and pour brandy
which I sip slowly, enjoying the sensation as it makes its
heady way down my throat. Smoke from my cigarette
palls the air. I laugh aloud. Living death. Entombed.
What nonsense. Have I really grown so melodramatic in
my final years that I can seriously entertain such
notions?

Earlier this evening, when Norah came in to check the
fire, I was sitting at the Steinway. A green vase was
reflected in its black case, holding leaves of preserved
beech. Copper, such a rich color, like the skins of onions.
Once, I played well, but for a long while I did not keep
it up, and then found how difficult it can be to regain a
wilfully discarded skill. She came over and needlessly
began to straighten the fringed Indian shawl which lay
across the piano's end. Something was weighing on her
mind.

"What?" I said, with a repressive downward inflection.

"Are you all right, Miss Mary?"

"I am perfectly fine, thank you."

"Because if you're not, how would I feel to hear it
from a stranger?"

"Your feelings are a matter on which I am not compe-
tent to judge," I said. My voice was disdainful, even
rude. I intensely dislike discourtesy, particularly in myself. I got up and walked across to the door. It is a
beautiful room, one of the few in the house which re-
flects my own taste, rather than that of the generations
of Cravens who lived here before me. A double cube,
ornately plastered ceiling, fine white marble fireplaces,
walls painted a deep leaf-green, furnishings yellow and
green and white. A great many plants everywhere, big
ones, flowing from pots set on columns or standing on
the green carpet. I wanted to blur the distinction between outside and in, especially once we had added the

big conservatory which attaches to one end of the room and is almost a continuation of it.

"There's no sense in keeping things bottled up, Miss Mary." Her voice came after me, pleading, but I ignored it.

Sense? What does sense have to do with anything? Where, for example, was the sense in that terrifying, bloody, debilitating war? "It'll be over by Christmas." Archibald Craven said that, right at the beginning. And Colin answered, throwing back the thick hair from his forehead, looking at me with the eyes of the girl with the green parrot on her finger: "It won't be over for years."

He was right, of course. Deliberately prolonged, some said, simply because they did not know how to get the fighting men home, or what to do with them when they got here. Those years changed us forever. My generation, my country. My Dickon. Him most of all.

Beyond the tall windows, the sky behind the moors is beginning to lighten. Flush of pink. The palest of creams. Like a rose. A blush rose. *Tha'lt be like a blush-rose when tha' grows up,* Dickon's mother said.

Soon it will be dawn. And then I shall go again to the secret garden.

1

Archibald Craven leaned his head heavily on his hand. Behind him, Pitcher bustled, clearing plates. The old man's clothes gave off a stale smell, unpleasant yet made familiar by long custom. Between his fingers Archie surveyed the dining-table and tried not to remember the cottages he had visited earlier in the day.

"I'm so terribly sorry," he had said three times that afternoon. "He was a fine man. A fine man." At each house, he had been offered a cup of strong-brewed tea, a fresh-baked scone on the best china; on the other side of the table, a stricken woman clutched a handkerchief and held back tears. Three different women, yet all reacting to his visit in the same way. They, and the others he had visited yesterday, the ones he would call on next week, presented an identical front, whether they faced him as mother, as wife, as sister or as daughter. In their eyes he saw always the same pain, the same anxiety for the future. He was exhausted by so much contained grief. It would have been easier if they broke down, if he could have offered comfort beyond the convention of words, if he could have reached out, felt the contact of human flesh beneath the shawls or the sleeves. Instead, they avoided his eye, twisting their handkerchief, fussing with teapots or children. It was as though demonstrated grief was something shameful, to be suppressed.

The woman on his right was speaking. ". . . so kind of you, Mr. Craven."

He pulled himself together, came back to the present and the dinner party he was hosting. "My dear Miss Ensleigh, it is the very least we can do."

Miss Ensleigh, the matron in charge of the convales-

cent hospital which had been set up in the West Wing
of Misselthwaite Manor, was a handsome woman, with
fine fair skin. He wondered why she had not married.
Perhaps she was yet another casualty of this war. Perhaps a fiancé lay dead in the mud of Flanders or the
trenches of Armentières.

"They do seem to be enjoying themselves." She stared
along the table and sighed. "Not that you can always
tell."

The English attitude, thought Archie. Like the be-
reaved women up and down the Dale, the men seated
at his table tonight gave no indication of the horrors
they had been through at the Front, showed little if any
of the pain some of them, at least, must have been feeling. Lost limbs. Torn flesh. Black patches over empty
eye sockets. Along with most of England, he had at first
believed the propaganda, accepted the necessity for this
war. Not any more.

The long table stretched away from him, crisply ta-
blecothed in damask worn thin and brittle as tissue
paper. Silver glinted in the light from the candles. The
Waterford glass shone. Gold rimmed Coalport plates,
each one decorated with a different hand-painted rose.
How many times, he thought, for how many years, have
I sat here, at its head? Tradition, custom, continuation:
I can never decide whether these things are meaningless,
or whether they are the very stuff of life itself.

Tonight, Pitcher had pulled out all the stops. Despite
the difficulties and deprivations imposed by the war, the
impressive standards expected from a formal dinner at
the Manor had somehow been maintained. Halfway
down the table sat his niece, Mary. The child was looking well this evening; she had obviously made an effort
for the sake of the wounded men invited tonight. He
had not seen her frock before: beaded green chiffon over
a blue underskirt, a kind of sea-green effect which suited
her blonde coloring. He thought vaguely of mermaids
and sea nymphs. She had taken her hair out of its usual
thick plait and put it up, which made her look altogether
different from the everyday Mary he was used to. As a
matter of fact, he had not fully registered until now quite
how grown up she already was. And how pretty she
might eventually be. It was the first time he had seen

any likeness in her to the feckless pretty creature who had been her mother. He supposed he must start to think about the mechanics of presenting her at Court—if such social niceties still continued after this damnable war was over.

So much investment lost, so much hope for the future gone. The blankness. Husbands. Sons. What must it be like to bear a child, to rear him, to love him, and then have him wiped out for what must seem the most futile of reasons? One cottage he had visited three times. Two fine sons gone, and a husband. The woman had one son left, fighting in France.

He touched his eyes with his hand and then gripped his mouth to still the shaking of his lips. The suffering . . .

He forced himself to concentrate on Mary. She was sitting next to the man Miss Ensleigh had earlier introduced as their newest arrival. Major Someone. Sandling? Shipbourne? He had been too concerned about the visits he had made earlier in the day to take in his name. Handsome, in a conventional English way: blue-eyed, fair-haired, his features very boyish under sun-bleached sandy eyebrows. His face was unnaturally pale, however, and the deep lines drawn around his mouth were those of pain rather than experience. Sambourne: that was the fellow's name. From an Indian regiment, originally. Called back to England and then sent to fight in the European theater.

Across from Mary sat his own son. Cowardly though the thought might be, unpatriotic, inglorious, a thousand times he had thanked God that Colin was too young to take part in this hellish business. He holds my heart in his hands, Archie thought suddenly. As his mother did before him. The thin young face above the formal dress-shirt and black tie shone with intelligence. The shock of black hair, the wide dark eyes, the mouth which moved perpetually to smile or argue or persuade. My son . . .

Colin was watching Mary. Although they were almost exactly the same age, she sometimes seemed ten years younger than he was. But perhaps she felt the same about him. His enthusiasms, for example: he knew they were childish but he could not help them. He had wasted the first ten years of his life lying in bed and he was afraid that however hard he tried, he would never catch up on all that he had missed.

He frowned. Usually Mary did not welcome admiring glances from men, especially ones as old as Major Sambourne, but tonight, for some reason, she was looking distinctly less stiff-necked and stony than she usually did. He hoped she was not smitten. Girls often were, according to the chaps at school. He doubted if any girls would ever be smitten with him: he was too odd-looking. Besides, they could probably tell that he did not really enjoy their company. At the local parties and dances which it was expected he would, as his father's son, attend, he always felt awkward. The girls he was supposed to partner seemed so ignorant, so uninformed. None of them was ever interested in any of the things which excited him. Was that the fault of their education? For a moment, he abandoned an earlier brilliant idea he had had of turning Misselthwaite into a center devoted to bringing leisure and pleasure to the working classes. Perhaps it would be more worthwhile to espouse the suffragette cause. Considered rationally, logically, it was outrageous that women did not yet have the vote. Was this his mission in life, after all? Rather than Colin Craven, Benefactor of the People, should he become Colin Craven, Emancipator?

Across the table, Mary laughed. Obviously the gallant major was amusing, as well as handsome. And a grown man, into the bargain, unlike Colin himself. What chance did a mere boy have against such competition? He thought of poor Faringdon, who had come to stay last Christmas and been so transparently keen on Mary. And then, inevitably and with pain, he thought of Dickon.

"Do you know," Major Sambourne suddenly said to the girl on his right; he had noticed her as soon as she entered the room and been delighted to find himself seated next to her at dinner, "you remind me tremendously of someone I used to know."

Mary smiled politely. "Do I?" He had no obvious disability; she wondered what was wrong with him that he should be convalescing at the hospital.

"Indeed you do." Major Sambourne drew in a quick breath and surreptitiously clutched at the seat of his chair, something solid to hold on to while he reorien-

tated himself. It happened more and more, this sudden
giddiness, this sense of not being quite sure who or
where he was. For a moment, talking to this delicious
young creature, he had almost seemed to be back in the
dust and heat of India, with the *memsahib* dead beneath
the muslin mosquito netting, still beautiful despite the
stench of sickness which hung about the room. He shook
his head hard. Since that blasted shell had landed so
close and scrambled his brains, shaking sometimes
seemed to be the only way to get his thoughts in order.
Like the kaleidoscopes they had had in the nursery as
children: shake them and the pattern changed. He gave
an unnecessary laugh.

The old butler was standing behind him, offering a
silver platter. Nausea moved faintly in his stomach but
he ignored it. Mutton, was it? Beef? It was hard to tell
the difference these days, since nothing seemed to have
any taste. Except drink. He picked up his empty wine
glass and put it down again before taking the silver
servers and helping himself to slices of bloody meat. It
was good to know that despite the war, standards were
being maintained, the old England was not yet dead, the
sacrifices had not been made in vain.

Mary looked along the table at Miss Ensleigh. When
they had met earlier, she had smiled, but in the matron's
expression there had been only—or so Mary imagined—
contempt. She knew why. At the end of term, instead
of coming straight back to Yorkshire, she had spent a
week in London, at Archie Craven's house in Fitzroy
Square. Shopping, the theater, meeting friends for lunch
or dinner: it had been a wonderfully frivolous way of
celebrating the end of term, of marking the freedom
from rising bells and dinner bells and end-of-lesson bells.
She had now been back at Misselthwaite for almost a
week and it would have been perfectly possible for her
to have gone over to the West Wing and volunteered to
help in some way. She could have read to the wounded
soldiers who were being cared for there. Written letters
for them. Served their meals. Even, much as she would
have hated it, scrubbed floors. Made herself useful in
some way. Instead, she had simply slouched about since
she got home. She was ashamed. She wished she had
put on one of her older dresses tonight, rather than this

new one. A vague idea of trying to look her best for the
soldiers who must have seen such horrors at the Front
had prompted her to wear it instead of something less
obviously fashionable: she could see that as far as Miss
Ensleigh was concerned, it was frivolous and a mistake.

She murmured something to the officer next to her.
Major Sambourne. He gave a quick meaningless laugh
and stared too hard into her eyes, until she felt thoroughly uncomfortable. He was probably suffering from
shellshock. She had read about it. Dulcie Lanchester,
one of the girls at school, had a brother who had been
sent home from the Front, suffering with his nerves. He
just sat in an armchair all day long, picking at things,
Dulcie said. Wouldn't go to bed. Drank whisky all night,
and screamed if anyone spoke above a whisper. Major
Sambourne did not look as if he sat about all day. Nor
could she imagine those strong blunt fingers picking,
picking—"anything," Dulcie said, "anything at all. Pick,
pick, pick. Tablecloths, bread, plants, books, he picks
them right to pieces."

"Where were you before you came here?" she asked.

Major Sambourne told her that his regiment had been
transferred from India to Africa and then to Gallipoli.
He said he had been slightly wounded there and sent
back to England, first to a military hospital at Haslemere
and then, just two days ago, up here. She did not ask
what his injuries were. Think of the horror if it were not
shellshock he was suffering from after all, but some
wound of a more intimate nature.

He was staring at her again. She wished he would
stop. She was not to know that the major did not see
her but another woman, one whose laughing eyes had
haunted him all through the war, whose image had remained in his heart as the ideal of womanhood. Never
mind that the eyes of this child seated next to him were
not laughing. Looked, in fact, as though they seldom did.
Never mind that although she was likely to be passably
pretty, she lacked that extra dimension of beauty which
Alice had possessed. The similarity was nonetheless
uncanny.

Alice. He had never managed to forget her. Although
he was now thirty, he had not yet married, precisely
because he could not rid himself of the thought of her.

And now, in front of him, was a child who resembled his lost love in almost every particular.

How many years ago was it? Only seven or eight, yet it could have been in another lifetime, another century. So young he had been, little more than a boy. He had traveled for weeks, from the soft airs of Hampshire to the inhospitable heat of India, to the dusty parade grounds, the alien sounds, the unexpected danger from snakebite and poisoned water. And she had been there, Alice, reminding him of his mother and sisters, of the green fields and gentle landscapes which seemed, then, so intolerably far away. Her image soothed him at night as he tossed in the heat and remembered his home; her soft voice and eager laugh cheered him when the crude ways of the mess had seemed too much for him. His fellow officers teased him because he looked so young. They asked whether he'd ever had a woman, made suggestions on how best to change his virginal state. They talked of bringing in a professional from the town to service him, offered to accompany him to the local houses of joy. He was able to ignore them because of Alice. He had wanted her. He had ached for her. They had often gone riding together, just the two of them, without an attendant *syce*. Sometimes he'd had to grit his teeth not to catch her in his arms, not to pull the ribbons from her hair and bury his face in it, not to tear at the bodice of her dress. He would remind himself that she was a married woman with a child. It made no difference. When she died he had thought he would die too. There had never been any other woman for him.

And now here she was again, recreated. Risen from the dead. Persephone, he thought, and realized too late that though he had meant only to think, he had spoken the word aloud. That damned shell . . . More than anything in the world, he did not wish to shock or otherwise alienate this child, girl, almost-woman, who was fashioned so closely to the likeness of Alice.

She was looking at him as though wondering whether he was mad. "Miss Ensleigh and her staff have been real bricks," he said quickly. "Have you any experience of nursing?" He shook his head violently again. Gave another bray of laughter. Of course she did not. She was barely out of the schoolroom, if not still in it. Alice, he thought.

"We've been learning some first aid at school," Mary said, "but nothing more than that."

"It's unpleasant work," he said. "The real thing, I mean."

"So is fighting in the trenches, I should think. Caring for the wounded men is something women can do to help the war effort," Mary said. Guiltily, she pushed away the thought of how little she herself had done. "I wish I were not so young. At school, we have gardens where we grow vegetables so that we can at least be self-sufficient."

He smiled, thinking her entirely enchanting.

"Every little helps," he said. "Do you like gardening?"

"More than anything. Do you?"

"I know very little about it. My mother . . ." His voice trailed, halted. His parents were still trying to come to terms with the loss of his elder sister. She had been a nursing sister aboard a transport ship which had been torpedoed off Malta by a German submarine. It all seemed terribly sad, suddenly. And dreadfully pointless. This bloody war. Even the women weren't protected. Tears came into his eyes.

Mary was horrified. A man crying. Should she pretend not to notice? That was probably the best thing. He would be embarrassed if she let him see that she was aware of his discomposure. She turned slightly. "Have you had a chance to walk round the Manor grounds since your arrival?" she asked, indicating the windows which looked out on to the park, though tonight they were closely curtained against the dark and cold.

"Not yet." Surreptitiously he touched the moisture in his eyes with his starched linen napkin.

"We have some very fine gardens here. A wonderful rose garden. An Elizabethan knot garden." She was not going to mention the other garden, the secret garden.

"Perhaps tomorrow you would be kind enough to show me some of the best places."

"It's hardly the right time of year, but yes," Mary said. "Of course."

Oh dear. She would rather have sat by some poor soldier's bed and read Dickens. Or possibly something

lighter. She did not want to tramp through the grounds
with this obviously suffering officer. And yet she could
see that he was—or had been—an attractive man. He
reminded her of someone. A memory of her father came
back to her: she had been standing on the wooden verandah of their house in India. She was holding her
ayah's hand, watching as he mounted his horse. The sun
had glinted painfully on the harness and the buttons of
his uniform so that she had been forced to screw up her
eyes in order to keep looking at him. Her eyelashes had
made rainbow bars across her eyes. Even now, she could
remember how the smile on his face had given way to
a look of resigned disappointment as he glanced down
at her and then rode away between the tall hedges of
croton which surrounded their bungalow, not looking
back to see her wave. By then it was too late to explain
that she was not being disagreeable again, it was only
that the sunlight was too bright.

"I don't know this part of the country at all," the
major said. "I wish I had a motor—from a distance the
scenery looks spectacular."

"My uncle," Mary lifted her chin at Archibald Craven,
"has a motor. He sometimes lets me and my cousin drive
his car. Perhaps he would—"

"I hope he does not allow you on to the road. Cars
can go at quite alarming speeds these days. Forty miles
an hour. More, in some cases."

"Only round the estate," Mary said reassuringly. "But
there was a senior girl at my school who went off to
France to be an ambulance driver with the First Aid
Nursing Yeomanry. Maybe next year, if the war is not
over, I could do that."

"An ambulance driver," said the major. The thought
of this lovely innocent in the mud and horror of France
was appalling. "You would have to deal with wounded
men, my dear."

"I know."

"The mutilations inflicted by today's modern weaponry are not pretty."

"I'm certain I could deal with whatever I had to,"
Mary said, though she was far from sure. If Dickon could
go to war, then she could too. If it lasted long enough.
She hoped that it would not. She hesitated to admit,

even to herself, that the reason she had not offered help to Miss Ensleigh and her staff was her terror that she would have to uncover wounds or bandage them up. She was afraid she would be sick.

"I wonder if you could," Sambourne said. How would she cope with the sight of men whose faces had been blown away, men whose limbs stank with gangrene, men who were no more than pieces of flesh kept alive by machinery? Blood. Pus. Severed limbs. The thought of her face to face with some of the horrific scenes he himself had witnessed appalled him. Again he remembered that white bedroom in India, the muslin curtains drawn across the windows, the crumpled linen on the bed, and his Alice—though she had never been his in any meaningful sense of the word—lying across the linen sheets, as lovely in death as in life, despite the contorted body and the ugly signs of cholera all about her. "Another day, you must allow me to show you about the hospital," he said. "I'm sure Miss Ensleigh would be agreeable."

"That would be very . . ." Mary did not quite know how to complete the sentence. Very what? Interesting? She could not in all conscience reduce the sufferings of the wounded to the status of mere interest. Kind? That was hardly the way to describe such a visit. "That would be very . . ." Again it was difficult to find the right word. In the end, she merely mumbled something vague.

Archibald Craven rose, glass in hand. "Ladies. Gentlemen. I give you King and Country," he said.

The company struggled to its feet, exchanged glances, raised their own glasses. Miss Ensleigh murmured patriotically.

Captain Hardman and Lieutenant Carrington spoke together. "King and Country." Behind their superficial expressions of cheer, memories twisted like worms. The left sleeve of Hardman's dress uniform was pinned to his chest.

Mary repeated the words softly, wondering as she did so why her uncle thought them appropriate tonight, as the old year waned. She had heard them so often but never really thought about them. At midnight the bells would peal out over the roofs of Misselthwaite, sound across the frosty moors, rise to the cold stars in the sky:

1918, the fifth year of war, would begin. King and Country: they were words that needed to be considered. What did her uncle mean by "country"? What did the word mean to the disabled men on the other side of the table, to the stranger at her side? Was it the land itself they had fought for, the moors outside the windows, the fields bounded by their stone walls, the cliffs which rimmed the island and all it contained of history: castles, cathedrals, manor houses, monuments? Or had they sacrificed themselves for a concept merely: England, green and pleasant, this blessed isle, a focus for the thoughts of those in exile? And why did they drink to the King instead of to the men who were fighting and dying to keep him safely down in Westminster?

Across the table, Colin banged down his glass. Wine slopped on to the damask cloth. He said loudly: "I refuse."

"What?" Archibald Craven stared at his son.

"I cannot and will not drink either to my king, for whom I have no regard," Colin announced, "nor to my country, which allows this slaughter to continue, day after day after day, which has killed off an entire generation for absolutely nothing, which seemingly has no more compassion for its citizens than a gamekeeper has for vermin, which—"

"Colin!" Archibald said sharply. "You are forgetting yourself."

"Why not drink instead to the men who are dying out there in their bewildered thousands?" Colin demanded. "The ones who lie wounded tonight in some damnable shellhole, waiting for rescue? The ones caught on the wire to be picked off at leisure by German snipers? The ones who even as we stand here tonight, are being blown apart, scattered across the mud?" Passion choked him and momentarily, the words failed to come.

Before he could open his mouth to continue, Captain Hardman said: "Good idea." He looked quickly at his host. "Here's to the men who so gallantly have laid down their lives for their country, who have offered up their futures as a sacrifice that we—that their children— may live in safety."

"No!" Colin moved away from the table. "Oh no. I won't drink to that, either. They did *not* lay down their lives. They didn't offer up their futures." He stood against the heavy sideboard with its weight of decanters and silver salts, its salvers and chased pitchers. He spread his arms wide. "They've had them snatched from them. Torn from them. They've been cheated, they've been lied to. They've endured horrors which no one— *no* one—should have to experience. And for what?"

The three older men gaped at him. "I say, young man," the lieutenant began, "I think you've got things a little twisted. It's not—"

Colin cut him off. "Do you know how many men died at the battle of the Somme? Four hundred and twenty thousand. Think of it. The enormity. Twenty-one thousand in a single day." Dramatically, he tipped his glass so that the wine ran on to the floor. "And you ask me to drink to my King? To my Country? I will not."

"We have guests," Archibald Craven's voice was cold, cutting across the performance Colin was giving. Yet his heart burned with pride and love. To have that fire in the belly again, he thought. To believe in something. Or, rather, to so passionately *not* believe in something. He swallowed his wine and motioned Pitcher to refill the glasses.

"I'd like to propose the health of our host," Carrington said pacifically. They drank, and Sambourne followed with a toast to the new year. Colin's outburst was lost in the departure of the ladies from the table, the passing of port, the cutting of cigars.

Later, when the guests had gone, Archibald Craven said: "Apart from your little . . . on the whole, I thought the evening went very well." He did not intend to reprove Colin for his words, merely to indicate that given the circumstances, they were inappropriate. He and his son stood with their backs to the billiard-room fire. "Would you agree, Colin?"

"Very much so, sir."

"That matron's a fine looking woman," Archie said, liberated from inhibition by the wine he had consumed and the whisky now in his hand.

"Is she?"

"Certainly. And your cousin Mary's growing into a charming creature, too."

"Yes," Colin said, frowning. Was his father drunk?

"Come along, boy. Don't be so pious. Of course she is." Archie tried to repress the memories of his lost wife, of whom this resurrected son of his increasingly reminded him. Same eyes, same expressions, same mouth. It was years since she had died, but not a day had gone by without him thinking of her. Missing her. He put down his glass. "If I could guarantee you just one thing, my boy," he said abruptly. "It would be a happy relationship with a good woman. A long-lasting one, I mean—"

"Father, please don't."

"—not one cut cruelly short, as mine was." There had been other women, of course there had. Not just in England, but in France, Italy, Austria. He had traveled Europe for ten years after the death of his wife, crisscrossing the continent like a damned railway line. But nothing, nothing, had given him anything more than a transient happiness, a momentary pleasure. He knew he would give every penny he possessed if she would only come back to him. He knew, too, that there was no reason why he should not marry again. Colin was getting on for eighteen. All too soon, he would be nineteen and then twenty, twenty-one—at which point there would be complicated legal matters to be sorted out. He experienced a moment of panic: what had he done with his life since Colin's mother had fallen from that tree and mortally injured herself? Nothing. Nothing at all. He guessed that, after an inauspicious start, his son loved him. As did his niece. Was that enough? Since Mary's arrival at Misselthwaite, he had been happy enough. His son was someone that any father could be proud of. But was it enough? He refilled his glass, noting the disapproving twist of Colin's mouth. He smiled wryly. Whether they love them or not, the young always disapprove of their elders. He had been the same. No doubt Colin's sons would feel the same way about their father.

"Do you still miss my mother?" Colin said.

"Always." Archie was suddenly serious. "Always. Every day I think of her. Miss her."

"That's terribly sad."

"In one way, perhaps. But in another, it shows that I've been lucky, don't you think?"

"How's that, sir?"

"That I met a woman and fell in love and never stopped loving her. How many men can say the same?"

"I don't know."

"But I do. Meet them all the time at the club. Talking about their wives as though they were maid servants. Or strangers. Hope that won't happen to you, my boy."

Definitely drunk, Colin thought. Some of the oldest boys in his house at school behaved like this, talked in that careful way, when they'd sneaked into the town and been drinking. "So do I, sir."

"Damn fine woman, that Miss Ensleigh."

"So you said."

"What did you think of Major Sambourne? Seemed very taken with our little Miss Mary, didn't you think?"

"Not really," Colin said stiffly.

"She'll be ready for marriage a year or two from now. I ought to spend more time in Fitzroy Square, I suppose. Introduce her about, do some entertaining so she can meet some eligible young men. I always envisaged—" he had some trouble with the word, "—envisaged her choosing a fellow like the major."

"That's—" Colin, outraged, broke off.

"That's what?"

"For a start, he's years older than she is. Besides—"

"Besides what? Perfectly suitable match. Asked Miss Ensleigh about him. Good family, reasonable expectations, all that sort of thing, for what they're worth these days. Not that I'm saying that Major Sambourne is the one. She's still far too young. But someone similar, that's all I'm saying. Someone like that."

"Father," Colin said firmly, "you've had more to drink than you ought."

"You're probably right, son," Archie Craven said. The pleasure he felt in saying the word, at the same time remembering the poor queer child Colin had once been, made him repeat them. "Son. My son."

"Father . . ."

"Yes. Help me up to bed, my boy. Had too much, I know. But in these damnable times . . ."

Colin looked at his father and his eyes smarted. His father was still a striking figure, despite the crooked shoulder and the lines on his face. Though his hair was gray now, with a thick white streak along the left side of his head, his eyes were full of something which Colin hesitated to categorize as fire but which, nonetheless, smouldered, lending him a hugely attractive air. He had noticed the way Miss Ensleigh looked at Archie. And that friend who had come visiting with her daughter last year—Mrs. Bedgrove, was it?—had certainly turned a fancying eye in Archie's direction. He prayed that his own life would not be as barren as his father's had been. He would see to it that it was not. He was clear about that.

"Take my arm, Father," he said. And the two men, the last of the Craven line, trod arm-in-arm across the oak beams of the billiard-room floor, each of them secretly exulting in the fact that they did so, father and son together.

2

When Colin reached his room, he found Mary sitting cross-legged against the headboard of his bed with his eiderdown tucked around her. She wore her woollen dressing-gown over a nightdress with a high collar. Her hair hung loosely on her shoulders.

"What do *you* want?" he asked rudely.

"A word with Colin Craven, Ham Actor. Or do I mean Colin Craven, Confidence Destroyer?"

"What do you mean?"

"You know perfectly well."

"Do I?" He gave her a lofty look. She was so pretty. There was a tightness in his chest which reminded him of the asthma attacks he was prone to when he was younger.

"Of course you do. Those men there tonight, do you think they needed to hear you ranting at them about the pointlessness of the war? Do you think it helped that lieutenant to have you shouting out casualty numbers? Did you think about his lost arm, or poor old Captain Hardman, trying to get about on crutches? Or that officer with the eyepatch? They probably agree with you, but they don't need to have it thrust in their faces like that."

"Nor does your precious major, either, I suppose."

"What are you talking about?"

"The one you were getting on so well with tonight."

"I was talking to him, if that's what you mean."

"From my side of the table it looked more like blatant flirting."

"What?"

"Hanging on every banality he came up with. Not to

mention simpering like a lovesick sheep every time he let out that dreadful laugh of his."

"I did *not!*"

"God," Colin said, moving his thin shoulders about contemptuously. "I thought I was going to be sick."

Mary pushed away the eiderdown and jumped off the bed. "How dare you!" she shouted. "How dare you say such things? Apart from anything else, that poor man's been through God knows what horrors, while all you've done is sit around at school, despising people who've had the courage to join up and fight for what they believe in."

Colin had intended to annoy. "Banality after cliché after platitude," he said. "It was like a never-ending stream."

Mary clenched her fists. Her eyes were fierce. "You are the most hateful, conceited little . . . *coxcomb* I've ever met."

"Coxcomb?" Colin tried to take hold of her hands but she evaded him. "How do you make that out?"

"You're always so certain that you're right, aren't you?"

"That's because I usually am."

"You can't imagine that any one else might have a point of view, can you?" Mary raged. "Or that your opinions might not be the only ones. Might even be *wrong!*"

He was suddenly alarmed. "Look here: you haven't fallen for this wretched major, have you?"

"Of course not. And I agree his laugh is irritating. But there was something rather nice about him." She looked away from him toward the window. The curtains had not yet been drawn and the glass was blank and cold. "And he's been in the war." Her eyes smarted. "You're so damn convinced that you know best, aren't you?"

There was a pause. Then Colin said quietly: "Mary."

"What?"

"I miss Dickon too, you know."

"I wonder what he's doing tonight?"

"Or if he's even alive . . ."

"Don't!" exclaimed Mary. "Don't say that. Whatever else happens, Dickon's got to come through. I wouldn't be able to bear it if he . . ."

"He was an idiot, joining up like that."

Mary grabbed Colin's left hand and squeezed the thumb back until he gasped with pain. "Don't ever say that again," she said through clenched teeth. "It was brave. He was brave. He did what was right."

"What they *told* him was right. It's not the same thing." Colin twisted his thumb out of her grip. She used to do this when they were children; it hurt then and it hurt now.

"He's a hero."

"You don't believe that. You can't."

"There was a piece in the local paper. Mrs. Medlock saved it for me. How he'd shown extreme bravery under fire. How his commanding officer said he wished there were more like him."

"Mary, don't be so naïve. There's probably a 'hero' in every town in England. There's probably an officer whose sole duty is to write to provincial papers saying exactly the same thing about some local soldier. It's propaganda, that's all. A way to persuade more men to join up and get themselves killed for the sake of three feet of muddy French farmland, so the generals can pat themselves on the back and tell the country we're beating the Hun."

"I don't believe you."

"Don't you read the real papers? Haven't you heard how we're sending men out there without the proper equipment, without sufficient training or weapons, without even coats or gloves? Haven't you heard about some of the terrible tactical mistakes that've been made? The complete disregard for lives? How troops are dying of fever and dysentery and pneumonia before they can even get to the Front?"

"No," Mary said, sounding sulky.

"And do you think Dickon's commanding officer will give a damn when he comes home again?" Colin asked. "*We* will. You and I and his family will. But not that CO. Not the men who sent him out there in the first place."

"But—"

"You must make yourself think about it, Mary. He could come back shellshocked. Or in a wheelchair, with his legs blown away. He wouldn't be able to work, in that case, but do you think any of the generals will see that he's clothed and fed and kept clean for the rest of his life? Someone will have to, but it won't be them. They'll just go back to their lives of privilege and indifference."

"Colin, I—"

"Did I tell you I heard from Faringdon?"

"No." Mary immediately felt guilty. Last winter, Colin had brought home friends from school: Faringdon and Eversholt. Faringdon had irritated her. Despite her scowls, he hung around. As soon as she had settled by the library fire with a book, or started off on a solitary walk, there he was. It was as though he had a sixth sense which alerted him whenever she particularly wanted to be on her own. He would smile at her, call after her in his rough boy's voice. She had been beastly. Shouted at him, frowned, told him to leave her alone. In the spring term, Colin had written from school to say that Faringdon had run away to enlist with his father's regiment. In the summer term, Colin wrote again: Faringdon had been shot through the head by a German sniper and though he had survived, was now lying blinded in a military hospital near Calais. "I wish, tremendously, that I'd been nicer to him," she said.

"I don't suppose he realized you were being horrid"

Mary frowned. "I hate the idea that if he should ever think of me, he'll only remember how unkind I was. That he'll always remember my face all screwed up and scowling."

"I'm sure he won't."

"It would have been easy for me to smile, Colin. And now he'll never see anything ever again. That's so dreadful. Worse, almost, than being dead."

"His people wrote to say that he's been transferred to a hospital near Scarborough."

The letter had come two days ago. Poor Faringdon, Colin had thought, reading the information it contained. Such a duffer at everything. He had surprised everyone by joining up so unexpectedly. He must have lied about his age. When the news of his wounding came through, the Head Man had preached a sermon about death and *pro patria mori* and what does it profit a man if he loses his own soul? The hypocrisy of it was sickening. The way the old men were sending boys off to fight this pointless war. The way they implied that the ultimate sacrifice was the only means of preventing the filthy Hun from overrunning the country. Such rot. More than half the chaps at school were in the OTC and spent hours drilling and polishing buttons and naming parts. What good would any of that do when the mustard gas blew across the trenches? How would it help them when a shell tore off their arms? When a bayonet was thrust through their chest? Had anyone prepared them for the horror of seeing a fellow human killed? Had they ever really thought about death or—even worse—about dying?

He had. He scarcely slept for thinking of it. For thinking of Dickon. His imagination did not spare him. Blood spilling from a khaki uniform. A blue eye dangling on what was left of a ruddy cheek. Ripped flesh. Guts, soft and pink as the herring roes he had seen in Whitby one summer. Screams in the night. Sometimes the screams were his own.

"Scarborough?" Mary repeated slowly.

"Yes. Why don't we go over and see him?"

Terror seized Mary. "I couldn't. I just couldn't."

"Why not?"

"His face might be . . . his eyes." She could not explain how impossible it was for her to visit Faringdon, who had once been a boy calling after her in the winter sunshine and now lay in perpetual darkness. Because she had been unkind, in some complex way she felt that the bullet which had severed his optic nerves was her fault.

"That's very selfish of you."

"I know." Suddenly, she held up her hand. "Listen, Colin." She ran to the window and opened it. A bell tolled.

"It must be midnight." Every year, Pitcher pulled at the bell rope which hung outside the scullery. Ringing in the New Year, as he had done since long before Colin was born, and his father had done before that. "What kind of a new year will this one be?"

"I don't know." Colin stood beside her at the window. The coarse wool of her dressing-gown brushed against his knuckles. His scalp tightened in the freezing air. "Things are breaking apart. The world has changed."

Sometimes he sounded so wise, like an old old man.

Mary did not doubt that he was right. Her throat ached
with the effort of not breaking down as she listened to
the long slow notes of the bells rolling among the slates
of the Misselthwaite roofs. Dickon. Faringdon. So many
dead. Wherever you went, you could not escape them.
Coffins. Weeping parents. Friends, brothers, cousins, fathers. How many more would die before this war was
over? The papers were suggesting that it might drag on
for another five, even ten years. Ten more years. I shall
be quite old by then, she thought. Nearly twenty-seven.

"Ring out the old, ring in the new," said Colin. *"Ring
out the false ring in the true."*

"What's that?"

"Tennyson. We did him last term."

"It's 1918. When will Dickon come home?" The wind
sighed in invisible trees, a restless melancholy sound.

"Who knows? And when he does . . ."

Colin knew that when the war was finally over, England would not return to what it had once been. The
country was metamorphosing like a chrysalis. He feared
that when it emerged, it would not be with the beauty
of a butterfly but with something much more sinister.
A generation had been lost. Butchered. For what? He
clenched his fists. He had no desire to fight for England,
not from cowardice, not even from some idealistic disbelief in violence. Simply because he did not believe that
anything would be gained by the millions of lives—not
just English, either—thrown away.

"Kiss me, Mary," he said suddenly. This would not
normally have been a wise request, but he sensed that
tonight, some of her prickles had softened.

"What?"

"Kiss me."

"But you're my cousin."

"So what? Kiss me for the sake of auld lang syne."

"Whatever that may mean." She turned her face up
to his and he felt the cold press of her lips against the
side of his mouth. She was small, maybe as much as a
foot shorter than he was. Her head came no higher than
his breastbone. "Happy New Year, Col."

He kissed her cheek. Above her head, his eyes were
closed. The feel of her skin under his mouth sent a

shiver through his loins. If only, if only . . . "Dickon," he said.

"I pray that he's safe. More than anything in the world I hope that."

In the wintry darkness, the great bell tolled on.

"Ring out false pride in place and blood, the civic slander and the spite," said Colin. He moved away from her, not wanting her to sense the excitement which had suffused the lower half of his body. He took her hand. *"Ring in the love of truth and right,"* he chanted slowly. *"Ring in the common love of good."*

"Is that why Pitcher's pulling at the bell?" Mary leaned back against him so that her hair covered his cheek and sent small currents through his lips when she moved. "For the common love of good?"

"No," said Colin. "But how I wish it were."

The frosty air pressed like a hand against Mary's face as she skated across the frozen surface of the lake. Ice rang hollowly beneath her feet; all around was the creak and groan of hoar-laden tree branches. Reaching the further limit of the lake, where the rhododendrons crammed blackly down the bank, she turned. Overnight, the temperature had dropped well below freezing. This time last year, there had been snow, as well as ice, white beneath the black trees.

Smooth as a pewter spoon, the surface of the lake curved toward the banks. Dark sky, black leaves, ice against snow, the disembodied glow of the sun sinking between banks of freezing fog.

Mary thought: Dickon. Where are you? What are you doing?

From the shore, a voice called and was caught among the leaves. Colin was skating toward her. He pulled up short when he reached her, his abundant hair briefly flying out about his face then settling again.

"I thought you'd be here," he said. She smelled wood smoke and the oiled wool of the black jumper he wore over corduroy trousers. His face had the same thick whiteness as chalk. "What are you thinking?"

She did not answer and he put an arm round her shoulders. "Mary. You are not going to cry, are you?"

"No." She shook her head. "Of course not. It's just . . ."

"Just what?"

"This wretched war," Mary said. Frowning, she took a deep steadying breath but it was no good. "People dying all the time. Faringdon . . . I wish I . . ." Tears filled her eyes.

"I know."

"I keep thinking of *him*. Of Dickon. What he must be going through."

Colin did not answer. He hoped her thoughts were less graphic than his. In the silence, they heard the cold wind between the rhododendron leaves. Across the lake, the ice sounded, the sharp crack like a pistol shot.

Is Colin handsome? she wondered. The senior girls at school, who used to ignore her until they discovered she had a male cousin, were always asking her that. "Is he handsome, Lennox? Does he dance? Is he good looking? Has he got 'it'?"

Not knowing exactly what "it" was, she was never sure how to answer. Had he or hadn't he? She guessed he probably had. But good looking, handsome? He was so familiar to her, so much part of her, that she could not consider him in the abstract impartial way such a question required. Was he? Compared, say, to a Greek god, he was not. His face was too thin, his eyes too big, his body too long.

She thrust her hands into her pockets; stupidly, she had come out without gloves. "As soon as I can, I'm going to leave school," she said abruptly.

"You can't do that."

"Why not?"

"You—you just *can't*." Colin looked at his cousin in dismay. If she left school, what would she do? Where would she go? Whatever she chose to do, it would be bound to take her further away from him. He could not imagine Misselthwaite without her. House, moors, lake, each separate tree, each blade of grass, individually or as a whole, she was part of it. "Anyway, you're only sixteen."

"I'm nearly seventeen."

"It'll be ages yet before they'd let you go."

"They can't stop me."

"You're a child still."

"But I feel I'm grown-up. And I know I should be doing something more important than piano lessons and dates of English monarchs and French conversation. I'm not like you, clever, going to university."

"You *are* clever," said Colin. "You're the cleverest girl I know."

"Since the only other girl you know is Eithne Blackhouse, that's not much of a compliment."

"I know lots of girls. *Dozens.* And none of them is a patch on you." He would have touched her face or the fair hair which curled beneath the woollen edges of her tam o'shanter. But he was afraid she would mock him if he did. Or, worse, turn from him, push his hand away.

Instead, she moved closer to him. He could feel her shivering against his jumper. "Whatever you say about the war, Colin, I can't not get involved. Not while . . ."

"While what?"

"While *he's* out there."

"So what are you going to do? Roll bandages? Knit socks for the troops? Hand out cups of tea and expect them to be grateful?" He dropped into a savage parody of a cockney accent. " 'Gawd bless you, lidy, and my the sun alwise shine on your sweet fice.' It's rot, Mary."

"I was thinking of nursing or something," Mary said, ignoring this. "I could probably pass for older than I am—"

"That's ridiculous."

"—if I put my hair up."

"You have to be well over twenty before they'll take you," Colin said.

"There must be something I can do."

"Do you want to die?"

"Of course I don't."

"Nurses are being killed, as well as soldiers."

"Last night, looking at those wounded officers, I felt ashamed of myself. I could have at least offered to help Miss Ensleigh in some—"

"How? By changing dressings on gangrened legs? Picking up severed arms from the floor of the operating theater?"

"Colin!"

"Do you want to help strange men to go to the lavatory?" Colin said brutally. "And then have to wipe their rear ends because they have no hands?"

Mary twisted violently away from him, almost falling on the slippery ice. "That's disgusting," she cried. "Why are you being so horrible?"

"It's not disgusting. It's the truth." He pulled off his gloves and gave them to Mary. "Here, put those on."

"Thanks," Mary muttered.

"Oh, Mistress Mary," Colin said gently. "You're even terrified to see Faringdon. How do you think you'd ever get on as a nurse?"

Mary knew he was right. If she was so squeamish that she could not even bring herself to visit a friend, what possible use would she be on a hospital ward?

Sensing her humiliation, Colin began to clown. He spun on the ice, then did a series of twirls and leaps around her, whooping as he went. "What do you think, Mary? Am I good?"

"Very good."

"Am I amazing?"

"Truly amazing."

"I'm going to become an Olympic skater, I've decided, the best there ever was, I might even become a professional. I could stage ice shows, or something similar, go on tour in America. What do you think, Mary? What do you really think?"

Was she laughing? Or at least smiling? In the pearly light cast by the backlit banks of mist, it was difficult to tell.

She said abruptly: "I'll come with you to visit Faringdon."

"Will you really?"

"When would you like to go? Roach would drive us, wouldn't he? Or maybe Major Sambourne. I was talking to—"

"Major *Sam*bourne?" Colin sounded outraged.

"I'm sure your father would let him drive the car."

"I'll be damned if I'm going to go with him. He's a total stranger. Besides, what would poor Faringdon make of some braying ninny like that? He'd think they'd let a donkey loose in the ward."

He sped away from her, the hiss of his skates sounding like fire. Major bloody Sambourne. Couldn't she see what an insensitive suggestion that was? He wondered what had made her change her mind. When they were children they did everything together, her and him and Dickon. Not now. She was always creeping away by herself, or staying in her room. He no longer understood her. The purity of unspoken communion had gone. The silly part of it was that he knew it had nothing to do with being a girl and getting moody, the way his friends at school described their sisters doing. It was because she was worried about Dickon. As, indeed, was he.

3

January 6th 1918

Dearest Mother,

I hope you are well as it leaves me at present. It is raining here again, very wet & uncomfortable for the men as there is no means of drying our kit. New Year's Day: who would have thought we should still be at it four years later? We were given a ration of brandy each & drank the King's health, also to the hope that we would not have to spend another New Year in the trenches. The cooks had made some special puddings & pies & we had roast fowl & plenty of vegetables, even though it is wintertime, & wine as well. Some of the lads made me stand up & sing, so I gave them "On Ilkley Moor Baht Aht," & soon they were all joining in. It was grand, & easy to forget for a few hours that we were at War. Then we had "Auld Lang Syne." I thought so hard of you & the children when we raised our glasses, & also of Colin & Mary. It is a long time since I last saw them, though I have had letters, of course.

Everything here is very gray & muddy & wet. The rain is not like our Yorkshire rain . . .

Nothing like. A hateful drenching non-stop downpour, that smelled of graves and decayed meat and cordite. On the horizon, there were puffs of white smoke, which on a windless day might hang unchanging for minutes on end. Pretty as elder flowers, each one signaling more bloody deaths. The insides of his thighs were chafed raw with the rubbing of his coarse rain-soaked uniform. Somewhere, a horse screamed. A trumpet of despair. Guts spilling on to the cratered mud. Guts and blood. That's all there was. And dreams. Such terrible dreams. Faces wrenched from their skeletons. Eyes lying like jewels on the palm of a severed rotting hand. The ponies. Manes of fire streaming in the wind. Nostrils full of blood.

At Misselthwaite, the bell would have rung out across the dale to mark the passing of the year. There would be snow on the higher moors. Frost sparkling. One year they had roasted a sheep on the shores of the frozen lake. Mary and he had skated across the ice, hand in hand through the glacial air. It was cold here, too, a terrible soaking cold which clamped their damp clothes to their bodies. Impossible to sleep. Shivering. That morning he had seen Hillman frozen like a log into the ice of a pothole. Frost whitened his eyebrows. The back of his head had been blown away.

St Valentine's Day, 1918
   My dear Mary, I hope you are well. I was pleased to hear of your expedition to York with your friend Major Sambourne & am glad to know that in spite of everything, you are still managing to have some good times. Thank you for the Woodbines & the jam. Knowing that it was made with Misselthwaite strawberries made it taste all the better. It quite hides the taste of the biscuits we are given as part of our daily rations.
   Yesterday I was reminded of you & Colin & the fun we used to have. One of the adjutants was playing a piano in an estaminet (French eating place, though this one was really the kitchen of a bombed-out farmhouse) where we were having egg & chips (a favorite out here). Someone else produced a mouth organ &, believe it or not, another man took a flute out of his kit, which he had carried around with him throughout the War & even into battle. Before we knew it, we were engaged in a right royal singsong, all the old favorites that we used to sing round the schoolroom piano at Misselthwaite. I have to confess that I felt a bit choked up when I remembered you playing, & Colin scraping away at his fiddle, & me singing along whenever I recognised a bit of tune. We got to singing our national songs. There was a Frenchman who gave us the Marseillaise, and Subaltern Foster did "On Ilkley Moor" and

*our youngest recruit sang a fine Cornish air, and the
Irish and Scots got in on the act too. & didn't our
boys just yell their lungs out when it was time for
"God Save the King"? Quite a concert party, we had.
To cool things down, they asked me for something a
bit more sentimental & I gave them I remember
Mary . . .*

And he did remember. Always. Her pretty fair hair
and the small frown between her brows. The smell of
her clothes. Starch and lavender. The sailor's middy she
wore over a short pleated skirt, and her long legs in
black stockings. The big knitted jumpers round her little
face. Three or four times he had visited the women who
serviced the soldiers. Five minutes to get the business
done. Spurious love. Thick peasant arms around his
body. "Mary," he had said quietly, at the moment of
climax. "My Mary." "Yess, Tommy," the women said.
"Marie. Good boy. Marie. *C'est bon.*" They were always Marie.

February 28th 1918
  Dear Sister,
  *I thought you would like to know that I have a new
friend, a kitten which I found in the ruins of a house
when we were marching to this encampment. The family which used to live there had all left, because they
have no food or anything to cook by. Most of the time
we are not hungry so I suppose we soldiers are luckier
than the Frenchies are. I have called the kitten Janey,
after you, & I carry her around inside my battledress
jacket. All the lads save food for her, she is very partial
to a bit of cheese. There is not much milk to be had
but she makes do. One of the men here has a terrier
and sometimes we go ratting, but the dogs do not take
to shelling as easily as the cats, and mostly we keep
them back at the horse lines. I hope you are being a
good girl & helping Mother as much as is possible &
attending to your books. One thing I have learned
from being here, is how important it is to get an education, it does not matter if you are poor as long as you
have something to turn over in your mind. One of the
officers has lent me some of his books, which I am*

enjoying very much. I daresay you are laughing at the thought of your big brother reading & the truth is that I would not have read this book at home, so you see even in War there may be good to be found.

Lies. But he could not write the truth, not all of it, even if the censors allowed. He longed to share the terror he felt, the way his body pulsed and drummed in time to the music of the guns, the sudden fits of demonic shivering which made it impossible for him to sit still, and only the thought of what the other men would say kept him from—or so he felt—juddering to pieces. Disintegrating. An ear here, a foot there, arms, legs flying about all over the dugout.

Most of the time, he tried not to think of home. He wanted no reminder of normality, for it only served to emphasize the abnormality of his daily routines, the degradation of the human spirit, the piling on of more than anyone could be expected to endure. He did not want his family to know any of it. Not the horror. Not the crippling fear. He wanted to keep untainted the memory of the pure air of the moors, where plover and skylark soared above the miles of golden gorse. He did not want them to know what he suffered.

The endless mud was like a sea. A vast ocean, stretching into the distance as far as the eye could see. Not inanimate, not simply earth and water, but a new world, with its own sights and sounds, its own moods. A whole crawling subterranean universe. It reared above the trenches, wave upon wave swallowing sandbags and motor lorries and stretchers, tin hats, letters and weapons, dreams, hopes, bodies and parts of bodies. The dead moved under the mud. And the horses. Stepping through the thick viscosity of it. Delicate legs treading deeper and deeper as it rose over their hoofs and fetlocks, up to their bellies and sometimes, as the push continued, to their mouths. They kept their heads raised to the sky until they sank, unable to move, nostrils, eyes, even their narrow ears swamped in mud. Breathing it until they died. He saw the mud as his personal enemy. Beneath that slick gray surface lay soldiers he had known, talked to, ridden with. At night, men sometimes drowned in it. Went into the trenches and stuck fast, suffocated in mud.

If the snipers didn't finish you off, the mud would. Those drowned men haunted him. Their mouths opened to curse him and he saw the maggots in their wounds, the mud which clogged their throats. When the sun shone and there was no rain, the thin crust dried to a lilac-pink which reminded him of the thin ears of the rabbits he used to watch on the moors at dusk. Tender, violet-veined ears. So thin the light shone through them.

He touched the skin of his eyelid. The tremor fluttered under his finger like a bird. The robin. He used to talk to the robin. If he spoke now, what would come from his mouth. Foulness? Black vomit? Maggots? Once he had stumbled over a man lying beside the road, asleep, or so it seemed until he had shaken his shoulder and realized that the exposed surfaces of the body were a heaving creeping mass of maggots, hard and glossy as corn-seed. At night, they crawled over him, too, their jaws working, the shiny ridged bodies covering him like a blanket, eating him alive until he woke, screaming, beating them away while his companions in the dugout cursed him in their sleep.

Last spring, in the country lanes, he had found a robin's nest with one blue egg in it. Although he had watched for a week, the parents had not returned. In the end, he had taken the nest back to his dugout and hidden it carefully among his spare shirts. He would give it to Mary. When the other pictures in his mind grew too fearful for bearing, he would think of Mary, and how she would break into that rare smile of hers.

"A robin's nest," she would say. "All the way from France? But it looks just like *our* robin's nest." And she would look up at him and there would be something painful under his ribs as he gazed down into her eyes.

"Mary," he would say. "Mary," and she would put her little hand on his chest and he would take her into his arms. Feel her against his heart. His fingers against her fine skin. He wished he had a photograph. Like the one Johnson kept in his back pocket, a snap sent from his girl, "Yours till hell freezes over" scrawled in the corner. In the old order, Mary would not have been for him, he knew that. She was a lady and he was just a rough countryman. Subaltern Forster had explained that this was what was wrong with the country, the social divisions which shut him off from Mary. He was not to think of himself as "just" anything. He and Forster stood among the horses, breathing the rich odor of animal sweat and hay and healthy dung, talking about rights and equality, about the changes which must take place in society, about the welcome they would all receive, all the brave heroes who returned to the land they had fought for. "O brave new world, that has such people in it," the subaltern would say. And shake his head a little, and smile. From a play by Shakespeare. In that new world, he would no longer be "just" Corporal Richard Sowerby. He would become a man among equals, a man fit for Miss Mary. The thought of it filled him with a sweet and fearful delight.

March 17th 1918

  Dearest Mother,

  I hope that you & the family are well. I am not too bad though troubled with my chest. Thank you for the soap. Also the parkin. I am sorry to hear that Martha has been poorly, hope this will not harm the coming baby. I hope I may have some leave due after it is born, it is a long time since I saw you. We are about a mile from the Front & doing nothing much at the moment but I keep myself busy, it is the best thing. Today I groomed all the horses I have charge of. They looked grand. I oiled their hooves & plaited their tails to give them some encouragement, which I could do with myself. Some of the men here find this whole business exciting, or say they do. One of them, Davey, a Cornish lad who is only sixteen yrs old, talks about it as though this were a game of football, but I only wish it were over & I could come back.

  I have been thinking a lot, Mother, while I have been out here. I have decided that I should like to work for myself, rather than for Mr. Craven, or for another employer, as Father does. It would be difficult, I know, but I think it would be best. I am not the same lad who went away to War. I have lost my ideals. You may wonder to see me write of ideals, & ask yourself where I have got such notions from, but out here, some of the barriers between people which we are used to at home have broken down. For instance, my Subal-

*tern used to be a teacher at home, he lives in York.
We talk together a lot because we both love horses. I
suppose you could say he has put ideas into my head
about a man's worth & the way we think about ourselves. I daresay I am not making myself clear & you
are wondering what I am going on about, but after all
this time of fighting for my country, I feel I am entitled
to a better place in it when I come home. I don't
know what.*

    *This morning I heard a bird. A blackbird. It is the
first one I have heard for a long time. Seems strange
to think that the song of a French blackbird is no different from an English one. Perhaps the German ones
are the same, too . . .*

Against the blue. The song. Like fresh water bubbling.
No trees, anymore. Just shattered trunks. Sometimes,
after a particularly heavy bombardment, the cruel smell
of the sap would drift across the endless mud toward
the trenches. No leaves. Not a blade of grass. Last spring
there had been dandelions, pushing through the pitted
ground. And away from the trenches, there had been
hedgerows full of violets. Dark sweet violets, the smell
intoxicating. He had thrown himself down and thrust his
face in among them. Breathed deep as though the rich
purple scent could obliterate the horrors. Thought of
Mary. Her face, that first spring in the secret garden.
Here, there were only craters, full of stagnant water. Full
of dead faces. Arms. Waving, waving. Beckoning. Join
us. That's what it came down to. Why are you still alive,
when we are dead? Why? He had no answer to that.
That morning, he had heard the bird singing. His chest
had flooded with heat at the sound. Fear. Cowardice.
He ground his teeth together, shutting out the hatred.
What were they doing, the generals behind the lines?
The lives of so many, so cheaply thrown away. Not just
men with families, but boys. Like Cornish Davey. Like
himself, those endless months ago when he had volunteered. A boy with his head stuffed full of dreams.

    Cowardice. Fight it. The desire to get away was so
powerful that at times he could smell it coming off him,
a foul sweat which stank stronger than the odors from
his own body. Sometimes two weeks would go by with-

out an opportunity to wash, or remove his boots. The
tic in his lower lid jigged against his eyeball. Fear. Fear
God. Honor the King. A single bird. Was it the last one
left in all this hellish landscape? One early dawn, he had
heard larks, high above him.

Now, he could hear horses neighing, terrified by the
smell of the thick black smoke which drifted toward
them from the battle lines and the constant artillery
bombardments. A nerve-racking orchestra. Field guns
drumming. The piccolo chatter of shrapnel. Shells whistling, long and eerie, ending in a bang. And all the time,
never ending, the screams and groans of countless men.
Even when they died, they continued to scream. He
heard them. All of them, every single one, screaming.
After the explosions stopped, he could still hear them.
His ears ached. And his eyes. Never enough sleep. He
longed for sleep but when it came, it was worse than
being awake. The images which disturbed his rest had
begun to invade the times he thought he was awake.
Sometimes he was not sure whether it was day or night.
Sometime he did not know whether an event had taken
place or he had simply dreamed it. Hours would go by
and he would have no recollection of them. Down in the
trenches, they were cut off from reality. He could have
been anywhere, in any time.

Some people thought that being in the horse lines was
an easy billet. He wondered if he had been attached to
stable duties through some word from Mr. Craven, or
because he had ridden down to York with the grooms
when the Misselthwaite hunters were handed over to the
regiment. Standing among the big haunches, warmed by
the steam of animal breath, listening to the quiet rustle
of hoofs on straw, was the only time in the past few
years that he had felt safe. The horses in the division
produced tons of manure each day. Manure bred flies.
Thousands. Millions of them. Flies bred disease. Sometimes the noise they made was so great that it even obscured the sound of an approaching shell. Often the
horse lines were more dangerous than the front for many
times the whizzbangs flew directly over the front
trenches to land at the rear. He had been there during
a direct hit. Guts and blood darkening the sky. Earth,
harness, fingers, hoofs, shreds of cigarettes and silver-

wrapped chocolate raining down on his startled upturned face. Beside him, a pair of legs had landed upright in the mud, puttees, boots, breeches, all complete. Johnson. He had recognized Private Johnson's breeches by the blue patch sewn on to the khaki, near the right-hand pocket. Johnson moved now through his nightmares. Beckoning. Why wasn't it you, Corporal? Why was it me, with the blue patch on my trousers and the picture of my sweetheart in my pocket?

April 19th 1918

Dear Colin,

Thank you for the chocolate. It was grand to get news from home, & I hope you will never think that I could ever be anything but interested in even the smallest details of what is going on at Misselthwaite. You can not imagine how we hunger for any sign that life continues as we remember it. It is the only thing that keeps me sane. This place is unimaginable. Literally unimaginable. I would not wish you to be here for anything. When I think of the poems we learned at school, like the "Charge of the Light Brigade," & the boys' stories we read glorifying War, when the truth is, it is very far from glorious. I think of those men marching into the Valley of Death, knowing that someone had blundered. I think of their fear, for every single morning I wake up & feel the same fear, & yet, like them, I am forced to carry on, knowing that my life is in the hands of incompetent blunderers. You should see what a direct hit by a shell can do to a man's body. You cannot possibly believe it. Nobody should have to. Maybe I can explain some of it to you when all this is over, & I come home, as I believe I shall. I cannot accept that God would allow me to be killed for a cause I believe in so little. When I joined up, I had some notion of laying down my life for my country. I thought that it was my duty to my King to go & fight the Boche. Now I see that I was mistaken. The Boche is no more than a man like any other man—like me. We were told to Honor the King but my King means nothing at all to me, any more than I do to him. My country I still have some affection for, but I am afraid that when I return I will not find it the same place I set out to save. There is something here which is horrible to see & that is the excitement some of the men feel just before an engagement, at the thought that they will be killing German soldiers. It is a terrible thing, to ask a man to kill someone. Luckily, spending so much of my time with the horses, I have not had to face this. I wonder whether I could do it if I had to. I think I could not for, as you know, I could not even fire at a partridge. I would then be shot for cowardice. But it would be the very opposite.

I wonder if you are right when you say that the tide of the War has finally turned. It is hard to believe it, out here. Some of the things you wrote about, such as your plans when you finish at Oxford, seem admirable & I hope that they will come to pass. I am sorry if I do not sound more excited, but I live at the moment from day to day.

Minute to minute. Second to second. Each sixty seconds got through was another minute nearer to the end. Two five-day stints of leave in the past two years, and little more before that. Not long enough to get all the way to Yorkshire and back. In one way that was good. How much more difficult it would have been to drag himself back here if he had seen the moors on a windy spring day, or smelled the grass under the sun. He wanted to feel his mother's arms about him again, as he had felt them when he was a child. Most of all, he wanted to be allowed to cry. His leaves had been spent in northern France.

May 25th 1918
Dearest Mother,
Thank you for the birthday cake & the presents from the children. Also for the new underclothes. You cannot imagine how unpleasant the conditions are here. I have not had my clothes off for more than ten days. I thought I should have to use my clasp knife to remove my socks this time. When your dear parcel came, I was due an hour or two off duty so I found my bit of soap & slipped away with my gray before they could give me some other task to do (they think it is better if they keep us fully occupied, even when

*by rights we should be resting). I say my gray: I mean
Jason, the dapple from Mr. Craven's stables, which
was allocated to the regiment, along with others which
have not survived. He is like a friend to me. The only
friend I have left. So we found a stream nearby & I
stripped right off & lay down in the water & let it
wash over me. It was very cold, but staring up at the
sky I was able to believe for a few minutes that I was
at home again, that this was one of the burns on the
moors, that I was still a boy called Dickon & not a
grown man who has seen too many horrors. I am
afraid, Mother, your boy has gone forever.*

The need to wash himself clean. Not just of his own
stink, but from the cloying smell of death. The trench
walls were made of the dead. In the churned mud which
ran knee-deep along the bottom were mess tins and helmets and boots. And worse. Much worse. Occasionally,
through some subterranean shift, the walls would move
and a mud-streaked half-eaten face appear, a shinbone
protrude from rotting khaki. Bony hands cradling eyes.
Gray, like Colin's. Brown, like Mary's. Blue, black,
hazel. Multicolored jewels. He had hobbled Jason at the
water's edge and the horse had stood patiently, cropping
the grass. Little ferns stood out from the banks, very
green against the reddish mud. A heron floated down,
further along the river's edge, and stood suspiciously for
a moment before turning its attention to the water. Rabbits hopped and nibbled; a small brown bird darted
busily here and there, foraging. From the breast pocket
of his khaki blouse, Dickon brought out the wooden
pipe he had brought with him from home, and began to
play a low chirping tune. The rabbits sat up. The little
bird turned her head and watched him. The heron swiv-
eled its arrogant gaze toward him.
    And then, high above, too far away to hear, a patrol
of English planes, SE5s, flew overhead. As he watched, a
formation of Huns drifted into view beneath the English
planes. Detached. Nothing to do with him. He saw the
higher aircraft strafe the ones below: Not a sound. Just
the smoke from the rear guns. A flash of red fire.
Flames, almost invisible against the sky. The silent explosion of white fire. The machine zigzagging soundlessly

to earth like a dying moth. Eerie. He watched three of
the enemy go down. Only two parachutes opened. The
remainder of the German planes turned back toward
their lines, pursued by the SE5s. He tried to play his
pipe, but could not. The madness of it. Men dying a mile
up in the air.

Last night, in his dreams, he had opened a parcel from
home and inside had been Colin's head, black hair falling away from the skull in rotting tufts, eye-sockets
empty. The rat-chewed lips had spoken. "I love you."
And then it was Mary's face, Mary's skull, and he was
lying under the mildewed blankets in his dugout, screaming, drenched in perspiration as he tried to wipe away
the images, tried to gouge them out with his dirty fingers.
Heart thumping in time with the guns and the rest of
the fellows complaining. "Pack it in, Corp," says young
Davey. "Leave him alone, chummy," says another.
"He's dreaming of his girl."

July 17th 1918
Dear Colin,
 *Thank you for sending the Woodbines & the Oxo
cubes, & also for the poem you copied out. I have not
heard before of Rupert Brooke but his poem is very
fine. I hope he did not truly believe that "Honor has
come back, as a king, to earth." I have seen many
things out here, but precious little honor. I do not believe that people at home can imagine the vileness I
see every day. It is now three years since I joined up
but I do begin to think that maybe you were right
when you wrote recently that the War may be winding
down. The men talk confidently of the Boche being
rattled. We take another field of craters & this time we
keep it. The shells fly less frequently overhead. I wonder what peace, if it really comes, will be like. I do not
think that men who have been through this hell will
ever forget it. It would not be possible to lay the memories aside & carry on. I think that in one sense I am
more frightened of what lies ahead, once the Generals
agree peace, than I have been in all the months I have
been out here.*
 *Now some bad news. Most of your father's hunters
were destroyed in earlier attacks but Jason, the dappled*

*gray, had survived it all. Last week, I am sorry to say,
he received a direct hit.*

Ah God. Breathing through his mouth, retching at the
rank stink of the horse's guts on his clothes and skin.
On his knees in the mud. The brave eye rolling toward
him. The nostrils wide and flared. "Jason." Stroking the
coarse mane while the horse screamed. Half the buttocks
gone. The tail hanging from a stump of tree, still
attached to a glistening piece of flesh. "Jason." The pitiful stretch of the neck. "My friend." Soothing words. A
hand on the smooth gray back. The dapples, delicate as
the mark left by waves on the sand, as the track of a
sparrow in the snow. Blood everywhere. Intestines spilling out into the mud. Sinking into the world below
where dead hands waved. Laying his head against the
wild beat of the heart, listening as it gradually stilled
and the mutilated body quivered and was still. For the
first time wanting to die too. A hand on his shoulder.
Forster. And behind him, the voice of the sergeant
major. "On your feet, soldier. We've work to do."
Screaming himself then. Leaping wild-eyed to his feet.
His face bloodied. "What did you say? *What?*" Tears
spurting. Heart breaking. Mouth full of hatred. "Leave
me *alone,* damn you." Wanting to maim. Wanting to
tear apart. To kill. And Forster, stepping between them.
"It's all right, S'arnt Major. The Corporal will be along."
Sobs shaking him apart. "My friend. He was my friend."
"I know, Richard. I know."

Dear God. How much do I have to bear? How much
longer can I endure?

September 3rd 1918
  My dear Mary,
  *Thank you for the Gillette & blades. I hardly know
myself, with such a smart razor. The cough lozenges
are also much appreciated. In spite of the warm
weather our clothes & kit never get really dry. I have
just spent more than twenty-four hours helping the
other men to repair breaches in the trench walls. Very
wet & muddy. When the mud dries on your boots it
hardens, almost like cement & it becomes difficult to
move in it. You would not like it here for there are*

*rats everywhere. I found one eating its way through
the book you sent me last time. I don't know if it was
the same fellow which had already consumed most of
my precious bar of soap. I am pleased to hear that
you are in London at the moment. Major Sambourne's
sister sounds very kind. I hope you are not too distressed by things you have seen at Victoria. Some of
the survivors are in a very bad way. As you say, such
brave fellows. What the shells can do to you is just
nobody's business.*

*I find it so odd that in spite of all the Hell which is
going on around us, we still find ourselves doing ordinary things. Walking. Riding. Picking rhubarb in
abandoned gardens. Last week I went for a stroll with
one of our fellows, a lad from Cornwall called Davey.
A dog joined us; a mangy-looking animal which set
up a couple of rabbits. You should have seen it go,
with young Davey running along behind, determined
to have at least one of the rabbits for our communal
stewpot. I could not help but remember the many times
we went walking on the moors, you & me & Colin.*

*I thought of you again last night. A nightingale was
somewhere nearby, singing. It is the first time I have
heard one over here. Is it a sign that this cruel War is
ending? This spring there are many more birds of all
kinds. I think it must be because suddenly the earth
is blooming again. Cornflowers, Dandelions, Poppies,
Clovers, Thistles. Yet for miles & miles ahead the landscape is distorted. You would cry to see what men have
done to these fields. Broken trees stand up in the mud
like big splinters. At night, when it is cold, mist hangs
above the shellholes, the way it does on the lake at
Misselthwaite. When they send up the lights, it looks
like the surface of the moon, green & ghost-like.
Things are a little easier at the moment. Colin thinks
it is the beginning of the end of the War.*

*How thankful I shall be to come home. I have not
slept properly for nigh on three years. Who could, with
the rats in the walls, the mice in the straw, the lice in
the blankets, which is not to mention the beetles, ants
etc. The lice are the worst. Keating's powder does not
affect them at all. They eat it as though it were some
delicacy & then come back to torture us afresh. I*

should not talk of such things to you, my dear Mary, &
a year ago I would not have done, but they have be-
come commonplace to the men who exist out here. I
am so glad you went to see Martha's baby before you
went to London. My Mother is pleased as punch to
have a grandson. I am now an uncle, which is very
strange.

Hands shaking. The letters dancing across the page.
Words forming which did not echo his thoughts. Concepts he could no longer understand. Mother. Colin.
Nightingale. Tree. What did they mean? What was a
tree? He knew such things existed. Could remember
them, even. But what did "tree" *mean?* Shivers. Jagged
lines across his vision. Somewhere along the trench
young Davey singing, singing. *Twenty thousand
Cornishmen . . .* and how many others? His heart beat
away inside his chest, but it felt heavy now. Weighed
down with loss. So many friends gone. Under the con-
cealing mud, did the dead men dance? He had heard
music at night. Seen their faces. Was it better to be dead
than to go on when it was no longer possible to go on?
The body did not give up, but the spirit did. Let me go
home. Let me. Oh God. Please.

September 1918
   My dear Colin,
   You were right. Again. It seems we are soon coming
home. Now that it is really going to happen, I almost
dread it. What can you know of me anymore? I have
seen too much. I have had the joy sucked out of me.
When I heard that the War was about to end. I took
one of the horses & rode away over the frosty fields.
There was a moon up in the sky, but no stars. I let the
horse go where he would. The cold wind streamed past
me & I felt nothing. No joy, no grief, no regret, no
wish for the future. Nothing. I am like a dry husk.
   It was good of you to say you would meet me when-
ever I reached London & take me home. I thought I
might spend a couple of days in London first. I will
come round to your Father's place in Fitzroy Square &
we could fix a time. But only if you are sure that is
not inconvenient. When I know the date & time, I will

send you a telegram. Even when it becomes official, I think it will be awhile before they get us out of here. The night they told us that hostilities were about to cease (though we are still being shelled), our Captain broke out the brandy & gave us all a tot. We were supposed to drink a toast to dear old Blighty. I was not the only man there who could not swallow it down. I have come through sound in wind & limb but so many of them have not. Recently I have been acting as orderly to the Captain. I cannot bear to think of the difference in his conditions & those of the men who fought the War. Many of our officers are brave & courageous, I know that. Hundreds of officers have died, I know that too. But the treatment of the ordinary tommy in the trenches makes me choke. But I must not go on. We can talk about this later. If you want to. You are two years younger than I am, in age, & about a century younger in experience. I do not say this in any patronizing way. I wish it were not true. I wish I had not seen a hundredth of the things I have seen. You could not imagine. When we meet, you must pretend you do not notice the shaking of my hands, or the fact that I break off in the middle of a sentence & forget what I was saying. If tears roll down my face, just look away. I am not aware myself of these things, except perhaps the shaking, but the men here tell me of it.

"You're a crock, Corp," they said. "Just a bleedin' wreck." The bleeding was internal, but he felt it nonetheless. A dried husk. The blood was the color of hatred. Gray and thick as the mud which had swallowed so many of the dead. And, in their dreams, the living.

4

All she could hear was the clamor of the wind. It pounded at her ears, whipped the ends of her hair spitefully against her cheeks, filled the immense sky with sound. She stood on the edge of a cliff of rain-slick black rocks which tumbled down to where a stream ran noisily between grassy banks. A flock of birds battled against the fierce air, heading for shelter. Winter had come early this year: the air was heavy with sleet that was gradually turning to snow. Thick gray cloud spread a ponderous light over the great treeless climb of the moors and the tops of the furthest hills were already white.

As she came nearer to home, she could see the lights of Misselthwaite. The trees of the park swayed beneath the onslaughts of the wind which rushed, clear and cutting as a piece of glass, from off the hills. Beyond them, the moors themselves were in constant motion, the coarse grass moving as though it were water.

She looked forward to the fug of the kitchen. Mrs. Medlock might have baked scones; there was butter from the home farm, and last year's raspberry jam. It was not really outside weather, but she had found it impossible to stay indoors. That very morning the news had been announced on the wireless: the war was officially over, the men were coming home. The house had seemed too small to contain the joy she felt. Seizing a coat, she had rushed out into the cold morning and walked until she was breathless, until her legs had lost their strength and she sank to the ground. Dickon was coming home. All these months, weeks, years, she had never dared to hope that he would survive, but against all the odds—Colin had told her the life expectancies of men at the Front—he had.

She laughed aloud into the wind and felt her laugh tossed roughly back into her face. Dickon was coming home, Dickon with his funny red face and round blue eyes. The three of them would be together again and everything would be the way it used to be. There was even a letter from him in the pocket of her skirt, though she had not stopped to open it after Archie Craven had come into the kitchen to give them the news.

"Do your very best for dinner tonight," he told the lady from the village who had taken over the kitchen when Cook left to work in a muntions factory, "and ask Pitcher to ice the champagne. This is an evening to celebrate."

"Is it?" Colin had come in behind him. "To celebrate what, exactly?"

"Just for tonight, Colin, let's be glad that it's over, shall we?" Archie put an arm round his son's thin shoulders. "We can start to count the cost tomorrow."

"We'll be doing that for the next fifty years or more," said Colin.

Mary was sitting at the big pine table, helping to prepare the vegetables which one of the gardeners had brought in earlier that morning. "I thought this was the war to end all wars," she said.

"If you believe that . . ." Colin sounded contemptuous. He picked up one of the circles of carrot which lay like a small sun on the chopping board and put it in his mouth.

Now, Mary rounded the side of the big house and made for the back door. The wind caught at it and slammed it back against the wall of the kitchen passage; it took all her strength to close it again. She saw Colin standing outside the kitchen door and smiled at him. "Isn't it wonderful?" she said. "Isn't it?"

She leaned against the wall and began to drag off her rubber boots.

"Mary."

She paused, assimilating the apprehension which swelled his voice. She did not answer, sensing immediately that something dreadful had happened, something not to be borne. Unwinding her woollen scarf she carefully hung it up.

"Mary, listen."

If she did not answer, if she methodically took off her coat, shook the flakes of snow from it, set her wet gloves to dry on the radiator, maybe he would not tell her whatever it was. Dickon's letter rustled in her skirt and briefly she closed her eyes, steadying herself for what was coming. Be brave, Mary, she told herself. Be strong. She pulled on her house shoes and did up the buttons. She stared down at the pitted red and black tiles, then up into her cousin's face.

In the backstairs gloom, she stood like a prize fighter, Colin thought. The upper half of her body leaned toward him, her hands were clenched into fists, her eyes were huge in her pale face. She knows, he thought. As I did, the minute my father called me in to his study. She doesn't need to be told.

He held out a hand and she took it. "Oh, Mary," he said, and his voice trembled then broke so that he could not continue. He pressed his lips together in an effort to stop himself from crying.

Calmly she said: "What's happened?"

"Dickon." Colin pressed a hand to his forehead. "His parents had a telegram last night. They came over to tell us. They're here now."

"Tell me." Mary was surprised at how detached she sounded, as though she were enquiring about a stranger, instead of one of the two most important people in her life.

In spite of his efforts, tears began to roll down Colin's face. "Missing," he said. "Presumed dead." The words had the solemnity of a morning bell.

"That can't be right. I heard from him this morning."

"Presumed dead." Colin's features dissolved, sliding like melted butter across his face.

"But I haven't even opened his letter," Mary said.

"Missing. Oh, Mary. What are we going to do without—"

"Is that all you know?" she interrupted, before he could complete the sentence she was already asking herself.

"So far. There was just the telegram. Apparently he went missing several days ago."

"Presumed dead," Mary repeated. "That doesn't necessarily mean—"

"It does. And we're going to have to accept it." Colin covered his face with his hands then buried his head among the piled coats and jackets hanging from the row of brass pegs. "He's never going to come back to us, Mary. Never again." His shoulders shook. "Dickon, Dickon," he said. He breathed in the odor of rubberized cloth and wet wool; the melted snow on Mary's scarf was sharp against his cheek. How many times had he worn these clothes to walk with Dickon and Mary across the moors? How many times . . . If Dickon was dead, then something dearer than life itself had been lost. Not just from the present but from the past as well. He saw the years behind like a rainbow-colored ribbon spread across sunlit pastures while ahead, they now stretched grayly over a barren inky plain.

"Don't give way, Colin." Mary's cool little voice broke into his grief. He felt her hand squeeze his shoulder.

"I can't help it." He thought of the tantrums which so often engulfed him as a child. How easy it would be to give way now, to beat his fists against the wall, to scream out his sense of anger and impotence as he used to do. He was old enough now to realize how little such rages achieved, yet, however temporary, there would be some comfort in breaking down. If he could only give expression to some of the pain he felt, it might ease the ache in his heart.

"Yes, you can," Mary said. "Besides, we have to be strong. Think how much worse it is for his mother and father."

Colin wanted to say that the Sowerbys had other children, that Phil already looked astonishingly like his older brother and would be a memorial to him, while he and Mary had only had Dickon. But it would sound graceless and selfish.

"You said they're here—we must go and speak to them."

"Yes." He stood up, wiped his eyes on his sleeve. In silence, they walked together to Archibald Craven's study.

Mrs. Sowerby was sitting in an easy chair, staring into the fire, while her husband stood at the window, looking out over the snowy gardens. The fall had been slight, no more than enough to outline the clods of turned earth in the flower-beds and lie along the ivy on top of the garden walls.

"Ah," Archie Craven said. "Here you are." He cleared his throat. He had already expressed his personal sorrow at the news, and offered the sincerest hopes that the outcome would prove positive. In his heart, he was afraid it would not. He wished that the Sowerbys would be less resigned, less stoical. It would be easier to offer comfort if they showed more of their feelings, instead of uttering philosophical inanities. He felt a sudden anger at them. Dammit: Dickon deserved more than this, more than his mother's straight back and fierce eyes, his father's twisting fingers. He would have liked to tell them how much he had intended to do for the lad, how he had envisaged Dickon working on the Misselthwaite land, starting out as a gardener or gamekeeper, and perhaps eventually, if he continued to show the qualities of industry and reliability which he had displayed before the war, rising to the elevated position of estate manager. He had even wondered about offering him a farming tenancy, giving him a helping hand, some encouragement to rise above his humble origins. With luck and hard work, he could really have made something of himself. He kept such thoughts to himself, not wishing to seem to be trespassing on someone else's emotions.

Mary walked across the room and touched Susan Sowerby's shoulder. "I'm sorry," she said. "I am so terribly sorry."

"Oh, Miss Mary . . ." Susan Sowerby stroked the hand which rested on the coarse wool of her shabby coat.

"We had plans, the three of us," Mary said. "Such plans . . ."

"I know, my dear. And you must go ahead without him. It's what he would have wished."

Again Archie Craven cleared his throat. Should he point out that the telegram had only said he was missing? Perhaps, after all, it was precipitate to assume that

Dickon was dead? "We don't know for certain that he—that he won't be coming back," he said.

"There's not much chance that he will," Sowerby said forthrightly. His eyes were clear and blue. Dickon's eyes, Colin thought. They showed no trace of tears. "They wouldn't be sending telegrams such as that if they weren't sure, would they?"

"They wouldn't let us suffer like this," agreed his wife. "Not if they thought there was still a chance." She clenched her work-roughened hands in her lap and folded her mouth together.

"I don't know," Archie said. He feared that they were right. On the other hand, the conduct of this war had been characterized by so much incompetence, so much carelessness, so much disregard for humanity . . . when the Sowerbys had gone, carrying their grief with them like an unwieldy bundle, he would make some telephone calls, try to find out more. Mrs. Ashton at the exchange would listen in to every word, but it couldn't be helped. "But I do know that it's a sad day for Misselthwaite and for the whole dale." He considered offering them a brandy, but again resisted the impulse, in case they should think him unfeeling enough to believe that strong drink could provide any comfort.

Mrs. Sowerby stood up. "We felt it was right to come and let you know," she said, looking at Colin. "Seeing as how you've been good to Dickon. To all of us. But we'd best be getting back. The bairns at home are all to sixes and sevens, as you can imagine. They'll need me there."

"Aye," said her husband. "And I'm expected back to work."

"Surely not, man," Archie said. "Not when you've heard such devastating news."

"If I don't work, I don't get paid," Sowerby said flatly. He moved over to the door, nodding to Colin as he did so. "Come along, Susan. It's a fair old walk home and there's more snow to come."

"We can get out the car," Archie said.

"We'll not bother you," said Sowerby.

"It's no bother at all. It's the very least I could—"

But Sowerby was shaking his head. "Thanks all the same."

"I'll walk with you some of the way," Colin said. "If you don't mind, that is."

"Of course we don't." Dickon's mother smiled at him. "It'll do us all good to get some fresh air into our lungs."

"Will you come, Mary?" asked Colin.

She shook her head. "No." She glowered, hoping her heavy frown would stop him asking why.

"Father?"

"I think not." Archie held out his hand to Dickon's parents. "If there's anything I can do . . ."

"Bring my son back," Susan Sowerby said. "That's all I want. Bring our Dickon safe home again."

Up in her room, Mary threw herself across her bed and lay with her face in the pillow. If Dickon was dead, she wanted to die herself. Sadness rolled through her and then ebbed, leaving an emptiness, as though all feeling, all emotion, had been sucked away. She felt nothing. Where was he now? Were those round blue eyes and funny face buried beneath the mud of France? She remembered him so clearly, the grassy smell of his rough red hair, the way he threw back his head and whistled like a bird, the sound of his laughter. She remembered him singing, standing behind the schoolroom piano while she played an accompaniment, his eyes fixed earnestly on hers. She remembered the two of them entwined, rolling over and over down the banks of the lake and splashing into the water, the silky feel of his skin in her arms. Had all that gone? She knew nothing of how he had died. Had he been blown to pieces by a shell? Had he felt any pain? Had he had time to realize that his life was over? She thought of poor Faringdon in the Scarborough hospital. The side of his skull had been streaked with a broad furrow of naked skin where the hair no longer grew. His sightless questing head had turned pitifully this way and that as she and Colin talked to him; he had tried to smile but could not hide the expression of strain on his face, as though he was desperately willing his eyes to see once more.

She hoped that Dickon's death had been quick.

Sitting up, she reached into her pocket and pulled out the green envelope. His careful dame-school hand had grown familiar over the years of war. She held the letter, not wanting to read it. It seemed strange that she could be holding a letter written when he was still alive, knowing that he no longer was. Missing, presumed dead. She allowed herself a glimmer of hope. Perhaps he lay wounded somewhere, still unconscious, unable to say who he was, unable to tell them that at home there were people who waited for him, people who loved him. But no. His parents were right. The authorities would never send a telegram like that if they were not certain of their facts. It would be too cruel.

Slowly she opened the letter.

Dear Mary, she read. It was very good to get your last letter & to hear how things are in Misselthwaite. I am so eager to get home. They say the War is ending but we are still being attacked by the enemy, though not all the time. I shall only believe it is finally over when I stand on the moors again &, feel the wind in my hair. I am sick & tired, Mary, worn out, the way my clothes are worn out. I believe I shall never be rested again. I keep thinking of when we were young, the things we shared. We were happy then, weren't we? I doubt that I can ever really be happy again, when so many of my fellows have died, in such ugly ways. You cannot—&, should not have to—imagine how such deaths degrade a human being. A man with his hands blown away, his head sheared off, his guts hanging out over his trousers, is no longer human. The smell of blood will stay with me until I die. I know I should not write such things to you, but now that the end seems close at last, I find I am sometimes near to bursting with the need to explain what we have suffered out here. I am afraid I am full of hatred.

Mary put the letter down. He had never written to her with such honesty before. He had mentioned the noise, the rats, the lice which infected his clothes, the mud which filled the trenches, but only in passing, as though they were incidentals to be shrugged off. He rarely spoke of his feelings. One of the reasons she loved Colin was that he so rarely tried to protect her from reality. However much she shrank from it, he dragged her from the flimsy shelters of pretense when she tried to hide, and forced her to look, to face up to things. Until now, Dickon had not done that. For the most part, he had written of the lighter side of his life, insofar as there was one. He had written to Colin of friends killed, and once, when a horse was blown apart, his words had almost bled onto the paper, but apart from that he had said little. And now . . . she looked down again at the schoolboy writing. Had he had some presentiment of his own death?

> But I know I should be thankful that I have come through so far without a scratch. Unless you count the nightmares which I suffer from. Oh Mary, I am afraid that even when I am back at Misselthwaite, I shall not see the beauty anymore. I am afraid that my eyes are too full of the horrors I have been forced to look at. I should not be morbid, I know. It will be so good to be with you & Colin again, to see my parents & brothers & sisters. I have been thinking that I should go somewhere when I get back, get some kind of training, though I do not know what. But I believe the Gov'ment is setting up schemes for the likes of me. I would like to hear what you think about this. When I get home.

He had ended with his usual signature then drawn a line from the word "when" to the bottom of the page and added "if."

Grief gathered inside Mary and moved fierily toward her throat, so that she was afraid she might choke on it. She leaped from her bed and went over to the chest of drawers which stood against the wall. There was a carved box standing on it, in which she kept her pieces of jewelery: a gold locket set with seed pearls which her uncle had given her, her mother's engagement ring, a diamond brooch that had belonged to her grandmother, a gold chain. Screwed up underneath was a tiny scrap of paper and she fished it out, unfolded it, smoothed it with her finger. *I will cum bak.* And above the roughly printed words, a sort of picture: a nest with a bird sitting on it. It was the first letter Dickon had written to her. Oh God, oh God . . .

She ran to the window, throwing it open and letting

the freezing air swirl around her. She wanted to cry but the tears would not come. How could it have happened, that a man survived the horrors of war for so many years and then, at the very end, went missing? How could God, Fate, be so unfeeling as to let it happen? She stared at the terrace below. For a moment she contemplated throwing herself out of the window. She imagined the flight of her body through the air, the shock and jolt as she thudded against the stone flags. It would be a quick death. Or would it? Suppose she lay there, not dead but crippled for life. Suppose she did not die but merely damaged herself so severely that she was condemned to spend the rest of her life in pain.

Reading the letter again, the words did not sound like Dickon's. For the first time, she understood how little the Dickon who might have come back to Yorkshire would have resembled the one who had left.

5

At Archie Craven's urging, they had come down to the house in Fitzroy Square two weeks ago.

"The place has been neglected for the last five or six years," he told Colin, "and I haven't the time to go and see what needs doing, now that we're getting back to normal."

"Normal!" Colin had uttered the word with scorn. "As if things will ever be normal again."

"Exactly so," said Archie. "However, I should like you to look the place over and draw up a list of priorities for me. Last time I was down there, the roof was leaking dreadfully. And the housekeeper tells me there is evidence of rot in some of the bedroom floorboards."

Colin had seemed less than enthused. "I don't suppose you want to come, do you, Mary?" he asked grumpily, and had seemed surprised when she agreed.

"An excellent idea," approved Archie. "It'll do you both good to enjoy yourselves for a change, get out and about, meet your friends and so forth."

An excellent idea, as her uncle had said. Except that so far, Colin had objected every single time Mary suggested doing anything in the least enjoyable. A concert at the Wigmore Music Rooms, for instance, or the new exhibition at the British Museum. Only yesterday, they had conducted the latest in a series of disputes.

"An exhibition of paintings: what a waste of time," he had said imperiously. "When there are so many more important things to be done."

"I don't see that art and music are unimportant," contradicted Mary. "Quite the opposite. Anyway, a year ago, when you decided to take up oil painting, you told me art was the encapsulation of the human spirit."

"I won't say I was entirely wrong," Colin said, "but my perspective might have been wrongly slanted."

"I see," Mary said, heavily sarcastic.

"Besides, photography is the coming thing, the new art form." Colin brushed the black hair off his brow. "The photographs from the Front are as impressive as any painting could be. I'm going to buy myself a camera and take it up seriously."

"Until another craze sweeps you up. Honestly, Colin, you're like a weathercock, going whichever way the wind blows."

"How utterly beastly you are to me." Colin threw himself on to the chair by the fireside. "Anyway, I've got to squeeze as much into my days as I can. You know I'm still trying to make up for lost time."

"Then come to the British Museum with me."

He gave her his most supercilious expression and did not bother to answer.

She had flounced out of the room, pausing at the door to say: "You can't live off your invalid childhood for the rest of your life, you know."

What annoyed her most was that in response to her own suggestions, all he had offered in return was a talk by some pacifist organization down in Blackheath or a reading of poetry by Balkan refugees at some dreary lecture room in Holborn.

It was nearly three months since the telegram had arrived announcing that Dickon was missing and there had been no further news. She knew Colin was still mourning him: so, indeed, was she. But she needed a change. Everything had been so dreary while the war dragged on. For far too long she had felt as old as the moors round Misselthwaite, and the limited chances for gaiety offered by the Yorkshire social scene only added to that feeling. But she was nearly nineteen and she wanted to be young, to be like the girls whose exploits she read about in the society pages of the newspapers, the girls who were rebelling against the stuffy conventions of their parents, who belonged to the smart sets, like those who surrounded the Prince of Wales or Lady Diana Cooper. She longed to smoke Turkish cigarettes and bob her hair and dance till dawn in smoky basement night-clubs. When she had finally understood that Dickon was lost to them, she had known she would mourn him for the rest of her life. Even now, she was pierced by sadness as sharp and cold as an icicle whenever she thought of him. And yet, with the war over, life was slowly beginning to return to some kind of normality, and with a certain surprise, she was realizing that there were limits to how much time a person could spend being grief-stricken.

"Mary! Mary, where are you?"

Signing the letter she had just finished and folding it in two, Mary quickly pushed it into an envelope and sealed it firmly. If he knew she had been writing letters, Colin would demand to know to whom; if he discovered that, despite his disapproval, she had accepted Lucy Gardiner's invitation to a musical soirée next week he would most certainly create a fuss.

"People like her can't be justified," he had announced a few days earlier, when the invitation had arrived. "Come the revolution, the Lucy Gardiners of this world will be the first to be lined up against the wall and shot."

"What a dreadful, intolerant, *horrible* thing to say," protested Mary.

"Why? She and her kind are leeches, sucking the blood from our society and giving nothing in return. The only thing they're fit for is filling space in the gossip columns. I don't suppose she's got a brain in her head."

"So what?" Mary had responded. "We can't all be little geniuses like you. Besides, I understand she's got several children, and a husband who needs her to entertain for him." According to the newspapers, Sir Mark Gardiner was some kind of financier attached to one of the merchant banks, though Mary was not quite sure what he did.

"Children. Entertaining. She's got an army of servants who do all the real drudgery, *and* she probably pays them a pittance. All she ever has to do is appear at the appropriate time in yet another frock and smile at people. Not exactly a worthwhile way to spend your life, is it?"

"She does a lot of charity work, too."

"Bridge and beetle drives," sniffed Colin. "I despise people like that."

"The only reason you despise Lucy Gardiner, whom you've never even met," said Mary, "is because you know she's Major Sambourne's sister."

"Why should that make the slightest difference?"

"Because you're jealous of him."

"Jealous? What is there to be jealous of?" His slate-black eyes bored into her. "Unless, of course, you're having an affair with him. Are you, Mary?"

"Don't be so offensive and ridiculous," snapped Mary. "And even if I were, it's nothing to do with you."

"Isn't it? You are my cousin, after all. I'm responsible for you."

"You certainly are not."

"And if I thought you had Given Yourself to the Laughing Cavalier . . ." Here, Colin had produced a cruel parody of Major Sambourne's tittery laugh, "I should have no alternative but to avenge your honor and call him out." He made several dramatic passes through the air with an invisible foil.

"I haven't seen him since he left Misselthwaite," Mary said, trying not to laugh. "That was ages ago." She had not added that, since then, she had received several letters from him. And he had kindly asked his sister to invite her to this soirée.

Today, however, she felt too tired to argue. In the moments of depression which so often afflicted her these days, and had done so ever since the telegram announcing Dickon's death, it sometimes seemed as though she spent most of her life standing up to Colin. The trouble with him was that he was so often right. Lucy Gardiner probably *was* frivolous, she probably *did* fill her days with trivial pursuits. Was that a crime? Like Mary's own mother, even if she did not make any significant contribution to the good of mankind, she undoubtedly cheered and amused, something which could not be said of Colin.

So now, hiding her letter under the blotter, she got up from the desk and moved swiftly to stand by the long windows so that Colin should not suspect what she had been doing. In the square, rain poured from a leaden sky. The rotting yellow leaves of winter still covered the grass and flower-beds, and lay piled up against the rail-

ings. In the bare branches of the plane trees, sparrows
sat huddled together; water darkened the roadway and
swirled in the gutters. In Yorkshire, the rain fell softly
over heather and gorse, filling the air with moisture
which lay against the face like a cobweb; here, it fell
sharply from gray skies, jagged as broken glass. It was
cold, too. She could see steam pluming from the nostrils
of the blinkered horse standing between the shafts of a
tradesman's cart which was delivering to the house
across the square.

She thought of sunshine, of the exotic India of her
childhood, of the vibrancy which she still remembered
clearly, of the warmth and color. There had been a procession, once, through the main street of the little town
near the cantonment. She remembered elephants tricked
out in glittering golden harness, barefoot men with dark
faces and wild eyes, the constant throb of drums. A boy
rajah, too, carried on the shoulders of his servants, his
silk tunic sewn with jewels. In retrospect, although she
knew she had not been particularly happy there, India
took on the magical properties of a fairytale, all gold
and red and azure, brilliant and strange. How different
from the subdued grayness of London in winter.

"Listen!" Colin staggered in to the room, hung about
with equipment, a tripod slung over his shoulder, both
his arms weighed down with boxes and bundles. "Look!"

Mary's eyebrows rose coolly as she turned towards
him. "Yes, Colin?" she said, in her most irritatingly languid tone. She was conscious of the picture she made,
standing against the light, framed by the long curtains,
her fair hair piled becomingly on top of her head. "What
is it?"

He took no notice of her attempt to establish superior-
ity. "I bought a camera. Look—here." He waved a box
at her. "You've got to pose for me right this minute."

"Pose?"

"I want to try it out, do you see? Take some pictures
from life. I can't afford to hire a professional model.
Besides, I ought to get some experience first."

"So I'll do?"

"Of course."

"What makes you think that I—"

"Come on, Mary. It's easy. All you have to do is sit

and read or knit or whatever it is you do, and I'll set up lights and things and take pictures of you."

"Fully clothed, I presume."

"Of *course* fully clothed." He considered the idea. "Though now you mention it . . ."

"No," Mary said. "Whatever you're thinking, I won't."

Though Colin had not for a moment envisaged photographing Mary naked, he could see at once what a brilliant idea it was. He had never seen her without her clothes, never even consciously imagined her in such a state. Once, as they changed under towels by the side of the lake, he had caught sight of her small breasts, the pinkness of her nipples, and been forced to dive into the water to hide his sudden arousal. And occasionally, when she sat against his pillows in her nightclothes as they talked before going to bed, he caught a flash of her upper thigh and the mesmerising shadows above. He had wondered then, and known that she would be beautiful.

Looking at her now, with the daylight sifting through the softness of her hair, he sighed internally. She herself was so *unsoft*, so prickly. And yet, occasionally, he glimpsed another Mary, one who waited, like a damped-down fire, for someone who would breathe on the embers of her, fan her into flame.

He began to clown. "I'm Dr. Dodgson," he said. He set up his tripod, mimed an eccentric Oxford professor taking picture after picture, "I'm Juliet-Margaret Cameron," became a plump lady photographer. He pretended to be a bemused sitter awkward under the camera's eye, he moved objects about on the tables, shifted furniture. He had always had a knack for imitation: one moment he was long and lugubrious, like the author of *Alice in Wonderland,* the next a fussy middle-aged female. Mary sat down on the horsehair sofa and laughed delightedly.

Colin rejoiced inwardly at her laughter, loving the way the soft dimples moved in her face when she was happy, which these days was all too seldom. It seemed to have been months since she had even smiled. Dickon's disappearance—he still refused to think of it as a death—had cast both of them down so far that at times he had wondered how they would recover. They were both orphans,

they had both had more than their share of childhood
difficulty; Dickon's appearance in their lives had been as
refreshing as the winds which blew across the moors.
Since Dickon had gone off to the war, Colin had had
plenty of time to analyze the relationship between the
three of them. He knew that he and Mary needed
Dickon to complete themselves. Without him, they were
too rich a mixture. Dickon diluted the intensity of their
natures, absorbed their more extreme tendencies, gave
them a sense of balance.

But Dickon was gone.

Mary said: "Oh, Colin. You are *such* an idiot."

"I know." He gave a rueful smile. Last night, Dickon
had come into his dreams again. "Colin," he had said,
reaching out a hand. His blue eyes had been loving.
"Wait for me," he said. In the dream, Colin thought that
he himself had cried out: "How long must I wait?" but
he could not be sure. There had been blood in the
dream, too, and a headless horse lying on the ground,
its shredded belly oozing green guts and vomit. He had
woken excited, and dismayed.

Lucy Gardiner's reception rooms were crowded. If Mary
were honest with herself—and though she regretted it,
most of the time she was—none of the people there was
particularly interesting. That did not worry her. After
the restricted social scene in Yorkshire, she enjoyed the
admiring glances which she received, the gallantries
which were offered. Looking about her, she wondered
whether Barney Sambourne would appear or not; Lucy
had not been sure whether her brother was going to
attend. Though scarcely recalling what he looked like,
she remembered that she had liked him, had felt sorry
for him, had enjoyed the two or three occasions she had
spent with him. And he had, of course, been responsible
for her friendship with Lucy, by giving her his sister's
address and insisting that she call when she was next in
London. Colin's accusations against him were ridiculous:
even if she had felt inclined to Give Herself to a man—
and these days, girls quite often did, or so she understood from whispered conversations between the girls
she knew—it would most certainly not be to someone
as old as the major, nor as damaged.

Standing near the fire, she laughed at something one of Lucy's guests was saying about the eccentricity of Erik Satie—not that it was particularly funny but she needed time to recall precisely who Satie was. A painter? An actor? A musician of some kind? At the same time, she asked herself to what kind of man she *would* Give Herself, supposing she were to do so outside marriage. The concept was unthinkable, but nonetheless, she thought it. The trouble was, she knew so few men. What about Colin? Apart from the fact that he was her cousin, she simply did not feel romantic about him. Dickon? Again the old griefs swept over her. So much promise. So much potential, not just Dickon but all those young men who lay dead. Could she have gone to bed with Dickon? He was not from her own social background, of course. And however much she despised herself for being a snob, she rather thought that would make some difference. Besides, he was only a boy. If she was ever going to Give Herself, it ought to be to a man, someone who would treat her gently, give her time to adjust to . . . well, to whatever it was that married women had to adjust. She was remarkably vague about the details.

She heard someone call her name. "Mary. Mary Craven." She looked up, glancing about.

"Miss Craven. Over here." And there, at the edge of the crowd around the fireplace, waving at her, was Major Sambourne. She smiled.

Watching that smile, Barney Sambourne felt his heart jump within his chest. *Alice.* He began to push through to her but she indicated that she would join him.

When she stood beside him, he took her hand and held it close. "It's so good to see you again."

"You too."

"My sister said she would invite you."

"Yes."

They smiled at each in silence, then Barney said impulsively: "Miss Craven, I should so much like to—"

"My name is Lennox, not Craven," Mary said. He had referred to her as Miss Craven before, both during his time at the Misselthwaite convalescent hospital in letters he had written to her but she had not liked to correct him then, thinking it might confuse him further. "My father was my guardian's brother-in-law."

The major gasped, swayed slightly, steadied himself by grasping her shoulder with his free hand. "Lennox?" he said. "Your name is Lennox?"

"Yes." His fingers were digging into Mary's back. She tried not to show her alarm. The blood had drained from his face and she was afraid he was going to faint.

Sambourne's mind flashed back to the dust and heat of India, and the heart-stopping shock of finding the *Memsahib* dead beneath the muslin mosquito netting. There had been a child, yes, Alice's child, though he had never seen her while Alice was alive. He dimly recalled walking through the deserted bungalow, trying to hold back his tears, and his colonel's exclamations as he opened a door to find a little girl standing stiffly in the middle of her nursery, still unaware that death lay on every side of her. The shock of realizing that Alice was dead had lent an air of misty unreality to everything else that morning, but now he remembered wondering why the child had been spared. Was it possible that this Mary was . . . ?

"You remind me so much of someone I used to know," he said, as he had said the first time they met. "Alice. Alice Lennox." Saying her name aloud for the first time in years made his head feel too large for his shoulders, too large for his tumbling thoughts, and he shook it hard, hoping they would reassemble themselves in due order.

Mary's face was as pale as his. Major Barney Sambourne. *Barney, there is a child here . . .* The words rang in her head. "My parents died of cholera," she said. "Out in India." There had been a jewel-eyed snake, she remembered, green as parrot feathers against the dusty floor of her nursery. And then the large officer she knew—Colonel McGrew—came into the room followed by the boy officer who used to stare at her mother. She had not thought of that day for years, had deliberately expelled it from her mind, but now it came crowding back at her: the windless heat, the wailing from the servants' huts, bugles sounding in the cantonment, the forbidden taste of wine dry in her mouth.

"Alice Lennox," Sambourne repeated softly.

"My mother." The skin of Mary's face felt as though it was too tightly stretched across the flesh beneath. She tried to produce a social smile but was afraid that if she did so, her cheeks might suddenly split like the tomatoes that Mr. Roach, the head gardener at Misselthwaite, grew in the greenhouses behind the stable block.

"This is wonderful," said the major. Suddenly aware of his hand on her shoulder, he thrust it into the pocket of his jacket. How young he had been then, barely twenty-one, a complete innocent.

"You knew my mother," Mary said. He was the first person she had met since leaving India who had known Alice. It occurred to her that Archie Craven must have done too but if so, he had never spoken of it. Nor had she ever asked. Perhaps her father had met her mother in India, rather than in England. She realized how ignorant she was about her own origins.

"I most certainly did, though I had no idea, when we spoke in Yorkshire, of who you were." Barney could not believe it: Alice, resurrected. Was it meant? Was he being given a second chance? His parents, his surviving sister, even Sir Mark, her husband, were constantly urging him to find himself a wife before he rejoined his regiment in India. This could be his opportunity to please himself as well as them. But she looked so young. "Miss Cra—Miss Lennox," he blurted, before he could stop himself. "May I take you out to dinner tomorrow?"

"Uh . . . that would be—"

"Or the day after? I know a really rather jolly little place near Piccadilly. The food's not bad. We could even dance, if you'd like." The possibility of holding Mary in his arms was so heady that it induced in the major a feeling of being afloat on a sea of cotton wool. He laughed shrilly, hoping that she would not notice his disorientation. "Do say yes, Miss Lennox."

"I'd like that," said Mary, though she was not sure that she really would. She saw the terror lurking at the back of his eyes and felt the stirrings of something she had never previously experienced: compassion. "But only if you will call me Mary. We're old friends, after all."

"Old friends." He could feel his palm sweating against hers and realized he was still holding her hand. He laughed again. "Yes, indeed. Old, old friends."

He is rather sweet, Mary thought, despite the laugh.

She had forgotten just how boyish his features were; despite that, he was not just handsome—in the same way as the Prince of Wales—but also distinguished. Mrs. Medlock, who had it from one of the nursing orderlies at the Misselthwaite hospital, had told her that he had received medals and commendations for his bravery. Other women in the room were eyeing him with approval.

What would Colin say when he learned that she had accepted an invitation from Major Sambourne? Just the two of them. For dinner, maybe dancing. She could easily imagine his scorn and disapproval. For a moment, and unaccountably, she thought of Dickon, and frowned, feeling the pain settle in her chest, a nugget of undigested grief. This would happen for the rest of her life, she suspected. It was something she would have to learn to live with.

6

Was there anything else in the world quite as delicious as champagne? Mary took another sip from her glass, shuddering with delight as the bubbles broke against her tongue. To be here, in London, at the whirling center of it all: this was what she had wanted for so long, this was life at its richest and most exhilarating. On a tiny stage at the far end of the room, a six-piece Negro jazz band perspired, faces shiny as syrup under the lights, their brass instruments flashing as they prepared to launch into the next set. The crowded basement smelled of damp and lipstick, sweat and cigarette smoke. The clamour of voices rose to the low ceiling and bounced back again to scatter over the heads of the revelers in disjointed syllables, pieces of words. Overall hung a harsh sweet odor which Mary could not identify but which often lingered in the air of the night-clubs Barney took her to; she thought of it as the essence of the after-dark excitement which she craved. It still seemed unbelievable that the years of dull routine, of school terms and school holidays, of war and loss and grieving, had metamorphosed into these mad gay evenings when she and Barney and their group drank champagne, watched the cabaret, danced cheek to cheek to the new tunes which swept across the Atlantic from America. Often at Misselthwaite, she had wondered whether she would ever reach the unattainable longed-for state of adulthood. And here she was, indubitably grown-up at last.

Across the bobbed and brilliantined heads of the waiting crowd she watched the trombonist raise his instrument to his lips. Behind him, the drummer grinned manically, showing teeth white as peppermints. He brushed his sticks in a crescendo over the drums in front of him and the waiting dancers cheered. The singer, a negress swathed in a sequinned dress which outlined every voluptuous curve of her big body, clicked her fingers as the pianist struck three soft chords. "Every time we say goodbye," she sang, in a voice that resembled nothing that Mary had ever heard before, the words flowing like dark treacle into the smoky atmosphere, "I die a little." The crowd listened in silence as the song sighed to its close and then, as she lingered on the last honeyed vowels, the trombone glittered, the horn leaned into a new set of chords, the tempo changed and suddenly she was shaking to the rhythm of "I Wish I Could Shimmy Like My Sister Kate." The crowd wedged together on the dance floor shimmied along, hips swaying, fingers snapping, the beads on their short dresses clicking in time to the music, fringed hems swinging, buttoned shoes tapping out the rhythms. The saxophonist stepped forward and took over the tune, the melody oozing like melted toffee from between his fingers, while the big singer jigged beside him, waiting to come back into the song.

Barney took Mary's hand and held it close. He said something to her, smiling, and she smiled back, not hearing him over the dum-dum-dum of the drums, the sliding throb of the trombone, the silky slither of the piano, but seeing her name in the movement of his lips. These days he was less prone to the sudden violent shakings of the head which had so alarmed her when she first met him up in Yorkshire; he had told her how the images would shatter like broken glass inside his skull and she hoped his increasing calm might have something to do with the security he clearly felt when in her company. They had been to the theater earlier that evening, to see a musical show, followed by supper at the Café de Paris, after which they had come on here to drink champagne. She opened her beaded evening bag and pulled out a silver cigarette case. She tapped the end of an Abdulla cigarette against the top of the tiny table at which they sat and waited for Barney to lean forward with a light. Predictably, home from Oxford for the Christmas vacation, Colin had created a fuss when he realized she had taken up smoking, told her in his most censorious voice that it was fast, she looked cheap, that the next thing they knew, she'd be dancing in the chorus at the Alhambra or taking a job in a Soho bawdy house, to which she had coolly replied: "How do you know I haven't done so already?"

She did not pretend that the war had been anything like as hard for her as it had for others. Apart from Dickon, she had lost nobody close to her, at least nobody she knew well. Nonetheless, along with the rest of the civilian population, now that it was over, she was happy to put the dreary wartime years behind her, to forget the terrible rollcall of the dead and the daily knife-edge of waiting for something indefinably appalling to happen. Dancing, drinking, driving into the country in Barney's sports car, wild picnics on the beach at Sandwich Bay, taking off at a moment's notice for some hectic treasure hunt, parties, parties, parties, bottle parties and masquerade parties and Come As Your Favorite-Person parties, shrieking laughter and impromptu frolic, all these helped the memories of the past five years to fade into oblivion.

At her side, Barney stood up and held out a hand. There was too much noise for him to ask if she would like to dance. He nodded at the crowded dance-floor and she stubbed out her cigarette and stood up herself, to move gracefully into his arms.

Dawn was already seeping into the sky as she leaned over from the passenger seat of Sambourne's car and lightly kissed his cheek.

"Oh, I say." He put his hand up to his face, fingers exploring the skin as though the kiss might have left an imprint.

"Thanks, Barney, for a blissful evening. I've really enjoyed myself."

"It was awfully good fun, wasn't it?"

"It really was."

"Listen, old girl." Sambourne squeezed his hands together between his knees, feeling the familiar panic flood into his head. Willing his brain to stay clear and controlled, he took a deep breath, hoping that he was not rushing things, that he would not ruin his chances by acting too precipitately. For the past few months he had been seeing Mary regularly, had dined several times in Fitzroy Square at the express invitation of her guardian, had stayed with them in Yorkshire, had even done some sculling on the Thames with the boy cousin, who was, in the major's opinion, a pretty tricky customer, always dressed in black like a damned ghoul, never said a word except to make some kind of disparaging or sarcastic remark. He had taken her down to Hampshire to meet his parents, arranged a luncheon party in his temporary bachelor flat so that his family could meet Archibald Craven and his son. By now he had probably got his foot in the door, made his intentions fairly clear, shown both sides of the family where he stood *vis à vis* Mary, but there was always the risk that she herself would turn him down.

"Yes, Barney?"

"The fact is, the regiment's been recalled to India," Sambourne said.

"You told me that a month ago."

"Yes, well, now we're really off." He could feel the blood rushing into his face; there was sweat in his armpits. Suppose he had read the signs wrongly and she had only accepted his company out of some misguided sense of duty. Suppose she started back from him, unable to disguise her repulsion or—much worse—her pity. "They've already started shipping the men back." The impulse to repeat the sentence at the top of his voice rushed into his head. He gripped the inside of his thighs with his hands and forced himself back into a calmer frame of mind.

"Ah." Mary did not seem to be aware of his confusion.

"So I was wondering how you'd feel if I—I mean, would you consider—would you—look, old girl, why don't we get married?"

Mary smiled to herself. For a moment she had thought he was going to duck out of it after all; she could see the effort he was making to keep himself under control. She had been expecting his proposal and had already made up her mind to accept. It would mean leaving, not just for years but possibly forever, all the things she loved and which, she recognized, had given her the peace and stability she had needed after the turbulences

of her early childhood. Colin and her uncle, Misselthwaite and the barren windy moors, London, too, and the
new friends she had made, and the excitements it offered. On the other hand, she had spent as much of her
life in India as she had in England, the one was as familiar to her as the other. And she would be going there
as a bride. A woman, no longer a girl. Marriage to Barney would mean an escape from Colin's bossy disapproval, from her uncle's anxious care, from the trap which
Misselthwaite had increasingly become. The months she
had spent in London had opened her eyes to the narrow-
mindedness of Yorkshire, to the dull provincialism of the
people she knew. And there was a rightness about returning to the place where she had been born.

Then, too, there was Barney himself. She put her hand
on his and felt the strong bones underneath the flesh.
He was so much more solid than the young men who
rushed her at the dances and parties they went to. So
much more mature. And, despite the invisible terrors
which sometimes shook him, more peaceful. He demanded so much less of her. It seemed to be enough for
him to be allowed to hold her hand occasionally, and to
gaze at her without speaking, his eyes full of the admiration she had never expected to receive from anyone. In
addition, he had known her parents. He was part of the
life she had experienced up to the age of ten, he and
she shared something which even her cousin did not.
She used to talk to Colin about life in India, describe it
for him, but he could never really have known what she
was talking about, because he had never shared it. Barney had. She was uncertain whether she loved him; she
was uncertain what exactly love was. But she did know
that he meant a very great deal to her. And that he was,
quite simply, nice. Good. Honest. Dependable. Once,
she had overheard two girls in the Ladies at the Crite-
rion, saying how dull Major Sambourne was, and had
been indignant on Barney's behalf. Anyway, who wanted
to spend their life with someone who sparkled and fizzed
the whole time? With someone like Colin? Apart from
the fact that such a person would make her feel fright-
fully dull herself, it was so tiring.

"Yes," she said quietly. "I think that would be a very
good idea."

It was the answer Barney had wanted; he did not find the coolness of Mary's response in any way unsatisfactory. She was like that, he had discovered: undemonstrative, self-contained. Calming. It was part of what he loved about her. He suspected that underneath the restrained exterior, she was capable of high passion; shame-faced at such thoughts but nonetheless eager, he keenly looked forward to releasing it.

"Mary." He turned her face to his and pressed his lips against her mouth. "Oh Mary, you've made me so happy."

He could never fully express how thankful, how unutterably grateful, he was to have been given back his love, his Alice. It was nothing less than a miracle. The images in his mind came and went in rainbow brightness now: the body lying on white sheets under the mosquito netting was no longer Alice's but Mary's, and this time, she would not be forbidden him. His own body swelled and bloomed with lust but he was determined that Mary should not be frightened by the dark strength of his longing. She was still so young, still so innocent. She must be protected, even from himself, if need be. He would have to be patient with her.

"I must go in," she said.

"I'll call on your guardian in the morning."

"I'm afraid he traveled back to Yorkshire yesterday."

"Oh." Sambourne very much hoped he would not have to speak to the boy cousin. Too ridiculous, really, a man of thirty asking for the hand of a girl from a boy scarcely old enough to shave. A hostile boy, at that. "What about the telephone? I know it's not the done thing but . . ."

"Never mind the done thing," said Mary. "I've accepted you and that should be enough for my guardian." Whether it would be enough for Colin was quite another matter. "We'll sort it out in the morning."

"Right-ho. Good night then, Mary . . . darling."

"Good night, Barney."

Mary opened the door of the house as quietly as she could and listened for a moment to the sound of Barney's motor roaring round Fitzroy Square and into the Euston Road. It was supposed to be the most exciting moment in a girl's life, the day she accepted a man's proposal of marriage and thereby offered him her future. Was it strange that she felt comforted rather than exhilarated at the thought of being engaged? Did it mean that there was something odd about her? Surely not: she was certain she had absolutely done the right thing. And, on top of that, India awaited her.

She was still smiling as she stepped into the low-lit hallway and turned to close the door.

"There you are." The voice behind her was cold and disapproving. But it was the undercurrents in it which made her whirl round, her turquoise evening cloak filling like a sail as she did so.

"What is it, Colin?" she demanded. She knew him far too well not to notice how strange he sounded, how unlike himself. There was a looseness about him, a sense of unleashing, as though the fastenings which contained his personality had suddenly been untied. In the half-light of the hall, the whiteness of his face was startling. He was wearing evening trousers but had removed his dinner-jacket and undone his bow tie so that it hung loosely round his neck. "Is something wrong?"

Slowly he shook his head.

"It's not . . . has something happened to your father?" Coming closer, Mary could see hectic spots of color lying along his cheekbones, as they used to when he was a child and running a fever. As always, when she looked at him, she felt as though she were gazing into a mirror. It was not that they resembled each other in the slightest, simply that they were two parts of a whole, only complete when together.

"Not my father." She could smell whisky on his breath.

"Colin: are you drunk?"

"A little, I think. Or maybe even a lot."

"If it's not your father, then who is it? *What* is it?"

Instead of answering, he reached out and stroked the top of her head. "I wish you had not cut it off," he murmured. He had a sudden longing to lie among the silky fallen sheaves of her wheat-colored hair.

She jerked away from under his hand. "Colin. What has happened?"

"You're not going to believe it," he said. His eyes had a disturbing glow to them: she was not sure whether he was enormously happy or suffering some appalling torment.

"Tell me, and I'll try." She followed him into the drawing-room, where the embers of a fire still burned redly in the hearth.

"Whisky?" he asked, tilting a decanter over a glass.

"Am I going to need it?"

"I think you might." He poured an inch of Glenlivet and handed it to her with a strange little bow. "Yes, I really think you might."

"For heaven's sake, Colin, stop being so mysterious." She tasted the spirit. "Otherwise I shall simply have to tell you *my* news instead."

"What's that?" Colin straightened his shoulders like a man anticipating a blow, and thrust one hand into the pocket of his trousers. She could see the knuckles clench. "On second thoughts, don't tell me."

She ignored him. "Barney asked me to marry him tonight."

"And?"

"I accepted."

He said nothing for a moment. The muscles along his jaw bunched and relaxed as though he were swallowing the words which would otherwise have rushed from his mouth. Finally he said, his voice low and furious: "You stupid, *stupid girl.*"

That was all. She had anticipated recriminations. She had thought he might rave at her, shout, raise all kinds of objections, do his unkind imitation of poor Barney laughing, point out a hundred good reasons why she would be making a mistake. This unexpected reaction unnerved her.

"What do you mean?"

"You don't belong with him, with that brainless ninny."

"He is *not* a ninny. He's good, and kind, and generous. And I—"

Colin interrupted. His mouth was scornful. "Please, Mary. *Don't* tell me you *love* him, or I shall throw up."

"You are just a stupid ignorant *boy,*" spat Mary. "Barney is a man."

"He can be a—a giraffe, for all I care," Colin said.

"The fact is that you belong here, Mary. With me." There was an odd tremor in his voice. "With us."

"There is no 'us' anymore." Anger had sharpened her voice. Why was he always so difficult? Why did he always disapprove of what she chose to do?

"Isn't there?"

"Unless you mean Misselthwaite," she said sourly. "Now that Dickon is . . ." She broke off, alarmed. Her cousin had crouched in on himself, as though he were about to spring into the air. The agate-gray eyes burned. "What *is* it, Colin?"

"Mary," he whispered. "He's alive."

"Who?" she said, even though she knew at once whom he meant. There did not seem to be enough air in her lungs. She breathed shallowly through her mouth and felt heat wash over her, followed immediately by an icy chill. *"Who?"*

Colin pressed his hand to his forehead, as though he felt giddy. He said: "Dickon. He's alive, Mary."

Dickon. The name fell into her heart. She spread a hand across her chest, feeling it leap there, under the bead-embroidered bodice of her dress. Dickon. What did that mean? Whoever Dickon had been, he was gone, dead, finished with. For a moment, her mind returned to the image of him she had held for so long—that wide mouth screaming, the blue eyes empty, his butchered flesh. When she had first heard of his disappearance, she had forced herself to accept that this, or some version of it, was how he was now, or had been, before his body began to decay. "Dickon's alive?" she said slowly.

"He's in a hospital at Bournemouth. Nobody knew who he was until recently."

"Why couldn't he tell them?" Already Mary did not want to hear the answer to her question.

"It's like a miracle. An answer to a prayer." Ever since the arrival of the telegram announcing Dickon's disappearance, Colin had set aside the atheism he had embraced at the beginning of the war and had reverted to the habits of childhood, praying every night that Dickon would come back even when it seemed impossible that his request would be answered.

"How did they find him?" Mary asked.

"One of his former officers just happened to be walking along the beach when the patients were being taken for a walk, and he recognized him."

"But why didn't—"

"Apparently he ended up behind the German lines," Colin continued hurriedly. "No one's quite sure how. The Germans put him into one of their hospitals there and it's only now that they're starting to sort things out, that he's been sent back to England."

"How do you know all this?"

"My father told me over the telephone, earlier this evening. The hospital matron wrote to Dickon's mother about it."

A kind of faintness surged over Mary. Too quickly, she swallowed the rest of the whisky in her glass and felt it burn the back of her throat. Resurrection. All these months, Dickon had been dead, and now he was alive again. How was it possible?

"They asked if someone would travel down to Bournemouth and bring him home," said Colin. "It seems he's not really fit to travel by himself, even though he's not— not exactly an invalid."

"Oh, Colin." The cousins stared fearfully at one another. Both of them remembered Faringdon in the hospital at Scarborough, sitting between them in the anonymous communal lounge, turning his blind head from side to side.

From Mary's expression, Colin knew that she shared his fear that Dickon was a lunatic, that the horrors of the trenches had made him mad. He doesn't even know who he is anymore, he thought. He had asked his father the same question as Mary: "Why couldn't he tell the authorities who he was?" and Archibald Craven had said merely that the details were vague, the matron's letter had been uninformative.

Will Dickon laugh the same shrill way that Barney does, Mary wondered? Will the same shapeless terrors fill his eyes every now and then, will he reach out for support while the frenzied thoughts leap about inside his skull? But his condition must be worse than Barney's ever was, if he couldn't even remember his own name. Last year she had worked alongside Lucy Gardiner at Victoria Station, helping on their way home the hordes of men arriving on the troop trains. Most of them had remained cheery, in spite of everything, in spite of missing limbs or damaged bodies. But some, helped along by VAD nurses or simply by their friends, clearly had no idea who or where they were. Vague smiles at nothing, vacant stares, sudden hoarse shouts, strange expressions contorting their faces: they had seemed demented. And perhaps they were. Was Dickon like that too?

A sudden selfish thought crossed her mind: soon I shall be married and sailing to India. I shall not have to see him reduced. She despised herself.

"Anyway, I said I'd travel down and get him," Colin said. "I thought you might come too."

Can I bear to? Mary wondered. "When would you go?" she said reluctantly.

"I'll contact the hospital tomorrow. We could drive the car down at the end of the week and then go straight back to Yorkshire."

"Yorkshire? But—"

"The sooner we can get him back and begin taking care of him, the sooner he'll start to get better." Colin sounded more confident than he felt. Unlike his cousin, he found it relatively easy to come to terms with Dickon's reappearance because he had never, deep deep down, truly believed that he was dead. To have done so would have had the same catastrophic effect as losing some essential part of himself: an arm, a foot, something which would render him permanently less than whole. However, Dickon alive was one thing; Dickon alive but no longer Dickon was quite another.

"I don't want to leave London at the moment," Mary said.

"What?"

"For one thing, I've just got engaged. And Barney's regiment's being shipped back to India. The wedding . . . there'll be so many things to . . . ." The sentence withered under Colin's glare.

His dark eyebrows drew together in a single outraged line. "Are you seriously suggesting that your trivial little affairs are more important than taking Dickon home?"

"Of course not. But I can't simply abandon Barney the minute I've agreed to marry him."

"Why not?"

"Because I've made a promise to him."

"Nobody's asking you to break the promise, as far as I'm aware. But surely you can see that Dickon must take priority? He's been through hell for the past few years, he's suffering from God knows what kind of mental and emotional stress, we're as much his family as Mr. and Mrs. Sowerby and the other children are, you know that as well as I do."

"Yes, but Barney—"

"For all we know, he may need us even more than them. I mean, he spent most of his time with us while we were growing up. In some ways, we probably know him better than anyone else in the world."

"I agree, but on the other hand, there's—"

"Mary, Mary." Colin shook his head. "I simply can't believe that after all he's had to endure, you could even *think* about leaving."

Exhilaration flowed through his veins. He was strong, he was the master. Mary would do as he said, he could see it in her uncertainty, the way she was biting her lip as she wondered what was best to do. He was absolutely confident that once the three of them were together again at Misselthwaite, she would realize how ridiculous it was that she should contemplate leaving them, sailing for India, especially with such a boring idiot as Major Sambourne. He and Mary and Dickon were part of each other: they belonged together. Nothing could alter that.

He moved over and took her hands in his. Squatting down, so that they were on the same level, he pulled her face toward him. "I don't mean to be cruel," he said, "but you can see how important this is. You said yourself that Dickon is a hero: surely he deserves the very best we can give him, after what he has sacrificed for us."

"I thought you didn't believe that the men at the Front sacrificed anything," Mary said. "I thought your argument was that they'd had their lives snatched from them."

"Of course," Colin said. "But that doesn't alter the fact that Dickon gave up a large piece of his life, whether you and I believe in the cause or not." He pulled her to her feet and put his arms round her. "It won't hurt Major Sambourne to wait for you a little longer, will it?"

"But why should he? He fought in the war too, you know. He's been damaged by the shellfire, just as much as Dickon."

Colin ran his hand down her back. One of the sea-green beads caught under his fingers and flew into the hearth to bounce against the tiles.

"Now see what you've done," Mary said crossly. She did not want to look at him. He was like one of the cobras which her *ayah* used to tell her about, the big hooded snakes which hypnotized their prey before they consumed it. If she allowed him to, Colin would swallow her whole, she knew. It was very clear in her mind: once that happened, she would never get away from him again, however much she struggled. But it was late, and she was tired.

"Let's talk about it in the morning," she said.

"It *is* the morning. We must contact the hospital in Bournemouth. We must make arrangements."

"I'm exhausted," said Mary. "I'm not going to discuss it anymore until I've had some sleep."

"But, Mary, that's—"

She cut across him. "If Barney can wait, so can Dickon. What difference will another twenty-four hours make?"

"You don't sound the slightest bit pleased about Dickon."

"That's stupid, Colin. You know how thrilled I am, how excited. But for the moment, all I want is a bath and my bed. After that, we'll sort things out, all right?" She felt older than Colin, and much more mature. She was engaged, after all. Her future lay before her, the milestones clearly marked—marriage, wifehood, children—and she intended to follow them, whatever Colin said.

7

Papery spirals of wood beneath his knife. Curling round his boots, pale as cream. Resiny. Pictures in his head. His father standing behind one of the old kitchen chairs, the younger children taking it in turns, sitting down one after the other, a sheet tied round their necks, *criss criss* as the scissors cut, hair falling, flowing across the flags of the kitchen floor. So many children, so much hair. A tide, a sea of it, gold and yellow and auburn, lapping at the door which led out on to the moors. Until he went away to war, he had never seen the sea. Now, he heard it all day, all night, sucking at the land like a hungry animal. Saw it, too. Sometimes they were taken for a walk along the front, the walking wounded, who showed no visible scars. An embarrassment, that was what they were. The townspeople averted their eyes when the straggling line of patients appeared. Crossed the road, some did, to avoid coming face to face with them. A land fit for heroes. That's what they had been promised. Pinch of salt, maybe, but they had still not been prepared for the reception they were given when they returned home. A fine welcome. No jobs. No pay. Men still in uniform begging on the streets. Even officers. Now that the war was over, everyone wanted to forget all about it. The wounded were no more than an unwelcome reminder of the hardships of the past five years.

He worked the wood with his knife, running the blade along the grain again and again, until a shape began to emerge. The shavings had the same aromatic scent as a pine forest. When he was a boy he sometimes went along with Mr. Craven's head forester on his walks of inspection. When Ted Langdale marked the trees by making a white nick in the scaly trunks with his knife, the same smell would rise from the bark. They carried bread and cheese in their pockets, a bottle of cold tea, and Ted often had something stronger, a drop of his wife's homebrew. Ted taught him how to tell if a tree was diseased or so old that it needed to be felled. "They've got their natural span, same as you or me," he said once. "They don't live forever any more than we do. Some of them'll last longer than others, of course, but in the end they all come to dust. In a manner of speaking, like." He would bring his pipe out of one pocket, a screw of tobacco out of another and start to light it with a match which he extinguished by putting it, flame and all, into his mouth. "And when they're dead, know what the difference between them and us is?"

Dickon had shaken his head.

"Difference is, boy, that they're beautiful in life and useful after death," Ted continued. "Now there's not many of us you can say the same about."

"Useful?" Dickon picked up his cue.

"That's right. The wood, you see. You can do anything with wood, depending on whether it's a soft wood or a hard. Anything, from building a house to carving a box for your sweetheart to keep her pretties in."

Once the bread and cheese was consumed and the homebrew gone, out would come Ted's knife and while he smoked, he would whittle away at a piece of wood, carving a spoon or a trinket or a whistle. Sometimes a living creature would emerge from his stubby fingers: a squirrel or fox, an owl.

More memories. Peaceful. Ted showed Dickon how trees differed from each other, how to distinguish each one not only by shape and foliage, but also by smell. Not just the woodland trees. One or two of the Craven forebears had been horticultural collectors, traveling to distant parts of the world to bring exotic specimen trees back to Misselthwaite. Ted told him there had been a Palm House, once. Out in the grounds somewhere, burned down years ago. Only the cedars left, being hardier. Ted liked the ones which stood on the lawns in front of the Manor. He knew the history of each tree, which one had been planted when and by whom. There was a magnificent cedar of Lebanon in which he took a personal pride. "Planted back in the eighteenth century," he told Dickon, "and still going strong. I reckon this tree was old when Mr. Craven's grandfather's grandfather's grandfather was a little lad." He took out his clasp knife, the blade honed to little more than a thin crescent of steel, and shaved a sliver from one of the sweeping branches. "Smell that, boy." If Dickon closed his eyes, he could still recall the strong sweet scent. "Used the cedar oil to embalm them mummies in Egypt," Ted told him. "And the wood to line trunks going out to India. And chests-of-drawers, too. Know why?"

"No, Mr. Langdale."

"Because God didn't make an insect which could get its teeth through the wood. Preserves things, you see. Fine ladies can keep their clothes safe from moth, too. But don't you go confusing the Lebanon with this tree here, which is also a cedar but isn't the same thing at all."

"I won't, sir."

"Different tree altogether. This one's a deodar. Shaped like a triangle—go on, boy, step back and look at it, can't tell nought about a tree until you look at it whole. Pointed on top, this one, whereas your cedar of Lebanon is flat. And there's the Atlas cedar, though we haven't got one of 'em here. Me grandad tried but couldn't keep it going, wrong soil, he said, and wrong climate. They likes their feet kept warm, do Atlases, just like me old mum in the wintertime."

Memories . . .

One of the nurses was coming, her feet click-clicking along the polished linoleum of the corridor. There were people with her, a man with a deep voice, a woman, young by the sound of it. He concentrated on his carving, the knife sliding over and around the piece of wood to suggest the curve of a belly. He hoped the visitors had not come to see him. There had been dozens of them in the past months, sad-eyed parents hoping to be reunited with a lost son, forlorn sweethearts, desperate wives with toddlers clinging to either hand.

"Suffering from memory loss," the Sister used to say

before opening the door wider. He had heard her several
times. "Doesn't know who he is, poor old chap."

They would stand in the doorway, looking at him, and
then quietly, or, occasionally, with a burst of sobs, shake
their heads. "No, Sister, he's not my son, my fiancé,
my husband."

But he knew very well who he was. He had told them
a hundred times. "Dickon. Dickon." But it was not
enough, and he was damned if he was ever again going
to call himself Corporal Richard John Sowerby. It was
not just the honest and ungrateful citizens of Bournemouth who wanted to forget about the war, who were
determined to pretend that it had never existed.

Not that forgetting was easy. He was plagued by waking dreams, during which he lived and relived in every
excruciating detail the events of that last day. It started
off the same as every other day, only worse. He would
remember it until he died.

*The war is supposed to be ending, yet they are still
under almost daily attack from the enemy. The nearest
railhead is twenty miles away and supplies have become
increasingly erratic, almost nonexistent. Sometimes they
have to ride ten miles from the lines to find a field with
any grass in it for the horses.*

*He is just back from such a ride, weary and aching for
rest, when Sergeant Phillips comes along the trench, calling for volunteers for a burial party. "What, in this lot?"
says Carter, listening to the sounds of the bombardment
whistling over their heads. "Not bleedin' likely, Sarge."
"They'll have to stop some time, lads, even Germans have
to eat," says the sergeant.*

*The men, having heard rumors that hostilities might
come to an end that day, are reluctant to expose themselves.
Meanwhile, there is rifle fire from the enemy trenches.
Machine-guns. Occasional shells still flying overhead. "Don't
they know the war's as good as over?" asks Rogers, and
the sergeant, po-faced, says: "Why don't you volunteer to
nip over and tell 'em, soldier?"*

*A smile cracks Rogers' grimy face as he tries to make
tea over a spirit lamp despite the fact that his hands are
shaking as though they'd been hung out on a washing-
line in a high wind. "Come along, lads," the sarge says.
"This burial party, now . . . I'd rather have volunteers,"*

but no one moves until, in the end, Dickon gets up, followed by Hill and Carter.

Later, when Captain Forster comes to collect them, someone says under his breath: "Can't you leave the poor buggers in peace?" and the captain turns. "No, I can't," he answers, sharp-like. "And there's reasons for that, as well you know. I'm not just talking about morale, lads, even if this show's about finished, nor about hygiene, though God knows both of those are cause enough. I'm talking about common humanity. I'm talking about the people back home, mothers and sisters, lads. Children, too. What would they think if they knew that you'd left their loved ones to lie rotting in some stinking shellhole when you could have helped to give them a decent Christian burial?"

"I'm a Buddhist, sir," says Farrell, cheeky, the company clown, and the captain turns on him. "Then God help Buddha, is all I can say."

He marches out, followed by Hill and Carter and Dickon, with Turnbull adding himself on, and Cornish Davey. There's more of them further along the trench, a group gathered from here and there in the company, stamping their boots on the duckboards to keep warm, waiting for the order to go.

None of them except Hill has been out on this fatigue before. On his advice, they put the mouthpieces of their gas masks over their faces. The nosepiece too. Wrap torn strips of sacking round their hands. "Maggots, lads," Hill says. "And where there's maggots, there's flies. If they've been out there for a while, watch out for the bloody flies."

They climb up over the lip of the trench. There's a bit of a moon. They can hear the Germans laughing, a snatch of song, and Dickon thinks, as he's thought so often before: "They're just men like us. Just men." They come to the first shellhole. "By God," says Hill, "blow me if that isn't little Hardiman. I was wondering why he didn't come around to nick one of me fags last night. Thought I'd got lucky, for once." They were mates, Hill and Hardiman, good mates, and Dickon knows that under the cheery exterior, Hill is probably weeping. "Let's be having him, then," says the sergeant, and Dickon gets down in to the hole, cuts away at the breast pocket of Hardiman's tunic, removes his paybook and red identity disk, and hands them up to the waiting men. "Leave the green one for identification," Hill says, leaning down toward Dickon, his mouth a black hole in his face. They reach for Hardiman's arm and legs and haul him out, place him on a stretcher. There are more bodies, scores of them, each one treated in the same way, run back to the trench and left there for others to deal with.

"All right, men," says the captain, one ear cocked towards the German lines. "Let's get a move on, shall we?"

"But there's more down here, sir," says Dickon. "At least two more. I can feel their—their heads, sir." He moves his feet and the stench brings vomit coursing from his stomach and into his mouth. "Oh, my God, sir," he says, when he can speak. "I don't know how long they've been here but—" The bodies are crawling with maggots. He shifts again, breathing carefully, releasing more of the dreadful stench. The two rotting uniforms are filled with something that has the consistency of cottage cheese. "The identity discs," says the sergeant, "look lively, lad." And Dickon bends down to cut away at the tunic, gagging, averting his gaze from the red-black faces of the corpses. "Been down there quite a while," he hears Hill saying. "You can always tell. They go red, see, before they go black."

They move on to another shellhole, another layer of corpses. One of them seems reasonably recent but when they lift it by the arms and legs, the limbs detach themselves from the torso, loose inside the uniform. Once, Dickon finds a couple of bodies crouched one over the other and lying around them, five separate legs, two wearing the remains of enemy uniform. They come across a German soldier, his blond hair pale under the moon, his face unmarked except for mud. His eyes stare at them: he could be alive, except for the blood which has dried in his ears. Turnbull lifts his foot and stamps heavily on the young face, cursing under his breath. He stamps again, his boot grinding into the dead mouth, and they hear delicate bones breaking. "That's enough of that, now," the sarge says, and they pass on. No time to bury the Germans as well, not this time round. Several of the corpses have been bayoneted, a sign of how close they are to enemy lines.

Dickon is aware that the Germans are no longer sing-

ing, that the laughter has stopped. He crouches at the edge of a shellhole looking down at the headless legless remains of a man, as rifle fire starts, followed by the rattle of machine-gun fire. The sergeant drops on top of him. "Down, lads," he says, but it is too late. Hill is caught, and someone else. Turnbull falls in beside them, first his chest and arms, then the rest of him, blood and worse spraying over Dickon and the sergeant. The captain is lying flat in the mud, immediately above them. "Oh my God," he says and then tumbles in. "It were Turnbull's fault they heard us, I reckon," say the sarge, keeping his voice close to a whisper. "Serve him bloody right." He groans, once. "They've broke me bloody arm, the swine."

They lie there. Time passes. The Germans stop firing, resume their talk. "What are they saying, Phillips?" the captain says, low-voiced. "Talking about a parcel one of them just got from home, sir," says the sergeant, who had signed on for language classes at his local Working Men's Institute before the war. "Got a cake, sir, and some hand-knitted socks. And a letter covered with hearts. His mates are teasing him about that, sir." "Just like our lot, eh Sowerby?" says the captain. Dickon answers: "No difference at all, really, is there, sir?" and the captain sighs. The moon disappears, there are stars overhead.

Cornish Davey is not dead. He lies just out of arm's reach, though the captain makes several attempts to get to him, to bring him down into the uneasy safety of the shellhole. "Give me a hand here, Sowerby," says the captain. "With two of us, we could just about get to him." Dickon peers over the rim of the hole. Davey's been shot through the chest. "He's dying," he says. "All the more reason, man," Captain Forster says roughly. "Let him die among friends." Dickon does not respond. He thinks: Davey's done for. I'm still alive. "Come along, Sowerby," says the captain, "I'm ordering you to give me a hand." Davey is muttering, a mad sing-song gibberish. Dickon says nothing. "Sowerby?" No answer. "Here's twenty thousand Cornishmen will know the reason why," mutters Davey, the breath whistling in his lungs.

"Reckon he's passed out, sir," says the sarge. "Think we'll be here all day tomorrow?" " 'Fraid so, Phillips," says the captain. "We won't be able to move until after dark." He calls again, sharply: "Sowerby?" before mak-

*ing another attempt to reach for Davey, while a German
sniper aims over their heads.* "Shall Trelawney die, my
lads?" *says Davey.* "I'd leave him be, sir," *the sarge says.*
"Just leave it be."

All day they watch the shells overhead. As well as
Davey, other men are out there, dying. No one can do
anything. Captain Forster has a book of poetry in his
pocket. The Golden Treasury. He reads to them: "Home
Thoughts from Abroad." "The Forsaken Merman."
Byron. "She walks in beauty," *says the captain, and
Dickon thinks of Mary.* "Oh to be in England" ... *They
are close enough to hear the German voices.* "He's talking about his girl again," *says the sarge. Dickon thinks:
I wonder what the German is for* "Yours till hell
freezes over"?

He has been waist deep in water for fourteen hours
when the captain finally gives the word for them to begin
the cautious move back to their own lines. As they start
crawling, there is a savage blast of air and Dickon is flung
towards the sky, feels his bones disintegrating, sees the
sergeant's face fly past him, hears the captain scream. He
lands face down in mud and lies there for a moment,
considering what to do. The pain in his legs is intolerable.
He does not know if he could manage to crawl the distance which lies between him and comparative safety. He
realizes that if he does not, he may die. At that particular
moment, the prospect is very appealing. It is, he suspects,
his last day on earth. He wonders how much longer the
war will go on. He thinks of Misselthwaite and his parents. A medical orderly once shared half a bottle of
French brandy with him and told him that of the men
who succumbed to their wounds, almost every one died
with the word "Mother" on their lips. "Mother," Dickon
says, his cheek pressed against the wet earth. He tries it
again. "Mother." It does not feel right. "Mary," he says.
"Colin." That is much better. "Mary." He starts to crawl.
For what seems like hours he inches forward, dragging
his useless legs behind him. After a while, the pain disappears. He tries to stand but cannot. He is cold, freezing.
He passes a corpse, a German, half in, half out of his
army greatcoat. Dickon wrestles it off and puts his own
arms into the sleeves. He finds his identity disks inside
his battle dress and pulls them off. Throws away his pay-

*book. Just in case. There is another enormous impact in
the air and again he is lifted bodily and propelled forward
before he is dropped to the ground again, legs first, and
falls unconscious, his body unable to bear any longer the
agony of his broken limbs.*

Much later, he woke from a medically induced stupor
to find that the hospital where he lay was a German
one. The war was over. How he came to be so close to
the German trenches no one was able to explain, though
he supposed he must have been dragging himself toward
them instead of toward his own lines. Perhaps the fact
that he was without identity disks, that he was wearing
a German army greatcoat, added to the confusion; it will
not be for years that he will discover he was found almost naked some yards behind the German lines. At
first he wanted to talk to his fellow patients and the
medical staff who cared for him, but could not make
himself understood. Once he had been transferred to an
English military hospital, he preferred not to. He wanted
to sleep. He wanted to be Dickon again, not Corporal
Richard John Sowerby. When they asked who he was,
where he came from he told them. "Dickon," he said.
"Dickon," and "Misselthwaite." He could manage nothing more and after a while, stopped trying. He wanted
to be healed from the horror and indignity he had undergone. He wanted to slough off the past few years, to put
them away, bury them permanently. Silence was one way
to achieve that.

He pulled his knife down the length of the wood,
drawing lines with the point, turning them round and
along so that the mane flowed over the neck and gave
the impression of movement. When there was a pause
in the shelling, he sometimes used to plait Jason's mane
and tail, threading in wild flowers if the season was right,
or pieces of bright-colored rag salvaged here and there
among homes abandoned by the French as the lines advanced and retreated. The self-imposed task was soothing, reminding him of happier days, of country fairs,
sheepdog trials, trotting races, the Misselthwaite rig always the smartest turn-out, and, once or twice, Dickon
allowed to sit up beside the groom, wearing a silk top
hat too big for him, as proud as a clothes-peg.

"Sheer coincidence," he heard the Sister say, outside

in the corridor. "Walking along the front . . . his former
captain . . . recognized him immediately . . . red hair,
of course . . ."

Sometimes when she mentioned the color of his hair,
they did not even bother to come into the room. Today,
however, was not one of those times. He bent lower
over the little carving in his hand. He wished they would
go away and leave him to himself. He was indifferent to
the future. There was the breath of a draught across the
back of his neck.

"Corporal," the Sister said. "Corporal Sowerby. You
have some visitors."

He did not turn. Footsteps approached. Someone
came round the table at which he sat and stood opposite
him. Lifted enquiringly, a voice said: "Dickon?"

The Sister gave a little laugh. "Dickon?" she said.

"That's his name," the same voice said.

"Well, if only we'd realized what he meant . . ." Not
that it would have helped identify the poor boy. She let
the sentence fade.

The second person joined the first and spoke his
name. "Dickon."

He looked up. Two people were watching him, two
strangers, a young man, a girl in a hat. Remembering
his manners, he tried to find a smile.

"Oh, Dickon," the girl said.

Colin could see that the man with the penknife had
no idea who they were. When he left Yorkshire for the
Front, they were still children. He stepped forward with
his hand outstretched. "Colin," he said. "And Mary. It's
so good to see you again, old boy."

Tears came into Mary's eyes; she bit her lip in an
effort not to cry. She hardly recognized in the stocky
young man behind the table the clear-eyed lad who had
gone off to war so long ago. There were lines around
his eyes and mouth which belonged to a much older
man; there was already gray in the sandy hair.

He stood up. He came to them, rolling slightly. His
broken legs had long since healed but one of them had
mended a fraction short. "Colin."

Colin took Dickon's hand in both his own, then suddenly threw his arms round him, holding the shorter man
against his chest. "You can't imagine . . ." he said.

Behind him, Mary waited apprehensively. The hospital's antiseptic smell was overlaid with something indefinably sad. Not given to abstractions, she nonetheless had a sudden conviction of tragedy ahead.

Dickon released himself from Colin's embrace. "Mary." He stretched a hand towards her.

"It's so good to see you," Mary said. She did not take his hand. Was this really their own Dickon or a stranger living in his body? Might it not have been better if he had, after all, not returned so dramatically from the dead? The table beside her was covered with what appeared to be literally hundreds of tiny carvings of horses. She was not sure whether she should embrace him as Colin had done. When they were children, she had not thought twice about it but the Dickon she had so often flung her arms around was not this young man who peered at them as though through a fog.

And yet, when he spoke, he appeared perfectly normal. "You've cut your hair off," he said.

"Yes. It's . . . it's the rage now."

"She walks in beauty," Dickon said.

"What's that, old boy?"

Mary wished Colin would not keep calling Dickon "old boy." He had never done so before: it seemed false and over-hearty.

"I thought of Mary," Dickon said. *The captain has a book of poetry in his pocket* . . . "It reminded me of Mary." He saw blankness in their faces.

"Did you do all these?" Mary said, picking up one of the little carvings.

"Yes."

"They're beautiful. I didn't know you could do things like this." She knew she sounded as bad as Colin: patronizing, unnatural.

He heard the sound of the shells again, the staggering blast of the air against his eardrums, the horse, torn and bloodied at his feet. "Jason," he said. It seemed necessary to explain. "The horse." Mud slippery under the knees of his battledress, flecks of blood on his hands again, something slimy caught on the rough edge of his thumbnail. He picked at it, head bent, then looked up. Two people watching him, strangers, though he knew them to be Colin and Mary. He sighed. Could they see the horse's blood on his hands, or was he still trapped in those waking nightmares which had not left him for months?

"It's a way of remembering him, I suppose," Colin said. He held one of the wooden horses and ran a finger down the curve of the neck. "How do you get the wood so smooth, Dickon? Do you use sandpaper?"

"Sometimes."

"And then what—linseed oil, to give it that shiny look?"

Dickon took the little horse from him and ran it down the side of his nose. "I do that," he said. "Over and over. Natural oil, see."

"That's a clever trick."

"Ted Langdale taught me."

"He'll be glad to see you back."

"How is Ted, anyway?" For the first time, a measure of animation came into Dickon's eyes.

"He's very well," Colin said. "He was wounded at Ypres and they sent him home. He's back at Misselthwaite now, and very glad we are to have him. Everything's been fearfully neglected these past few years."

"Your family is longing to see you," Mary said. "They're all well. Martha can't wait to show you your two nephews."

Dickon backed away, knocking over his chair as he did so. "No," he said. "No. Not yet. I'm not ready." *And twenty thousand Cornishmen knew the reason why.*

"What for?" asked Mary. "To go home?"

"Not ready," repeated Dickon.

"But you'll be better off there than anywhere else, won't you? With the people you know best. Your family."

"That's just it. They don't know me, not at all. I'm not what they expect, what they think I am. I don't even know myself anymore. And . . . and . . ." Dickon was growing agitated. His whole body trembled; a soundless clangor filled his head. "I need more time, much more time." Tears sprang from his eyes and rolled down his face. He wanted to add that he could not bear to mix the horrors of the war and the peaceful places he remembered, in case the first leaked into the second and destroyed them. But it was impossible to articulate the thought to these two who knew nothing at all of what he had been through.

"Then we'll take you with us to my father's place in Fitzroy Square. The car's outside," Colin said. He kept his voice calm, though Dickon's sudden disintegration was horrifying. Shellshock: they had heard of it, but not really experienced it before now. For the first time, he began to understand what had lain behind Barney Sambourne's insane laughter, the fierce shakings of the head. He took Dickon's arm. "You can rest up there, Dickon. We can show you some of the sights. You've never been to London before, have you? Just passed through, hmm? Well, we can do absolutely anything you like: theater, music hall, go on the river, Kew Gardens, all sorts of jolly things, just name it . . ." Talking gently, he steered Dickon out of the room.

Mary was full of admiration. He was showing a sensitivity which she knew she herself did not possess. Dickon frightened her. He seemed as alien as a bushman or an aboriginal: she was not sure how to approach him. Colin probably felt much the same, yet he was able to push the feelings to the back of his mind. Why couldn't she do the same?

"Will you be taking the corporal away, then?" It was the Sister, who had been waiting in the corridor.

"I should think so."

"I'll get one of the girls to bring his bits and pieces around to the front of the hospital, not that the poor dear's got a lot." She paused, head on one side. "Known him long, have you?"

"Yes."

"Only we haven't got much out of him in the time he's been here. Bit of a mystery man, is our Corporal Sowerby."

"We grew up together," Mary told her. "In Yorkshire."

"Yorkshire, is that where he's from? Beautiful up there, I'm told. He'll be glad to go home."

"Yes, I expect he will." Mary smiled politely. "Thank you for all your care and attention. I'm sure his family are immensely grateful."

The woman sighed. "It's little enough we do, when all's said and done. Quite frankly, I don't know if we do any good at all. We can provide them with the physical things they need, like a good night's sleep and warm clothing and three meals a day, but after that, we're pretty much in the dark. It's the minds that are affected, not the bodies, and that we're not properly equipped to deal with. Especially when we haven't been through it ourselves."

"Time," Mary said. "Perhaps they'll begin to forget after a while."

"Oh no. I don't think so. I doubt if the memories they brought back from the front lines are the kind that fade."

Her words were frightening. If Dickon retained that blankness, that otherness, for the rest of his life, was there then no hope that the three of them would regain their vanished closeness? Waiting in the chilly Palladian-inspired hall of the country house turned hospital, she realized that the question had no meaning since she herself, by accepting Barney's proposal, had already chosen to break away from the other two.

"He's asleep," said Colin, coming into the drawing-room where Mary sat staring into the fire.

"Or he wants you to think he is," she said.

"Why would he do that?"

"So you'll go away. Can't you see how much he wants to be left alone?"

"Do you think I'm crowding him? Coming on too heavy?"

"I don't think it's anything personal. But I do think you're deceiving yourself if you think it's going to be easy to get back the old Dickon. In fact, I'm not sure you ever will."

"Don't say that." Colin dropped something into Mary's lap. "Look. It was with the rest of your kit sent back from France."

Mary looked down at the intricately woven circle of twig and hair and moss. "A bird's nest."

"A robin's nest, to be precise. He found it in a ditch, somewhere in France, and kept it for you. This goes with it." He placed a blue egg inside the nest.

Mary stroked the smooth interior. "Colin." The emotions she ought to feel would not come.

"What?"

"You know when we fetched him from Bournemouth, he said that he wasn't what his family thought? That they didn't know him anymore?"

"What about it?"

"We don't know him anymore, either. But, equally important, he doesn't know *us*." She had a sense of her own image, unchanged by time; carried inside Dickon's head through the horrors of the trenches. "I mean, whatever he thinks we are is based on what we were when he went away to fight in the war. But we're both different now. We've grown up."

"Does that matter?"

"I'm afraid of letting him down in some way, not matching up." She picked up the nest. "I mean, once I would have been thrilled to have a robin's nest, but it means nothing to me now. Nothing at all. Whereas Dickon thinks it does."

"Can't you pretend to be pleased?"

"Of course. But that's not the point. He's got to come to terms with the way we are now. Otherwise we'd be cheating. It wouldn't be fair to him." She got up from her chair and faced her cousin squarely. "And I don't intend to hide the fact that I'm going to marry Barney. Nor that I'm going to India."

"But he's expecting you to go back to Misselthwaite."

"I can't help that."

"Even if it affects his chances of getting better?"

"I can't be responsible for him," Mary said stubbornly.

Colin felt as though he were sliding down a slippery slope. However much he dug in his heels, there was no way to halt his inexorable descent. He had hoped that concern for Dickon would put a stop to Mary's plans. He had gambled on her losing interest in Barney Sambourne in the greater need to rehabilitate their friend. But the fear he was experiencing was for himself as much as for Dickon. Without Mary, without the possibility of seeing her, being with her, watching her face light up, hearing her laughter, there seemed little point to his life. He had not believed that she would go through with the marriage. It seemed impossible that she would not come to her senses and realize the complete unsuitablility of the major to be her husband. With panic, he saw that for once he was wrong.

"Is that why you wouldn't come to Trafalgar Square with us? And why you refused to join us at Kew?"

"That's part of it. But I also didn't come because I wanted to see Barney."

"You always were a selfish little bitch," Colin said.

Mary's mouth opened. Tears of shock and anger came into her eyes. Never, in the whole of their intertwined lives, had Colin spoken to her so woundingly. "What?"

"I should have realized that you would always put yourself first."

"You've become an insufferable prig," retorted Mary, rallying. "Are you seriously suggesting I should break my engagement and dedicate myself to nursing Dickon back to health?"

"It doesn't sound that bad a prospect to me."

"I hate ill people. I hate sickness and hospitals. I'm just no good at that sort of thing, as you very well know."

"Let's hope poor old Barney doesn't catch malaria or something."

"If he does, there'll be servants to look after him."

"God, Mary. I never realized just how callous you were."

"That's because you've never given a thought to anyone but yourself in the whole of your pampered life. Remember those stupid tantrums you used to throw? The way you terrorized the staff at Misselthwaite?"

"It's years since I was like that. And it's thanks partly to you, Mary. You never allowed me to feel sorry for myself, and I'm truly grateful for that."

"One minute I'm callous and the next you're grateful to me."

"*Please,*" Colin said. "Don't marry Major Sambourne."

"What?"

"Mary." He was as serious as she had ever seen him. "It'll be the biggest mistake you've ever made."

"The biggest mistake I've ever made was ever listening to you about anything."

"Mary." Colin caught at her arm as she flounced towards the door. "Don't let's quarrel. Even if you don't stay long, will you at least come back to Misselthwaite when he feels ready to go?"

"I'm not going to promise anything."

It was a concession of sorts. Colin judged it wiser to change the subject. "When we went to Kew yesterday, he really enjoyed the tropical houses. I was saying what fun it would be to build something like that at Misselthwaite and he got all excited. I wondered whether it might not be a good idea for him to go and get some training."

Accepting Colin's olive branch, Mary said: "What kind of training?"

"I don't know. Agricultural, or horticultural, perhaps, so he could have a decent job on the estate. Maybe even veterinary. You know how he seems to have a special rapport with animals."

"He used to. We don't know that he does anymore. Anyway, shouldn't you discuss it with him first? You might find that he's got ideas of his own about what he wants to do. Perhaps he doesn't want 'a decent job on the estate,' thank you very much. You seem to think that he's going to be perfectly happy to go back to where he was before this war started, that he'll be pleased and grateful to let you organize his life for him." Mary remembered a conversation with Susan Sowerby shortly before the telegram arrived, in which Dickon's mother had indicated much the same thing. "You may be surprised."

"I'm only trying to help him," protested Colin.

"How kind of you," Mary said sarcastically. "Give him a nice toy to play with and hope that'll keep him happy, is that it?"

"If you'd bothered to come with us yesterday, you'd have seen for yourself the way he lit up at the thought of a Palm House at Misselthwaite. He told me something I didn't know myself: that years and years ago there actually used to be one, only it burned down. I only suggested he take a course because then he'd have some idea of how to go about creating one—"

"Provided that's what he really wants to do."

Up in her room, Mary was conscious that she had behaved badly—or less well than she ought to have done. It was obvious that Colin had Dickon's best interests at heart, and she ought to be more encouraging. The robin's nest lay on her dressing-table, a symbol of something, though she did not really know what. In any case, she was impatient to start her new life as bride, as wife, as, eventually, mother. Dickon, poor damaged Dickon, was part of the old life she would be leaving behind.

8

Mary Sambourne could not remember when she had last felt so miserable. Or so bored. The two things she had been counting on—India and marriage—had both let her down. At first, India had been as she remembered it: full of color, mystery, enchantment. Somewhere beyond the thick hedges of plumbago which surrounded her bungalow, it was still there, but as the wife of an officer, she was not allowed to enjoy it.

"Not allowed"—that implied there was a book of rules which could be studied but the pressure was much more subtle than that. She was perfectly at liberty to do as she pleased. She could dress like a native if she wished, talk like one, eat the same food, move out of the cantonment and set up house in a native hut. No one would stop her. She would simply find herself socially ostracized, not just by the English but by the Indians as well. As a child, a neglected child at that, Mary had been free to wander where she would; the houses of the native servants were as familiar to her as her own. But as an adult and a married woman she was learning that if she wanted to be invited anywhere—and there was no question that she did, because without the constant round of parties, visits and sports, life would be unbearably tedious—she was going to have to conform to the unwritten rules. And there was Barney's career to think of, too. He had already pointed out that proud of her as he undoubtedly was, it simply did not do for the colonel's wife to hear Mary conversing in their own language with the servants, even though she was perfectly capable of doing so. When she asked why not, he had talked of the dangers of "going *jungli*" and the social suicide it en-

tailed. Mary had stormed and raged, but he was ada-
mant. By speaking to her *ayah* in Hindi, he implied, she
would be letting down both the Raj and the British Empire. Not to mention Barney himself. It seemed melodramatic stuff to Mary, and naturally she ignored his
injunctions, but did take care after that not to be
overheard.

The cantonment was like a prison. After a few months
here, she was sick to death of the vapid company offered
by the other English wives. Of meeting the same people
over and over again. Of gossip about military matters.
Of tedious discussions about the horrors of Indian servants or the cost of sugar or rice. Often, she imagined
the scorn Colin would display if he were to see what she
was reduced to. The other day she had actually found
herself debating the best way to remove stains from a
Kashmir shawl.

It had all been so different on board. The journey out
by steamship from Liverpool had given her no inkling
of what it would be like when they rejoined the regiment. There were glee parties where she had played the
piano, there were concerts, games on deck, fancy-dress
parties—she and Barney had won a prize for their cos-
tumes at the Gala—even a military band since there
were troops aboard going back to their station on the
North West Frontier. There was a well stocked library,
and the chance to go ashore. In Port Said, Barney had
bought her a striped shawl and a *topi*, which he insisted
she would need in India; she had bought him a pair
of exquisitely embroidered slippers. They had had their
fortunes told by a man in Turkish trousers and a fez,
and learned that they would have a long and happy life
together and produce eleven children: "A regular cricket
team," Barney said, which Mary had found delightfully
comic. Once past the Suez Canal, they had been able to
leave off their winter clothing and bring out their summer dresses. At night, the steamer left a trail of fiery
phosphorus in its wake; by day, whales swam alongside
and schools of flying fish shot past them like a shower
of silver needles. As it grew hotter they had their bed-
ding taken up on deck and slept out beneath the stars,
while the Southern Cross glowed in the black sky. She
had never wanted the voyage to end.

And then the day came when they could smell India on the breeze. Eyes shut, she stood at the rail breathing the familiar compound of spices and jasmine, cooking oil and the smoke of burning cow-dung. She was coming home at last. It was easy, at that moment, to believe that the past few years had never happened, that she was still Mary Lennox, the imperious ten-year-old daughter of the beautiful Memsahib. India called to her: the noises, the gaudy colors, the teeming crowds, the beauty. As they steamed toward Bombay, she squeezed Barney's arm in rapture, and smelled the bay rum on his hair as he bent to kiss her cheek, happy to see her happy. Driving to their hotel through the streets of Bombay she had drunk it all in. After the pale Londoners, how exciting it was to see every possible shade of skin color, such diversity of feature from European to the Mongol peoples of the North East, from the Goan half-castes to the fierce horse-trading Pathans, from the handsome faces of the Rajputs to the pale Nepalese. And in among the brilliant saris and saffron turbans, the bullock carts, the temples, the stone figures daubed with red paint, the careless heaps of vegetables and flowers, the variety of buildings from classical European to the ramshackle native houses painted in pink or blue or yellow.

The journey northwards had been equally enjoyable. They had traveled by train for most of the way, passing from the lushness of the south to the sun-baked plains of the north. They had broken their journey in order to take a river trip and she knew she would never forget the peaceful beauty as their boat glided between the low banks. They spent all day under an awning, ate their meals on deck, watched the huge sun spread itself across the immensity of the land and color the water crimson as it set beyond the palms.

Then things had changed. Barney had his own bungalow at the cantonment, and she had at first been kept busy organizing that, unpacking their wedding presents, making her husband's sparse bachelor quarters more comfortable with chintzes brought from Home and shawls and brass Benares pots. The servants had been welcoming to their new *memsahib,* particularly when she spoke to them in their own tongue. Being a new bride meant she was given a certain amount of precedence at social occasions, and though she did not really care for such things, it had been enjoyable to be made a fuss of. A number of the more senior officers had served with her father and, she supposed, though this was not mentioned, flirted with her mother; they and their wives had taken her under their wing, much to Barney's delight. She had planted a garden and given the *mali* strict instructions about watering. She had joined the tennis club, and given her first dinner party.

But now she was bored. Although she and her husband were invited everywhere, they met the same small circle of people wherever they went. And though during the day, Barney was able to go off and do whatever he did—she was not exactly clear what that was—there was no such relief for her. Like all the other wives at the station, she was supposed to find a sufficient outlet for most of her energies in supervising her household. If she had spare time, she spent it with the other wives.

The household was not difficult to manage. She had a staff of fifteen indoor and outside servants, who took care of most of the domestic details, and because she spoke their language, and understood the various restrictions placed on them either through religion or caste, she had no trouble with them. She had become a voluminous letter writer, but had quickly realized that there was a limit to how many letters any one person could write, especially when the mail took so long. There was her garden, of course, and her piano. Colin's wedding present to her had been a black-lacquered Conway; every time she lifted the lid she thought of him, and of Dickon and wondered how they were getting along, whether Dickon's visions of hell were fading, whether Colin had succeeded in interesting him in something. Pressing the notes, she would tell herself that although she was occasionally assailed by emptiness at the thought that they might not meet again for years, or ever, it would nonetheless not be strictly true to say she missed them, or Misselthwaite. They were part of childhood, and must be put aside now that she was a married woman. And would probably be a mother one of these days. Not that motherhood sounded particularly pleasant. She had already heard every last thing she ever wanted to know about Fiona Stuart-Fraser's three miscarriages and Monica Streatham's most recent delivery from which she still had not fully recovered, and Grace Bellington's four sons, all away at school in England. There was also the sad little wife of Captain Blair, who had given birth six times and lost each child before it reached the age of two.

The thought of having babies was not one Mary cared to dwell on. It seemed horrible to think that having gone through all the danger and inconvenience of producing them, you then had to send them away when they were seven or so and not see them again for years, unless you were very rich and could afford the journey Home, in which case you saw them perhaps every year or two. Some of the women chose to accompany their children, which meant they had to leave their husbands, sometimes for years. Looking at the women around her, Mary had quickly realized the unpalatable choice each had to make: either they neglected their children or their husband. Whichever they chose, they could never win. Trained from their earliest years to be good wives and mothers, the demands of Empire made it impossible for them ever to be both.

Despite the predictions of the Port Said fortune-teller, she was fairly sure she did not want children. Certainly not eleven. On the other hand, she was not at all clear on how to prevent them from coming. Barney had proved of disappointingly little help. In fact, Barney was proving to be much more than a disappointment. Occasionally, as Fiona or Grace or Monica started again on stories Mary had already heard scores of times, she longed to interrupt their by now tedious accounts and come straight out with the question to which she was desperate to know the answer: was she the only woman in the world who dreaded the moment each night when her husband got into bed? And if so, was it because of some peculiarity about her own husband, or did all wives go through what she did each night? Was it meant to be so painful and unpleasant? Why had nobody explained? Warned her? Perhaps part of the problem had been the fact that her family only consisted of Colin and her uncle; neither of them could reasonably have been expected to talk of such things. Even Lucy Gardiner, from whose house she had been married, had said nothing beyond making some light-hearted comment about the first night being the worst and to remember that Barney was still a decent old chap at heart, because they couldn't really help themselves, poor dears. Mary had not had the slightest idea what she was talking about.

The odd thing about it was that he had not been like this on the journey out. They had shared a bed, and she had found it the most comforting thing in the world to snuggle against him each night, to kiss his cheek and murmur good night before falling asleep in his arms. If she had had a mother, would she have been given some indication of what might happen once they reached the cantonment and the privacy of their own quarters? Often, lying awake while Barney slept peacefully beside her, she had wept, vowing that she would never let a daughter of hers go so unprepared into marriage. It was horrible. Vile. Made all the more so by her own ignorance. She had seen Dickon's . . . male thing (she knew perfectly well what it was called but even in the privacy of her thoughts, could not bring herself to use the word) once when she had been walking on the moor and come across him swimming naked in one of the deep water holes below Skag Pike. It was soft, curled, like the marble cherub's in the library at Misselthwaite. Not in the least like the aggressive purple thing which Barney had.

The first time he pressed it against her, she could not think what he was doing. She thought vaguely that he had brought his parade stick into bed with them. Instead of the gentle kisses they had exchanged in the past, his mouth had chewed hers as though it were a piece of candy. There was hardness and pain between her legs. Barney grunting. Sighing. "Thought I'd let you get used to me first, old dear. Didn't want to rush you." And something invading her, hurting. She had thought she still had some choice. She had tried to struggle free, saying this was not something she wanted, but it was too late, he was moving up and down, panting, she was sure she was bleeding, he was groaning into her, murmuring. "Alice," he said. "Alice." She felt a disgusting stickiness. He had fallen against her side and begun snoring. His arm was heavy across her body. She lay awake and felt stuff oozing out of her. She cried. Barney's hand had twitched across her nipple. "My darling. That wasn't so bad, was it? I tried to be gentle." Breath of whisky and curry powder. Whiskers scraping her face. Her hand taken, wrapped round his . . . male thing. Growing between her fingers. "Rub it, my dear." Pulling back, she said: "No. No." He had ignored her, pulled her hand up and down himself, groaning with what she assumed was pleasure, then rolled on top of her though she pushed him away, brought her knee up. "Little hellcat. I always knew you'd be a fiery one." She hated him. She scratched him but it was no use. He had spread her legs apart and she felt the rhythmic pushing again, like the pump in the stable yard at Misselthwaite and then more of the slimy stuff. Someone should have said. She should not have been sent off to this, a kind of sacrifice. Her own husband had become a stranger to her, someone she did not know, who had the right to squeeze her breasts and enter her body, someone who said each night that it would get better though it never did, that he loved her, that life would be wonderful with her at his side. That he was a lucky man. That dreams so seldom came true, but his had done so.

Mary searched the faces of Fiona and Monica, of Grace and the captain's sad wife, for signs that they too endured this nightly humiliation. There were none. At least, none that indicated they suffered as she did. Had she, then, married a degenerate, a man set apart from the rest by the perversity of his desires? Was she alone in finding the ritual so unbearable? Sometimes she thought it would be less bad if he would just hold her for a bit, if he would behave more gently toward her before he got on with his manly business, but she had not dared to suggest this in case he accused her of being an unnatural wife.

Mary was not to know that Barney was as ignorant as she was, that until he had finally plucked up the courage to approach her after their arrival in their new home, he had been as virginal as she. Nor was she aware that he despaired at his inability to make his young wife happy. Like her, he wished that someone would give him some advice. He would have asked a brother officer but was terrified of looking like a fool, or—even worse—of having his failing bandied about the Mess, becoming a laughing stock. Did their wives shrink from them as his did? Did they weep after the deed was done? Was he too forceful? Not forceful enough? Was there some vital piece of technique which he was omitting? Where could he turn for help? He hated to see Mary's tears. He hated the fact that she never reproached him, never sighed or, after that first time, tried to prevent him from making love to her. He was sure that the act of love should not merely be endured, as she seemed to endure. When she accepted his proposal of marriage, he had thought himself the happiest of men. It had never occurred to him that there would be any further problem. He had waited, not wanting to scare her. Approaching her for the first time, he had felt as though he might burst with desire for her. Her body, beneath the muslin nightshirt she wore, was like satin under his hands. He had wanted to rush, but held back, terrified of scaring her. Her little breasts. The roundness of her hips. He could have stared at her all night, but the sight of her on the white sheet had in the end proved too much for his self-control. Although they had been settled into their new life for months now, he could not get enough of her. Sometimes he came home in the middle of the day, in order to make love to her, though he tried hard not to inflict his desires on her too often. He was unaware that the name he had called, that first time, had not been Mary's but Alice's.

Mary's garden was not flourishing. The seeds she had brought from England germinated well enough, but once the *mali,* under close supervision, had transplanted them, they seemed unable to withstand the harsh soil, the fierce heat. Despite his watering, they wilted: it had become a battle between her and the sun. She was determined that the roses she had brought with her, carefully wrapped in flannel kept damp through the long voyage out and the further train journey north, would flourish. Although she did not, she told herself, pine for Misselthwaite, she was nonetheless conscious of a certain need for something of the home she had left behind. She had planted larkspur, sweet-peas, phlox, snapdragons: she watched over their flowering as though they were nestlings or orphaned lambs. But when—if—they flowered, there was no scent. And they bloomed all at the same time, with no regard for proper season.

Languid Fiona told her she was wasting her time. "It won't work, my dear," she said, elegant beneath a lace parasol. "You can't fight India, you simply have to go along with it."

"I know that," Mary said, conscious of her flushed red face, the way her hair had lost its bounce in the heat. "I was born here."

"So you said. Which would lead one to suppose that you would know the futility of struggling against the way things are."

"I still think that if you take care, you can make a garden like the ones at Home."

"But why on earth should you want to?" Fiona was genuinely mystified and, looking at her cool face, Mary did not attempt to speak of the gardens at Misselthwaite, nor of the way she had been changed from a scrawny unhappy little girl by the magic of an English spring. In India, there was none of the slow change from seed to bud to flower. There was little waiting, no anticipation, everything bloomed riotously and at once. She was not stupid enough to try to keep India out of her garden. She was perfectly willing to allow bougainvillaea and plumbago their place, as long as they did not crowd out the less flamboyant English flowers.

Rocking on her veranda, a glass of lime and iced soda water in her hand, Mary was aware that she was not happy. She had expected to be, and the gradual realization that she was not had come as a cruel blow. Apart from his behavior in bed—or perhaps her own response to it—she had nothing against Barney. He was kind, he was attentive, she was really very fond of him. The round of activities which filled her days—riding, tennis, dances, reading—was unutterably tedious; yet when she tried to remember what she had done with herself in London, it seemed very much the same sort of thing. So where did the difference lie? Was it the fact that in England she could always get away from it if she chose? Or was it the nearness of Misselthwaite? Was it in having Colin always close at hand? She had sometimes hated him for the way in which he niggled at her, picked her up on every careless thought and unconsidered word, yet she realized now that irritating as he could be, he nonetheless stimulated her. Here, there was no escape. She was condemned to this society, these people, this way of life, until Barney resigned his commission or retired. Often, the thought was intolerable.

She took up archery. She threw herself into her piano playing, although the Conway needed tuning almost every week. She gave musical evenings, or card parties, as did the other wives. She rode for hours, sometimes getting up as early as four o'clock and foregoing breakfast in order to stay out in the cooler weather of early morning. It was only then, riding through miles of paddyfields, through villages where the people came out to watch in silence as she flew by, past beanfields which in the right season gave off the most delicate of scents, that she could feel free, that she could recapture the essence of herself. But even so, she was not alone. The countryside was too dangerous for a woman to venture out by herself and there was always the company of the two *syces* which Barney insisted must go with her. Sometimes she and Fiona would go on horseback to a tea or tennis party, staying so late that it was dark when they set off home again and then they would ride slowly home under the moonlight or, if the night were dark, behind the bobbing hurricane lantern of the *syce,* past coffee plantations or through rustling bamboo groves. Magical rides, Mary found them, and the only sure way to calm her restless spirit.

Increasingly, she looked forward to the mail from Home, particularly to Colin's letters. She had no desire to return to England but nonetheless found herself eager for even the smallest detail of what Colin and Dickon were doing. It saddened her that, though *she* could picture exactly the places they visited and the people they spoke to, the two young men could not reciprocate. When Colin spoke of Pitcher or Ted Langdale, she could instantly conjure them up in her mind: Pitcher in his stiff wing collar, Ted in his baggy coat of thornproof tweed. When he wrote about the Lower Copse, the new crops in Top Field, the refurbishment of the drawing-room, they were places she knew intimately. Her own life, of necessity, remained mysterious to them. If she mentioned Monica Streatham's recent river picnic, Colin could not begin to visualize the flat-bottomed boats pushing off from shore, the semi-naked boatmen, the palm-fringed river, smoke rising from distant hamlets, the elaborately turbanned *chuprassis* holding cotton umbrellas over the ladies' heads. If she spoke of a gymkhana or of amateur dramatics at the Club, they remained nothing more than words. Nor, even though she described to them in minute detail her everyday routines, could Colin or Dickon possibly imagine the slow swish of the *punkah* as it pushed the hot still air back and forth over her head, the particular sound a gecko made as it dropped from the ceiling on to the cloth stretched across the top of the bed she shared with her husband, or the exotic patterns of the shawls with which she covered the cane furniture on the veranda. When she told them that she had served a curry at a ladies' luncheon she had recently given, they could not really appreciate the nuances that this departure from the norm involved, even though she explained that the English generally turned up their noses at native cuisine, preferring to eat the dishes they were accustomed to at Home, or even serving food out of tins.

They could not smell India, taste, partake of it. She could tell them, but the only way they would share it truly would be if they came out to visit her. Gradually, this possibility began to assume an almost feverish importance to Mary. If they came, Colin and Dickon, she knew she would feel less lonely. When she next wrote of the sun setting across the dusty plains, or described a procession of elephants in the nearby town, they would have experienced it for themselves and the three of them would thus briefly be reunited.

My dearest Mary, Colin wrote. *It was so good to receive your latest letter which arrived just a few days before I returned to university for the start of the new (and final!) term, so I was able to share it with Dickon. I did enjoy hearing about your dust-up with your head servant, who sounds almost as autocratic as old Pitcher. I would so much like to see the two of them together: would they come to blows, I wonder? We were absolutely riveted by your story of the monkey*

*running up and down the dinner-table snatching food
from the plates of your guests. Even Dickon laughed
aloud and for a moment I felt as though the dear old
fellow was himself again. Alas not. My father tells me
he is deeply worried about him, and so are his parents.
It is nearly eighteen months since we brought him back
to Misselthwaite and he still shows no inclination to
do anything with himself. His mother says he suffers
appalling nightmares and I swear that since you left
us, he must have carved a thousand more of those little
horses. I remember his letter telling me that Jason had
been blown up by a shell, but had no idea he was so
attached to the horse. Or is the horse no more than a
symbol for all the other deaths he witnessed while on
active service?*

*I have been reading the works of Dr. Freud recently
(have you heard of him in your outpost of Empire? He
is an Austrian doctor with some extremely interesting
theories about the way our minds work) and am even
thinking of pursuing the study of Psychiatry further. It
might enable me to help Dickon more than I can at
present. As you know, I do not like being so helpless.*

*The summer term at Oxford is full of the usual de-
lights. Punting, cricket, reading poetry under the willows to girls in pince-nez. Why is it my fate to be
pursued by girls in pince-nez? And why, when I have
weakly given in to their blandishments and agreed to
punt them up or, as it might be, down the Cherwell,
do I always end up eating soggy tomato sandwiches
and reading poetry to them? Life is a mystery, Mary,
and one of the biggest mysteries of all is how I manage
to survive when you are so far away. Please do not
run away with the idea that I miss you or anything
like that, but I have to say that I do occasionally feel
a pang at the memory of your funny face all screwed
up as you berated me for some sin of either omission
or commission. There are many things I would enjoy
sharing with you. At least, as I punt my pince-nezed
ladies toward Marston Ferry and back again, I can
remind myself of the few golden afternoons when you
graced Oxford with your presence.*

*My father tells me about the great excitement being
generated by the building of a cinema in Middleburn.*

This is an epoch-making event for Yorkshire. Father is making plans for a ball to celebrate my coming of age next year and I have told him I would like him to book the cinema for the junketings. How nice it would be if we could sit there in the darkness, a glass of champagne to hand, and watch Charlie Chaplin or Cowboys and Redskins flicker away on the screen. Instead, I shall have to put on a white tie and dance with hundreds of hideous girls and be nice to everyone— and you, of all people, know how difficult I find that. Besides, who wants to have a ball all to themselves when the cousin who should be sharing it is miles away, doing impressive things at gymkhanas, and dealing with overexcited monkeys?

You ask what books you should be reading. I have prepared overleaf a book list for you. The titles marked with a star I have taken the liberty of asking Hatchards to dispatch to you as a gift from one who considers himself fortunate to be your friend as well as your cousin, and I hope you will enjoy them. I can especially recommend the Herbert Read book. He seems to me to have a particular facility for . . .

Mary put the letter down on her writing desk. She was seized with a fierce desire to be at the ball to mark Colin's majority next year. She too would be twenty-one; ordinarily it would have been an event they celebrated together, as they had shared so many other birthdays. Was there any possible way she could persuade Barney to let her go Home for it? It was not so much a question of the cost—both she and Barney had private money— as the prevailing mores. Even if Barney were to agree, what would the gossips and scandal-mongers have to say about a bride going Home for a visit so soon after coming out here? She wondered whether she could invent a sick relative, or develop the symptoms of a disease so rare that only a specialist doctor in London could possibly cure it.

Both were impossible, she knew that. Pacing the veranda, she told herself that it was ridiculous that a grown woman should be so hemmed about. If she wished to go back to England, she ought to be free to do so without having to scheme and plan. But she was not. Were she to insist on going, Barney would see it as a betrayal not just of him personally but of his military career. "What would the colonel say?" he would wonder, his boyish face creased in a bewildered frown. Though it was not the colonel they had to worry about so much as the colonel's lady. Even if she defied the conventions and went back to Misselthwaite, Mary knew that when she returned to India she would find herself pushed right to the edge of the social group, despite her current favored status. The *memsahibs* would not tolerate the idea that not everyone shared their high opinion of the society they had created out here. Abandoning her duties as a wife to return Home for something as frivolous as a coming-of-age ball would be taken as a clear sign of dissatisfaction, a setting of herself above the other women there, an indication that she considered herself superior to them. Which, frankly, in many instances, she did.

Someone was riding up the drive between the thick bushes of plumbago. A visitor: good. Barney had been away on maneuvers with his platoon for the past week and she was sick of her own company. Someone to gossip with would be welcome. She stood with her arms twisted around one of the wooden uprights which supported the thatched roof of the veranda. It was bound to be someone utterly boring: had it been Fiona or Monica, they would have sent a *chit* to warn of their arrival. As the horseman rounded the hedge, she recognized Basil Crawford and wished she had gone inside before it was too late.

Beastly Basil thought she had forgotten him, but she had not. It was he who had christened her "Mistress Mary quite contrary" when she was waiting to go home to England after the death of her parents. It was Basil who had interfered when she was trying to build a garden under a tree in his father's horrible bungalow, and informed her with relish that her uncle was a hunchback. On arriving back here, it had come as an unpleasant surprise to find the Rev Crawford still at his post as the regimental padre and even more of one to discover that Basil himself was now a junior officer.

"Mrs. Sambourne," Basil said, lifting his *topi* and

handing the reins of his horse to the servant who had appeared.

"What do you want?" asked Mary disagreeably.

"I merely came to call, since I had an hour or two at my disposal, and Mrs. Stuart-Fraser told me that she believed that with your husband away, you might be free this morning."

"She had no right to say any such thing." Mary called for lime and soda to be brought, and for gin to be added to Basil's.

"Except that she knows how I dote on you," Basil said.

"That is exceedingly foolish of you. I'm a married woman." Mary was furious that Fiona should have colluded with Basil in this way, especially when she knew how much Mary despised him.

"Why should that stop you?" asked Basil. He came closer to her. "It never stops Mrs. Stuart-Fraser, after all."

"She is a very different person from me," said Mary. Fiona had been in India for several years and had long ago given in to one of the accepted ways of passing the time—flirtation. Everybody flirted, despite the sharp eyes of the *memsahibs* which were always alert to any sign that a wife was Getting Up To Something. "And if I wish to behave as the other ladies do, it would certainly not be with you." She was irritatedly aware that every remark she made sounded like nothing more than the placing of another counter in the elaborate game of intrigue and romance.

"Oh come, Mrs. Major Sambourne. How can you be so cruel?" Basil cut a dashing figure in his uniform, and knew it. His hair was dark and romantically curly. His features were good. As a boy, his eyes had been, she remembered, blue. Over the years they had darkened to gray. To anyone else, he might have been handsome but Mary could never forget the way he had incited the other children to mock her, to sing "Mistress Mary, quite contrary," to her face.

"Perhaps I learned it from you," she said, turning away from him.

"From me? I assure you that I would never ever be

cruel to you," he said. "You're far too beautiful, for one thing."

"For goodness sake . . ." She scowled at him.

"And looking particularly stunning this morning, if I may say so."

Mary said nothing. She had not yet changed out of the jodphurs and short-sleeved blouse she had worn for her morning ride and did not like the way his eyes lingered on the swell of her hips under the thick cloth.

"But that is not the only reason I've come," he continued.

"Oh?"

"I have two other commissions to execute." Basil pulled at his drink and tapped the side of his calf with his parade stick.

"What are they?" Mary saw no reason to be polite.

"Firstly, I should be honored if you would attend the polo game on Saturday as my guest. I shall be riding, and it would spur me on to know that you were watching me."

"I can't imagine why." But there was no real acerbity in Mary's tone. Basil Crawford was an outstanding horseman; despite her antipathy toward him, she had admired his skill and daring on several occasions. Although they could not have been more physically different, she was always reminded of Dickon when she saw Crawford on horseback: in both cases, it was impossible not to appreciate the rapport which existed between horse and rider.

"Do say you will come, Mrs. Sambourne. Without your presence, there would be no point to the afternoon."

"You mentioned two commissions. What was the second?" Mary held her glass against her flushed face. Were she not married, would she find the lieutenant less offensive?

"Ah yes. One of the planters sent a boy up last night to say that a traveling theater company is on its way and will be here in the next couple of days. They specialize, it seems, in Shakespeare. I came to beg that you will allow me to escort you to at least one of their productions."

Again Mary was torn. She did not want to set tongues

wagging by appearing in public on the arm of Lieutenant Crawford. On the other hand, she did not want to miss an event so out-of-the ordinary as a professional production of Shakespeare. She could, of course, ask to join someone else's group: Fiona or Grace would certainly be making up a party to attend as soon as they heard the news, but it would be humiliating to have to make the request.

"I'm not sure that my husband . . ." she began, playing for time. "Perhaps I could send you a *chit*."

When he had gone, she lay back in her chair and closed her eyes. Restlessness filled her. Yet it was more than mere discontent. For some weeks now she had not felt really well. And although it was too hot to eat very much, she was nonetheless getting fatter. The waistband of her jodhpurs was cutting into her stomach and last night, dressing for dinner, her frock seemed to have shrunk around the bust. She thought with horror of the adjutant's wife, or the colonel's: what a hideous prospect if she were to end up like either of them, women in their early forties who had simply let themselves go, always picking at bits of this and that, forever popping tidbits into their mouths without thought for their figures. But she was not even twenty-one: surely she could not already be going the same way.

The heat was stifling, the air as thick and sluggish as warm oil. Normally she did not find the hot weather bothersome, but today, sweat lay along her arms and forehead. The *punkah-wallah* sat cross-legged in one corner of the veranda, half asleep as he pulled at the cord which moved the fan back and forth. She thought of going to her bedroom and trying to sleep but knew she would be as uncomfortable under the mosquito netting as she was out here. Trying to analyze what was wrong with her, she wondered if she were one of those unfortunates who did not fit in anywhere. At school, she had been one of the odd-girls-out, because of her exotic background, her dead parents. In London she was a provincial, at Misselthwaite a sophisticate. A square peg in a round hole: wasn't that the phrase? A fish out of water. There was no place to which she could rightfully say she belonged. She envied Colin: Cravens had lived at the Manor for generation after generation. The house held

their history. Dickon too. His forebears had lived in the
dales for as long as Colin's. Whereas she . . .

Tears filled her eyes and she angrily wiped them away.
These days, she wept far too easily. How she despised
self-pity. There was something she wanted, but whenever
she tried to pin down what exactly it was, she could
only come up with the thought of Dickon's mother, her
strength, her goodness.

Her *ayah* came out on to the veranda, carrying food
on a tray.

"I don't want it," Mary said.

"But *memsahib* must eat."

"I'm not hungry."

"If not for you, then for the new one." The *ayah*
placed dishes on the little table beside Mary: cold roast
fowl, cheese, rolls of bread, slices of mango, ripe strawberries. "It is important to eat."

"What are you talking about?" Mary's head began to
hurt. Oh no, she thought. Please not that. And if it was
that, how could it be that her servants were aware of
the fact before she herself was?

"Eat," the *ayah* said placidly. "Eat," and smiled at
her mistress in such an infuriatingly knowing manner
that if she had possessed the energy, Mary might have
slapped her.

9

Lying above Scarston Fell, Colin opened his mouth to the wind and felt it hit his lungs like a draught of cold water. "She's pregnant," he shouted.

"What?" Dickon cupped his ear against the rush of the air.

"She's going to have a baby."

"How do you know?" Dickon did not need to ask to whom Colin referred.

"I had a letter from her this morning." Most of the time, Colin managed to ignore the fact that Mary was married; he preferred to consider her absence as temporary, even though she was half a world away. But with a baby on the way, that would no longer work. He was going to have to accept that she was permanently gone, she was not going to come back to them.

"Does that make you jealous?" Dickon thrust his face close to Colin's in order to be heard above the gusty air.

"Jealous?" The question was disconcerting. "Why should I be? She's my cousin."

"What difference does that make?"

"Naturally I'm very pleased for her." The roughness of Dickon's hair brushed Colin's cheek. It smelled wholesome, like a horse's hide, of oatmeal and grass.

"I'm not."

"Why do you say that?"

Dickon rolled over and stared at the sky, at the same time reaching out an arm to bury his fingers in the thick fur of the young collie who lay stretched beside him. "Because I don't think she's ready for it, for motherhood. She's little more than a child herself. I don't believe a baby will make her any happier."

"You think she's unhappy?" Colin was not proud of the way his spirits lifted at hearing Dickon's words. Far below, the river wound away down the valley between flat banks of shale. Plovers dipped and wheeled above their heads and they could hear the distant squawks of gulls which had flown inland on the wind in the hope of easy pickings. Colin had been trying to capture the scene with his camera and rather thought that this afternoon he had been successful.

"Don't you?" Dickon asked.

"She certainly talks a lot about being bored."

"For her, they're the same thing." Like Colin, Dickon learned the news of Mary's pregnancy with dismay rather than with pleasure. Not only was it an ineradicable marker of the fact that she belonged to another man, it also confirmed her distance, her difference, from them. All these months, some diehard instinct within himself had hoped that she would eventually come home. He did not know her husband, had seen him only once, on the wedding day. He had seemed worthy but unexciting, the sort of man Dickon had learned to trust during his years as a soldier. Not at all the kind of husband he would have expected Mary to choose. Though, watching the pair of them make their vows in the fashionable London church, he was forced to admit that, until then, he had not envisaged Mary as the one making the decision. He had always thought of her being chosen rather than choosing.

He desired her. Had done for years. He wanted her in the ways that men did want women; he wanted to make love to her and feel her respond to his ardor. Dressed in the unfamiliar formality of morning dress, he had watched her walk away from him down the aisle toward the altar where Major Sambourne waited, and had known true despair. Yet he had not expected her necessarily to want him, nor that his own desires would be fulfilled.

"I miss her," Colin said.

"Yes." If he had ever thought about it at any level above the intuitive, Dickon would have assumed that Mary and Colin would make up the couple, were couples to be formed. He had, nonetheless, taken it for granted that for a while, at least, all three of them would have

some time to be together, to form an adult version of
their youthful trio. But she was already engaged by the
time they caught up with each other, and therefore out
of bounds, both to him and Colin. When he could bring
himself to think about this, Dickon knew that it was a
sorrow he would have to endure for the rest of his life.

Colin began packing up his photographic equipment.
The wind blew his black hair back off his thin face; he
looked as he had done when he was a boy, still coming
to terms with his own physical potential. When he was
finished, he slung the various boxes over his shoulder,
while Dickon picked up the tripod and folded the legs
together. As the two young men continued their walk,
each preoccupied with his own thoughts, he whistled for
the dog to follow. It was no longer necessary for them
to talk. On Dickon's return to Yorkshire, Colin had presented him with the collie, saying, as he handed over the
small warm bundle: "He was the quietest one in the
litter. Didn't make a sound, just looked at me with his
head on one side, begging me to pick him."

"Beggar," Dickon had said. He pressed his cheek
against the puppy's head and Colin could almost see the
ice around his heart begin to crack. The three of them,
Colin, Dickon and Beggar, had walked the moors for
months on end, day after day, regardless of the weather.
By constantly asking questions, by refusing to let Dickon
stay silent, he had forced his friend to articulate his experiences in the trenches. It had not been pleasant for
either of them. Purging himself of the horror, Dickon
had wept, screamed, cursed. Colin had cried too. Day
after day, he had held Dickon's head against his chest
and waited until the fits of shuddering died down. He
had gripped Dickon's hand as his bitter words poured
like vomit into the clean bright air of the hills. The apoc-
alyptic scenes that Colin pictured inside his head might
not correspond exactly to Dickon's experiences: he knew
that they were as grievous and as intense.

Since then, Beggar had been joined by other animal
companions. There was the baby badger rescued from
the jaws of a moor farm terrier. There were a couple of
kittens which Dickon had managed to save from drowning. And, most recently, he had acquired a baby owl,
whom he had named Forster, after the teacher friend he

had served under in the horse lines. Watching him trudge the moors with Beggar at his heels and the badger in his pocket, Colin was reminded of the Dickon he had first come across in the secret garden, with animals at his feet and his pet squirrels romping nearby. As the weeks passed, it gradually occurred to him that he knew Dickon better than he would ever know anyone else; he had seen further into his heart and his mind than wife or parent or lover would ever do. Sometimes he wondered if he knew Dickon better than Dickon knew himself.

Dickon wished he could fulfil the expectations that Colin had for him, but he was determined not to be rushed. He had to recover, he knew that as instinctively as he knew how to bind the broken wing of a bird. Plans swirled in his head as he waited for the moment when he could finally unlock the cage which the years of war had erected around him. Of one thing he was sure: he was not going to enter the employ of Archibald Craven, however beneficial or benevolent a master Mr. Craven might be. Nor would he follow his father and go down the mines. With his brothers working, and some of his sisters employed in the nearby mills, there was more money coming into the household than there had been before the war, and fewer people to be provided for. That eased the pressure on him. He was going to work for himself, in that much he was determined. He had discussed it with his parents and they concurred. "After what you've been through, son, it's no more than you deserve," his mother had said and his father, slower to speak, had nodded agreement.

No more than you deserve. She was right. Nothing could make up for the experiences of war, but they had at least given him a sense of his own worth. However poor a living he might make, he would never again be beholden to anyone. From now, until the day he died, he would retain control over his own life. His hopes were humble. He did not expect great wealth or renown. Self-respect would be enough. The ability to hold his destiny in his own hands. One of the most terrifying aspects of the war had been the realization of his helplessness to change things. He was no more than a cog

in someone else's machine. Never again. Never. Come
what may.

There was no way he could express his gratitude to
Colin for the patience and kindness he had shown. When
the time came, he hoped that his desire for indepen-
dence would not seem ungrateful. He had kept in touch
with Captain Forster, who was now back in York at his
teaching job. He had traveled over by bus to take tea
with him and his wife, and they had talked for hours
about the new world to which they had returned. Land
fit for the dole queue, more like, Forster had said, for
all the prosperity of the war years. Aye, money made
out of our sufferings, said Dickon. And you mark my
words, Forster told him, things'll go from bad to worse,
and lucky to find any sort of a job at all.

Soon, Dickon was sure, he would be clear about what
his place in that world was; for the moment, he was
content to let the poison work its way out of his system.

"I wish I knew what I was going to do, now that I've
finished at university," Colin's words echoed Dickon's
own thoughts.

"When you were a boy, you were going to be a Scientific Discoverer. After you'd been an Athlete."

"You remember, then?" Colin wanted to ask if those
long days in the secret garden had meant as much to
Dickon as they had to Mary and himself; he suspected
that they had not. But Dickon had not then been in
need of regeneration. He wondered how often Dickon
thought of that time, and of the Magic.

"Of course I do." Words crowded Dickon's throat, so
many of them jostling to get out, that he did not elaborate, not knowing where to start. The two of them, the
sallow bad-tempered little girl and the invalid boy, had
been in such obvious need that they made him feel invin-
cible. Watching them grow, watching the color come into
them and the way they budded and bloomed, knowing
that he himself was responsible, had given him a sense
of protectiveness toward them which nothing, whatever
happened in the future, would ever change. He loved
them: it was as simple as that. It was a quite different
love from the one which bound him within the circle of
his warm-hearted family, and based on different premises, different needs. Interdependence. Shared experi-

ences. And perhaps a touch of Colin's Magic. "Of course," he repeated, looking away so that his face would not betray the emotions that Colin roused in him.

"I've got a fairly good degree, you see," Colin said earnestly, "and absolutely no idea what I want to do with myself."

Dickon leaned on the tripod and laughed. "Your problem is, you've got a sight too many ideas. One minute you're going to direct Charlie Chaplin films in America, the next you're wondering whether you should go into politics, the next you want to be a trapeze artiste in a circus."

"Yes, well, that was only for a couple of days," said Colin. "I couldn't see past those spangled tights."

"You'd have looked right smart in them, I reckon." Dickon grinned. The wind rippled his russet hair; cold made the freckles stand out on his face.

"Dickon . . ."

"What?"

"What I wish more than anything in the world is that . . ."

"Yes?"

"That the two of us, you and I, could somehow work together. Set up a partnership or something."

"Doing what?"

"That's just it, I don't really know. I don't mind what it is. I'm not particularly proud, I'm not worried about being 'in trade' or anything snobbish of that sort."

"That's easy said." Though who, thought Dickon, was likely to look down on Colin Craven, of Misselthwaite in Yorkshire, and Fitzroy Square, London, even if he sold shoes in the Tottenham Court Road for a living?

"I mean it. Any gainful occupation would suit me, though I'd particularly like to build something up from scratch. You know, invent some product and then promote it, watch it grow."

"Scientific Discoveries, eh?"

"Something like that."

"I won't be at any man's beck and call."

"I understand that."

"I'd be a liability to you, Colin. I'm not clever, like you. And I don't want to leave Yorkshire. My roots are here."

"So are mine. That's the beauty of the idea of the two of us doing something together. For one thing, I can't just abandon my father, and for another, I've got too many responsibilities to Misselthwaite. One of these days, the estate will be mine, and it's my duty to see that it's passed on to my heirs in the best possible condition. But that doesn't mean I—*we*—couldn't . . . I don't know, go into business together."

"Whatever I do," Dickon pointed out one afternoon as they sat in the secret garden, "I shall have to start at the bottom and work my way up. I'm not like you, I haven't got any capital to invest."

"Capital's not such a big problem, if we can only hit on the right idea. My father has influential friends, and there's money coming to me as soon as I turn twenty-one—not a lot, but enough to get us started."

"I don't know how I'd feel about that. I'd want to come in on equal terms."

"That's the whole point," Colin said, speaking fast, elated as he saw that he had caught Dickon's interest, "We *would* be equal. Whatever we went into would need both of us. We've got different skills to offer."

"I haven't got any skills."

"Of course you have. You can turn your hand to anything." He looked round at the flower-beds, the bulbs which Dickon had planted years before. "Like gardening, for instance. Your sister Martha told Mary that you could make flowers grow out of a brick wall. And your mother always says that you just whisper things out of the ground. I've seen you do it myself."

"Gardening . . ." Dickon said slowly.

"And anyway, once we'd decided on something, we could always go away and learn what we need to."

Yes . . . Dickon was aware of something he had not experienced for years. Anticipation. A slow stirring of the pulses. Interest in the future. Although what lay immediately ahead was unforeseeable, he realized that beyond the mists of the unknown there might, after all, be a place for him.

"We should sit down with a piece of paper and list our assets and abilities," Colin said another time, as they came down from Skag Fell. "Between us, we must be able to come up with an idea. It could be something expensive, like turning out luxury custom-built motors, or something really simple, something that everyone will wonder how they could possibly have managed without, as soon as they hear about it."

"Such as?"

"I don't know." Colin looked about him as though hoping inspiration would leap out of the scrubby grass under their feet. "What about a hand-held camera, for instance? Instead of lugging all this equipment about, you'd just have the thing slung round your neck on a strap. Think of it: it could revolutionize photography."

"I don't know nowt about cameras."

"What about something you *do* know about? What about a gadget that would—that would peel potatoes, for instance? Or, if one already exists, a *better* gadget, a new and improved gadget? I bet every family in the British Isles eats potatoes at least once a day: suppose you could make it quicker and easier for housewives to get the peel off."

Dickon thought about the chore of potato peeling in a big family like his own. "Tha's on to something there," he said slowly. "Reckon they'd be putting up statues and turning you into a saint in no time."

"It was just an idea. Someone's probably already thought of it. But I'd be willing to wager that if we thought of all the little things that annoy us every day, and worked out a way to eliminate them, we'd make our fortunes." He glanced at his friend and added: "If a fortune is what you're after, of course."

"Wouldn't mind being rich," said Dickon. "Wouldn't mind a great house and a carriage with my coat of arms on the door, nor one of them big motor cars."

"We could have race horses, and own a box at Ascot."

"We could buy our own circus so's you could have them spangled tights after all."

"We could buy a pleasure yacht and sail to Monte Carlo."

"We could visit Mary," Dickon said.

"What about a chicken farm?"

"Chickens stink."

"Doesn't your grandmother have a secret recipe for

lemon cheese which we could pack up in pretty jars with rustic tops on, and make a fortune?"

"Doesn't yours?"

"I've never had a grandmother," Colin said dolefully.

"You must have done. Everybody's had a grandmother."

"Not me," Colin said.

They were in the secret garden again. Colin sprawling on a bench, while Dickon sat against the trunk of an apple tree, with Beggar at his side. It was quiet here. The high ivy-shawled walls fended off any noise; even the wind was subdued.

"Could we set ourselves up as interior designers? Gold lamé couches and potted palms in the lavatory. It's the very latest thing in London, so I've heard."

"What do we know about gold lamé?"

"How about turning ourselves into high-class mail-order grocers? I think I should like to dispatch pheasant under glass and smoked salmon down south. We could catch the salmon ourselves." Colin sketched the sign in the air. "Craven & Sowerby, by Appointment, Purveyors of Fine Food to the Upper Classes."

"That lot catch their own salmon and shoot their own birds," said Dickon.

"An electric toothbrush. A patent hair restorer. An automatic clothes press, a—"

"Tell you what: you've come up with all sorts of ideas over the past few days, but the first one were the best."

"What was that?"

"The patent potato peeler. There'd be a real market for it. I talked to me mam and dad about it, and they said the same."

"Really?" Colin loved to listen to Dickon's slow flat voice. He remembered Dickon here as a boy, talking to the robin and the rook, his wild rabbit in his arms. He remembered the sureness of him, the solid security which he exuded.

"And there's another thing I like," Dickon was saying. His eyes were closed. If he opened them, he would be looking straight up at the sky through the intricate lacings of the apple boughs. It was exhilarating to be up on the moors, with the wind blowing away the bad thoughts, the cruel nightmares. But here, in the secret garden, was the peace he sought.

"What's that?"

"Your idea of a palm house. Always liked it, from that time you took me to Kew Gardens. Maybe we could go into the palm-house business. I had a word with Ted Langdale about it: he says he reckons there's lots of fine houses would be interested in something like that."

"How does he know that?"

"He knows a lot about trees. When he hears about a rare one, he'll travel miles to go and look at it. There's plenty like him, not just those with the interest, but some of 'em rich collectors, like your great-great-great-grand-father used to be."

"Haven't they already got hot houses?"

"Some of 'em have, and some not. But them as hasn't might be interested in hearing more about it. And them as has will have let 'em go during the war."

"I like it. We could produce a brochure. With pictures. I could take photographs and we could send it round to potential customers."

"Ted says there's books in your father's library with pictures of the one which burned down at Misselthwaite. I was thinking we ought to look at them, learn something about it." His wide smile lit up his face and for a moment he looked like a boy again. "Build one here at Misselthwaite first, mebbe, as an example of our work. Stock it. See what works and what doesna. Ted would help us. People could come and see if they liked it, and then order ones for theirselves."

Colin's heart hammered. He thought: Dickon has returned. Or, at least, he's on his way back.

If only Mary were, too.

10

The baby was named Charlotte Alice, after Barney's dead sister and Mary's mother. Fiona and Monica stood as godmothers at the christening ceremony, which was held in the garrison church, and Barney's closest friend, Captain George Fleming, acted as proxy godfather for Colin. Afterwards, there was a gathering in the Mess, with champagne and canapés, and Barney expansively handing out cigars. "To celebrate the birth of my daughter," he kept saying. "My beautiful daughter."

But Charlotte was not beautiful. She was a sickly yellow baby, who clearly had not enjoyed the transition from the safety of her mother's womb to the cold world outside. However much the *ayah* soothed and rocked, she fretted; she refused to settle and was always difficult to nurse. Day and night, her thin relentless wails filled the bungalow, dragging at Mary's taut nerves until she thought she might disintegrate with the tension.

Sometimes, on the few occasions when the baby was quiet, she would stand beside the cradle and look down at the jaundiced little face on its pillow, wondering when she would feel the first stirrings of maternal love. It would be so much easier if the child did not scream all the time, if it did not have the same scrawny ugliness as a new-hatched starling. Mary could muster up nothing but disgust for the red cheeks covered in a band of miniature pustules, the eyes creased like a Chinaman's, the blatant nakedness of the overlarge skull. She was frightened by the vein which throbbed on top of the head; she was intimidated by the child's vulnerability, the ease with which its life could be ended. And as she thought this, the toothless mouth would open and the endless crying would begin again, and putting her hands over her ears, she would rush from the room.

Barney doted on his daughter. He would sit for hours in the rocking chair in the nursery, crooning at the ugly little bundle on his knee. "Babies are like that," he told Mary, when she complained about Charlotte Alice's appearance, and he would lift the child above his head then pull her back out of the air and into his neck so he could cuddle her close. "She'll grow out of it."

He marveled at the minute fingernails, the restless twitching limbs, the way the baby would react to sound or to light. He brought presents home: a wooden toy from the bazaar, a bracelet of thin gold links to fasten around Charlotte's wrist, a green plush elephant. Mary had found the whole business of childbirth both degrading and painful: that the end result should be nothing better than this noisy unattractive creature seemed monstrously unfair. It was all very well for Barney, she would think resentfully, as she was roused yet again from sleep by the baby's cries, by the slap slap of the *ayah's* feet as she walked across the nursery floor, by the creak of the rocking chair. He had not had nine months of getting fatter and fatter, of swelling breasts and ugly marks across his stomach, of backache and indigestion, of being taken over by an alien creature. He had not experienced the terrible pain of the contractions as the child worked its way out of the womb, nor the hideous sensation of being split apart as its head burst from his body. Nor did he have to feed it, to have those vampire lips clamped to his breast as though he were no more than some farrowing sow whose only function was to provide sustenance.

Was there something wrong with her? Was it normal to dislike your own child? Was she an unnatural mother? She did not know, and there was no one she could ask. During visits to her friends, she watched them with their children, envying them, wondering if she would ever achieve such easiness, such obvious love. Her secret was not one she could share. The other women might turn from her aghast, were she to admit that she found Charlotte repulsive, that the feel of the squirming little body under its layers of lace and broderie anglaise filled her with repugnance. The only one she could have confessed her feelings to was Colin: there had never been any need for pretence between them. But Colin was thousands of miles away, and Mary hesitated to commit her doubts to paper. Besides, she could not bear the thought that if she did so, she might lower herself in his estimation.

There was an even deeper trauma. Sitting on her veranda in the long afternoons, under the slow creak and swish of the *punkahs,* she would hear the distant screams of her daughter and face the possibility that this sense of alienation was what her mother had experienced toward herself. She remembered clearly the feeling, as a child, that while other children belonged to their parents, she had never seemed to be anyone's little girl. While she felt no love for her own child, she did feel responsibility and had no wish for Barney's daughter to suffer from the same feelings of inadequacy as his wife.

I was taken care of all my life, she thought, but never cared about. At least Charlotte has her father. Or did my own father love me as a baby, the way Barney loves Charlotte now, only to grow to dislike me as I got older? Was I so unlovable? Somewhere, at the roots of herself, she felt a deep misery on Charlotte's behalf, a desire that the little girl should not one day be asking the same questions.

And each time her thoughts reached this point, she would force herself to visit the nursery, to push aside the gauze-covered cage which guarded the crib from insects and take the hot little body in her arms. The softness of the baby's skin moved her. But if the *ayah* dared to give the slightest indication of pleasure at the sight of mother and daughter together, Mary would scowl and hand the child back, before stalking away with some dismissive remark.

One thing was clear to her. She would never have another child. If she could possibly help it, she would never even get involved in the kind of nighttime activity which might lead to a child. To this end, she held Barney at arm's length for at least three months after the birth and then winced and bit her lip as she submitted to his first tentative resumption of embraces until, after a while, he gave up attempting to make love to her. He was a decent man. And an inexperienced one. The thought that his advances might be painful to his young

wife was enough at first to help him bear his enforced
celibacy with resignation. Later, he consoled himself
with the knowledge that if he grew desperate, there were
other places where he could find what he wanted.

Mary thought him happy enough. After all, she had
given him his child and there were a myriad flirtations
to be carried on with the other women at the station.
Not to mention the relief afforded by discreet visits to
establishments in the town.

Colin has gone to London, Dickon wrote, *to see his
father's lawyers & one or two other people. He is hoping to persuade them to back us in our new enterprise.
Between ourselves, Mary, I believe he is not only concerned with raising money but that there is also a Romantic Interest. Although he has never spoken of such
a thing to me, I cannot help noticing how excited he
is when he journeys south, & how invigorated when
he returns home. But what could be more natural? He
is a young man, after all, & it is only to be expected
that he will fall in love.*

Why does he write as though he himself were fifty
years old and long past love? Mary asked herself crossly.

*Meanwhile, I am traveling round the north of the
country, visiting the established arboreta, the grand
houses with orangeries & conservatories, trying to discover what exactly the requirements are when people
decide to build up a collection of exotic or tropical
plants. As I believe Colin has told you, we plan to start
by rebuilding the Palm House which used to stand in
the grounds here at Misselthwaite. That way we can
make mistakes without endangering any reputation we
might later have.*

*I hope you & your small family are well. India
seems to me to be a most exciting country in which to
live—but then I remember clearly the tales you used to
tell of life there, & the elephants & rajahs & turbanned
nabobs. Perhaps, if Colin's schemes ever come to anything, we may even find ourselves in India: we think
that as well as building the palm houses, we should
learn about the specimens which would grow in them,*

so that we can advise our "clients." If that should happen, of course we shall hope to visit you. By then, you may have other children . . .

Reading this, Mary scrumpled the letter up and threw it into a corner of the veranda. She could not bear the way he wrote as though she no longer belonged to them, as though her life had nothing whatsoever to do with theirs. Nothing could be further from the truth. She lived for the letters which arrived from them both; she was as involved with the new project as they were, had even written with ideas about the regeneration of the Palm House. Years and years ago, old Ben Weatherstaff had pointed out the site where it had once stood and told her that his grandfather had made sketches of it, which were kept wrapped in brown paper, under Ben's bed. How dare Dickon exclude her like this, when it was she herself who had suggested that they visit the old man's niece to see if the sketches were still available? And weren't the two of them using them now, in conjunction with the plans in Archie Craven's library? Wasn't it thanks to her that they even knew about them?

And there was another thing . . . Scowling, she marched across the wooden boards of the veranda and picked up the scrumpled letter. As she did so, Fiona Stuart-Fraser came riding between the plumbago hedges, and gave her horse's reins to the *chuprassi* who appeared from behind the bungalow.

"Goodness, Mary. How cross you look," she said in her languid voice. She came up the steps, pulling off her *topi* and tossing it on to the bamboo table against the wall. "What on earth's the matter?"

"Nothing."

Spotting the envelope in Mary's hand, Fiona said: "Is that news from Home?"

"Yes." Mary thrust the letter into the pocket of her frock.

"Not bad, I hope."

"Not really." It depended, of course, Mary thought, clapping her hands for iced soda and limes to be brought, on how you defined bad.

"I came to visit my adorable godchild," Fiona said. "Where is she?"

"In the nursery, I imagine. Unless the *ayah's* taken her out in her pram."

"Really, Mary. Sometimes I ask myself if you have the slightest interest in that baby."

Mary caught the inside of her lower lip between her teeth then, taking the plunge, said quickly: "Fiona, do you really think Charlotte is adorable?"

Fiona seemed astonished. "But of course. Too exquisite for words."

"But that impetigo on her face . . ."

"That's nothing. Lots of babies have that."

"And the way her face is, those slanted eyes and everything."

"She'll change."

"Fiona, did you—" But Mary still did not have the courage to ask if her friend had disliked her own children when they first appeared.

"Did I what?"

"Nothing."

Motherhood was one of those universal ideals to which everyone subscribed. Everyone knew about the bond between mother and child, that tie stronger than steel, more enduring than mountains. Mary remembered standing in the National Gallery in Trafalgar Square, staring at da Vinci's *Virgin of the Rocks,* while Colin waxed lyrical about the beauty of the mother and child relationship.

"How would you know?" she had asked scornfully. "You've never *had* a mother, and you're never likely to *be* one."

"Everybody knows," he responded, in his lofty crushing way, before moving on to stand before a Caravaggio or a Cranach, she could not now recall which. She remembered, too, Martha Sowerby bringing her first-born son to Misselthwaite, and the tenderness with which she held him up to be admired, the love which had transformed her homely face as she looked down at him cradled in her arms. Mary had so much hoped that, as a mother herself, she would feel something of that same unquestioning devotion.

When the servants had left, after bringing iced drinks and a tray of sweet cakes, Fiona said archly: "I saw Basil Crawford this morning."

"Did you?"

"The poor boy is sick with passion."

"Really?"

"Yes, really, Mary."

"For himself, I suppose you mean. I've never seen a man who spends more time looking in the mirror."

"For *you*, idiot. Why do you think he's still single, when all winter long the Fishing Fleet has been casting its collective nets over him?"

"Basil's matrimonial state is of complete indifference to me."

Fiona leaned forward and took one of Mary's limp hands in hers. "Tell me, my dear," she said. "Do you and Barney . . ."

"Do we what?"

"You know. Are you still . . . *you* know?"

The color rose in Mary's cheeks. Had Barney said something in the Mess? Did the entire cantonment know that she no longer had marital relations with her husband? And if so, did Basil Crawford think that entitled him to make moony eyes at her or, even worse, did it give him the expectation that she might eventually succumb to him physically? She was about to make some furious riposte when Barney himself appeared, home unexpectedly early. In spite of her anger, Mary could not deny that he made a handsome picture, back straight, head up, his uniform crisply ordered, despite the heat of his working day.

Fiona jumped to her feet, exclaiming. "Oh my, your husband . . . I should go home."

"Please," Mary said. "Do stay."

And Barney, dismounting, strode up on to the veranda and said he would not hear of her ending her visit early on his account. "Especially when you're looking so awfully jolly." He smiled and stroked his blond moustache.

"Why, thank you kindly, Major Sambourne," Fiona said, head tilted flirtatiously to one side, face flushed with excitement. Barney's eyes, too, held a hot predatoriness which Mary had not seen since the early days of her marriage.

From the back of the bungalow drifted a smell of cooking and the voices of the servants, a sudden uproar from the baby and the soothing tones of the *ayah;* Mary

was seized with a longing for the moors, for the undemanding peace of Dickon's company, for the stimulation
of Colin's. She stood up. "I must speak to the
servants . . . some refreshments . . ." she mumbled, and
escaped into the house.

As a child, she had always assumed that life would
continue to be uncomplicated, that in due season, she
would become an adult, fall in love, be married, have
children and grow old. It had become obvious that the
certainties on which she had counted were proving to
be built on sand. Marriage, India, motherhood: she had
thought them the prelude to adventure. She had never—
still did not—envisaged the complications which beset
her now. She threw herself on to the rattan chair in a
corner of the shaded living room.

What did Dickon mean when he wrote of Colin having
a Romantic Interest? He could not have. He had no
right to. Who was she? Some bright pretty bluestocking
from one of the new London colleges? A girl he had
studied with at Oxford? She refused to believe it:
Dickon must have got it wrong. Her own life seemed to
have come to a full stop, while Colin and Dickon were
only just embarking on theirs.

There was an ache in her heart; bitterness threatened
to overwhelm her but she pushed it away. However
much she might want to, she was not going to indulge
in self-pity. She had made her own bed and now she
must lie on it. A Romantic Interest . . . fiercely she
wanted to know more. On the other side of the thin
wall, Fiona and Barney murmured together, the sun
throwing their shadows against the house. She got up
and paced about the floor. She wanted to know here
and now, she wanted to know immediately everything
that there was to know about Colin and this girl. But
there was no telephone available. And even if there
were, she could not use it. And even if she could, even
were she to find Colin at home, how would she put such
a question to him? What would he think of her? The
idea was absurd.

She took Dickon's letter from her pocket. His schoolboy hand continued down the page and over it, as dogged and unadorned as he was himself. She pressed it
hard against her face and breathed in. Did she imagine

it, or could she really smell the essence of him in the paper: that familiar odor compounded of grass and earth and goodness? How she missed him. Missed them both. Perhaps he was wrong about Colin: she herself had seen him so many times, flushed and excited, drunk on ideas. She often mocked him for his insistence that he had to live at double the speed of everyone else, but perhaps he was right after all.

Fiona was laughing on the veranda. Barney too. The smell of burnt meat and spices mingled oddly with the scent of sandalwood from the ornamental boxes stacked on the table. She was seized with urgency. Time was slipping by. Life was slipping by. It seemed altogether imperative that she find the space she was meant to occupy; already one thing was sadly clear to her: this was not it.

She had always been abstemious. Occasionally she took a glass of wine at dinner; less often she might join Barney in a small brandy. Her present unhappiness, and the knowledge that much of it was her own fault, began to lead her toward recklessness. One glass of wine no longer seemed sufficient, especially when three or four induced a gaiety of spirit in which it was possible to forget the disappointments and fears of the life she had chosen. Prismed through alcohol, the constant round of dinner parties and dances, fancy-dress balls and whist drives assumed a brighter glow. The other guests appeared wittier, prettier; she herself sparkled. It was even possible to view Basil Crawford more favorably. As wine heated her blood and gin loosened the inhibitions of her upbringing, she began to think that perhaps she had been stupidly prejudiced, that she had condemned him for what, looking back, she perceived had been nothing more than boyish pranks. He was, after all, a personable young officer, well-thought of by his superiors and much in demand by the *burra memsahibs* on the station. His professed devotion to herself was not only flattering but also—to her surprise—lent her a certain social cachet.

"If they want to be sure of Basil accepting an invitation, they know they have to ask you as well, darling," Fiona drawled one afternoon, as she sat on the veranda of Mary's bungalow, playing bridge with Grace Bellington and Monica Streatham.

"It's all such nonsense," said Mary, nonetheless flattered.

"Maybe," said Grace, "but it's nonsense you can't afford to ignore." She slapped a card down on the table and waited, hand already poised to collect the trick, for the fourth card to be played.

"Not if we want to maintain any kind of social life," said Fiona. "Goodness: where *should* we be if we were to be dropped?" Her tone was ironic; Mary was never sure to what extent Fiona was serious when she said such things.

"She's right," agreed Monica, arching her back and pressing one hand against her waist. She did not look well. Her last confinement had been particularly painful and there had been complications during the birth which had left her weak and exhausted. There were dark shadows beneath her eyes which had not been there two years before, when Mary had first arrived in India, and recently, her body seemed to have reduced to little more than skin and bone.

"Are you all right?" Mary asked.

"Just a touch of backache." Monica concentrated over-intently on her cards.

"Backache?" Grace said sharply. "Why?"

"I went riding this morning—I probably overdid it."

"But you're not well enough to be out on horseback." Monica tried to ignore the remark.

"You know you're not," persisted Grace.

Monica laid her cards on the table in front of her. "The truth is," she said slowly, "I'm pregnant again."

Her friends looked at each other. Congratulations ought to have been offered, but all three of them knew that another baby so soon after the last was hardly a matter for felicitation. Not only was the climate out here unconducive to good health or an easy pregnancy; the standard of medical care was sadly lacking. Although she was the youngest there, as hostess, it was left to Mary to get up and put her arms round Monica's thin shoulders.

"I hope you're pleased about it," she said warmly, unable to think of anything more suitable to say.

"I'm not, actually. As a matter of fact, I think this child will kill me," Monica said, in such a drab little voice that it took all the melodrama from the words.

"Haven't you heard of Marie Stopes?" Fiona demanded. The women looked at each other. Mary said: "I haven't."

"I'll lend you a copy of her book," said Fiona. She turned back to Monica. "Can't you do something to prevent this baby coming? These days, it's not necessary to get that way."

"We've taken—I've done what I could. I don't know what else there is."

"You could always try abstinence," Fiona said in her languid fashion.

"Yes," said Monica. "We could. But . . ." She broke off.

"But your husband refuses," retorted Fiona. "Is that it?"

Monica bent her head. "The doctor told him that another baby would be dangerous," she said. "But when he comes home from an evening in the Mess, it's not always possible . . ." again she stopped speaking before the sentence could be completed.

"Pig," Fiona said forcefully. "They're all brutes and pigs."

"All of them?" Mary asked. "Surely not." She intended to be sardonic but feared she merely sounded as though she asked for information.

"When it comes to the bedroom, they are," asserted Fiona.

Grace ignored her. "How far along are you, dear?" she asked Monica.

"Three and a half months."

Grace, older than the other three, stared hard at Monica. "That far? Then I'm afraid riding—or anything else—won't be much help."

To everyone's consternation, Monica broke down. Hiding her face in her hands, she began to sob wildly. "What am I going to do?" she wept. "I've tried everything and nothing seems to have worked."

"Darling," Fiona cried. "Why didn't you come to me

as soon as you realized? There's a woman in the bazaar who's positively brilliant."

"I'm so terribly afraid," sobbed Monica, her voice muffled by her hands. "Quinine . . . gin . . . suppose I've caused some damage . . ."

"It'll be all right, dear," soothed Grace, but her face was grave.

"I don't want to die. What about my babies if I don't survive? Who'll look after them?"

Mary was horrified by Monica's anguished cry. How terrible it would be to die in a strange country, far from family and friends, to know that one would be leaving behind a grieving husband and orphaned children. She had always liked Major John Streatham, who had struck her as a gentle and civilized man. That he could be so selfish as to jeopardize his wife's health, indeed her very life, let alone the happiness of his children, with his incontinent demands made her realize how lucky she was that Barney did not insist on his matrimonial rights.

Inside the house, she could see one of the servants moving about, taking in every word. No doubt every detail of what they had been discussing would be passed around the cantonment: there were no secrets out here, not even at the highest level for everywhere there were prying eyes and listening ears. She called sharply for more iced soda and lime and felt no twinge of guilt as she added gin to all four glasses.

When the ladies had departed, she lay back on the rattan chaise and closed her eyes. Her head swam slightly: the first drink had swiftly been followed by a second and she held a third in her hand. That evening the colonel and his lady were hosting a dance at the Club; it seemed strangely heartless to contemplate such entertainment in the face of Monica's domestic tragedy, although death was an inevitable figure in the pattern of service life in India. Marrying Barney, she had always supposed it would be. Yet she had imagined that when it came it would be manly, heroic: swords waving, gallant soldiers holding out against the onslaught of savage hill tribes, bravery in the face of impossible odds. Instead, it occurred with appalling suddenness from all manner of mundane causes: dog bites, infected insect stings, dysentery, even from a common cold. Mary had attended five funerals already that year, two of them children, one of them an army wife: Monica's fears were very real.

On the other hand, what would be gained by staying away from the dance, even supposing Barney would allow it? The simple answer was: nothing at all. Besides, she had a new dress for the occasion, ordered specially from the Army & Navy Stores' catalogue and skilfully adapted by a native seamstress. And it was rumored that there was actually to be a live American band, transported up-country especially for this evening by the colonel's youngest son, who was spending a few months with his family after leaving university. It would be foolish to miss such excitement simply because Monica was feeling depressed.

As she and Barney dressed that evening, the *ayah* carried Charlotte Alice in. Thinking of poor Monica, Mary looked at her daughter more closely than usual. Despite an unpromising beginning, the child had turned out well. As she bounced about on their bed, Mary was surprised to feel something akin to pride as she took in Charlotte's golden curls and wide blue eyes, charmingly set off by the blue glass beads she wore over a dress of crisp white broderie anglaise. There was no denying that she was a pretty little thing. Barney was handsome, too, and she herself . . . she surveyed the reflections in the mirror and was satisfied. Briefly, she was aware of—not exactly of happiness, but certainly of contentment.

Barney sensed it. He stood behind her, smiling. "My lovely Mary," he said huskily.

"Thank you," she said and, softened by alcohol, for once she smiled back.

He slid a hand down her bare shoulder and into the bodice of her dress. His hand touched her nipple and she was surprised by the leap of feeling she experienced. When she did not rebuff him, he stroked her white skin before taking her breast in his hand. Behind them, Charlotte Alice gurgled and bounced.

He lowered his mouth to her piled hair. "Oh God," he breathed. "Mary, my darling, it's been so long . . ."

She reached up and touched his wrist. "I'm sorry."

"If we weren't going out . . ."

"But we are."

"Tonight?" he said. "After?"

She touched the pearls at her throat. "Perhaps," she said, and did not hide the promise in her voice.

Charlotte Alice fell off the bed on to the floor and began to snivel. Before the *ayah* could pick her up Barney had done so.

"Who's a brave soldier, then?" he asked, tossing her into the air. "Who's Daddy's darling?"

"Me, me," squealed the child, tears forgotten as her father swung her to his shoulder. He brought her over and put her on Mary's knee.

"Give Mamma a kiss," he said.

For once, Mary did not pull away from the little hands which clutched at the bodice of her dress as the tender lips pressed her cheek. The child stared up at her mother and Mary felt a rush of some emotion too complicated to make sense of. She laid a finger against the blue veins which lay below the skin of Charlotte's temple; so soft, so delicate. She marveled at the intricacy of the mechanisms which operated the rounded limbs, the pumping lungs, the flutter of eyelashes. What a piece of work is man, she thought. Her head throbbed. In the mirror, she saw a familiar icon: Mother and Child, Madonna and Infant, a tableau of domestic bliss. She thought: Have I reached it at last, that normality to which I have for so long aspired?

Then Barney spoke. "The two most beautiful women in the world," he said, "and both of them are mine."

The possessive note in his voice shattered her mood like a hurled bottle. She kissed Charlotte's cheek and stood up, the child clinging to her like a monkey. She felt the old disengagement from her daughter as she handed her brusquely back to the *ayah*.

The Club had been decorated with balloons and banners interspersed with large portraits of Negro jazz players: Louis Armstrong, Johnny Dodds, Jelly Roll Morton. In an attempt to transform the big room into something approaching the intimacy of a jazz cellar in New York or London, small gingham-clothed tables had been placed about the room, each holding an empty bottle with a candle stuck into the neck. Despite pots of flowers set along the stage at one end of the room, it was impossible to disguise the underlying smell of mold and sweat

and vegetative decay. Mary regretted the wine she and
Barney had shared with Fiona and her husband prior to
arriving. Against that moment of intimacy achieved with
her child, this all seemed tawdry and unreal. How many
gatherings had she attended here? How many more were
there still to come? It was so meaningless. She was
frightened by the hatred she suddenly felt. Was it the
wine which had affected her vision, so that instead of
things entire, she could only focus on a series of details?
Aggressive scarlet lips here, voracious dimples there, the
straining buttons of a waistcoat, the spotted tongues of
flowers, the dangerous music of bottle clinking against
glass. She was acutely aware of sounds around her, so
much so that for a moment she wondered if she were
drugged. Water being poured from a jug sounded like a
Niagaran cataract; the scrape of a match against a box
rasped with the thunder of grinding millstones; feet on
the parquet floor boomed like war drums.

Basil Crawford presented himself. "A dance, Mrs.
Sambourne," he said, bowing slightly. "May I have the
pleasure?"

"A dance?" She leaned her unsteady head on her
hand. He was once more a boy, jeering behind a tree,
jumping sheet-wrapped from a cupboard, scornful in
her dreams.

"A waltz, I believe."

"Very well, we shall waltz together, you and I," she
said.

He did not appear to notice her detachment from the
scene as he took her into his arms and led her gracefully
on to the floor.

"You're such a good dancer," she said. "Everybody
knows that."

"Thank you."

"I thought there was to be a jazz band."

"They are to appear later in the evening," said Basil.
He tightened his grip. "Which is why I have asked you
to dance now, so that I have an excuse to hold you in
my arms."

Normally, she would have frowned at this, and pulled
away. Instead, she leaned into him, resting her head
against his shoulder and closing her eyes, aware that the

burra mems would be watching with disapproval and, for once, not caring.

Bending his head, he moved his mouth against her neck. "You don't need me to tell you that you're the loveliest woman here tonight," he said. His hand on her back pressed closer so that she thought she could feel the hot blood under her skin.

She wanted to believe him. "Why did you tease me so dreadfully?" she asked dreamily.

"What?" He stiffened.

"Why were you so cruel to me when we were children?"

"When we were—but I didn't even know you then." Holding her away from him, he looked into her eyes.

"You cannot have forgotten. After my parents died, I stayed with you for several weeks," she said. Was it possible that it had meant little to him then, and even less since? That all these years, the baggage she had carried around with her had been empty? "You *must* remember."

"Why have you not talked of this before?" he said.

"Because I couldn't bear to."

"And why can you tonight?"

Did he smell the alcohol on her breath. "Because it's time, perhaps," she said.

He dropped his voice. "You look terribly unhappy."

"I am," she told him. "Oh Basil, I'm so desperately sad. I always have been. Especially when I stayed in your house and you were cruel. Do you honestly not recall?"

"I recall only a thin pinched girl who was bad-tempered and rude. But that cannot have been you."

"And my gardens: you must remember how you interfered and tried to make me do something different, and then stamped on the flowers and went away," Mary said. She wanted to be light and flirtatious but knew she only succeeded in sounding deadly serious.

"If I did, I would give the world not to have done," whispered Basil, "I would do anything to make you happy, anything to make it up to you . . ." and she believed him because she wished to.

She danced with Barney and with Major Streatham, though to her mind he had become little more now than a raging sexual pervert. The colonel walked through a stately two-step with her, and his son, fresh from Oxford, twirled her through the gyrations of some new dance from America which, seeing it as though through the wrong end of a telescope, tiny and far away, she recalled dancing in London before her marriage, when she was young and carefree.

During the interval for refreshments, she found Basil at her side again. "Mrs. Sambourne," he said urgently, "do please step on to the veranda with me. I must speak to you."

"What is it?"

"Come with me." He touched her hand and she followed him through the crowded room. The big doors stood open, although it was scarcely cooler outside than in. The night air was thick with the harsh scrape of insects, oily as butter against her overheated skin. Somewhere close by, monkeys screeched angrily at each other; distantly, she thought she heard the growl of the jungle and was vaguely aware that beyond the high enclosing shrubbery of the compound lay a mortal danger.

11

" 'Capability' Craven," Colin said. "What do you think?"

"As a name, or as a character description?" asked Dickon.

"Both. Or 'Potentiality' Craven might be better?" Or 'Conservatory' Craven: I like that. It'll remind our customers of what we're trying to sell them, you see."

"Ha'n't you dreamed up a name for me, too?"

"Sowerby doesn't lend itself to this sort of thing, but I rather like 'Prospect'; don't you? 'Prospect' Sowerby. It offers a pleasing sense of rolling vistas and at the same time, of promises fulfilled. And if we really are to go into business as professional landscapists, with orchid-houses, orangeries, palm houses, arbors, follies and gazebos a speciality, not to mention temples, pavilions, pagodas and grottoes, then we must use every chance we have to make people think that we're the fellows to hire when they want their gardens done over, don't you agree? We shall have to learn to put ourselves about. And we'll also have to produce a catalogue or a brochure or something of that sort."

Colin twisted around in his chair to glance up at Dickon who stood beside him, looking down at a sketch of an extravagant structure of glass and steel which resembled nothing so much as a miniature Taj Mahal.

"It might be a good idea to get some clients before we go spending money we haven't got to promote ideas nobody seems to want," Dickon said.

"Which comes first, though? The clients or the ideas? Besides, we're building a reputation. Lots of people have been to look at the Misselthwaite Palm House, and we've had several jolly keen enquiries."

"That's all they've been so far: enquiries."

"We knew it would take time. We budgeted for that. Anyway, I'm absolutely convinced that those people across the dale at Silthorpe Hall are going to engage us. They were terribly enthusiastic about our plan."

"I shan't be buying champagne until they've signed on the dotted line."

Nonetheless, Dickon could not help smiling. He agreed with Colin: the Silthorpe Hall people were almost certain to engage them to lay out the neglected grounds of their newly-purchased mansion. And he was well aware of the importance of Colin's enthusiasm and energy in getting their fledgling business off the ground. Like a spring high up on the dale head, Colin was a constant source, bubbling with ideas. It did not matter that many of them were impractical, some downright ridiculous; in among the absurdities was enough flair, even genius, to keep them going for years. Once they got started.

"You know as well as I do that we can't fail," Colin said. "Ever since the end of the—" Hastily he changed tack, not wanting to remind Dickon of the war, well aware of the fragility of his friend's hold on the present. "There's been a wholesale redistribution of wealth in the past few years, and lots of new money is being spent by people who're not exactly sure what they want—or ought—to spend it on. Which is where we come in. We tell them that just as they would employ someone to decorate the interior of their houses—"

"Gold lamé, is it?"

"—So they should also hire someone to decorate their grounds. And who better than Craven & Sowerby?"

"Or 'Conservatory' and 'Prospect' as they're known to their friends."

"Landscape Artists," Colin said grandly.

"Artists: is that what we are?"

"I don't see why a garden shouldn't be a work of art, do you?"

Leaning closer, in order to look at the sketch on the table, Dickon laid an arm across Colin's shoulders. "No. Happen I don't."

Colin was often overwhelmed by his emotions. At the touch of Dickon's arm, a wave of love suffused him, so much so that he had to repress the desire to leap up and hug his friend. He held back, imagining all too easily the astonishment on Dickon's face if he did. The initial recoil followed by a slow accumulation of suspicion. The Dickons of this world did not show their feelings. Nor, for that matter, did most of the Colins.

He tapped the drawing in front of him. "What do you think?"

"Mary's idea, isn't it?"

"That's right."

"Full of good suggestions, is our Mary," Dickon said. "I know."

"Pity she's not here with us. Reckon she'd be a right help."

"How I wish . . ." Colin began. Was this how twins felt, parted from each other? Or Adam, sacrificing a rib for a helpmeet? The analogy was confused, he realized, but that did not help the sense of something missing. It had been well over three years, nearly four, since Mary sailed from Liverpool and he still missed her as fiercely as the day he waved her off. Dickon probably felt the same, though he was not given to expressing his emotions. "I don't know about you," he said, "but recently I've been encouraging her to take an interest in our plans. It gives her something to occupy her mind with."

"Aye. Since that friend of hers died, she's not seemed too happy."

"Sometimes she makes it sound as if it's one long party out there in India, but I imagine it's a hard life in many ways."

"Especially for the women. It seems hard to believe that a woman can still die in childbirth, like her poor friend."

"I don't suppose it's much of a picnic for the men, either. But then these notions of Empire and colonies and so forth are horribly outdated, don't you think? The grandeur that was Greece and all that rot—imperialism always depends on someone weaker than yourself being ground down."

"Ask me, there's quite enough exploitation at home,

without going halfway around the world to exploit some poor bugger with a different colored skin."

"Exactly. I've been doing some reading about India and although we may have conferred a few benefits out there, we've also behaved quite atrociously on occasion."

"Will she ever come home, Colin?"

"Bound to, old man. Absolutely bound to. One of these days."

Dickon pulled his armchair closer to the fire and adjusted the wick of the oil lamp behind him so that the light shone more brightly on the page of his book. He was living in rented quarters above a shop in the main street of Middleburn: three cramped rooms, a dismal kitchen and a WC downstairs in the back yard. It might not suit the newly monied businessmen who were their potential clients, but to someone who had grown up as one of fourteen people in a four-room cottage, it was a palace. There was enough space for him and his animal friends, and even room for his siblings to spend an occasional night when they came to visit him.

Despite Colin's desperate sensitivity about the war, he was perfectly well aware of how Mr. Lewin, the new owner of Silthorpe Hall—and all the others like him— had made his fortune. Armaments, in Mr. Lewin's case. Supplying guns and weaponry to the British Government. Was it any worse than the black marketeers? The purveyors of sub-standard footwear? The military and naval suppliers? The shippers and coal-merchants, all the commercial concerns which had helped to prolong the war, and made themselves rich through the deaths of their fellows?

He tried to sweep the thoughts from his mind, knowing that if he did not, he would find himself in the midst of the nightmare again. Though it was not only at night that the war years came to him. Or even in sleep. One of the surprising things was the random way whole hours of the experience could return at any time, as clear as if they were happening there and then. No warning, no signs, simply a transportation from whatever simple activity he might be engaged on—washing up, eating supper, walking along a pavement—to the bloody muddy hell of the trenches. He hoped very much that Colin did not realize to what extent he was still haunted by it all. The long weeks and months during which the two of them had walked the moors had been helpful, and healing. But they could not eliminate what was branded on his soul.

He poured ale from a jug fetched from the pub earlier in the evening. The silver tankard had been a present from Colin: it was engraved with some Latin inscription—*Amor vincit omnia*—which Colin had explained was about love and friendship. It was his most prized possession, not because of any intrinsic value it might have, but because it was so indubitably his. Apart from his army kit, the first thing he had ever owned which was not a hand-me-down, not a possession shared, not second-hand or passed on, but *his,* chosen especially for him, marked with his name.

He reached down and scratched Beggar behind the ears. The dog sighed comfortably before laying his aristocratic nose across his master's shoe. In his basket by the fire, Brockie stirred, shaking his heavy head before lumbering bow-leggedly around and around the room, stretching his muscles in preparation for the moment when Dickon would let him out into the darkness to hunt the night away. Meantime, on Dickon's knee was a book borrowed from the Misselthwaite library, an illustrated anthology of medieval times. Entranced, he turned the pages and read of enclosed gardens, monastery cloisters, the symbolism of plants, of the Rose, the fountain at the center of a garden, of earthly paradises. It had not occurred to him before that a garden represented a refuge, whether from the wrath of God, the venality of mankind, or the torment of the soul. Yes . . . reading that, he realized that the war had never intruded on him among trees, flowers, natural things. He was enormously excited by the intellectualization of concepts to which he had hitherto responded entirely from instinct.

Taking another book from the pile beside his chair, he was held spellbound by Persian miniatures, Indian manuscripts, tomb paintings from Egypt, mosaics from ancient Rome. A garden was as fundamental to Man's spirit as God or as love. The Lady with the Unicorn, *à mon seul desir,* the Romance of the Rose . . . the *hortus conclusus,* he read, the cloistered garden with the waiting Virgin at its center. He was part of a long tradition, a knight of courtly love in pursuit of his Lady, his Rose, his Mary, and finding her waiting, as he had found her long ago, at the heart of a secret garden.

Staring at the pictures, he marveled at the delicacy with which those early illuminators had used silk and wool, paint and ink, to recreate the natural world. So much else had changed over the centuries, but the little flowers—primrose, bluebell, buttercup, violet—remained as they had always been.

He wished she would come back. He knew it was impossible, that her destiny bound her to her major. He wondered how things might have been if he himself had come back earlier from the war. Or less damaged. Would she have looked at him then? Or would he still have felt that he had no right to her, not until he could provide for her as she deserved? If only it were possible to talk to someone about her, to express the heart-bursting emotion which occasionally threatened to swamp him, reduce him. It was his guess that Colin felt the same way. It would be very damaging to the partnership between them if they both wanted the same woman, even if she were as unavailable to the one as to the other.

Colin, however, was less single-minded where Mary was concerned. Of the two of them, Dickon imagined that it would be he himself who ended his days alone. Colin might love Mary, might be every bit as passionate about her as Dickon, but he had responsibilities; he would have to find himself a wife eventually, in order to pass on his name and his inheritance. In fact, as he had written to Mary, Dickon rather suspected that Colin was already looking about him with this in mind. There was no denying the alacrity with which he visited London at least once a month, or the sparkle which hung about him on his return. Only love could produce that particular glow.

Dickon was a pragmatist. Most of the time, he was not cast down by the reflection that he loved a woman he could not have. He did not expect to deny himself the pleasures of the flesh, nor saw any reason why he should. But his heart: that was different. His heart had been given away years ago, and he felt it unwise, unfair, to marry when he loved elsewhere. Sometimes, waking from damp dreams, he speculated on the possibility of Mary returning alone to England. A widow, fetching in black, needing an arm to lean on, a shoulder to weep on, her children in want of a father, the gallant major gradually fading from her memory until she was ready at last to trust herself to the one who had waited for her, oh so faithfully, and with such dogged devotion, through the years. The prospect pleased him, though he occasionally felt a twinge of conscience at the thought of poor Barney Sambourne, dead on some remote mountain pass in the Punjabi hills, simply in order to feed his fantasies.

He picked up another book. Colin's latest idea was that they should study orchids in order to provide a comprehensive service to those of their clients who might be interested in exotic tropical greenhouse plants. Cymbidiums, he read, Cattleya . . . and without warning, he was back.

They move on to another shellhole, another layer of corpses. Again, as so often before, he lifts a corpse from the rusty water where it lies rotting, and the limbs come clean away in his hands, the flies surge in a fizzing cloud, their metallic bodies huge and bloated with blood. The stench hits the back of his throat; he gags. Is it Turnbull? Is it young Davey, only sixteen, with his sweet voice and country boy's cheeks? He tugs at the identity disc and the corpse's head falls to one side as the chain pulls through flesh no more substantial than cheese. Maggots. Swollen fingers as monstrous as black puddings. Arms waving from the shellholes. Fleshless mouths, teeth whose complicit grin warns him that it'll be his turn next, his turn to lie drowning, decaying in the mud. He screams, over and over, sweat running down his back despite the cold, the freezing winds which howl across the featureless plains of mud. Oh God, he screams, how much do I have to bear?

Somewhere they are beating a drum, a warning drum which marches alongside the rhythm of his heartbeat . . . and there was someone knocking at the door, Colin's voice in the street below.

"Dickon! Are you asleep? Wake up and let me in."

Accompanied by Beggar, Dickon stumbled down-stairs, stupid with remembered pain. "What is it?" he said, peering out into rain and darkness. "What do you want?"

"Got any of that beer left?"

"Beer?"

"I know you had some because I dropped into the pub and they told me you'd been in earlier."

"That's right."

"It's cold out here," Colin said plaintively. "And wet. Are you going to let me in or not?"

Dickon pulled himself together. "Of course. Come on up." Shivering, he followed Colin back up the narrow flight of uncarpeted stairs to the upper floors.

"You've made it nice and cozy here," Colin said, look-ing around, while Dickon fetched another glass and filled it with beer.

"Yes." Dickon's head still echoed to the sound of ar-tillery fire. He felt very tired.

"You'll be wondering why I'm here."

"Aye."

"I've just got back from visiting friends in Oxford."

"I can tell."

"Can you?"

"You always have the same air about you when you come back from the south," Dickon said gruffly. He did not feel like explaining that Colin's seal-sleek satiated look was a dead give-away, an open announcement of sexual satisfaction. He was not sitting in judgement on his friend: he himself probably took on the same appear-ance after a visit to an accommodating woman he knew ten miles the other side of the Manor. He wondered what she looked like, Colin's lady-friend, whether she was someone suitable, someone he could eventually bring to the Manor to meet Archie Craven as a prospec-tive bride, or merely a physical stop-gap until he found a woman to assume the role of Misselthwaite's mistress.

"Gosh. Do I?" Colin seemed a little disconcerted. "Anyway, I came to say that I've got guests arriving for a visit next week, and I shan't be available for a couple of weeks."

"I see." An unreasoning anger filled Dickon. He sat

heavily down in his armchair and glowered at Colin. "Not available, is it?"

"Dear, oh dear." Picking up one of the books on the table, Colin held it lightly against his chest. "Do I detect just the teensiest touch of bad temper, or am I imagining things?"

"I thought we were trying to establish a business together."

"We are."

"So how come it's 'not available for a couple of weeks'? Or are you just playing about, Colin? Just doing the Oxford dilettante bit? Farting about, keeping yourself amused until you think of some other brilliant idea to throw yourself into for all of two months?"

"Hang about. I'm not—"

"Is that all it were to you, this landscaping lark? After all, it's not as if you need the money, is it, Mr. 'Potentiality' bloody Craven? It's not as if you'll ever have to work for a living, not like us common folk."

"Could you just calm down, Dickon?"

"Why should I? I've put a lot of me time into this project. I've been thinking about nowt else for weeks and then you waltz in here, patronize me in my own home—"

"I did not patron—"

"—tell me you're ever so sorry, dahling, but you won't be bloody available because some lah-di-dah friend of yours from Oxford wants to come up and compose sodding sonnets about butterflies on the heath or delicious little villanelles or summat."

Colin almost laughed. Dickon had met some of his more effetely precious friends earlier in the year and was taking them off to a T. But the savagery in his tone made it clear he was not joking. "What on earth are—"

"Or do I have it wrong? Is it your more manly, murderous types of friends who's coming up this time?" Dickon could feel his north-country accent swelling in his mouth as he let the anger take hold. He ought not to let himself go like this, but, as always, the nightmare angered and scared him and he deliberately wallowed in his rage although he knew it had nothing to do with Colin.

"Manly? Murderous?" Colin raised a fastidious eyebrow in a manner calculated to annoy Dickon still further. At the same time, his heart thundered with apprehension. There was real dislike in Dickon's eyes. *He knows. He knows or he's guessed. And either way, what do I do if he accuses me? Confess? Admit it? Go further and spill the entire bean pot?* He wished he could anticipate Dickon's reaction if he were to do anything of the sort.

"Your hunting, shooting and fishing types," Dickon said. "If it moves, shoot it. If it flies, it dies: isn't that what your lot say?"

"I wasn't aware I had, as you put it, a lot."

"No? Well, you have. You and all the people like you. You think you're so bloody original, don't you, but you're a type, Colin, a paradigm, that's what you are, nothing more than a paradigm of the kind of class system I spent five years in the fucking trenches to preserve."

"Oh, please," Colin said, with weary indifference. He had a fleeting vision of himself as a matador, darting hither and thither across the bloodied sand with a sword in his hand while in front of him a bull swung its heavy head and roared, wondering where the next thrust was coming from. "Not the war again, for God's sake. Can't you give it a rest? I mean, we all know you single-handedly saved us from the onslaught of the Hun, and we're really awfully grateful, but isn't it time we all moved on?"

Although he managed to swing a nonchalant leg as he sat on a corner of the table, he quaked inwardly even as he finished speaking. The dog was watching him, lips lifted away from its teeth. A rumbling growl rippled the fur of its chest. Even the badger had stopped stumbling around and around the room and was staring at him with small suspicious eyes. *How could he have said something so utterly appalling? And to Dickon, of all people?* It was not as if he even believed what he was saying. *How would Dickon ever be able to forgive him? Had he gone too far?* They had never quarreled before, not even exchanged harsh words. It was difficult to be sure exactly why they were quarreling now. He had never heard Dickon swear until tonight.

"Right. That does it." Dickon rose to his feet. "I've had enough."

"Enough of what?"

Although Dickon was several inches shorter than Colin, at that moment, enraged, he seemed twice the size of the younger man. "Out! This minute."

"What?"

"You heard. Out of me house, you workshy, arrogant over-privileged little shit. And don't ever come back."

"Dickon, I—"

"Get out. Now."

And before he quite knew how it had happened, Colin found himself leaping down the steep stairs with Beggar nipping at his heels, while Dickon stood at the top, like some furious god. Sitting in his car while rain drummed on the windscreen and the winds roaring up the dale sucked and blew at the canvas roof, he rested his forehead on the dashboard. Oh God. He'd been drinking on the train journey back: the railway carriage had been freezing and the brandy in his hip flask had seemed the only way to combat the cold. And it had been a bloody awful visit, too. He was not cut out for philandering. Maybe if he got married . . . Bitter laughter bubbled from his throat. That was certainly one way to ensure a deliriously happy future, both for him and whichever poor girl he chose. There were only two people in this wide world whom he could contemplate marrying and neither of them was available to him. It was the word "available" which had seemed to set Dickon off—why was that?

Available: he considered it for a moment, while rain leaked through the roof and trickled down the inside of the screen. A damned irritating word, he supposed, especially if uttered in a particular way, in a particular accent.

But was that enough to send Dickon into such a fury? Perhaps something he'd been reading had set him off. Colin had recognized some of the books by Dickon's chair as coming from the library at the Manor. He wondered now whether Dickon, too, was reminded of Mary as he studied those wonderful paintings of impregnable rose gardens and milk-white unicorns with slanted eyes? He groaned. Oh, Mary, Mary . . . How was she? Miserable, undoubtedly. He did not derive the faintest satisfaction from this, although he had told her repeatedly what a mistake she was making, to marry Major Barmy Sambourne, a cruel jibe he had restricted himself to making no more than half a dozen times before the inexorable moment when she walked up the aisle to meet her bridegroom. It had made no difference whatsoever. Even if she had had hesitations about the wisdom of what she was doing, she would never have said so. Particularly after his comments. She was as stubborn as he was. It was one of the many reasons why he loved her.

His head throbbed with a combination of alcohol, guilt and despair. Oh God. Cold water dripped on to the back of his neck. Sadly, he wished that they could all go back to the days of youth and innocence. And now he had alienated Dickon, whom, of all people in the world, he would least wish to hurt, who was, in any case, hurt enough already. What had he been thinking of? He knew the answer to that. It was as though the three of them, Mary, Colin and Dickon, were trapped on some terrible treadmill, endlessly circling around each other, longing to be together and forever driven apart.

The hip flask cut uncomfortably into his buttock and he reached toward it, then stopped. Better not. He'd already had more than was good for him and it was going to be difficult enough to negotiate his way home in the dark across the moors without more alcohol slowing down his reactions. *If it flies, it dies:* where had Dickon picked up that curious saying? Despite himself, he snorted with laughter. *Delicious little villanelles . . .* he might be a humorless old sod on occasion but Dickon had Freddie Avery's mincing ways down pat. He recalled Dickon's face last summer, when he finally realized that Freddie was wearing lipstick. This time Colin laughed aloud. His laughter turned suddenly to weeping. Into his mind came another memory of Dickon, in the orchard at Misselthwaite, knee-high in foxgloves and drooping grasses, head bent. He was watching the butterflies which rested on his out-held hand, sipping as though they tested his sweetness. Red admiral, painted lady, purple emperor: *Look, Colin, look at them.* Their wings fluttering like dusty breaths, scales glinting in the fruity yellow light. And tortoiseshells, hovering over the windfall plums, silvery fritillaries drifting through the pear trees.

If he had lost Dickon . . .

There was a burst of laughter in the street, people straggling from the pub, a woman's voice calling across the wet cobblestones as they dispersed between the stone houses.

If he had lost Dickon for the sake of Bertie and Freddie and others like them, then he had struck a damn poor bargain. Get out and never come back, he'd said. Patronizing, he'd said. Thinking back, Colin accepted that it might have sounded patronizing to say that the place looked nice and cozy, even if it was not meant that way. Nor would the old Dickon have seen it as such. It was only since he'd got back from the war that he'd developed this prickly sensitivity.

Colin started the motor, determined that he would telephone as soon as he got home and put Bertie off for next week. Or better still, send a telegram. That way, he wouldn't have to face Bertie's shrill protests. Dickon was absolutely right: if you were a businessman, you couldn't just arbitrarily take time off to enjoy yourself with a group of varsity friends you didn't even like very much. He would telephone Dickon, too. Except that, now he thought of it, Dickon did not have a telephone, and was unlikely to answer the one which had been installed in the shop below. Would it be better to turn around right now and go back, make his peace, or should he leave it until the morning, when they'd both have cooled down? He decided to wait. He wondered if his father was waiting up for him. He had wired ahead to say what time his train would arrive. He drove carefully: the road was no more than a muddy track across the moor and rain did not improve the going. This was not a night on which to find oneself mired to the wheelhubs. He might die of exposure if he were to get bogged down. He tried to remember if there was a flashlight in his baggage and decided there was not. Beyond the beams of his headlights there was nothing but blackness, miles of wild moor, and not a fellow human to call on for help if he should need it, not a light anywhere in the whole vast night.

What a contrast, he thought, as the miles slowly slipped away beneath his wheels. Last night in Oxford, it had been all starched shirt fronts and ancient silverware, medieval beams above his head, port laid down half a century before, a syrupy madeira as sweet as sunshine. They had walked back to Freddie's rooms beneath walls older than time, while sonorous bells sounded the hour and black-gowned proctors prowled the streets, to oysters and champagne and civilized laughter. While tonight, he might as well be lost in the jungle.

He reached the gates of Misselthwaite. It was even darker here, under the trees. After a while, he could make out the arching branches of the drive and through them, dimly, lights. His father had left the shutters and curtains open to welcome him back. He pulled up in front of the main door and sighed with relief. The quarrel with Dickon still nagged at him, but at least he was safely home. Archie Craven waited for him in his study. A fire blazed in the hearth; whisky and soda sat on a silver tray at his elbow. "My boy," he said.

"Are you well, Father?"

"Very. Did you have a good trip south?"

"Indeed."

"And how's business?"

"Ah." Colin poured himself a small whisky and splashed soda into it.

"What's wrong?"

"I stopped in to see Dickon on my way back and I fear I may just have brought Craven & Sowerby to a somewhat premature conclusion."

"Wound it up, do you mean?"

"Not exactly."

"But why?"

"I don't know—envy, perhaps." Because he recognized it now, the envy which had suddenly hit him as he took in Dickon's snug sanctuary, the warm lamplight, the books, the air of contentment. He had wanted to be part of it; he had felt excluded. "To be precise, I've been so rude to my partner that he may never forgive me."

"Dickon? Whatever you may have said, he's not one to bear grudges." Archie pulled his half-hunter from his waistcoat and flipped open the lid. "Though you must have been in unreasonable temper indeed to discover something to be rude to Dickon about. A more good-natured man it would be hard to find."

"Oh, Father." Colin sighed heavily. "Do you ever

wonder what on earth it's all about? Why we bother to go on living?"

"Often, Colin."

"And what do you conclude?"

"Why, that we only have one life to live, and must go on with it to the end, that if we feel it is meaningless, then we ourselves must give it meaning."

"Do you ever think of Mary?"

"Of course. I would be an unfeeling brute if I did not, considering that I regard her as my own daughter."

"I wish, more than anything in the world, that she would come back."

"We must face the fact that even if she did, she has other responsibilities now." Archie Craven glanced at his son's bent head and frowned. Was Colin suffering the pangs of unrequited love? He had always hoped that the two cousins might one day unite as a married couple—it would have been a most fitting match in any number of ways—but they had never shown any inclination to fall in love and it had certainly not occurred to him that his son could be carrying a torch for Mary after all this time. Though if he were, then it explained a number of things which had recently begun to niggle at Mr. Craven. The boy was still young, of course, much too young to think of settling down. On the other hand, in the heedless fashion of youth, he might have been expected to be falling in and out of love with various young women, be they eligible or ineligible, but this he had apparently failed to do. Not that, according to the reports Mr. Craven occasionally received from friends in London, he did not enjoy a full social calendar. But up here, in Yorkshire, he seemed to prefer the company of young Sowerby, or one or two of the friends he had made at university. Certainly nothing in the way of what he believed nowadays were called girl-friends. But if he still sighed after Mary, then the reasons were obvious. Archie felt sorry for his son. He knew all too well what it was to love in vain, to hanker after something which could never be. Just so had he himself been after the death of his beloved young wife.

"It is perhaps the oldest of all clichés," he said gently, "but time does eventually heal all wounds. Even though it may take longer in some cases than in others." In his

own, of course, it had been more than ten years before
he had been able to return to Misselthwaite, or visit the
walled garden where Colin's mother had suffered her
fatal accident.

"That must surely depend on the type of wound, sir."
Colin longed to ask about his father's own love life, but
dared not. He had long suspected a partiality toward
their lively London cousin, Mrs. Ledworth—and remembered still the brightness of his father's eye when it
rested on Miss Ensleigh, the matron of the convalescent
hospital set up in the West Wing during the war.

"I've been thinking," Archie said, though in fact the
thought had only occurred to him in the last few minutes, "that we should entertain more, see something of
the young people of the district, hold a few gatherings
here. You'd enjoy that, wouldn't you, my boy?"

"Very much," Colin said. It was the truth, though his
enjoyment would come more from seeing his father's
pleasure than from any of his own.

"We are, after all, the foremost family in the area,
and it behoves us to set an example. I don't believe
we've really entertained since your twenty-first ball, and
it seems a shame to have paid for the redecoration of
the ballroom only to use it for the single occasion."

"I quite agree. We must set about it at once." Colin
felt a lift of the spirits, an urge to begin drawing up
lists, finding caterers, organizing a band. Already he was
assessing the eligible widows and unmarried ladies of
their acquaintance. If his father were to remarry—and
there seemed to be no reason why he should not nor
why he had not already done so—he imagined he would
feel nothing but disinterested delight. And it would certainly take away some of the pressure he felt to produce
a wife himself.

12

Adjusting the angle of his hat, Colin paused for a moment on the top step. In Hyde Park, trees were greening; there were daffodils in the windowboxes of the house from which he had emerged and sparrows fussed busily in the gutters. He took a deep breath. "Spring," he murmured. "The sweet spring."

The roadway bustled with traffic. Horse-drawn conveyances. The chauffeur-driven cars of the wealthy. Tradesmen's vans. People hurrying along the pavement. Pulling on his gloves, he watched the busy scene with a pleasure made all the more satisfactory by the knowledge that eighteen months ago, everything had looked as though it might be about to fall apart. It had taken weeks to coax Dickon out of his black mood, weeks during which Colin had been forced to examine himself and come to some decisions. Dilettante. Workshy. They were harsh words, and although not strictly true, he recognized in himself a tendency to dart from one enthusiasm to another without any real application. Everything came easily to him, that was one trouble. Another was the fact that he had no real need to work. If he wanted to, he could simply have helped his father run the estates at Misselthwaite until it was time to take them over himself. That was what many of his friends did, and never appeared to feel that they were wasting their time.

It was not enough for him. He wanted to create something solid and lasting, and in those miserable weeks during which he wondered if Dickon would ever speak to him again, he had realized that Craven & Sowerby provided him with the ideal opportunity. He had busied himself as never before while he waited, drawing up plans, talking to architects, corresponding with the Patent Office, traveling all over the country, anywhere there might be a potential customer. By the time Dickon had gruffly agreed to a meeting, he had the foundations of the business comfortably set up. All that remained after that was to persuade Dickon that the whole project was unworkable without him.

"What do I know about plants? About gardens?" he had asked. "You're the genius. I can handle the paperwork and make the contacts, but without you, there's no business."

"Oh aye." Dickon sounded sceptical.

"You know everything about green things," Colin continued. Although he knew better than to say so, he guessed that Dickon had been as unhappy about their quarrel as he. "And what you don't know, you feel. It's instinct with you. You can see how stone and plant and water go together. All I can do is organize things."

"I'll think about it."

He did so. And told Colin he would be glad to join forces with him. Since then, Craven & Sowerby had gone from strength to strength. Their distinctive green vans, painted with white trellis-work, the attractive Art-Nouveau lettering, were seen everywhere. Although one or two rivals tried to set up in competition to them, Craven & Sowerby was widely recognized to be the best. There was a huge demand for their services as money flowed freely in the expanding post-war economy. Four months earlier they had decided that, after all, they would have to leave Yorkshire and base themselves in London, and had opened an office in Mayfair.

Colin had never before tasted the fruits of real success. Whether at school or university, academic study had never stretched him; to have built something from scratch and watched it prosper: that, he found, was truly worthwhile.

He was about to step down on to the pavement when his eye was caught by a young woman on the other side of the road. Nondescript, dressed in slightly shabby mourning, at first sight there was nothing to distinguish her from a hundred other similar young women. The casual observer might have taken her for a stenographer, or a governess, though a second glance would have revealed that she bore herself like a lady, that her shoes were expensive and her clothes, though worn, were of good quality. In her hand she carried a leather music-case and as Colin watched, frowning, she hurried down the street and turned the corner in Grosvenor Square.

For a moment, he had thought it was Mary there, on the other side of the road. But it could not possibly be. He had caught a fleeting likeness, nothing more. Mary would not have been dressed like that, nor moved with such an air of anxious haste. Besides, how could she possibly be in England? She would most certainly have written to let him know the minute there was the slightest chance of her return. He walked on toward Bond Street. He and Dickon were the tenants of offices above a florist's shop, specifically chosen because of the horticultural connection. Mounting the stairs, he pushed open the green painted door with its highly polished brass furniture and went in. Fanny, the girl who sat behind a typewriter at the desk, smiled cheerfully.

"Good morning, sir," she said.

He hung up his hat. "Anything urgent?" he said.

"A couple of definites, three maybes and a no thanks," she said efficiently.

"Which was the no? Those people in Cornwall?"

"That's right."

"Good. I wouldn't have enjoyed working with him."

"A nasty fat pig, I thought him," Fanny said. "Couldn't keep his hands to himself, either."

"Who can blame him?"

"Get along with you, Mr. Craven."

Colin grinned at her. Never really at ease with any but the closest friends, he enjoyed the bantering relationship which had sprung up between them. "The people I've just been to see in Green Street appear very enthusiastic. They've recently inherited a place from his uncle and want to rehouse his collection of orchids."

"That'll be one for Mr. Dickon, then."

"Quite." Colin went into his office and sat down behind the desk. Despite the success of his visit to the house in Mayfair, he felt unsettled, disinclined for business. The sight of the young woman in the street had brought back the realization of how much he longed to see his cousin again. And thinking of her, he realized for the first time just how long it had been since she had last written; he supposed she was busier than she used to be, now that she had a growing child to care for, and her position in the local society was more assured. In one of her letters, she had spoken of a school for native girls with which she found herself involved, and of her attempts, along with some other women, to integrate the ladies of the British and the Indian armies, a difficult task, given the deep-dyed suspicions and fears which existed on both sides.

Leaning back in his chair, he tried to recall when her most recent correspondence had arrived. Could it possibly be as long ago as three months? In fact, now he thought more carefully, he realized it must be six, if not nearer seven. Even taking into consideration the time it took for letters to arrive, it was most unlike her to leave such a gap. Lately, he himself had been somewhat neglectful about writing to her, with the London office to set up and all the planning and organization that had required. Even so, seven months was a very long time.

On impulse, he picked up the telephone and asked the operator for Lady Gardiner's number. He assumed she was connected; these days, just about everyone was.

Within a few seconds he heard the voice of her parlor maid. He gave his name and asked if he might speak to the lady of the house. "I'll see if she's at home, sir," the prim voice said.

He waited. After a while, the parlor maid returned. "I'm afraid she's not here, sir," he said. Behind the words, he detected a strong hint of triumph and wondered why. There was no reason for Lucy Gardiner not to speak to him, unless she were otherwise occupied. He could visualize the parlor maid now: thin gray face, thin gray hair, a thin gray body. A disapproving old hag, as he remembered. Florence, that was her name. He had escorted Mary to some occasion at the house, and probably been rather unguarded in his views about the idle rich.

"What a pity," he said politely and put down the receiver. He did not for a moment believe that Lucy Gardiner was away from home. She had probably refused to speak to him for no more important reason than that she was in the bath, or communing with her dressmaker.

Nonetheless, imagination stirred by the young woman glimpsed in the street, he decided that he would call around there this afternoon, say he had had word from Mary, that she had asked him to pass on some message, something like that. Though as the cousin of her sister-in-law, he surely needed no excuse to call.

"I'll see if her ladyship is at home," Florence said frostily.

Colin forebore to remark that he knew perfectly well that she was. having seen her standing at the first-floor window, not ten minutes earlier. It was a convention that, he supposed, had its place from time to time. He hoped now was not one of them.

"Since I was unfortunate enough to miss her ladyship this morning," he said pleasantly, "and I happened to be in the neighborhood . . ."

"Very good, sir."

A few minutes later, Florence returned. She held a silver tray toward him containing a short note. "Her ladyship cannot see you," she said, her mouth twisted with pleasurable disdain, "and asked me to give you this."

Bewildered, before he could quite take in the import of this, Colin found himself standing on the top step, with the door of the house firmly closed behind him. Walking round the corner, he read the note.

I am sure you understand why I cannot possibly speak to you. In the circumstances, may I ask that you do not call on me again.

It was signed with initials.

To what circumstances did she refer? What harm could there be in talking to him? He felt astonishment rather than anger. Even a faint amusement. The woman was certainly brainless enough to have confused him with someone else; he wondered what social solecism that someone else had committed. His resolve to question her about Mary hardened.

He showed the note to Dickon. "Happen she's mistook you for a former lover," Dickon said, hardly able to contain his laughter.

"Whatever's behind it, I find it bally insulting," declared Colin. "I don't want word going around that there's something shady about Colin Craven. Could turn out to be not only bad for business, but rather dire for my social standing."

"How do you reckon to put it right, then?"

"I haven't worked it out yet."

"You could wait outside her door until she comes out."

"I haven't got time to waste. I'll have to find some event she's attending and beard her there, if I can."

It was two weeks before Colin was able to contrive a confrontation with Lady Gardiner. During that time, he had found himself watching the busy London crowds with more than usual attention, in the hope of catching sight of the woman with the music case again. He was increasingly worried about the breakdown in correspondence with Mary, and had sent her a long letter urging her not to neglect her family in England. It was with a certain measure of relief, therefore, that having forced himself to attend a private view of the latest Hungarian artist to have been taken up by the critics, he saw Lucy Gardiner standing alone on the other side of the room. He had expected her to be there; the event was being sponsored by a cultural group of which she and her husband were patrons and he pushed his way through the crowd, eager to talk to her.

"Good evening, Lady Gardiner," he said, when he finally reached her side.

He was taken aback by the look of icy contempt which she gave him. She tried to sweep past him without speaking, but he prevented her from doing so by placing himself squarely in her path. "Why are you trying to ignore me?" he asked.

"It must surely be obvious," she said haughtily.

"I'm afraid I have no idea what you mean."

"Come, Mr. Craven. Do you imagine that I would accept what you say?"

"Indeed I do. And since you clearly do not, I insist on an explanation."

"Insist? How dare you?"

"Wouldn't it be simpler if you clarified what it is I am supposed to have done?"

She hesitated. "You really don't know?"

"Absolutely not."

Doubt was taking hold. "I can't believe you're serious, Mr. Craven."

"Never more so."

She bit her lip, her eyes searching the room for her husband. "When this dreadful business first came to light, I did wonder whether I should contact you, but since there was nothing any of us could do, my husband decided it would be best if we simply severed all connection."

"I'm sorry," Colin said, "what dreadful business?"

She was not listening. "Naturally, my poor brother is distraught," she continued. "He even talks of resigning his commission and returning to this country."

"But why?" Colin tried to imagine what could have driven Major Sambourne to contemplate such a step. There must have been some mention in Mary's last letter which he had not understood. "If they did return, we would, of course, be delighted to have Mary back among us, but I'm sorry that her husband is upset."

"Upset? He is far more than upset. I'm afraid this may have broken his spirit as well as his heart. He doted on Mary, and as for that unfortunate child . . ." She shook her head. "When you called at my house, I hoped it might be to tell me that your cousin had come to her senses—but I was obviously wrong."

"Lady Gardiner, I really do not have the least—"

"Though I can't honestly say that I wish to see her, after what she has done to my poor brother, and I very much doubt whether my husband would approve of a meeting between us. Modern we may be, Mr. Craven, but I do consider there are standards to be maintained, even despite the grievous loss she has undergone. And quite between ourselves, I don't know that—"

"Lady Gardiner," said Colin firmly, raising his voice a little. "Please believe me when I say that I don't know what you're talking about. Grievous loss? Your brother distraught? A dreadful business? None of this makes any sense to me at all."

She was disconcerted. "You really mean it, don't you?"

"Absolutely, I assure you."

"But Mary must have told you."

"We have not heard from Mary for some time, which

is why I contacted you. I've been much occupied by the pressures of business—" even in the midst of his apprehension, Colin was conscious of what a fine ring the phrase had "—and until now, hadn't appreciated exactly how much time has passed since her last letter."

"It must be deliberate," exclaimed Lady Gardiner. "Her family . . . where else would she turn if not to you? I had assumed . . ." She raised her hand to her face. "Oh dear. I do hope there isn't another disaster waiting for us."

"What disasters have there already been?" Colin asked. He had warned Mary years ago that this woman was as empty-headed as a budgerigar; then, it had been a statement made out of intellectual conviction rather than any real acquaintance with her; now he saw only too clearly how right he had been.

"But I can't believe you haven't heard about it all."

"Please, Lady Gardiner: believe it."

"She hasn't told you?"

"Not a word."

"Dear, oh dear. I wish my husband would join us." Lucy had no wish to be the one to give the bad—the appalling—news to this rather fierce young man, who, it was now obvious, had no notion of the events of the past few months. She had always felt that for some reason he despised her, though they had met no more than half a dozen times. She touched the crepe band on her sleeve.

"What exactly has happened to my cousin?" Colin spoke as though to an idiot child, trying to keep his voice gentle and his manner calm, though he wanted to shake the wretched woman until her teeth rattled? Had there been some kind of uprising in the Punjab? Had the major committed some terrible breach of military etiquette? Had his military honor been impugned? Cowardice? Unspeakable vice? A native mistress? Something serious had occurred, but what could it be?

"Oh dear, this is so awful, and to think that you know nothing about it . . ." fluttered Lucy.

Colin held on to the fact that whatever Lady Gardiner was nerving herself to tell him, at least Mary and her family seemed not to have been harmed. "Nothing at all," he repeated.

*   *   *

Half an hour later, he was hurrying back to Fitzroy Square. Dickon had agreed to dine with him that evening, but would not be arriving for at least another hour. If there was one thing Colin needed at that moment, it was Dickon's calm solidity. Reaching the house, he changed his mind about going in, and instead, walked on toward Regent's Park. Lucy Gardiner's revelations had been so unexpected that he had scarcely known how to respond. Even more extraordinary had been the realization that at this crisis in her life, Mary had deliberately chosen not to share it with him. Where was she? To whom had she turned instead?

"Left him," Lady Gardiner had said. "Just walked out. Left a note saying she would tell him where to send her things. Such a scandal."

"Has she returned to England?"

"Who knows? She could be anywhere. She could be in Australia, for all we know. She always was a willful girl, and though my poor brother is far too loyal to say so, reading between the lines I should guess she led him quite a dance."

"But when did all this happen? How long ago?"

"I suppose it must be seven or eight months now." Lady Gardiner thought about it. "Yes, at least seven months."

"But why didn't she let us know?" Colin was ashamed to realize just how long had slipped by without him growing anxious about the lack of correspondence from his cousin. If he had been a kinder, less selfish person, he would have realized weeks ago that something was badly wrong in Mary's life. "And where on earth can she be?"

Walking toward the Zoological Gardens, he was tormented with the idea of Mary alone somewhere, suffering. Why had she not called on him for help? She must know that he would do anything for her, anything at all. He did not wish to think about his bruised heart; Lady Gardiner had been too delicate to come right out and say so, but she had hinted at some scandal which he had taken to mean that Mary had fallen in love with another man. Was she living with him in sin somewhere? Was that the reason for her silence? Was she feeling too guilty and ashamed to contact him or her uncle? Or

Dickon? And at that thought, Colin stopped suddenly on the sanded path of the park. Was it possible that she had been in touch with Dickon, swearing him to secrecy? The very thought made him sweat with jealousy and longing. No. Dickon was too straight to keep such a secret. Dickon would never countenance such a thing. A woman who had left her husband and set up with another man? Never.

He turned back toward Fitzroy Square. Dickon would be arriving soon; the two of them could talk it out and see what was best to be done.

"Poor lass," Dickon said. He stood in front of the fire and shook his head. "Poor little lass."

"I could hardly believe it when that—that flibberti-gibbet finally got it out," said Colin. "If only we knew where she was."

"She's run away. Not just from him, her husband, but from all of us. Best leave her to make her own mind up about whether she wants to see us," Dickon said. "It's plain that wherever she is, she wants nowt to do with any of us at present."

Colin followed his own thoughts. "She'd obviously come back to England, after she left her husband."

"Would she?"

"Of course. Where else would she go? Calcutta? Paris? New York? She knows nobody there."

"Mebbe this fellow of hers is from New York. Or Paris. He might even be a black man, for all we know, an Indian, who's took her to Calcutta or Bombay. It's not unheard of."

"She's here, in London," Colin insisted. "I know it. I can feel it."

"Wherever she is, about all we can do for her is pray," Dickon said.

"I'm going to do more than that."

"What, exactly?"

"I don't know," Colin said wildly. "But something."

"Poor lass," repeated Dickon. "Best leave her alone. She must be grieving."

The thought of Mary weeping in some lonely room made his heart sore. He did not think she had run off with another man, that would not be Mary's way. Deep down, he agreed with Colin that she had indeed returned to London. It was the logical thing for her to do. But even if Colin did succeed in tracking her down—and it was a thousand to one chance that he would—there was still no way to make her come back to them against her will. But if she *is* here, he thought, and we find her, she'll not get away from me again.

13

Mary stepped out of the front door and closed it carefully behind her before setting off. Pretending to tuck her scarf more firmly into her coat, she surreptitiously examined the faces of the passers-by. Although the chances were slight that, in a city the size of London, she would run into someone she knew, she dreaded the possibility. And there was Barney, too: she was terrified that, in spite of all she had done, he might still try to find her, try to persuade her to come back. Most of all, she shrank from the idea of enountering Colin or Dickon, and was careful to avoid going anywhere near Fitzroy Square. She did not go out into society. For one thing, she had no wish to take up again with any of the crowd she had known before she married, and had therefore told no one of her return to London. For another, she had very little money to spare. And finally, she preferred to spend the evenings in her room, trying to teach herself the Pitman's shorthand system. Having taken painful stock of herself and her abilities on the long sad journey back from India, six months earlier, she had realized how few marketable accomplishments she possessed. Even if anyone were willing to engage her, what could she do? She was too woefully ignorant to become a governess. She could not sew. Although she painted well enough, her little talent was not enough to earn her a living.

It had been a humbling experience to discover just how unemployable she was. Her education had fitted her for nothing; it had never been expected that she should have to earn her own living. She saw now how shortsighted this was. All girls should acquire some skill: after all, however secure their situation might seem it was impossible to predict what the future might hold. The only thing she was reasonably good at was playing the piano. Accordingly, she had placed advertisements in two or three newspapers and, somewhat to her surprise, had received replies. Currently, she possessed half a dozen little pupils. The pay, however, was appalling and the work tedious. Looking down the Situations Vacant lists, she had noticed that typewritists and stenographers were earning twice as much per hour as she felt able to demand and she had therefore determined to become proficient at both typewriting and taking letters down in shorthand from dictation. To this end, she had purchased a second-hand upright typewriting machine, which she had seen in the window of a pawnshop, and carried it back to her lodgings in a cab. There had been a number of expenses connected with the scheme which she had not foreseen, such as the purchase of paper, fresh ribbons and a manual of instruction, but it was cheaper than enrolling in one of the schools which existed for the purposes of training women into secretarial skills, and it also left her free to teach during the day.

She walked through the park. She had an appointment in Notting Hill, with a Mrs. Carstairs, and hoped that she would be engaged. If so, she would gain three new pupils at once; apart from the money, the advantage of taking on all of the Carstairs children would be that she could take them one after another, without having to travel about London between lessons, which was not only expensive but was also very wearing on the shoes. She had never thought about such things before but these days, they dominated much of her life.

A drop of rain darkened the sleeve of her coat, and another. She looked anxiously up at the gray sky. If it rained, she would have to decide whether or not to take a cab: it would be an expensive luxury considering that she did not yet know whether she would get the job. On the other hand, she would present a less than impressive picture if she appeared at the door soaked to the skin. She began to hurry, hoping the rain would hold off until she reached the Carstairs house.

She shivered. Although it was a late spring day, the temperature had dropped during the night, and the wind was unseasonably cold. The coat she wore was too thin to withstand much more than a mild breeze. She had brought few suitable clothes with her from India: her flight from Barney had been precipitate and, in addition, she had felt it a matter of honor to bring with her only such garments as had been purchased with her own money. One of the few exceptions to this was the cashmere shawl which Barney had bought for her during their stopover in Port Said. To leave it behind would have seemed an additional rejection for the poor man, and she did not wish to hurt him more than she had already done. None of what had happened was his fault. She was the only one to blame.

Sometimes it seemed to her that all she had done was cause pain to those she loved. She hated to think what her uncle must have felt on receiving the letter she had written while in Calcutta awaiting a passage home. She had described only the barest facts and had asked for his forgiveness, but she knew he could not help but be grieved, perhaps even angered, by the knowledge that she had defied society's rules by abandoning the husband she had publicly promised to love, honor and obey. The good husband. For adding to her despair and self-recrimination was the awareness that Barney was a fine man who had never treated her with anything but kindness and love.

Colin and Dickon would also be shocked by the news—she assumed that, as she had requested, her uncle would have passed on such information as she had given him—but she hoped that they might better understand her feelings of shame and guilt for running away from a situation which had grown intolerable, and why she felt she must drop out of their lives, even if temporarily. What she had not been able to explain, and perhaps never would, was her own sense that she had no right to expect their love or forgiveness. For as well as being a wife who left her husband, she was also a mother who did not love her own child. It was impossible not to feel that this failure trangressed some fundamental human law and rendered her unfit to take her place alongside other more decent people.

One day, perhaps, when the wounds were a little less raw, it might be possible for them all to meet again; she hoped so. Occasionally, when her situation appeared at its most disheartening, she contemplated throwing herself on her uncle's mercy, but the thought that, because of what she had done, he might refuse to see her was so terrifying, that she preferred not to put him to the test.

When she had first arrived in London, she had thought herself much better off than other women who had been forced by circumstances to earn their own living. There was a little money in a London bank account, although she did not wish to use it: it would almost certainly result in a letter from the bank manager to her uncle, and would necessitate leaving an address through which she could be tracked down. There were also various pieces of jewelery she could sell if it became necessary. With what she was able to earn from giving music lessons, she calculated that if she were careful, she could manage for nine months or so, by which time she hoped to have become a proficient enough stenographer to get a better-paid job.

Meanwhile, she was lucky enough to have found a cheap attic room in a Bayswater lodging house whose owner seemed kind. There were other boarders living there: dull people with miserable faces. She did not talk to them nor they to her. She had passed herself off to Mrs. Bentley, the landlady, as a widow; to the woman's enquiries, she had simply pressed her lips together and shaken her head, implying that the circumstances were too painful to discuss.

Mrs. Bentley had not pressed the matter. Although Mary was not to know it, she was aware that young Mrs. Thwaite, as Mary called herself, was brought up in better circumstances than those in which she now found herself. A nicely spoken young woman, Mrs. Bentley considered her, and clearly not used to fending for herself. The landlady had a keen eye for detail: she had noted the quality of Mary's shoes and gloves—always the sign of a lady—and the expensive materials of her wardrobe, and considered that she brought a certain cachet to the lodging house, so much so that she had already decided that when the day came—as she was sure it would—that Mrs. Thwaite found herself in difficulties over the next week's rent, she would be understanding about it.

She was not above a little genteel snooping when she

could be sure that Mrs. Thwaite was safely out of the house, and had found two or three really good pieces of jewelery among her possessions. A double string of pearls, for instance, which must be worth a bob or two, a couple of fine diamond brooches, a solid gold bracelet and matching choker. No photographs, however. No personal items which might give a clue as to the young widow's background. She was not entirely sure that her name was really Thwaite but so far had discovered no evidence to the contrary, and really there was no reason not to take her on trust. So far the rent had been paid on time, and she scarcely ate enough to bother dirtying a plate for, which, as Mrs. Bentley pointed out to her friend down the road, was all money in the pocket, breakfast and dinner being included in the rent, and a roast dinner on Sundays.

When shown into her presence, Mary swiftly decided that Mrs. Carstairs was not a person in whose company she would have chosen to spend two minutes. As it was, she was forced to endure nearly half an hour of questioning as to qualifications and teaching methods, and even to play two or three pieces as a demonstration of ability, although it was obvious that Mrs. Carstairs did not know Chopin from Tchaikovsky. She also wished to see references, which Mary, blushing with mortification, had to say she had forgotten to bring with her. The truth was that she had none, nor, in the panicky moments during which Mrs. Carstairs gazed at her in obvious disbelief, did she see where she was going to acquire any. The parents of her other pupils, perhaps? Her dislike for the woman increased by the moment and her nerves were raw by the time Mrs. Carstairs rose and said that she would let Mrs. Thwaite know her decision after talking it over with the children's father.

"Let me know?"

"I assume that is the normal procedure, is it not?" Mrs. Carstairs's fishy stare was cold. "You have an address to which I could write, I imagine."

"But—" Mary tried to hide her dismay. To her horror, she could feel the onset of tears. She needed the job and the money it would bring: her earlier estimate of how long her funds would last was already proving woefully short of the mark. Despite the lack of references, she had hoped that she would be told immediately whether she would be suitable or not.

"The musical welfare of our children is very important to us," declared Mrs. Carstairs, "particularly now that Mr. Carstairs has been appointed to the board of his firm and will naturally be expected to attend charity concerts and the like."

"I see." It seemed something of a *non sequitur*. Had it not mattered so much, Mary might have asked whether the lessons were for the children or for the husband. Mrs. Carstairs went on to say how very fond she was of Handel's Water Music and the symphonies of the divine Mozart. To have walked all the way across the park for such an indefinite conclusion was irritating enough in itself; to have to listen to her potential employer discoursing on matters about which it was obvious that she knew nothing was almost unendurable. Or would have been, if she had not reminded herself that this kind of thing was part of her punishment for running away from her duties as a wife and mother. "How long will it take you to decide?"

"You surely realize that we have other teachers of pianoforte to interview," said Mrs. Carstairs superciliously.

Exhaustion made Mary suddenly bold. "Naturally." She spoke with an hauteur at least the equal of the other woman's. "But you will appreciate that I myself have a waiting list of would-be pupils."

"Oh?" A look of uncertainty crossed Mrs. Carstairs's face. "I hadn't realized that you—"

"Because three children were involved, I decided to come to see you first," Mary said coldly. "Perhaps you will give me your decision in the next few days. Otherwise I shall feel free to assume that you have found a more suitable teacher for your children."

"I will of course let—"

"And I must add that I shall obviously wish to audition them before I can agree to take them on. If they show no aptitude, I'm sure you will agree that it would be a waste of my time and theirs to try to teach them."

Without waiting for words of dismissal, Mary rose to her feet and began pulling on her gloves. She could see

Mrs. Carstairs noting the quality of the fine French leather and wondering how a humble music teacher could afford them. She hoped she would spring to the conclusion that this was no ordinary teacher but one so much in demand that she could charge accordingly. Likewise one whose services should be snapped up at once.

Once out in the street, she let out a pent-up breath. She had taken a gamble in not being cringingly grateful at the prospect of teaching the Carstairs children; she could not help a certain inner pleasure as she remembered their mother's face and the expression on it as she took in the fact that the music teacher had come with the intention of vetting the potential employer rather than the other way about.

Her next pupil was the daughter of a widower in Belgravia. Mr. Vernon's house was elegantly appointed, full of well-kept furniture and a good deal of choice silver and porcelain. Mary enjoyed her weekly visits there, partly because the luxuriousness of the house was such a pleasant contrast with her own lodgings, and partly because ten-year-old Dora Vernon was the most promising of her pupils. She had told Mr. Vernon so on the last occasion she encountered him, when he had unexpectedly arrived home a few minutes before the end of the lesson and then insisted that she take a glass of madeira with him before setting off home.

It was beginning to rain in earnest by the time she arrived in Eaton Square. Standing on the doorstep, shaking her umbrella, she hoped it would have eased off before it was time for her to walk back to Bayswater. Mr. Vernon was at home that afternoon and during the lesson, she was very conscious of him standing at the door of the parlor, listening intently as she instructed Dora in some of the more difficult passages of the piece she was preparing, and suggested new exercises for her to practice before the following week.

At the conclusion of the lesson, he again asked her to step into the drawing room. "There is something I wish to discuss with you," he said, when she was seated. "Last week you said that my daughter was very promising."

"So she is."

"Her mother was very gifted," he said. "She was French, had studied at the Conservatoire. She always hoped that at least one of our daughters would follow her in this, but the other two, I'm afraid, did not take to the instrument."

"I expect their abilities lie in other directions," Mary said tactfully.

"Perhaps. However, what I wished to ask you, Mrs. Thwaite, was whether you might be induced to increase Dora's lessons from one a week to two?"

Mary tried not to show too much elation. It would not do to indicate just how welcome the extra income would be "I would have to look at my timetables," she said primly.

"Of course. A busy person like yourself . . . I quite understand."

"But it might be arranged," said Mary. "I can let you know next week."

"The sooner the better, don't you think?" Mr. Vernon looked up at a portrait on the wall which showed a pretty blonde woman in a blue dress seated beside a table on which stood a bowl of nasturtiums. Mary could not help thinking that the flowers were better painted than the person. "Dora's mother. A sad loss for the poor girl—for all of us."

"There can be nothing worse than to lose a mother when one is still a child."

His eyes were fixed on her in bright enquiry. "You have suffered a bereavement yourself, of course." He nodded at her mourning.

"Yes." Mary folded her mouth together. If he started to pry into her affairs . . .

"Then you will know something of what I feel. It worries me to know that Dora is being deprived of a mother's love at this delicate stage in her life. Her sisters are considerably older and away much of the time, which adds to her isolation."

"I see." Mary tried to remember what little Dora had told her of the other daughters in the family: twenty and nineteen, she thought, one of them studying art in Paris and the other at the Sorbonne. "But she seems a very happy child to me." It was impossible not to think of her own daughter, and tears came suddenly into her eyes.

"My dear Mrs. Thwaite." Mr. Vernon was immediately at her side, one hand on her shoulder. "I'm so sorry. Is there something I can do? Something to drink, a brandy, perhaps?"

"Nothing." Horribly embarrassed, Mary dabbed at her eyes. It would not do for the parents of her pupils to have a weeping music teacher on their hands: words would get about and she would not find further employment. She tried to visualize Colin and the scornful expression he would assume if he were present at her moment of weakness. "Thank you, but nothing."

Awkwardly, he bent and took her hand. "Mrs. Thwaite, I have been meaning to ask you for a couple of weeks. It would give me the very greatest of pleasure if you would do me another small favor."

"What is that?" Mary said.

"You are a musical person, obviously, while I am not. I like a good tune, but the finer points of music escape me."

"I see." What was he leading up to? Did he want to take piano lessons himself?

"I happen to have been given tickets to a concert at the Wigmore Hall next week and would much appreciate it if you would be willing to accompany me and perhaps educate me in some of the subtler details which I might otherwise miss. My dear wife tried hard to increase my understanding but with little success, I fear."

"What sort of program is it?"

"Some Schubert, some Beethoven. And one of those European composers: Stravinsky."

"I adore Stravinsky."

"Do you indeed?" Looking down at the bent head of the music teacher, James Vernon congratulated himself on the fact that she had obviously forgotten telling him so last month, information which had prompted him to order the tickets for the forthcoming concert. "Then may I hope that you will take pity on my ignorance and come with me?"

She looked up at him. Such a pretty creature, he thought. Or would be, if she were not so thin, so exhausted. Yet the faint lines of grief and experience which showed around her eyes only added character to her features. "I should like that," she said warmly.

"I'll send my car for you, then."

Mary did not want his chauffeur to see where she lived. She decided that she would accept his offer and then, at the last minute, arrange to meet him at the concert hall. "Thank you." She was conscious of excitement. It was so long since she had enjoyed an evening out, and Mr. Vernon was a more than acceptable companion.

"And you will consider fitting in an extra lesson for Dora?" he said

"I'm sure it will be possible."

Rain drummed at the windows. Vernon frowned. "You must let me send you home in the car."

"No!" Mary's refusal was overly vehement. "I wouldn't dream of inconveniencing you to such an extent."

Vernon was about to say that it was no inconvenience, that in any case he paid his chauffeur to be inconvenienced. But although he had never experienced poverty, and hoped he never would, he was sensitive enough to guess that she was living at an address which was less than fashionable, somewhere she did not wish his driver to take note of and perhaps pass back to him. He did not insist. "In that case," he said, "I shall see that you take a cab." He would instruct his man to find one and give him instructions to slip the driver the fare.

Waiting on the top step of the Vernon house, while the manservant searched for a cab, Mary had the sudden impression that she was being watched. With her free hand, she pulled the collar of her coat higher about her face, at the same time looking about, but could see no one who appeared to be displaying the slightest interest in her. The square was virtually empty, the rain keeping most people indoors.

Later that evening, Vernon sat before the fire in his study with a glass of port in his hand, wondering about the young music teacher. He had recently found himself thinking quite a lot about Mary; there was a hint of mystery about her which intrigued him. Where did she come from? How many pupils did she have? Did she make an even halfway decent living? He doubted very much whether her background and upbringing had fitted her for the kind of life she was at present leading, but she had not let that deter her. He admired that. It showed courage. She was obviously not trained as a teacher—probably not trained as anything. At least his own daughters had had it drilled into them from an early age that they must gain some kind of qualifications. The death of his wife from influenza had come as a terrible shock; he had often thought since of what might have happened if *he* had been the one to succumb. How would the rest of his family have managed? Even though they would not have been left destitute, what personal resources would they have had?

The port was smooth on his tongue. It had been put down in his grandfather's time and enough remained to see him comfortably through his own lifetime. One of the sadnesses of his otherwise easy life was that there was no son to inherit the family name and, in his own turn, pass it on. He had loved Francine, grieved hugely at her death, but recently he had begun to wonder about the feasibility of remarrying. He was still on the right side of fifty, well set-up, not entirely hideous, if the women with whom he had enjoyed several short-lived liaisons were to be believed. There was no shortage of money: as well as the town house, there was the Norfolk estate and the shooting lodge in Scotland. He knew himself to be both kindly and tolerant. Why should he not have a son, after all, especially if he were to choose a wife still in her twenties, still young enough for child-bearing?

Resolutely he pushed Mary from his mind and turned to the architectural plans which had been delivered to his house earlier that day. His dead wife had loved Norfolk, more particularly Haslingfield, his country seat, much of which had been left almost untouched for more than a century and he had decided to develop and improve the estate, now that the war was done with. When she was alive, they lived down there more or less permanently, and some of the plans he was determined to incorporate in the overall designs had originally been hers.

He had discussed his ideas with friends who had similar works in progress, and there had seemed to be almost unanimous agreement as to the best firm to approach. One of the central tenets in Vernon's life was the opinion that if you paid for the best, you got the best. Accordingly, he had gone to the place in question and asked them to carry out his commission. The two young men who had sat on the other side of his desk and expounded their plans for the grounds in Norfolk made a nicely contrasting pair: the one dark and enthusiastic, bubbling over with ideas, the other phlegmatic, keeping a restraining hand on his partner's exuberance yet with plenty of excellent suggestions of his own to make. Mr. Vernon himself had grown quite excited as they talked: he always admired enthusiasm, especially when combined with expertise, and there was no doubt that these two knew exactly what they were doing. It had never occurred to him before to view the making of a garden as an art form; the books they had brought with them one afternoon, urging him to read them before their next consultation, had changed that. He had begun with a few general rather staid ideas; now he felt like a man with a mission: nothing less than the transformation of Haslingfield. The two partners had instinctively seemed to know which of his ideas he was set on, and which he was prepared to be flexible about. Francine had always wanted to build a summer house in the grounds, a relatively simple notion which he had put to the contractors as no more than an addition to his other plans. They had responded with a a fervor which quite surprised him, discussing the relative merits of loggias and arbors. Chinese pavilions and Ottoman kiosks, *treillage* versus wire work, timber versus brick or stone. He was looking now at an exquisite design, something like a Hindu temple, which they had produced for his consideration. Nothing could be more alien to the Norfolk landscape, the large East Anglian skies, yet, the more he studied it, the more right it seemed, exactly what Francine would have wanted. He could clearly picture it set back from the ornamental lake which had been the contribution of one of his forebears. It would be reflected in the shallow waters, a symbol of the Empire which had made England great. And when he remembered that two of his great-uncles had served in India, and a cousin was out there now . . . what could be more fitting?

He had missed his wife dreadfully in the past four years but never more so than now. He longed to share

his excitement with her, he longed to see the look in her
eyes when she raised her head from the drawing and
nodded slowly, a smile gradually spreading across her
face. None of the women he habitually saw would have
the faintest concept of what he meant or why the design
so pleased him. He wondered what the little music
teacher would make of it and tried to imagine the circumstances in which it would be possible to ask her.
None sprang immediately to mind.

"I wonder if that really was Mary I saw," Colin said, for
the fiftieth time.

"And supposing it was?"

"Then we'd at least be sure she was back here in
England. According to Lady Gardiner, it was months
ago that she left India. If she's not here, where can she
possibly be?"

"I've told you before, Colin: if she wanted us to know
where she was, she'd have contacted us. Poor lass is still
grieving, must be. She needs time to herself."

"That's why I want to find her. So I can tell her that
we want to help. That we love her, dammit."

"Leave her alone, Colin. Whether it's Mary or it's not,
leave the poor young woman alone."

14

"Lovely, aren't they?" Mrs. Bentley said.

"Beautiful." Mary buried her nose in the huge bunch of daffodils and narcissi, iris and tulips. Simple flowers, sweet scents. How like him to know that she would prefer them to hothouse roses.

"I kept them in water so they'd stay fresh. You can borrow the vase, if you like."

"You're very kind."

And you, my dear, are very lucky, thought Mrs. Bentley, watching from the shadows of the hall as her top-floor conversion—it sounded grander than attic—made her way upstairs, her face pressed into the flowers. Someone was obviously courting the young widow. This was the third time in two weeks that flowers had been delivered for Mrs. Thwaite. And not from some back-street flower-seller, neither. The florist's van was a smart cream affair with an address in Mayfair painted on the side. There'd also been a delivery, earlier in the week, of half a dozen books—three of the latest novels, a poetry anthology, a book about opera and another full of beautiful reproductions of paintings—from that shop in Piccadilly *and* a big basket of fruit from Fortnum's. Oranges, apples, beautiful ripe pears. Very nice too, though it might have been better to spend the money on a new coat for the poor thing, something thick and warm to replace the thin one which was all she had.

Take him, Mrs. Bentley would have said, were Mary to have asked her advice. Even if he's old, take him. He's obviously rich, and let's face it, my dear (this was one of the landlady's favorite fantasies, Mary and herself seated on either side of the plush-covered table in the

basement, talking about life and love and men), let's
face it, shop-worn goods are lucky to find a buyer. Beggars can't be choosers, she might have added, pouring
more hot water on to the tea leaves and passing a slice
of seed cake, no more than young widows can.

Up in her room, Mary took off her coat. How like
him, she thought again. Although she rarely smiled, her
features softened. How very like him. She knew she
could never feel love for him, but she admired and re-
spected him, enjoyed his company. Their acquaintance
had grown considerably over the past weeks: they had
attended several concerts, and visited the theater a number of times. They got on well together. As her hands
moved among the leaves, she remembered the last time
she had arranged flowers and, before she could push
them back, memories washed over her like blood gush-
ing from a wound.

The vase then had been glass painted with a intricate
pattern of green and blue, bought in the bazaar. The
flowers had been flashy, fleshy: cannas, asters, bird of
paradise, begonias. Beyond the shaded living room, the
afternoon sunshine was piercingly bright. She set the
flowers on a carved sandalwood chest, hardly able to
bear their strident colors, and went over to sit at the
black Conway. She pressed down a chord but only one
of the notes sounded. She had not been able to play the
instrument for months. The keys, from which the ivory
was lifting, stuck together and either played late or not
at all. Even when they produced a sound it was out of
tune, for the climate did not suit the delicate structure
of a piano.

There had been no note with the bouquet, nor any
need for one. It had become an accepted thing on the
station that Basil Crawford—Captain Crawford as he
had become—was pursuing young Mrs. Major Sambourne and that she was not averse to his attentions.
Though the first of these assumptions was correct, the
second, in fact, was not. Mary could not think of Basil
without her cheeks flushing. She wished he would leave
her alone, yet, at the same time, she was excited by his
obvious ardor. He both intrigued and disgusted her. She
was filled with self-loathing as she found herself wonder-

ing what it would be like to have him make love to her,
whether he would awaken something within her which
had hitherto lain dormant. So far she had done nothing
more than exchange a few snatched kisses, yet she knew
that if he continued to press her for more, she would
inevitably succumb. The prospect had the fevered gleam
of some flesh-eating orchid in a jungle, the dubious
beauty of oil rainbowed in a puddle of dirty water.

From the verandah, she looked down at the garden.
The withered grass and dried-up flowerbeds were somehow symbolic of her own hopes. India had seemed like
a garden, green, abundant, full of promise; in reality, it
had proved no more than bare soil, barren and dusty.
She had tried to transplant herself and had failed to put
down roots.

Dispiritedly, she trailed into the bedroom and, remov-
ing her dress, lay down beneath the mosquito netting.
There was to be yet another dance that evening at the
Club, the last of the current season. The thought of it
tired her: the futility, the sameness, the predictability of
the conversation, the food, the music, the company. She
thought of Basil. Already she could feel his hands at her
waist in the darkness of the Club's verandah, the brush
of his fingers across her breast, her feigned indifference
to the electricity of his touch. She knew so little about
love, lust, sex, whatever you chose to call it, yet she
recognized that Basil roused her, that she wanted to feel
him do to her the things she hated Barney doing. With
Basil, it would be different, of that she was sure.

Somewhere in the rear of the bungalow, Charlotte Alice
grizzled; for the past few days she had been listless and
discontent. It was the heat, Mary decided, the heavy pre-
monsoon heat, which bore down upon the parched earth,
squeezing it like an old-fashioned press until the air
seemed as friable as glass. Every afternoon, clouds
sagged against the hills then moved away in a rumble of
thunder without releasing the longed-for rain. Just before darkness fell, an irascible little breeze would blow
dust across the cantonment, penetrating the soft tissues
of nostril and eyelid, giving a gritty coating to the
tongue. Even the old timers found it hard to bear; tempers grew increasingly volatile and morale quivered on
the edge of breakdown.

Mary and Barney left at seven. Just before they set off, the *ayah* brought Charlotte Alice in to say good night to her parents. Mindful of her carefully-arranged hair, Mary bent to give the child a perfunctory kiss. Barney held his daughter close, gently rubbing his chin against her cheek, blowing softly into her neck, but for once she failed to laugh. He looked at her with some anxiety. "She seems rather hot," he said, to the hovering *ayah*. "I hope she hasn't got a fever."

The girl shrugged. Although she did not say so, she wondered what he expected. The monsoon season was almost upon them, and daytime temperatures were already in the low hundreds. It would be cooler up in the hills—but Missy Mary never joined the other women there, much to the chagrin of her servants, who lost a considerable amount of caste because of this. It was not as if she stayed behind because of her husband: the entire staff was aware of the lack of nocturnal activity at the Sambourne bungalow, and equally aware that unlike so many of the *mems,* Missy Mary was not having an affair, despite the gossip overheard in other bungalows.

"I wonder if we ought to send a *chit* to say we can't make it," Barney said. "What do you think, Mary?"

"I think you're making an absurd fuss about nothing," Mary said disdainfully. She sipped from the glass of gin and lime set among her boxes of powder and cream then hung jewels in her ears: gold fashioned into the shape of a serpent with ruby eyes and an emerald at the tip of its tail. They were a gift from Basil Crawford, the first of any value she had accepted and she was aware that by wearing them tonight, she was giving him a clear message. Her boldness both exhilarated and frightened her. In the mirror, the rubies caught the light as she turned her head; in her eyes she could read her own determination.

Barney laid a worried hand against Charlotte's forehead. "She's definitely got a temperature."

"We're only a mile away if anyone needs us," Mary said impatiently. Having keyed herself up to indiscretion, she was not going to stay tamely at home on account of a child who was slightly under the weather. "She'll be perfectly all right." She spoke to the *ayah*. "And if not, you'll let us know, yes?"

"Yiss, yiss," nodded the *ayah*.

"Just don't put too many covers over her when she goes to bed," Barney instructed. Mary was already turning again to gaze at her reflection in the mirror as the child was led away.

Everyone had gathered on the verandah to watch the fireworks. Behind Mary, Basil Crawford stood very close, so close that she could feel the buttons of his uniform through the thin material of her dress, and the heat of his body. His hands moved upwards to her waist; his mouth was on her neck as he whispered: "Your earrings are charming, Mrs. Sambourne."

"They were a gift," she answered, leaning back against him. Her breasts seemed to swell as his fingers touched her nipples. Desire melted her; she felt as though she were made of golden honey.

"From someone you care for, I hope," he said softly, his breath stirring her hair.

"Maybe."

His hands grasped her hips and pulled her so close that she could feel the hard swelling inside his trousers. Above their heads, rockets filled the night with glittering showers of purple and gold, which lit up the sky as they drifted slowly down to earth. Roman candles burned a lurid red; Catherine wheels fizzed and spun, shooting off explosions of dazzling sparks. The night coruscated with stars; the acrid stink of gunpowder hung above the watchers like fog.

"Mary," Basil said, his voice urgent. "I want you. I must have you." Passionately he pressed his mouth against her throat. "Oh, Mary." Longing had thickened his voice.

Rockets leaped upward. Red, purple, green, silver, they burst against the heavens and broke into a thousand pinpoints of light which fell like drops of colored mercury into the Club gardens, throwing the shapes of shrub and tree into sharp relief.

"Come with me," Basil said suddenly. He pulled her after him, down the steps and on to the grass. Nobody saw them leave as another quiverful of fireworks arrowed upwards in a hissing whoosh of flame.

"Where are we going?" Mary said.

"Just away from the others." He led her around the side of the building and then stopped, pushing her roughly up against the wall. "Oh my God," he said, as he began to cover her face with fierce kisses. "I've waited for this so long."

Mary gasped as his tongue filled her mouth. Barney had never . . . As his hand reached inside the bodice of her dress and covered her breast, she found herself kissing him back. "Jesus," he moaned.

Was this what she had read about in books? This searing, desperate need. "Oh," she said. "Oh . . ."

"Mary, I . . ." Basil pulled her down on to the lawn beside him. They moaned together in the shadows of the Club. His hands tore at the front of her dress as she fell backward. He pulled her skirts up to her waist.

She lay with her mouth open, panting under the sparkling sky. Ribbons of color streamed across the sky. He opened her as he fumbled with his braces, wrenched at the buttons which secured his clothes. "Hurry," she said.

He pushed into her. It was no more than a few seconds before he came, moaning with bliss as Mary's body began to move in a series of ecstatic leaps. She had never felt such uncontrolled physical pleasure before. Dimly she was aware of someone shouting her name as Basil lay over her, his damp cheek pressed against hers. She simmered like a volcano, ready to erupt again while, above her, the fireworks burned.

Barney was calling her but she could not have moved had her life depended on it. "Oh my darling Mary," Basil said. He began to move again inside her and she found herself responding, grasping his head, holding his mouth to her breasts, giving herself up entirely to him.

"Oh God," she whispered. Pleasure surged through her once again. "I never knew . . . I didn't realize . . ."

Deep in the rational part of her brain, a voice said coldly that she was behaving no better than an animal. It spoke of betrayal, of vows made and now broken. Even as her body jerked once more, she felt the seeds of shame sprout. How would she ever look Barney in the face again, knowing what she had done? She was a married woman, yet she had shared the most intimate of acts with this virtual stranger, knowing all the while

that he meant nothing to her. There could be no excuses.
Filled with disgust for herself, she pushed him away.

"What is it?" he said.

"I must go," she said. "The others . . . they'll be
wondering . . ." She stumbled to her feet, tugging at her
clothes, smoothing down her dress, trying to rearrange
her hair. They would know, all of them, what she had
been doing. Already their sharp eyes pierced her, their
knowing smiles smothered her. She must find Barney
and go straight home.

Basil hurried after her. "What's wrong?" he said.
"Didn't you—didn't I make you happy?"

She made no reply. Happy? She no longer knew what
happiness meant, but certainly it was not to be found in
such activities as she had just indulged in, whatever her
treacherous body might try to say.

His hand grabbed at her skirt and she turned on him.
"Don't touch me," she said. "Don't ever . . ." She
wanted to explain her distress but they were at the corner of the building again, slipping back up on to the
veranadah, mingling with the crowd. They could not
have been gone more than ten minutes. Down on the
grass in front of the Club house, the servants darted
about with fiery torches, setting light to a final pyrotech-
nical set piece. As the touchpapers caught fire, the words
GOOD NIGHT LADIES AND GOD BE WITH YOU
were spelled out in fizzing letters, and underneath that:
GOD SAVE THE KING.

The spectators clapped and cheered. A general movement back inside began. Major John Streatham material-
ized out of the dark. "Oh there you are, Mrs.
Sambourne," he said. He seemed worried. "Your husband was looking for you."

"My husband?" The words sounded strange, as
though Streatham had chosen them deliberately to emphasize the inexcusability of her recent behavior.

"One of your bearers arrived here," explained
Streatham. "Your little girl has been taken sick."

"Oh my God," said Mary. Could retribution be so
swift?

"Major Sambourne couldn't find you so rode home
without waiting."

Mary looked wildly around. "I must get back immediately."

"Let me drive you." It was Captain Crawford's serpent voice.

"No!" She almost shrieked the word, not caring what Streatham thought . . .

"But my car is just outside in the—"

"No," she repeated more calmly, aware of the expression of shocked surprise on Streatham's face. "I would really prefer . . ."

"Very well. I'll arrange some alternative transportation for you," the major said stiffly. As she followed him across the room, she realized that he thought she was the worse for drink. She could feel Basil's semen trickling down her leg, over the top of her silk stocking. She was sure that everyone else in the whole room could see it.

Outside, Streatham ordered the colonel's driver to run Mrs. Sambourne home. As he handed her in, he said awkwardly: "I do hope your child has recovered by the time you get back. You know how it is with children out here . . ." And wives, she wanted to retort. As the person directly responsible for Monica's death last year in childbirth, he was hardly the man to sit in judgment on her.

The colonel's car smelled faintly of good cigars. Although it was luxurious, she sat on the edge of the leather seat, silently urging the driver to go faster. As they turned into the gate of her bungalow, she saw that all the lights in the house were on. Stepping out of the car, she heard the muffled sound of a drum from the servants' quarters, and the sound of weeping. What could have happened? But as she ran up the shallow steps of the verandah, she already knew.

Barney was seated at his daughter's side, his head in his hands. When she came in, he lifted a tear-stained face. "Where *were* you?" he demanded. "I looked everywhere."

She heard him, but the words fell toward her as though they were feathers in a vaccuum. She stared beyond him to the little white bed. Under the mosquito netting, the child lay still. Mary remembered a jeweled green snake, the feel of the wooden floor beneath her

bare feet, how she had slowly pushed open the door of
her parents' bedroom to see her mother's body under
the mosquito netting. Then I was a child, she thought
bleakly, who saw my dead mother without understanding; now I am a mother and, although I do not understand why, my child lies dead before me.

Barney stood. He came over and gripped her shoulders. "Where have you been?" he asked. There was
whisky on his breath. "What were you doing?"

What would he say, Mary wondered, if I told him that
I was lying tumbled on the ground with my skirts thrown
back like a common servant girl, while a man I scarcely
know pumped his seed into my willing body? She wished
she could feel something: grief, pain, remorse, but she
could only remember how good it had been. She was
aware that she would live with the guilt of that moment
for the rest of her life.

"She asked for you," Barney raged. She felt his spittle
on her face. He shook her violently. "Our daughter
asked for you as she died and you weren't there." He
began to sob, remembering the beautiful woman dead
on the white sheets, and a child alone in an empty room
with wine stains round her mouth. "I wish I'd never met
you. You've been . . ." He turned away from her, his
shoulders defeated. Alice, Charlotte: both so beloved,
and both gone. "Ah God," he said, his voice breaking.
"My little Charlotte. My precious daughter . . ."

Mary knew she ought to offer comfort, she ought to
say something. But what was there to say? In this country of sudden deadly diseases, there was no point in asking which specific one had killed her daughter. She
stared at her husband's bent head and realized that
whatever had once bound them together was over: She
blamed herself. Only herself. All along she had behaved
abominably, selfishly. She recalled her reluctance to visit
poor Faringdon in hospital, her rejection of Dickon, her
inability to love little Charlotte Alice. There was only
one honorable course left to take. As soon as the funeral
was over, she would leave.

15

If Mrs. Bentley, Bayswater landlady, had had any doubts about the eligibility of the unknown suitor courting her top-floor conversion, they were finally resolved one Tuesday a week or two later. That was the day she responded to a knock at the door and opened it to find a young man holding in his arms a large white cardboard box tied with dark brown cord.

"For Mrs. Thwaite," he said. "Is that you, love?"

"Who's asking?" countered Mrs. Bentley, a woman skilled in the ways of delivery boys and not one to stand for any sauce.

"Only Madame Zoe's, that's all."

"Down Bond Street, you mean?"

"That's right, love."

Mrs. Bentley snatched the box from him. "That's quite enough out of you, my lad," she said. "What is it?"

"A coat, they said." The boy grinned. "Who's Mrs. Thwaite, then: your mother?"

Carrying the box into the hall, Mrs. Bentley decided her friend down the road must have done a good job with the iron curlers yesterday; it was a long time since anyone had cheeked her like that.

When Mrs. Thwaite returned, Mrs. Bentley handed her the carton. "It's a coat," she said.

"A coat?"

"So the delivery boy said. From Madame Zoe."

"What's that?"

"Ever such a chic place in Bond Street," said Mrs. Bentley. The question added another piece to the unfinished jigsaw that was Mrs. Thwaite. If she'd never heard of Madame Zoe, she was either deaf and blind, or had been out of the country. And since there was nothing wrong with her hearing . . . Like Lucille and Worth, since the war Madame Zoe had become one of London's leading couturiers, Britain's answer to the fashion houses in Paris: Chanel, or Madame Paquin's. Despite her circumstances, Mrs. Bentley was a keen follower of fashion. She and her friend down the road spent many a happy hour poring over the fashion magazines, their hair tied up in scarves, cigarettes at the ready and a pot of tea always on the go. "I'd like to know what my Harry would say if I went down the pub dressed in that," was her friend down the road's favorite comment as she studied some flimsy creation of silk and feathers designed for Ascot or a Buckingham Palace garden party, while Mrs. Bentley, contemplating an evening gown in brocade velvet, usually contented herself with a judicious: "Wouldn't be seen dead in it, dear, not if you paid me."

Mary was about to carry the box up to her room, but just in time she saw the naked yearning in her landlady's eyes. It is possible that the Mary of a year ago might have wanted to know what her private affairs had to do with someone like Mrs. Bentley. Now, she paused on the stair and said: "Would you by any chance have a good sharp knife? I've only got a pair of nail scissors and I don't think they'd be strong enough to cut the string."

So part of Mrs. Bentley's fantasy came true. She found herself waving Mrs. Thwaite to the basket chair beside the coke stove while she rummaged through a drawer in the built-in dresser for a carving knife. "The kettle's on, Mrs. Thwaite," she said happily. "Can I offer you a cup of tea?"

"That would be marvelous," said Mary. "It's so cold outside."

It was not until the tea had been brewed and poured that Mary began to cut the string around her package. Lifting the carton lid, she found layer after layer of brown tissue paper ("Not brown, *bronze*," corrected Mrs. Bentley. "That's Madame Zoe's trademark color.") and underneath, a coat of fine brown wool with a heavy fox collar.

"It's beautiful." Mary lifted it out and held it against her. "What do you think?"

"Ooh, Mrs. Thwaite. It's gorgeous. Goes ever so well

with your hair, too. Slip it on and let's have a look at
you."

Mary did so. "Well?"

"Lovely, dear. Really beautiful. Ever thought of working as a mannequin?"

"A mannequin?"

"You know, dear. Modeling and that. You've got just
the figure for it. All skin and bones, more like a boy
than a full-grown woman, if you ask me, but that's what
they want these days."

"No, I've never thought of that line of work." Mary
smoothed the coat over her hips, stroked the fur collar.
"Isn't this splendid?"

"Ever so chic," agreed Mrs. Bentley. She put her head
on one side. "Any idea who sent it?"

Mary tried to look nonchalant. "I can guess."

"Obviously dead keen on you, dear. Madame Zoe
doesn't come cheap, believe you me."

"And obviously I can't accept it."

"What?" Mrs. Bentley could hardly believe what she
was hearing. "Not acc—" She stumbled over the words.
"How do you mean, dear?"

"A gift like this—clothes, I mean—isn't it a bit intimate? Doesn't it kind of imply . . . you know what I
mean."

Mrs. Bentley was not sure, but she was not going to
let on. "He'd be ever so insulted if you sent it back,"
she pointed out. "And hurt, too, more than likely."

"That's true."

"You've never given him no cause to think . . ." The
landlady nodded her head knowingly a couple of times
and raised her eyebrows. "No encouragement, nothing
like that?"

"Good lord, no," said Mary hastily. "Absolutely not.
I mean . . ." She tried to think whether she could be
said to have "encouraged" Mr. Vernon.

"Nice gentleman, is he?"

"Very nice indeed."

"I can see he takes a real interest in you, dear." And
in your shape, Mrs. Bentley added silently. The coat was
a perfect fit.

"Yes. I teach his daughter piano, you see."

"And where would he live?"

"Belgravia."

Decent address, noted Mrs. Bentley, who kept up with such things through the gossip columns. *Very* decent. "And a place in the country too, I'll be bound."

"Yes. In Norfolk, actually."

"Very suitable, dear. Very." Obviously he was able to provide for Mrs. Thwaite in the manner to which Mrs. Bentley suspected she was accustomed.

"Suitable?"

"I always think a gentleman should have two addresses, don't you?" Mrs. Bentley said quickly, hoping Mrs. Thwaite would not perceive the way her thoughts were tending and take offense.

"I don't think I've ever considered it," Mary said doubtfully. Now that she did, she saw that her landlady was right. Just about everybody she knew had two addresses, if not three. "But you think it's all right for me to keep the coat?"

"You'd be mad not to. Especially with winter still about."

"You'll manage all right until I get back from Misselthwaite, will you?" asked Colin.

"I think I'll be able to cope," said Dickon, looking up from the catalog of roses which he was studying. The office cat lay on his knee, furling and unfurling its claws. "I've done it before."

"You won't be bored without me?"

"Won't have time. There's a deal of stuff to attend to. Fanny's snowed under right now."

"Which is a good sign. When I get back, we may have to think about taking on more staff."

"Right. And I've me brother Phil and me sister Janey coming to stay, too. I'll be showing them all the sights—it'll be their first visit to London."

Colin felt in his pocket and fished out two sovereigns. "Give them one each, from me, will you, old man? It's no fun coming to London without a spot of cash to spend."

"That's right thoughtful of you, Colin."

"I envy you," Colin said wistfully. "I wish I had a brother and sister to take about."

"It'll be exhausting, I don't doubt." Dickon laughed,

his big hand curved over the delicate shape of the cat's skull. "I've had me orders. Buckingham Palace. Big Ben. A ride on a bus. The Tower of London. Madame Tussaud's. It'll take me a month to recover."

"If my father didn't need me, I'd stay down and join you," said Colin. "I don't know when I last visited the Tower."

"Are you well?" Dickon thought that his friend seemed less so than usual. The flesh had fallen away from his face, giving his head the same bony over-sized look as when he was a child; his agate-gray eyes were huge and sad. "Are you well, Colin?"

"Reasonably." Colin did not want to talk about the attacks of breathlessness which had begun to afflict him recently. The Harley Street doctor he had visited put it down to pollution from the increasing numbers of motor vehicles clogging the streets, and advised him to go abroad, or at least, back to Yorkshire. Colin did not want to do that. It would mean leaving Dickon down here alone, for a start. Only the other day he had unexpectedly said that he had no intention of returning north, for the forseeable future, at any rate.

Wryly, Colin reflected on other changes. Dickon himself was different. In the years since the end of the war, he had filled out, grown at least five inches. Now that the firm was doing so well, he had money enough to dress well, use a good barber in Jermyn Street, buy handmade shoes. The result was a fine-looking man, clear-eyed, glossy-haired, handsome as a fox. There was an air of confidence about him which it pleased Colin to see, though at the same time it saddened him a little. He often wondered whether Dickon kept a discreet mistress, or if there was someone he loved. Recently, he looked as if he guarded a secret which gave him a purely private satisfaction. Colin knew that were he to ask, Dickon would simply turn those sky-blue eyes on him and not answer. He was so close-mouthed, so Yorkshire. Yet sometimes it seemed that all was not as well as it appeared. There was a line between Dickon's brows which spoke of pain; an anguish which came and went behind his eyes, as though he were still haunted by demons. What shape did they take, Colin asked himself?

Of what horrors did they shriek when they crowded into Dickon's dreams? Were they anything like his own?

"So you see, Mrs. Thwaite, you'd be doing me such a favor," Mr. Vernon said earnestly, some days later, as Mary was preparing to return home after one of Dora's piano lessons. As had become usual, he had called her into the drawing room and offered her a glass of sherry. "I have no one else to turn to. No one else whose opinion I would value as much as yours."

"In that case, I'd be delighted to come," said Mary.

"We could simply make a day of it," said Mr. Vernon, carefully hiding the pleasure her acceptance gave him, continuing the pretense that he only wished her to come with him in order to advise him. "Set off early in the morning and get back late at night. Norfolk is a good drive from here, but perfectly possible in a day. However . . ." He paused. This was a bird not easily caught, a bird who would flutter through his fingers if he came too close, whose confidence needed to be gained before there was any chance of snaring it.

"Yes?" Mary said.

". . . we could go down and stay overnight. The housekeeper wouldn't require much notice—and the cook would be simply delighted to have the opportunity to produce dinner for us. Since my wife died, she's had very little chance to display her talents."

Overnight? Would that be wise? Would he expect her to—what would he think if she agreed? Mary had no way of knowing whether he regularly took women down to his place in the country, whether the servants were used to it. "Well, I—" she began.

"If you're worried about the proprieties of the thing," said Mr. Vernon, "I can arrange for other guests to be there."

"I'm sure it will be—I certainly didn't mean to imply—"

"As a matter of fact, that would be an excellent idea," said Mr. Vernon, perceiving that he had made a slight blunder in not making it clear earlier. "I'll send out invitations immediately. Just a few neighbors, you know. You needn't worry."

"I won't."

"I'll drive us down myself," Mr. Vernon said. "I'll pick you up just after lunch, then."

He wanted to tell her how pretty she looked in her new coat, how becoming the fox fur was against her fair hair. If fair was the right word for something so fine, so varied in color. As a child he had been told of Rapunzel spinning gold in some towered room: he imagined that the stuff she span might have been very like Mary's hair. The time for saying such things had not yet arrived, however. He would have to wait.

Almost unconsciously, Mary found herself playing the role of hostess. Mr. Vernon's neighbors differed hardly at all from the people who dined at Misselthwaite Manor: stolid country gentlefolk, of fixed ideas and predictable reactions, who, nonetheless, she recognized as possessing a solidity which acted as the cement which bound together the social disparities and contradictions of modern-day England. Colin, she knew, would have been contemptuous of them but looking around the table, she saw only a group of kindly, dutiful people, whose sons governed and died for the Empire, who served their country in Parliament, who saw no reason to lower their standards.

She was the youngest by twenty-five years, apart from the curate, a prematurely aged thirty-three-year-old, whose pained expression and sudden tics she recognized instantly. Shellshock, she thought, remembering Barney, remembering Dickon. He told her that he had taken a First in Greats at Cambridge, that splendid things had been predicted for him; she could see that now this rural retreat was probably as far as he would go.

She was wearing one of the dresses she had brought back with her from India. It was no longer in the height of fashion, but still more up to date than any of the other women's gowns. She wore the pearls her uncle had given her for her twenty-first birthday: two matched rows with a diamond clasp set with a large sapphire. They compared favorably with the jewelery of the other women.

How impossibly young she looks, Vernon thought. And how serious she is. Where does she come from? Watching the ease with which she turned from dull old

Colonel Jepson on her left to that strange young clergyman on her right, it was clear that she had been born and trained up to this sort of thing. Even if she had not . . . He was determined that he must push his suit harder: little Dora was ecstatic about her, which was as much encouragement from outside himself as he needed. So far he had not dared to enquire into her past, sensing in her a desire for privacy so profound that it would be almost impossible to plumb its depths. Perhaps he should make his intentions a little clearer, and thus give himself more right to ask.

Mary caught him watching her from the other end of the table and gave him a brief smile, gone as soon as started. She was afraid that she had allowed herself to be maneuvered into a compromising position by agreeing to come down to Norfolk with a man she scarcely knew, a man, moreover, from whom she had accepted gifts which, with hindsight, she could see it might have been better to refuse. The fruit, the books, the flowers: it had been such a pleasure to taste a little luxury again after so many months of deprivation that she had scarcely thought about it. But now she could see how unwise she had been. Acceptance was perhaps exactly the "encouragement" about which Mrs. Bentley had spoken. And there was the coat, which it would have been an almost unbearable sacrifice to refuse. She had been wrong to keep it, she could see that now. On the other hand, she told herself, listening to the clergyman as he reminisced about his university days, this *was* the twentieth century. In her relationship with Mr. Vernon, she had done nothing to be ashamed of. Besides, she liked him. Was that so very wrong?

She was impatient for the morning, when he would take her over the Haslingfield grounds and show her his plans for their improvement. He had spoken of water gardens, of lime walks, of some pavilion he was building, which stood beside a shallow lake. In a sense, it would be like going back to Misselthwaite. And thinking this, she realized that much of Mr. Vernon's attraction lay in his resemblance to Colin. Not physically, of course. But they both possessed a habit of enthusiasm, of eagerness. They were both so full of zest. She caught Vernon's eye again and looked down at her plate. Euphoria turned to

melancholy. Having allowed Colin into her mind, Dickon
inevitably followed. Without them both, she was a cripple, she recognized that. She was an emotional ampu-
tee, the best part of her cut off. If only it were possible for
her to go home to where she belonged: she dared not
try, knowing that she was too vulnerable at the moment
to withstand the pain it would cause her if they rejected her.

The morning room at Haslingfield was much brighter
and airier than the one at Misselthwaite. A woman's
hand was evident in the simple yet elegant furnishings,
the gleaming white paint, the chintzes. Above the mantel
hung another portrait of the former Mrs. Vernon, better
executed than the one in London; she sat beneath a tree
with dogs at her feet and a landscape of fields and woods
extending behind her. Apart from the painting, there
were no other pictures on the white walls, none of those
eccentric touches which were so much a part of Misselthwaite: no dusty paintings of girls with green parrots on
their finger, no carved ivory elephants or cushions housing a family of mice, no shrunken heads in a glass case
or maggotty little collections of birds' eggs in narrow-
drawered cabinets.

"Ah, Mrs. Thwaite," said Vernon, as Mary entered
the room. "I trust you slept well." He hoped she would
not ask him the same question; he might otherwise be
tempted to tell her just how distracting he had found it
to know that she lay asleep only a few doors away from
his room.

On a table in front of him lay an open portfolio. "I've
arranged for our designer to meet us here shortly," he
said. "Unfortunately his partner won't be with him, but
that doesn't matter. Now come and tell me what you
think about this, before we go and look at the place
properly."

Mary stood beside him as he discussed his plans. He
smelled of bay rum; he wore good tweeds and brogues,
every inch the country gentleman. She felt a sudden
yearning for the safety which she knew he would offer
if she allowed him to. Her attention was caught by the
edge of a drawing hidden by a design for a walled rose
garden. "What's that?" she asked.

"Charming, isn't it?" Vernon uncovered the illustration. "That's the elevations for the summer house being erected beside the lake."

Mary found that she was looking at a refined version of her own rough sketch, scrawled months earlier in the margin of a letter to Colin. For the first time, it occurred to her who Vernon's landscapers must be. How could she not have realized before? She had been privy to their plans for so long, she had shared in so much of their excitement as the business took off and expanded. Why had it not been her immediate thought when Vernon told her of his plans for landscaping the grounds of his country house?

And now one of them was here, would be joining them any minute. She could not cope with it. "I—I'm not well," she said. "I . . ." She put a hand to her forehead.

"My dear Mrs. Thwaite." Before she could say anything further, Vernon had opened the French doors and was leading her outside. "A breath of fresh air, perhaps. I trust that yesterday's journey was not too much for you. Or perhaps something you ate last night has disagreed with you . . ."

"No. It's . . ."

Woman's problems, Vernon thought. With two grown daughters, he was well aware of the inconveniences which women suffered. "Would you like to lie down? With a hot water bottle, perhaps?"

Suffused with embarrassment as she realized what he meant, Mary shook her head. "If I might just return to my room for a while . . ."

"Of course, my dear."

Mary turned back toward the morning room. Hiding away would only postpone the confrontation. She doubted whether Vernon would drive her back to London without insisting, however gently, that she look at his projected works. And he would naturally wish the contractor to be present as he did so.

But even as she was about to step through the windows, there were footsteps ringing on stone flags and someone whistling, and a man came round the side of the house toward them. "Mr. Vernon," he began, then stopped dead.

Mary pressed her hands against her breast. He was so . . . the only word which came to her mind was "beautiful." So beautiful. But then he always had been. He was taller than she remembered him, with the same brown shine on him as a horse chestnut which has burst from its shell. He came toward her, his rolling uneven walk sweeter and more touching than she could have ever imagined. He took her hands and held them to his chest.

"Mary," he said softly.

"Oh Dickon." Oblivious of Vernon, her eyes closed, she raised her head and felt his lips warm against her trembling mouth. "Dickon."

"My Mary," he said. Swiftly, he hugged her close then let her go.

Behind them, Mr. Vernon was talking. ". . . know each other?" There was astonishment in his tones.

"Used to, sir," Dickon said. "Once upon a time."

"And where was that, Mrs. Thwaite?"

"At Missel—in Yorkshire," Mary murmured.

Vernon sensed that the atmosphere had changed but was still too surprised at seeing little Mrs. Thwaite being embraced by what was, in all honesty, little more than a glorified gardener, to be able to analyze quite how. Perhaps he had been mistaken in the piano teacher. Perhaps her background was somewhat less elevated than he had assumed. Not that such a consideration would make him change his mind about her suitability to be his wife. Not yet, at least. A tactful word could be dropped, however. If she were to become the future mistress of Haslingfield, there could be no question of intimacies with the hired help, whatever the custom might be in Yorkshire. Presumably her family had hired the firm of Craven & Sowerby for the same reason as he had.

"Shall we go and inspect the works?" he said, trying to keep his tone genial, though he was still astonished at the familiarity she had accepted or, at least, shown no objection to.

"That would be lovely," Mary said.

"Aye," said Dickon.

He was not surprised to come across her here. Ever since he had seen her coming down the steps of Mr. Vernon's town house, he had known it was inevitable

that they would meet when eventually the right moment
came. This was obviously it. She was still much too thin,
but some of the edge of unhappiness he had noted in
her earlier, when he first caught sight of her in London,
had been smoothed away. He wished he could reach out
and touch her face. If he could just do that, he thought,
he could make do until they were alone. The longing
burned in him to feel again the woman he had dreamed
about for years. If only Mr. Vernon would go away.
"Shouldn't you be wearing a coat, Mary?" he said. "It's
none too warm."

Mary, Vernon thought indignantly. Who does the fellow think he is? The other one—Craven—was very
much more of a gentleman. "Let's go back inside the
house and I'll get the maid to bring it," he said. "Mr.
Sowerby, you won't mind waiting outside a moment
longer, will you?"

"Not in the least," said Dickon. He smiled his big
crooked smile at Mary. "I've waited long enough already, a few more moments won't hurt."

"My dear Mrs. Thwaite, I do apologize for him," Vernon said as they reentered the morning room. He
reached for the bellpull beside the hearth. "I can repri-
mand him, if you wish."

"There's no need," said Mary.

He looked at her and it was as though someone had
switched on a lamp inside her. It was most extraordinary:
she positively glowed. He decided that he would hesitate
no longer. Once back in London, he would insist on
taking her out to dinner and he would ask her to marry
him. If a simple matter like meeting Sowerby again
could cause her such delight, what would she look like
when she was mistress of his heart and his home? The
prospect was delicious. Waiting for the servant to bring
their coats, he moved toward her and put a hand on her
arm. "Mrs. Thwaite, are you fully recovered?"

"Recovered?" Mary could only think of Dickon, of
the love which had poured from him when he saw her,
as though a spring had been unblocked, a dam broken.

"A few moments ago you did not feel well."

"Oh," Mary said, recollecting. "Yes, indeed, Mr. Vernon. I'm better now. Much much better."

"I'm so glad." He helped her on with her coat, arranging the fur collar around her face, his hand lingering against her neck. It was a long time since he had touched a woman so young, and he found the thought of further physical pleasures quite intoxicating.

Outside, Mary heard Dickon whistling. A robin's call. A thrush's song. She felt as though she were one of the roses in the secret garden of their youth, growing quick and fair again, the dead wood cut away. She ran to the tall windows and stood straddling the threshold, half-in and half-out of the room. "Come on then, Mr. Vernon," she cried joyfully. "Show me your summer house beside the lake."

The three of them set off together, Mr. Vernon and Mary in front, Dickon keeping a little behind. In that coat, with the fur framing her face, she looked like a Tartar princess. There was a grin on his face which he could not have suppressed for any amount of money. She was back. That was almost enough. The rest, he knew, would follow. And meanwhile, in this if in nothing else, he had shown himself to be Colin's superior. Instead of blundering in, he had waited, had followed, had noted, as he had done so often on the moors above Misselthwaite. It did not do to rush. How many years ago had he told Mary that you had to move gentle and speak low when wild things were about? He laughed aloud for pure joy.

Mary turned and looked at him over her shoulder. Her answering smile was one of complicity. Her dark eyes shared his secret though what exactly that might be was still unknown. My little wench, he thought tenderly, smiling again at his own sentimentality, tha'art safe as a missel thrush with me.

They came to the crest of a rise in the ground. Below them, the ground fell away to a lake, with a stone bridge built at one end. A building stood to one side, reflected in the flat surface, a small Mughal temple such as Mary had ridden past many times in the fresh mornings of India.

"There, Mrs. Thwaite, what do you think of that?" Vernon said, coming to a halt in front of the group, raising his stick to point out the summer house.

But as he spoke, so did she. "Oh Dickon," she said. "It's fair graidely."

"Aye, that it is," Sowerby answered.

"I'll warrant it's th' graideliest one as ever was in this world." She spoke as if reciting from a much-loved childhood story.

"I never seed one as graidely as this here," said the landscape designer, staring at the music teacher.

"It's mine, isn't it?" Mrs. Thwaite said, and to Vernon's astonishment, she was flying past him, running across the rough grass, graceful as a deer, with Sowerby chasing after her, both of them laughing, leaping across the tussocks, she with her skirts flying, he following like a wild animal, a fox, running low to the ground, no longer a man but something wilder and more elemental, a force of nature, not to be gainsaid. Mr. Vernon shivered as he heard them laugh. Though not a fanciful man, he could have sworn that from the little temple he heard the swirl of pipes playing a pagan tune. At the door of the summer house, he saw her turn, saw him sweep her up into his arms, saw their faces meet, saw all his hopes disintegrate as he heard her say:

"Dickon. My darling Dickon."

And heard Sowerby reply: "Home at last."

16

"Dickon, does tha' like me?"

"I like thee wonderful."

Mary splayed her hand on Dickon's bare chest, just above the heart. She gave a small contented sigh as she burrowed her head against his shoulder. "You were the first person who ever said he liked me. It was in the secret garden: do you remember?"

"I remember everything."

"I'll never get tired of hearing you say it."

"Nor me of saying it."

"Never?"

"Never. Never."

"Oh Dickon."

Later, Mary said: "We'll have to tell Colin. Not about us, I don't mean. But at least where I am."

"He'll not understand why you didn't tell us."

Mary sat up, the sheets falling away from her. "But I *did*. I sent a long letter to my uncle, trying to explain about things, how I simply couldn't go on living with poor Barney when I didn't love him, and about the death of my little girl." Even to Dickon, Mary could not bring herself to admit how she had failed to love the child. "I wrote from Calcutta and said that when I got back to England I had to be on my own for a while and that I hoped he would understand."

"None of us knew any of this."

"But . . ." Mary held her face between her palms. "Oh dear. The letter obviously went astray. What must you have thought of me?"

"We reckoned you were busy with your new life."

"So how did you find out I wasn't?"

"Colin fancied he saw you in the street one day, and got in touch with Lady Gardiner when he realized how long it was since any of us had heard from you." Dickon reached for her and pulled her down beside him. "But I knew where you were. I saw you one afternoon, coming out of Mr. Vernon's house in London."

"Did you?" Mary remembered an afternoon, weeks ago, when she had been convinced that someone was watching her.

"I followed your cab, found out where you lived."

"Why didn't you tell me?"

"You weren't ready."

"It wasn't *you,* was it? Who sent me all those things: the books, the fruit?"

"Happen it might have been."

"You dear thing."

"And the coat."

"That really impressed my landlady."

"I'm right glad to hear it," said Dickon, "though it was *you* I was hoping to impress."

"Madame Zoe," said Mary. "How would a simple boy off the moors know about Madame Zoe?"

"She's got a shop just down the street from our office. I asked our receptionist about her."

"And I thought it came from poor Mr. Vernon."

"Poor Mr. Vernon. He's behaved like a gentleman, any road. Kept us on to do his improvements, in spite of everything."

"Yes. But we still have to tell Colin that we've met, even though we don't have to tell him that we . . ."

"That we love each other?"

"Mmmm." Love: what exactly did that mean? Mary was not sure she knew. Nor was she inclined to confess to a feeling she did not consider herself capable of experiencing. Being with Dickon was like fitting two pieces of a puzzle together, the setting right of a mistake which should never have been made. But was it love? Until she knew, she was reluctant to commit herself. She said slowly: "I can't believe that my letter didn't arrive."

"When should we speak to Colin?" asked Dickon. "What shall we say?"

"You could tell him the truth, that you saw me by

chance and followed me to where I was living, spoke to me, something like that."

"That might be best. He's been fair miserable without you, Mary. I reckon he'd be so pleased to have you back that he wouldn't ask too many questions. He's been looking proper peaky recently, just like he did when he was a lad. You could be just what he needs to bring him up to scratch again."

"I wonder." Mary's hesitation stemmed from a fear that she did not deserve either her present happiness with Dickon, nor the forgiveness of Colin and his father.

"He's up north at the moment. At the Manor. You could go up and see them."

"I can't. Not on my own."

"Leave it to me. I'll think of something."

"The way you always did."

"Aye."

After a while, Mary said: "Dickon."

"Yes, lass."

"Does tha' like me?"

"Oh Mary. I like thee *wonderful*."

A hazel-edged country lane, bare branches frizzed with young green. Bird song. Shells bursting miles to his rear, no louder than the pop-guns his little brothers used to play with. Somewhere, a voice singing. Twenty thousand Cornishmen shall know the reason why. Peace, of a sort. Then, leaning down to pat Jason's mackereled coat, his hand sank deep. Torn flesh and shattered bone. Intestines writhing in his fingers like bloody worms. A brave eye rolling. The delicate legs staggering in the roadway, while an incongruous robin sang in the hedge. The mouth opening to scream and scream again, the sounds echoing those emerging from his own throat.

He was jolted into wakefulness by Mary shaking his shoulder. "What is it? My God, Dickon, wake up!" Aghast, she knelt beside him, one hand lifted disbelievingly to her mouth.

His throat was still stiff with screaming as the gradual realization came that it was over, that instead of the stenching mud, the spilled guts, there was a loving woman at his side, linen sheets beneath him, blue bedroom curtains gently billowing against a vase of white narcissi.

"Jason." He shook his head. "I was dreaming of Mr. Craven's horse." And of Davey, young Davey with his bright fair head and countryman's cheeks, who had died with a song on his lips, while Dickon cowered in the mud and refused a helping hand.

"Was that the gray?"

"That's it."

"It's all right," Mary soothed, cradling him against her naked breasts. "It's over. You're here, safe."

Cruel as cold water, acceptance splashed over him. "I'm never going to be safe. Never again. Wherever I am, it's in my head, I carry it with me. I can't escape."

"Do you often have these bad dreams?"

"It's not a dream. That's what's so terrible. It's real."

"Once, maybe. Years ago."

Dickon squeezed her hand. "Always. Every time." He turned his head into her hair. In the past couple of years, the frequency of the nightmares had diminished almost to extinction. In the last month he had woken three times in the same panic of sweat and tears. Why should the foul images have begun to recur now, just when he finally possessed what he had so long desired? Was it because of his ever-present heart-deep fear that he would not be able to keep her?

Mary held him tightly, pressing her body along the length of his, trying to contain her own fear. Dickon had always been the keystone of their tripartite relationship, the nucleus round which she and Colin revolved. Yet, just now, he had been almost unrecognizable as Dickon, his limbs rigid, his face convulsed with horror. But if he could no longer be relied on to be strong, what certainty was there left? *I can't escape,* he said. Neither could she. Although it did not manifest itself in nightmares, she could not rid herself of the image of her daughter on her deathbed, could not forget the fact that she had been rolling on the ground with a stranger while Charlotte called for her. She would never be able to forgive herself.

"We're coming down to London the day after tomorrow," Colin said.

"We?" For a moment, Dickon's hopes flared. How much easier it would be for him and Mary if Colin were to announce that he had fallen in love, was engaged, was bringing his fiancée to London to be introduced to his friends.

"My father and I."

"To Fitzroy Square?"

"Of course. Look, why don't you come to dinner on Friday? Just us, nothing formal. My father will like to hear about the business from you. He never quite believes it when I say it's going well."

There was a pause. Dickon said: "May I bring someone?"

"What kind of someone?" Jealousy sharpened Colin's voice.

"A . . . friend."

"I hardly thought you'd want to bring an enemy to the house."

"A woman."

Colin swallowed. "I look forward to meeting her, old man." Up in Yorkshire, he defeatedly hung up the receiver. He'd always known that it would come one day, Dickon meeting someone, falling in love. But did it have to be so soon?

"I'm frightened," Mary said, as they mounted the four shallow steps to the front door. "They're my family, all I've got left. Suppose they turn me away."

"Why should they do that?"

"A woman who's run away from her husband? And since they didn't even get my original letter of explanation, they must have thought I didn't care enough about them even to let them know I'd returned. They're not going to welcome me with open arms after that, are they?"

Dickon took her by the elbows and brought her up against his chest. He wished she would talk about the little lass who had died, but whenever he tried to discuss it, she pressed her lips together and turned away from him. He imagined that when she was alone, she wept for her lost child; he sensed that over and above her loss, there was some sharper edge to her grieving. "Remember that they love you, Mary," he said. "We all love you. It's enough for us that you're back."

"I wish I could be as sure as you."

Dickon rapped at the brass knocker and, as soon as the parlor maid opened the front door, said: "Good evening, Grace. Don't announce us. We'll just go up and surprise them."

Grace began to speak, then caught sight of Mary. She pressed her fingers to her lips. "Oh," she exclaimed. "Oh, my dear Lord. Oh, Miss Mary, you're back."

"Hello, Grace."

"Oh, Miss Mary. Cook and I were ever so sorry to hear about your little girl. Them dratted Indian fevers. I knew no good would come of you going out there. Cook's cousin's boy's out there, and he says he doesn't think he's been on top of himself since he set foot on foreign soil."

"It's not a healthy climate," Mary said.

"Mr. Craven and Mr. Colin will be ever so glad to see you."

"I hope so, Grace."

The two Cravens were standing side by side with their backs to the coal fire when Dickon entered the drawing-room. As he walked toward them, Archie Craven said: "Dickon. My dear boy. It's good to see you."

"You too, sir." Dickon half-turned to where Mary hesitated on the threshold. "As I said, I brought someone with me."

Colin and his father looked beyond him at the figure which waited beside the door. For a moment, social smiles of greeting hovered on their faces, then Colin was moving rapidly across the thick Turkey rugs, his face alight. "Mary!" He embraced her roughly, tightly, crushing her against his shirt, her shoulders familiar under his hands. "Oh, my Mary."

"Dearest Colin." She stretched up to kiss his cheek, but he turned his face so that mouth met mouth. His lips were cold. She remembered kissing him one winter night, with the kitchen bell pealing through the darkness, summoning in the New Year. So much had happened since then. In the years since their last meeting, his resemblance to his father had grown more marked, though his eyes were still the same blacklashed slate gray his mother's had been. There were lines in his face which she had not seen before; she could tell immediately that he was not happy.

"This is . . . where have you been? How did Dickon . . . ?" Colin looked from one face to another. "How long have you . . . ?"

"I told you she wasn't ready," Dickon said, and through the blood which roared like a river through his ears, Colin thought he heard the sound of a thrice crowing cock. Betrayal: the word rang in his head. He wanted to beat the walls, drum his heels against the floor as he used to when a spoiled tantruming invalid. Don't leave me out, he wanted to shout. I belong with you.

". . . complete coincidence," Dickon was saying to Archie Craven, who held his niece's hands with both of his, his face alight with joy. "Saw her in the street—just as Colin had . . . back to her lodgings . . . enquiries . . . spoke . . . persuaded her to . . ."

To what? Colin would have liked to ask. The two of them had the shiny conjoined look of a double-yolked egg. How long had Dickon known where she lived? Why had he not told Colin?

He stood at the edge of the room, looking at the other three tableauxed against the flames in the grate. Mary was crying, her head turned into her uncle's shoulder, and Craven's eyes, too, were wet. On Mary's other side stood Dickon, his mouth curved in a wide smile which to Colin's jealous gaze, had the same possessive pride as a farmer with a prize sheep.

"But my dear child, why didn't you tell us what had happened?" Archie asked.

"I did. Of course I did. But it seems that a letter went astray." Mary explained, seeing again the airless hotel room in Calcutta, the *punkah* endlessly turning, turning on the ceiling, heat sweating through the blinds, insistent, debilitating. She had felt as though she were slowly being suffocated in a viscous soup of sorrow and shame. There had been voices outside the window, cries and shouts, a snatch of plaintive music, the clatter of wheels; if she lifted a corner of the blinds she could see the swarming street below, a vivid life continuing while hers disintegrated.

"We should mark your return in some way," Archie said. "Drink your health." Belatedly he recalled the deserted husband, the dead child he had never seen. There were ramifications to Mary's return which he felt diffident about exploring. What had she been doing in the months since leaving India? How had she lived? Where had she been? "We should wish that the coming years may be happier for you." He turned to his son. "Don't skulk over there like a thundercloud, Colin. Come and join us."

During dinner, they discussed with some animation the firm of Craven & Sowerby. To Colin's over-sensitive ear, Mary displayed a deeper knowledge of their business affairs than she could have picked up in casual chat with Dickon. They'd been meeting for weeks, it was obvious. And had excluded him. It was like the secret garden all over again, with Mary and Dickon busy about their private affairs, while he lay helpless on his bed, dying, for all they cared. There was an occasion on which he had raged, called her selfish, sneered when she had referred to Dickon as an angel. Which he was, he was. Articulate child though he had been, he had found it impossible then to describe his sense of being on the wrong side of the door, shut out. He felt it again, now.

"Do you have plans?" he asked his cousin. "Something you want to do with yourself?"

She hesitated, looking from him to Dickon and back again.

"What?" He leaned toward her. It was so wonderful to have her back again, though she had changed, had lost some of the edge which used to be one of her defining characteristics. "Tell us."

"I've taught myself to use a typewriting-machine," she said. "And to take down shorthand, though I haven't had much practice at it."

"You want to be a stenographer?" Archie Craven said, trying to conceal his concern. It was hardly a suitable occupation for his niece.

"Not just any stenographer," corrected Mary. "What I'm hoping is to find some up-and-coming firm in need of the excellent secretarial services I could offer, where I could make a positive contribution." She smiled teasingly at all three of them. "A landscaping company, for instance. With offices in Mayfair, perhaps."

"You want to come in with us?" Colin said.

"Would you have me?"

"Would we?" He leaped up from the table and began

to pace the carpet. "What do you think, Dickon? Do you think the three of us could work together? Would she listen to us or would she be always contradicting?"

"I reckon it's a good idea," Dickon said.

"But do we even need another partner?"

"I'm only offering to be a humble stenographer."

"Humble?" said Colin, lifting an eyebrow. "I've been thinking for a fair while," said Dickon slowly, "that we could just do with a woman's touch."

"But this particular woman?" All Colin's doubts had vanished. Although there were parts of his life which were less than satisfactory at the moment, he suddenly felt happier than he had done for some little while. "Could we stand her bossy ways?"

"I am *not* bossy."

"Why don't we give her a trial, same as we'd give anyone else? She could go down with you to that place in Surrey, see how we go about things, see if it suits her." Dickon wondered why Mary had not mentioned her idea to him before. Perhaps it had only come to her on the spur of the moment. Even so, it was a brainwave. Her letters from India had been full of good suggestions. He suspected that she would prove to be valuable in precisely the areas of the business where he and Colin were less astute.

"You can start as soon as you like," Colin said. "Next Monday?"

"I have one or two matters to clear up," Mary said. It would be unfair to desert her little pupils until other arrangements could be made for them.

Colin addressed Archie. "Don't you think it's an excellent idea, Father?"

Mr. Craven was so relieved at the knowledge that his niece was not going to be taking up a post in some seedy office in the worst part of London, surrounded by her social inferiors, that he gave immediate approval to the scheme. It led him neatly on to the subject which he had discussed some months before with Colin. "You should see the ballroom at Misselthwaite," he said to Mary. "We had it completely restored and redecorated for Colin's coming-of-age dance, but it has not been used since. It seems such a waste."

"I believe my father is hoping to marry me off," Colin

said. His pale face was flushed; hurt pride and injured hopes had caused him to drink more lavishly than was usually the case.

"There are a number of reasons why it would be a good idea to hold a Misselthwaite ball," Archie continued, ignoring his son's interruption. "In my . . . in your mother's day, my boy, dances at the house were a regular thing, and I should so much like to see the custom revived. People would make up house parties, you know, and bring their guests over. Since the war, there has been so much less of that sort of thing. But with Mary back . . . and your business doing so well, the three of you about to join forces—"

"And your birthday is coming up soon, Father," Colin said. "Don't forget your fiftieth birthday. That's an achievement in itself."

"For a long time, it was not one I ever thought I would live to see," Craven said somberly.

Colin reached into the inner pocket of his jacket for a fountain pen and notebook. "How many guests can we dredge up between us?" he said. "How many beautiful maidens for Dickon and eligible men for Mary?" Though he studied them both closely as he said this, neither showed any particular reaction.

"What about yourself, Colin?" asked Dickon.

"Exactly," said Archie jocularly. "A beautiful maiden for you is a priority. As the heir to Misselthwaite, you have a definite duty to perpetuate the line."

"Indeed, sir."

Mary was taken aback by the stricken look which briefly crossed Colin's face. Had the romantic interest of which Dickon had written so many months ago come to nothing? Had the girl, whoever she was, rejected him and thus broken his heart? Indignation at the girl's cruelty filled her yet she was surprised at her own feeling of relief. She wanted Colin's happiness, of course she did. But not at the expense of their closeness.

By the time they moved into the drawing room together to take coffee, it had been settled that there would be a dance held at Misselthwaite in early summer, as soon as the warmer weather arrived. While Colin threw himself moodily into an armchair, away from the fire, Craven and Dickon settled on a sofa, chatting idly.

Then Archie said: "Play for us, Mary. Sing to us. It's been so long since we heard your sweet voice."

He wished he did not feel so contented with his little circle since it was inevitable that it would once again be broken—and he tried to stifle the selfish thought that Mary belonged with them more than she could ever belong to someone else. Poor Major Sambourne: how unhappy he must be. And Mary too, of course, though she had so far resisted all his conversational efforts to find out what had occurred over the past months.

Mary obediently seated herself at the piano. Hands drifting across the keys, she softly sang first one old favorite and then another. "Pale Hands I loved," and "Genevieve," and "Drink to me Only." After a while, Dickon joined her and stood with one hand on her shoulder, his rich voice joining hers, before he sang alone: "Sweet Afton" and "How Happy Could I be with Either?" looking into the far corner of the room, one hand on his breast. And though he was the least self-satisfied of men, he could not help reflecting what a distance he had come, from the barefoot rough-headed lad from the moors to this elegant London drawing room. Colin, too, came over to stand on Mary's other side, and join their song, his light tenor sweet as milk among the melting sounds of soprano and bass. They smiled, not really seeing each other but remembering, thinking their private thoughts, content for the moment to be together again.

If only it could always be like this, Archie thought from his place on the sofa. If only things did not have to change. For a moment, he had a presentiment of disaster, but shook it off, taking another cigarette from the silver box on the table beside him and lighting it, watching the three through the thin blue smoke, remembering how they had been as children together, inseparable, indivisible.

17

Northerners move more slowly than the people of the south. Even though the war was now more than six years behind them, the return up there to the hospitable ways of pre-war years had been very gradual. Among the Yorkshire gentry who had been the Cravens' acquaintances, too many people had lost the taste for entertaining, some through bereavement, some because of change in fortunes. The Misselthwaite ball was greeted with eager anticipation. All over Yorkshire, silk dresses were taken out of their storage bags and tails coats examined for moth.

August that year was hot. For once, the wind which endlessly stirs the heather on the high moors had calmed; it was possible to have the windows on to the flagged terrace open long after the sun had gone down. Nor did the marquee erected in the garden whip and tug at its moorings like a ship anchored in a storm, the way so many of those present remembered it doing on the occasion of Colin Craven's coming-of-age.

In the Great Hall of Misselthwaite Manor, Mary stood beside Colin and his father. Their guests, many of whom had known her since she was ten years old, had heard enough of her sad history to believe that grief at the loss of her daughter had driven her back to the security of her own childhood home. It was not behavior to be particularly recommended, nor was it how most wives would react to such a loss, but it was certainly understandable and, in these modern times, even acceptable.

Besides, they whispered to each other as they passed beneath the huge central chandelier in the hall and up the grand staircase to the main guest suite where they were to leave their cloaks in the care of two undermaids, Mrs. Sambourne was so pretty. Almost, in the opinion of one or two, beautiful. Hair like the pale stems of wheat, eyes as dark as slate, flawless skin . . . "Passable, my dear," said the redoubtable wife of the Lord Lieutenant to a fox-furred dowager of her acquaintance, "not a patch on her mother, of course, but passable." She dabbed at her weatherbeaten complexion with a powder puff and added the discreetest touch of lipstick to her mouth. "Very passable."

"You knew the mother, then?"

"Met her a couple of times, after she became engaged to Lilias Craven's brother, Captain Lennox."

"I never met Mrs. Craven. All that business, her death and so forth, was while we were still attached to the Chancellery in Bonn, before Frank came into the Grange."

"Of course."

"Anyway, I'm glad to see young Mrs. Sambourne has the good taste not to wear any jewels," said the fox-furred lady, tugging at her corsets and wondering why they felt so much tighter than they had yesterday. "Given the circumstances, anything flashy really wouldn't do."

"The circumstances, Cynthia?"

"Well, you know what I mean," Cynthia whispered, as a group of younger women came in, laughing and chattering. "The Case of the Missing Husband and all that."

The Lord Lieutenant's wife ignored her. "A girl always looks well in pearls, and those—"

"A girl? My dear, she is—or *was*—a married woman."

"—are a particularly fine set." The Lord Lieutenant's wife was a close friend of Mr. Craven, who had asked her to do her best to scotch any gossip about poor Mary.

"A gift from the husband, do you suppose?" asked Cynthia, diverted, but keeping her voice low.

"The necklace is from dear Archie, as I understand it, and the earrings belonged to poor Lilias."

"Archie must be delighted to have her back."

"I believe he is."

"And up here, at least the poor girl needn't suffer any ostracism. We are, after all, a fairly broad-minded society."

"There is no reason, these days, why she should be ostracized anywhere. She's of good family, well-educated, well brought up. We must move with the times, Cynthia. After all, there are few of us without a skeleton or two in our closets."

And Cynthia, whose particular skeleton was well known though never mentioned by her Yorkshire neighbors, not only took the hint but stopped other gossip where she heard it.

It was rehabilitation of a kind. Nonetheless, Mary, who had a good idea of the way the conversations were likely to go upstairs, over the pincushions and the lavender water, found it something of an ordeal to be acting as hostess for her uncle and her cousin. At least she looked well and did them credit. Her balldress—by Madame Zoe—was of forest-green taffeta; the double row of pearls at her throat was matched by a pair of pearl teardrop earrings which had been Colin's mother's. She wore no wedding or engagement rings, only a baroque pearl set in plain gold on her right hand and, on her left, a ring of twisted gold strands, yellow, rose and white.

It was a gift from Colin and Dickon.

"It's us, do you see?" Colin had said, as she opened the box which he had handed her on her first day as a partner in Craven & Sowerby. "The three of us."

Behind him, Dickon had said nothing, though his crooked grin was as wide as a crescent moon.

"We had it made specially to commemorate the three of us working together," Colin said. "At Garrards, in Piccadilly. What do you think, Mary, do you like it?"

"I love it. I shall never take it off."

"I designed it myself," said Colin. "At first I thought of hearts or clasped hands or something of that sort, but I decided it would be too sentimental. The simpler the better: it's more *us,* don't you think."

"Speak for thasel'," Dickon said. "I'm not so simple as you make out."

"Do you know what I think?" Mary said to him, her forehead earnest.

"What's that, lass?"

"I think Colin should take it up."

"You're right, Mary," agreed Dickon, grinning. "Eh, I can see it now, the Royal Warrant over the door and painted along the front, in big letters, Colin Craven, Jewelery Designer."

"Do you know, I wondered about—" began Colin eagerly, before he realized too late that the others were teasing him.

"Remember when he was going to be an Athlete?" Mary said.

"And a Scientific Discoverer."

"And a Lecturer. And later we had the Olympic Skater and the Photographer and the . . . um . . . the Actor, when he was at Oxford."

"There was the Psychiatrist, too. An' don't forget the Trapeze Artist."

"You didn't, Colin." Mary's face was creased with laughter. "A *Trapeze* Artist? I don't believe it."

"He's made it up," said Colin. "Absolute nonsense: I never said anything of the sort."

"It were the spangled tights," Dickon said, straight-faced. "Fancied himself, he did, swingin' up there in pink underbritches with silvery bits on em."

"I simply said I thought I had the sense of balance that was needed to become a circus performer," Colin said in a dignified way, "and my legs are—if I say so myself—rather good," but the other two began to howl, falling over the office desks, gasping for breath with tears streaming down their faces. After a while, even Colin himself had to join in.

Remembering this, as more guests swept in through the big open doors to be greeted by their hosts, Mary found it difficult not to laugh aloud. She knew she did not deserve the happiness she felt. She had not earned the right to forget the bad years, nor the wrong she had done Barney and little Charlotte. Especially when Barney had acted with such decency. He had concocted some necessary business in England and then allowed himself to be discovered *in flagrante* in a Brighton hotel with a young woman paid especially for the purpose, in order that Mary might divorce him and thus retain a measure of respectability. Mary had found the whole episode embarrassingly sordid, particularly as she felt entirely to blame and it was then that Barney, the blood rushing beneath his fair skin, had confessed that he had not been entirely faithful and added that people who lived in glass houses shouldn't throw stones, should they, old girl? Mary suspected that what he really meant to say was: "Let him who is without sin cast the first stone," but she was nonetheless immensely grateful to him for behaving so well.

She did not speak of it to her uncle or cousin, afraid of their embarrassment, and hers. Nor did the guilt leave her, but guilt was as tiring to live with as grief, and for a night or two, here and there, she might, she thought, be allowed to push it to one side.

Through the open doorway of the ballroom, she glimpsed Dickon's russet hair. In tails, he looked—not handsome, because his features could never be described as classically good, but . . . beautiful, she thought to herself. He was, quite simply, beautiful.

Beside her, Colin murmured from the side of his mouth: "I hope I didn't forget to tell you, Mistress Mary, that you look ravishing tonight."

"You did, actually."

"Dance with me later, hm?"

"Lots of times. And before *I* forget, Colin, let me say I think you look pretty marvelous yourself."

"I do?"

Archie Craven pulled his gold watch from the pocket of his white waistcoat. "We've been here over an hour. I think you two young things might be released from greeting duty."

"Thank you, Father." Colin took Mary's arm. "A glass of champagne, I think—"

"Or two."

"Definitely two." He looked down at his cousin and felt a kick in his chest. God, she meant so much to him. Even on her worst days, when she was scowling, or out of humor, he loved her. Simply that. It was one thing he had over Dickon, for as he had predicted, the three partners had their differences. But whenever Mary began—metaphorically—to kick the furniture, it made no difference to him, whereas Dickon was both amazed and appalled, taking her bad tempers personally. With all his heart, Colin wished that things were different. He had guessed that she was conducting a love affair with Dickon and the certainty pained him whenever he thought of it, but for once in his life he had managed to keep his thoughts to himself. He pretended not to know; he hoped they were fooled. More strongly, he hoped that neither of them would end up being hurt. "Champagne, and then several turns around the floor. What do you say?"

"What I say is, I jolly well hope you've learned to do the foxtrot while I was away. The last time we danced it together I thought I should have to have surgery on my toes."

"My foxtrot is renowned the length and breadth of Yorkshire," Colin said.

"I'm sure it is. But not for its grace and style."

They went into the dining room where supper was being laid out on tables covered with a damask cloth. Standing in a corner, away from the servants, Colin raised a glass. "To you, Mary mine."

"To us, Colin."

They drank, arms linked together, staring into each other's eyes, silent. After a while, Colin leaned down and kissed her cheek. However much he might wish it, he was afraid that she could never be his, but nonetheless, there was a physical pull between them which he had never felt for any other woman. Oh, if only . . . For perhaps the first time since he had met Dickon, he saw the ties which bound the three of them together as chains, rather than as connecting links.

"Come on," he said suddenly. He tapped his patent-leather dancing pumps against the floor. "My feet are itching."

At the side of the ballroom, half-hidden by one of the gilded pillars which supported the gallery along one end, Dickon leaned against the wall and watched them. So dark, so fair . . . They made a good couple, the two of them, a right handsome one, if the truth be told, especially dolled up in evening dress, but she was his, not Colin's. The thought did not give him any satisfaction: his gain could only mean Colin's loss, and that did not please him. Unlucky Colin would never know what it was like to lie beside her in bed, to feel her small breasts in his hand, or kiss her soft belly until she moaned. He remembered his first sight of her, a scrunched up, sour-faced little miss with something so damaged inside her that he had made a vow then and there that he would

die rather than ever hurt her. She was like the kitten he
had found once, outside the back door of a farm where
he was delivering vegetables for his mother. Half-
drowned, it had been, and huge-eyed, its little face so
pleading, so vulnerable . . .

He straightened himself. This would never do. Another moment and he'd be blubbing like a baby. He
looked around for someone to dance with and saw a
plain girl, the daughter of a farmer over by Bowlby way,
sitting alone, trying not to look as if she minded.

It was later in the evening that Archie Craven stood
with his son at the door of the ballroom. All the windows were open to the warm night breezes and the
sound of laughter and conversation came from the lawns
outside, but the dance floor was still crowded.

"Young Dickon looks happy," Archie said.

"Doesn't he." And why shouldn't he? thought Colin.
He had Mary in his arms and was twirling her up the
middle of the room between two clapping lines of country dancers. "Who could blame him, when he dances
with my cousin?"

Stealing a sideways glance at his son's expression, Craven's heart leaped. As a young man, he would have
walked the world over to pick Lilias a blade of grass,
had she so desired. Was it possible that Colin . . . could
it be that after all . . . He cleared his throat. "Ever been
in love, my boy?"

Colin, his eyes still on the couple coming back down
the set, nodded. "All my life, Father. All my life."

"We have to delegate," Mary said, some months later.
"We've *got* to. Some of the paperwork, a lot of the routine stuff, could be given to an office manager." Her
brows were drawn together as she stood clasping a file
and glaring at Dickon.

"And I say we can handle the work between us,"
Dickon argued stubbornly. It was a sentence which had
been repeated several times already.

"The more successful the firm gets, the less we see of
each other," said Mary. "And one of the points about
joining forces was that we work together. Another is
that we ought to tailor each project to the individual
needs of the client."

"Isn't that what we've been doing?" asked Colin through the open door of his office in the next room.

"Not quite. The danger is that we'll get so swamped with stuff that we'll do what you've done here, Dickon." She slapped some papers down on the desk in front of him. "Look at this. These are exactly the same designs as you used for that place down in Surrey."

"So? I went down there and walked over the land with the owner," Dickon said. His face was red, though Colin could not tell whether with rage or embarrassment. "What he wanted was exactly what the chappie in Surrey wanted. Where's the crime in giving it to him?"

"But he's in Devon, and it simply doesn't work," Mary said. "Anyway, I know this place: I went to school with one of his daughters and I've stayed at the house. I couldn't believe my eyes when I saw that you were planning to set a delicate little ornamental pergola up against a great sweeping view of Dartmoor. It looks fine in Surrey but in Devon it'll look quite ridiculous. You need something heavier, something monumental in stone."

"Who says?"

"*I* say." Mary slammed her hand against the side of the wooden filing cabinet in the corner so that it gave out a hollow booming noise. "Me, Mary. Little though I might mean to you."

"What's that supposed to—"

"And what's more, you've even used the same costings as for Surrey."

"What's wrong with that?"

"But they're bound to be different, if for no other reason than that it's a lot more expensive to move the equipment and supplies we're going to need through those narrow Devon lanes, not to mention the distance from the nearest source of materials. You don't seem to have taken any of that into consideration in your estimates."

"Are you telling me I don't know how to do my job?"

Oh dear, thought Colin. Here we go.

"Of course I'm not." Mary stamped her foot with exasperation.

"Then what exactly are you saying?"

"That we're getting careless."

"We, lass? *We*? Far as I'm aware, you weren't involved in this project, neither was Colin. So at the end of the road, it's me you're bloody blaming, and nobbut me."

"In this instance, yes, you," Mary said. Her temper was up now and the scowl on her face was ferocious. "But we're all likely to do the same thing sooner or later, simply because we can't keep up with the volume of demand for our work. It's *good*, that we've got so many orders, but the reason we're successful is because we give individual attention. As soon as we start getting blasé—"

"Blasé, is it? What's that, a fancy word for sloppy?"

"Maybe it is," yelled Mary.

"In that case, mebbe it's better I—"

"Oh sit *down*, Dickon, and listen to what I'm saying. Which is that we cannot go on dashing all over the country *and* dealing with all the boring routine stuff. We need a bookkeeper, at the very least. And," she took a deep breath, "while we're on the subject—"

"What subject's that, then? How Dickon Sowerby don't know what's what? Is that what you're saying, lass?"

"*Don't* call me lass," Mary said.

"I always have."

"You don't call Colin 'lad,' do you?"

"That's different."

"Why is it different?"

Colin sank lower in his chair. Poor Dickon was falling into every trap Mary set him. Any minute now, he was going to utter the unforgivable word and then the fat really would be in the fire.

"Because you're a woman," Dickon said, all too predictably.

"A *woman*!" exploded Mary.

"Aye."

"So it's all right for you to patronize me, because I'm a *woman*, is it, but not Colin?"

"Patronize? What're thee on about, la—Mary?"

He's like someone playing Blind Man's Bluff, Colin thought, blundering about, never sure where the next buffet's coming from and incapable of avoiding it, even if he did.

"I thought I was an equal partner in this concern," Mary was shouting. "Please correct me if I was wrong, but I thought that, male or female, we all had equal status."

"Of course tha—"

"I know I haven't been in it as long as you have and, of course, I wasn't involved in the preliminary setting up and so on, but I believe I'm right in thinking that you incorporated a number of my suggestions, I *believe* you asked my advice which I gladly gave and was *delighted* to see that you took. But when one partner feels free to condescend to another in the manner you've been doing to me—"

"Condescending? What're you—"

"—when one partner clearly feels that women are somehow inferior to men, then perhaps it's time for me to go."

She doesn't mean it, old boy, Colin thought, at his desk next door. He was keeping his head down, not moving a muscle in case Mary turned on him next. She's goading you, that's all, trying to get a rise out of you—not that she's aware that that is what she's doing. She's looking for a reaction, but you shouldn't give her the satisfaction. She has no more intention of going than I have.

But Dickon was not privy to these unspoken messages. He half-rose. "Go? You mean . . . *leave* us?"

"It may be for the best," Mary said, pursing her mouth.

"Leave Craven & Sowerby?"

"The way things are going, yes, it might be the easiest solution."

"Colin," Dickon said. It was not a wail, but pretty close to one.

Colin straightened, tried to look serious. He had called Mary's bluff too often in the past not to be able to handle the situation. "Do you want us to take this as a verbal resignation, Mary?" he called through the open door. "If so, I'm afraid it can't take effect until we have it formally backed up in writing."

"What?" Mary was clearly disconcerted. She had forgotten about Colin.

"Correct me if I'm wrong, but listening to the two of you, a resignation is what it sounded like to me. And if you really feel you must go, then far be it from Dickon or me to stand in your way."

"But—"

"Don't you agree, old man?" Colin said loudly.

"Um—" said Dickon.

"It's a pity, really." Colin got up and came round his desk to stand in the doorway of Dickon's office, arms folded. "Because Mary does have such marvelous ideas. And she always knows exactly what she's talking about—as you were saying just yesterday, weren't you, Dickon?"

"Er . . ."

"But if Mary thinks she's being patronized, then obviously she's going to feel happier working somewhere else."

"I didn't exactly say that," Mary said.

"Sounded like it to me." Colin moved nonchalantly across the room. "Anyone want tea? I'll ask Fanny to bring some in."

As he went out of the door, Mary glowered at Dickon. He wanted to tell her that she looked beautiful when she was angry; some instinct made him think better of it. But it was true. That flush on her fine skin, above the cheekbones, and the way her hair quivered, her eyes flashed at him . . . They were going to a cabaret show together that evening, after dining at the Café Royal. He hoped she would be in a better mood. It was wrong of her, he reckoned, to speak to him like that, as if he were some kind of a servant, but maybe she didn't know she was doing it. But even so, whatever she said, he was a man and she was just a lass: she ought to show him more respect. He hoped she would come home with him at the end of the evening. He hoped that very much.

When Colin returned. Mary said: "There's another thing I want to talk about."

"What's that?"

"Nurseries."

"Don't tell me you're *enceinte,* Mary," Colin said.

A queer mottled color reddened her cheeks. "Don't be so ridiculous," she snapped. "And so vulgar."

"Then you mean nurseries for plants? Flowers? That sort of thing?"

"Of course I do. It seems to me that we could save a lot of money by supplying our own plants rather than buying them in. And we could also offer guarantees of replacement and so on much more easily."

"You're talking about capital investment."

"I know." Mary scowled. "But we should be expanding. Not much, but a little. We're certainly doing well enough—I looked at the figures last week and they're excellent. Now we need to plough profit back into the business. We need extra clerical staff, as I said, though that's not so much expansion as efficiency. But the nursery idea is—"

"An excellent one, if you ask me," Colin said. He wondered where she had picked up such a sense of good business practice . . . He was still marveling at the way she had insisted, right from the beginning, that they pay themselves a proper salary, where he and Dickon had been content to draw money for their personal needs when they needed.

"You do?" Mary had expected more opposition.

"Certainly. What do you think, Dickon?"

"Eh?" Dickon sounded bemused. She was a proper little businesswoman and no mistake—but he checked the thought. She would take strong exception to such a patronizing opinion. Sometimes he was bewildered by the speed of exchange between the two cousins. They seemed almost to read each other's thoughts. Occasionally he felt as though between them they were trying to take something precious away from him. "Yes. Mebbe. We'd have to talk about it more."

"Something else I want to talk about," said Colin. "That man who spent his holidays in France as a child and wants to recreate that kind of garden—do any of us know anything about French gardens?"

Nobody, it seemed, did.

"What I suggest," Colin said, "is that since Dickon has a bit of the local patois, he goes over to France and motors about for a week or so, has a look at the grounds of some of the palaces—Versailles and Fontainebleau, *par example*."

"France, is it?" said Dickon.

"It would be research, do you see? And a nice excuse for *une petite vacance*."

Dickon shook his head. "Not me."

"Why not?" asked Colin.

"I'll never go back there. Never. I've spent all the time in France that I want to."

"But that was ages ago. And anyway, it was different then. I thought you'd enjoy a bit of time off," said Colin. "Wine, women and song, old man: doesn't it tempt you?"

"Not in the least." Dickon's face was closed and stubborn. "From now on, England'll do me fine."

"Heigh-ho," sighed Colin. "Then I may have to go myself."

"When would that be?" asked Mary.

"I thought in a couple of weeks."

"Can I come too?" Mary said suddenly. "I've never been to Paris: it would be wonderful to see the Louvre, the Left Bank, Notre Dame, all the things you read about in the papers."

"Sounds like a good idea." Colin raised his eyebrows at Dickon, knowing better than to suggest in any way that he sought Dickon's permission for Mary to accompany him. When Dickon nodded, he added: "On second thoughts, an *excellent* idea."

"I don't know about this," Dickon said. He stared doubtfully at the tiny stage where an enormous man strutted back and forth dressed in a sequinned flapper dress. A diamanté band with a feather stuck into it was tied round his shaven head and his grotesquely lipsticked mouth bawled a song of such depravity that Dickon thought he must be hearing wrong.

"Don't know about what?" Mary asked.

"It's not right. Not with ladies present."

"Don't be so old-fashioned," said Mary. "Or so Yorkshire."

"I am Yorkshire, Mary, and I say this isn't right."

"I think it's rather amusing, actually." Mary's voice was contentious.

Dickon sighed inwardly. She'd been like this recently: sharp and edgy, seemingly ready to quarrel about the least thing. Something was bothering her, he could tell. "Mistress Mary, quite contrary," he said.

"What?"

He tried to put his hand over hers but she snatched it away. "*What* did you call me?" she said dangerously.

The blackness of her eyebrows against the golden color of her skin and the fairness of her hair . . . "Nothing much."

There was a misery inside him. He had thought, perhaps simplistically, that once they finally came together, as he had always hoped they would, everything would be wonderful and they would live happily ever after, like the fairy stories she used to read aloud when Colin was not well. But it had not turned out like that. For him, it was enough just to be near her. He wanted the things most men, he imagined, wanted: a fireside, children, food on the table and a loving wife. By loving, he supposed if he was honest, he meant sexually loving, as well as heart loving, and most of the time, Mary was both. But she was not his wife, and there were no children. She had refused to marry him, although, now that she was free, he'd naturally asked her; he had swallowed his prejudices and suggested she move in with him if she was not yet ready to remarry, but she had rejected that idea as well. When he asked her why she had looked away and played with the gold ring he and Colin had given her, and said nothing.

"What can you expect?" his mother had said, when he had blurted out the hurt this caused him. "What can you expect, son?"

"I love her, Mother. And I know she loves me." Even though she would never say so, never admit her need for him.

"But . . ." Susan Sowerby had laid a gentle hand on her boy's rough red hair. ". . . she's a lady, Dickon. And you're a—"

"—a man," Dickon had said, his inability to change things already choking him, the words squeezing painfully from his throat. "A man as good as any other. And better than some, though it's against my beliefs to say so."

"She knows that."

"Then why, why does she turn me down?" Dickon wished he were a child once more and could bury his head in his mother's breast. She had always made everything come together again, when things temporarily shattered, but this time, he knew, she could not.

"You have to face the fact, son, that she'd never marry the likes of you. Not because she doesn't know what a fine man you are. Not because she doesn't love you—it's plain as the nose on your face that she does—but because even the bravest woman would quail at the thought of going against her own class and her own kind."

"But—"

"And those are things which love can never overcome."

"Not Mary," cried Dickon. "She's too strong to take notice of such things."

"She's a woman like any other."

"I won't believe that she won't have me because I'm not her social equal. Not until she tells me so," and Dickon remembered standing among the horses in France with Subaltern Forster and discussing the brave new world they were fighting for, where everyone would be equal and snobbery and class prejudice would have been swept away.

"It's not fair of you to force her to give her reasons," Susan said.

"Why not?"

"She'd find it mortal hard to tell you she didn't think you matched up to her socially—for all that it's the truth. Best settle for what you've got," said Susan and he looked up sharply, wondering if his mother had any notion of the dazzling moments he and Mary had shared and seeing from her face that she had.

Settle for what you've got . . . while the man on stage behaved in a most indecent manner with a silk stocking and a bunch of grapes, Dickon sat hunched on the too-small gilt chair and knew that what he had got was not enough for him. He remembered another of Mary's stories: about a fisherman who was granted three wishes and how they all went wrong. I only wanted but one wish, he thought unhappily. And although it came true, it seemed to be going wrong too.

His mother had been right. He wasn't sophisticated enough for Mary. Not quick-witted and clever enough. Not well-born enough. Not like Colin. And there were the dreams. He knew his nightmares frightened her. They frightened him. And since he had realized that what he had so much longed for was unlikely to come true, they were getting worse, more frequent. His professional sense was being called into doubt, too. Mary had been absolutely right about the design for the chappie in Devon: he *had* taken a short cut, used plans already drawn up for another client. Sometimes he started to cry, for no reason, sitting in his little house in Pimlico, sobbing his heart out. Calling her name. Beating his fist against the table at the wrongness of things, the unfairness, while Beggar growled softly and nudged his foot. Not that he cried when Mary was there, of course, though by God, he sometimes felt like it, so hopeless were his dreams. But it didn't do for women to see the weakness of their menfolk. He hadn't cried for years and now he seemed to be at it every few days. He wondered if he ought to visit a doctor. Recently, he had been haunted by a sense of doom, as if something heavy was about to fall and crush him. It had been like that at the Front, the same kind of feeling that however hard he tried, he couldn't escape from whatever it was.

"I'm sorry, Dickon." Mary put her hand on his arm. "I'm sorry about being so bad-tempered. Not just this morning, but now. And you're right: that man is rather beastly, isn't he?"

"He is that."

"We could go," she said softly.

His flesh stirred at the meaning in her eyes. He touched the back of her hand with his finger.

They got up and pushed through the crowded room toward the exit. At one, an unruly group of effeminate men objected as Dickon's coat caught at the edge of their table and threatened to overturn it. He stared down at them with contempt: one of the fellows had plucked his eyebrows like a woman's, and another was wearing rouge, he'd have sworn, with a bead hanging from his ear. Disgusting. Degenerate. He hated that kind of thing. He'd seen enough of it in the army to last him a lifetime. Even been approached himself, once, by a captain who'd

been at the next table in a pub one evening, when he'd
decided he couldn't stand the company of his fellow soldiers for another minute. He'd been nice enough, at the
start. They'd talked of books and that, about the way
the world would be when the war was over. The officer
had ordered a bottle of wine and they'd shared it.
Dickon hadn't had the least idea until they came out
into the street that the other man was that way inclined.
He'd been a gentleman about it, not forced himself on
Dickon or tried to pull rank, nothing like that. Nonetheless, the encounter had left him feeling soiled, even
though he hadn't even shaken the chap's hand.

Making love to her was so far removed from a merely
physical act that he could not express it even to himself.
It had an element that was almost religious. Part of it
was a yearning not just to be with her, but to *be* her,
even though he knew that in some way, he already was,
just as she was, in a certain sense, him. When she moved
under him, he was as awed as a priest performing some
mystic ceremony. When she called his name, it was as
though the gods cried out. And when his guts melted,
when he rushed, gushed, overflowed into her adored
body, he was at once god and sacrifice, pained as well
as pleasured, at once freely soaring above the earth and
bleeding on the altar with a knife in his heart.

"Do you love me, Mary?" he asked, needing to hear
it said.

"Mmm."

"Say you love me," he urged, but she did not, nor
ever had.

She cried, afterwards. When he asked her why, she
said she didn't know. He thought she did. Perhaps she
felt the same inexpressible unfulfillable yearnings as he
did. He found himself wondering about the young men
at the cabaret. What they did together he was not sure,
but he could not imagine that they could feel anything
like his own ecstasies. He hoped Mary had not noticed
them or, if she had, that she had not realized what kind
of creatures they were.

18

They drove from Calais to Paris, taking their time. It was a new experience for them both: each wondered how it was that they had never been together away from home before now. The first evening, they reached a small town and put up at the first hotel they came to, drawn by shabby peach-colored plaster, wooden balconies, shutters in faded gray. Wisteria climbed untidily over the front; there were cobbles in the courtyard, and the stamp and whinny of horses behind the main building.

They booked adjoining rooms. The proprietress spoke at great length about the local amenities—the ancient church, the river, the Roman antiquities in the little museum—before handing over the keys. Tired, they went down to dinner early and sat alone in the tobacco-and-garlic scented dining room, while outside, people at small tables drank *digestifs* and talked zestfully about nothing very much. There was a sense of gusto about the way they discussed life's small mundanities which, more than anything else, proclaimed that this was not England.

Colin ordered the local wine, which came in a tall carafe. While waiting for their food, they ate crusty bread and hard fierce olives. Wine softened the abrasions which occasionally lay between them. As they waited for coffee, Colin put his hand over Mary's and said: "You're my best friend, you know."

"What about Dickon?"

"Him too. But you and I are cut from the same cloth: we understand each other better than he'll ever understand either of us."

"That's very true."

"Are you happy, Mary?"

"Do you mean now, this very minute?"

"That'll do to start with."

"Then yes, Colin. I am. I'm always happy with you."

He twisted the three-stranded ring on her finger. "It's always been that way, hasn't it? Ever since we were children."

"Even when we were fighting."

"Perhaps especially then." They laughed, pleased with each other, with this place at this time.

"Shall we take a turn down to the river that Madame was so insistent we should see?" Colin asked, as they wandered out into the foyer.

"Why not?"

They strolled through quiet streets until they came to an old stone bridge across the river. It was almost dark, the fading light reflecting on water where swans fought effortlessly against the swirling current. Hyphens of light shone in the shuttered windows of houses already made indistinct by nightfall; honeysuckle trailed over walls of gardens which backed on to the river, scenting the breeze. Further down, on the opposite bank, untidy willows leaned over the water and a few swallows still swooped and circled in the search for insects. A bell tolled the hour from a nearby church, the sound rippling across the water meadows as it must have done for hundreds of years.

"How still it is," Mary said.

"You can hardly tell that the place was in the thick of the fighting only a few years ago."

"If we looked, we'd probably find enough reminders," Mary said. "Madame was saying that some of the houses further down the street had been damaged by shell fire."

"Strange that Dickon is so dead set against coming here."

"He's still very fragile. Still has terrible nightmares."

Colin did not want to think about how she knew. He envisaged her in bed with Dickon; like a knife the memory of her sitting dressing-gowned against the pillows of his bed came back to him. "I wish we could have stayed like that forever," he said.

She followed his thoughts so closely that she must

have been thinking the same. "Things change. It's part of growing up."

"I never wanted to, though lots of people do. Boys I was at school with, for instance, chaps at Oxford: they couldn't wait to be men. Whereas I, I've always wanted to hang back, to say, 'Just a minute, not so fast, let me enjoy this, let me take my time.' "

"Me too." Mary turned to face him, leaning one elbow on the weathered stone parapet. Her hair blew softly over her eyes and he reached up to stroke it away. His hand lingered on her cheek.

"Mary . . ."

She leaned toward him. "Colin."

Knowing her so well, he sensed in her some purpose, some determination. There was wine on her breath; light from a window in the nearby houses centered her dark eyes. Excitement flickered in his belly. He brought her closer to him and kissed her mouth. It was cool, yielding. He could feel the softness of her tongue. Breathing deeply, he cupped the back of her head and held her face to his. Every strand of her silky hair seemd to vibrate under his fingers. "Mary," he said again, his lips moving on hers as he spoke. Under her thin dress, he was aware of the roundness of her breasts.

"Shall we go back to the hotel?" she said, her voice quiet.

Somewhere a dog barked, a woman shouted. Possessed, he took her hand. Beneath them, the river chuckled thickly as it slid between the ancient arches of the bridge. They walked past the bright-lit windows of bars, past a black-skirted *curé* who murmured as he scuttled by, past tables set out behind potted box hedges where dominoes clicked and glasses clattered. Back at the hotel, they crossed the foyer to the stairs. The dining room was crowded now; in the lounge, a woman sang with melancholy of lost love and dead flowers.

Outside Mary's room, they paused. Colin put his arms around her, surprised at how slight she felt in his embrace. Yet, at the same time, how solid. Again, and more strongly, he was aware of some undivulged purpose in her, dark and fierce, not to be gainsaid. Her hands were on his back, her lashes touched his cheek. The need for her was explosive. He reached behind her and turned the handle of the door, then lifted her. Carrying her inside, kicking the door shut behind him, he laid her on the bed. Looking down at her, he knew that this was the defining moment. If they went on with what had been begun, what waited to be continued, there could be no going back. He had a second of time to decide whether to step back and away, or to lie down beside her and do with her in reality the things he had so often done in imagination, and then accept the consequences such action might bring.

She lay against the pillows, her face unshielded by the protocols of every day. Her mouth seemed swollen by his kisses; her eyes invited. As though sensing his hesitation, she tugged gently at the neck of her dress so that it opened wider. He saw the spill of her breasts. Wonderingly, he reached out to touch the white skin. In that moment she was transformed for him, no longer Mary, cousin, friend, but Woman, all women, mysterious and new.

He fell on to the bed, pulling at his clothes, speaking her name over and over, as though it were a lifebelt to which he needed to cling. She found herself showing the way, and was astonished at his lack of knowledge. He came as soon as he felt the surrounding warmth of her, barely inside her body, but almost immediately was ready to take her again. Again she guided him and this time it was a longer, more reciprocal pleasure. At his climax he murmured her name and then Dickon's, and she thought of how, even here, in this most intimate of sharings, there was always the three of them, and never simply two.

They drove on to Paris. Colin took her to dinner at Maxim's and afterwards to the Moulin Rouge. His experience of Paris was heightened by the knowledge that he had woken beside her that morning and would fall asleep, sated, beside her at the end of the day. Yet his physical pleasure was not unalloyed. He was disturbed by the swells of her body: the fleshiness of breasts, the roundness of buttocks, the soft doughiness of stomach. She was lovely, he knew, but he could not appreciate her beauty. And he knew also that he did not satisfy her, that he could not produce in her the same shuddering pleasures that he himself experienced. Although she never said so, he knew she loved him, but he did not think she took the same enjoyment from him. Perhaps her husband had been brutal; perhaps she had been traumatized by the loss of her child. He had read enough to know that for women, the fear of childbirth often overlaid the pleasures of lovemaking. Once, he spoke of preventative measures, thinking this would ease the tensions he sensed in her but she grew angry, shaking her head violently on the pillow, shouting, and he did not bring it up again.

One morning, she stayed late in bed, refusing breakfast, saying she felt unwell, so he went walking about the city. The grace and exuberance of its architectural landscapes attracted him in a way that London did not. Everything, the open air cafés, the elegant women, the flower-sellers, the music on the streets, the rich display of the shop windows, spoke of a tolerance of the frailties and frivolities of the human condition which contrasted strongly with the pinched hypocrisy at home. In the Faubourg St Honoré, he passed a shop selling luxury goods intended for those who already had everything they could possibly need: enameled cuff-links, silver hip flasks, yew-bladed letter openers with lapiz handles, crystal paper weights. On impulse, he went in. He loved giving presents, far more than receiving them. Examining the discreetly lit glass shelves, he saw a cigarette box of fine green shagreen, lined with cedar wood and bought it for Mary. For Dickon, he bought a malacca cane with a silver head. He could just imagine the dear old chap saying: "Eeh, there's grand for you," something like that, and never making use of it, but pleased just the same to have it. He bought cufflinks of jade for his father, a heavy silk scarf for Medlock. She would be able to show it off among her friends at Thwaite and thus get double the pleasure. Further down the street he passed a *chocolatier* and bought a heart-shaped box of chocolate truffles for Mary.

By the time he returned with his purchases to the hotel, she was up, pale and heavy-eyed. They were to spend a couple of days in the country outside Paris with an old friend of Archie Craven's: from there they would drive out to Versailles, to examine the grounds, and visit

a number of private gardens in the area, to discuss design and organization, ways and means.

Their business concluded, they returned to a hotel to
spend a day or two of holiday, since neither had ever
visited Paris before. They went one evening to the
Opéra, to hear *Otello*. Sitting in the darkened amphithe-
ater, Mary took hold of Colin's hand while the Moor
sang his impassioned way to murder and tragic death.
Do I feel jealous? he wondered, as her fingers pressed
his and, on stage, Iago fanned the fires of Otello's suspicion. Does it disturb me that Dickon has made love to
my cousin?

He thought it did not. His own love for her lacked
that element of worship which existed in Dickon but it
was something he could not grudge his friend. Perhaps
he was abnormal in this but he could not conceive of
himself being jealous of Dickon. Once, maybe. There
had been times in childhood when he would gladly have
spirited Dickon to some desert isle in order to keep
Mary at his side instead of out in the fresh air of the
secret garden. But that was years ago. While Otello wept
over the body of his innocent wife, Colin decided that
he did not feel strongly enough about anything to kill
for it. But he had no need to. Mary, his father, Dickon,
Misselthwaite: his loves were all unthwarted. Even when
Mary had sailed for India he had been angry rather than
desperate. In his heart, he had always known that sooner
or later she would return. In the darkness of the audito-
rium, he pondered the possibility of her remarrying another man and leaving once more . . . but she would
not, he was certain. It occurred to him, not for the first
time, that there were ways in which he might ensure that
she stayed. He had not thought she would be amenable
to them but now, as the music reached a somber climax,
as Otello drew his sword and prepared to die, as Mary
clutched at his arm, he wondered whether things had
changed. If they had, how well it would fit with what he
perceived as his duty.

They walked back to their hotel arm in arm. "What
it must be like," Mary sighed, "to be so passionate, so
involved."

"Are you not, then?"

"Not with anything," she said. "There are people I

love, of course . . ." she pressed his arm against her side
". . . but I fear I must be a very cold fish. Perhaps I lack
some essential element."

It was so exactly what he himself had been thinking
that he stopped. They were in a tiny deserted square lit
by gas lights in moon-white globes; all around them, narrow houses leaned inwards, enclosing them. Impetu-
ously, he grabbed both her gloved hands and pressed
them to his heart.

"Mary!"

"How gallic you've become, *Monsieur* Craven," she
said, laughing.

"Listen." He raised her hands and kissed them.

"And so gallant."

"Don't," he said. "Don't laugh. I was never more serious in my life."

"What is it?"

"Marry me."

The laughter died from her face. She stared up into
the tangled branches of the plane trees which stood
around the square. In the white light of the gas lamps,
her face was pale, considering. "But we're cousins.
First cousins."

"Why should that matter? Think of it, Mary. You and
me—and Misselthwaite. It's so suitable."

"Suitable," she echoed sadly. "It's that, yes. But is it
right?" Her voice was so low that she might have been
talking to herself.

"If you mean Dickon . . ."

"I didn't. But go on." She sagged against him and
sighed a little, as though in relief that something desired
had been achieved.

"If you mean Dickon . . ." Colin found himself floun-
dering. It was a little thick to propose to a girl and immediately suggest that if she wished to, she could
continue to sleep with another man. For himself, he genuinely did not mind. And Dickon: surely he too would
see the advantages of the plan. After all, he could hardly
imagine that Mary would marry him, could he?

He could. And had. The frozen look on his face, the
movement of his mouth, when she told him that she was
engaged to Colin smote Mary to the heart. She had re-

fused his proposals in the past, assuming that he would understand the social impracticalities of such a marriage. It was not that she hesitated to defy the system in which she had been raised, simply that it did not occur to her to do so. The love she felt for Dickon was elemental rather than pragmatic; her feelings for Colin were more complicated. For both, her need was ungainsayable. Now she saw that Dickon had truly expected that they would live together as man and wife. It was impossible for her to spell out to him why this was not feasible. She hoped that one day he might understand. She loved him. His pain was terrible to see, the worse for not being expressed. She longed to hold him against her heart, to soothe and comfort him. "I'm sorry," she whispered.

He did not reproach her. "I'd thought we'd get wed," was all he said, looking down at the floor. "I thought . . ." He could see how far ambition had outstripped practicality. What made it worse for him was the fact that although she did not give expression to such an opinion, he was aware that she shared his own view. How could he, a cottager's son, have imagined for an instant that a lady like Mary would consent to be his wife?

But he had. He had.

Once, in the Misselthwaite woods, he had found a fox caught in one of the gamekeeper's traps. The mangled paw was beyond repair. He had killed the animal as cleanly as he could, but not before he had seen—and shared—the agony in its eyes. This was far worse. He knew now why his nightmares had returned: in the place where he kept his most private thoughts, he must always have been aware that he could perhaps have but he could never hold her.

She reached a hand toward him. "Dickon, you know that I . . ."

"What?" If she said she loved him, perhaps he could endure this more easily. Because truly he understood that they could never have been man and wife, even if for a while he had been mad enough to believe that they could. He moved toward her. "What is it, Mary?"

"I . . ."

"Yes?" He took her gently in his arms. Her bones seemed more brittle, now that she was no longer his. He looked into her eyes. If she would admit it, he thought he would be able to carry on.

"I . . ."

"Tell me."

"I'm sorry," she repeated lamely. "So very sorry."

"I love you," he said. Perhaps he was luckier, after all, than she was. He could love and say so; she could not.

He went away. He did not tell them where. He traveled as far north as he could and, for nearly a month, he and Beggar tramped the heather-clad hills of Orkney, like yet different from the moors he loved so well. As darkness fell each evening, it was not difficult to find a crofter willing to give him shelter and food; by day he walked with no more than a slice of bread and cheese in his pocket, and thought about the future. He faced a choice, perhaps the final one. To stay with them, or to go. But he knew he could not leave. Where else would he turn? Who would have him? The world beyond the other two was pale, ghostly, another zone of reality, filled with insubstantial shapes. Even his family lived in that unfocused region: his mother, his brothers and sisters. Mary and Colin alone conferred color and validity. He could no more break away from them than he could have sprouted wings and flown. He came to terms with the fact that he was enchained. During the years at the Front, he had promised himself that he would never again follow another's orders. He would arrange his own destiny. He would remain outside the stockades behind which people liked to barricade themselves because it was easier to have someone thinking for them than to think for themselves. Now, as he examined the last few years, he recognized that instead, he had willingly walked into a cage, one made all the more secure because its door stood wide open. He could leave whenever he wished. No one would make the slightest attempt to prevent him going, which was precisely why he would stay.

For a while, he contemplated killing himself. He had faced death before: it did not seem so very dreadful, out here, in these lonely hills. With the spring of heather under his feet, bird song and scudding cloud above, it would be easy to disappear. No one knew where he was;

it might be years before his body was found and identified. Only the thought of his mother's tears held him back.

And something else.

Standing to one side of his mind, just beyond his vision, knowledge waited like a polite stranger to introduce itself. One day—not yet, but soon—it would step right up and shake him by the hand. He thought he could wait that long. As the days passed, his pain did not lessen but he grew more adept at handling its unwieldy bulk. With only Beggar for undemanding company, the long vistas of hill and water and wide pale sky worked upon him like a healing balm. Each night he slept without dreaming. By the end of four weeks he had achieved a kind of peace.

When he returned, they were married. It had been a quiet affair, Mary told him. Archie Craven had been informed by telegram, otherwise there had been no guests, no celebrations. She knew he would understand, she said, but he did not. Not really. Where was the point in keeping quiet about what should be the most joyous of occasions? Perhaps she felt embarrassed because of the pomp and expense of her first marriage and how it had come to nothing in the end. He thought of how he had hoped to make Mary his wife; of the chapel at Misselthwaite, crammed with his brood of siblings, the people he and Mary had known since childhood. He thought of his mother's blue eyes filled with pride and daffodils blowing in the churchyard; he cursed himself for a sentimental idiot.

Marriage did not seem to have changed the working relationship between the three of them. Mary and Colin, who had for the moment taken up residence in Fitzroy Square, appeared no more affectionate to each other than previously, nor less affectionate to him. There was no attempt by either of them to shut him out. Spending the long evenings alone, he sometimes wished there had been. It would have helped, perhaps, if he could hate them but he could not. He wanted to go home. He saw himself as condemned to a lifetime of standing on the edges of someone else's existence. It was not to be borne.

With the ever-increasing improvement in communications, he decided that there was no need for him to be in London at all. As soon as they had settled on a person to take over the management of their business affairs, he would let out the small house he owned in Pimlico and return to Yorkshire. The gorse-covered moors called to him once again; each morning he woke with images of curlews and badgers in his head, rain-lashed granite and rabbit-nibbled turf. He had enough money put by to buy another house for himself, somewhere with a garden he could tend. He had no intention of abandoning the business, but increasingly he longed to wake without the clamor of other people in his ears. He wanted to look from his window and see space, see quiet, not houses and pavements and bustle. London tired him: on the moors, it was possible to go for a week without seeing another soul.

Colin was delighted when he told him of his decision. "That's marvelous," he said. "I was afraid Mary would be lonely . . ."

"What do you mean?"

"She's going to move back soon too."

"What? But . . ."

"She's decided she's had enough of London for the time being," Colin said. "She says there are too many people, too much noise."

"Does she now?"

"She says she needs space around her. She's restless for the moors, you see, and for Misselthwaite."

"Aye, I know how she feels."

"And if you're there too, old man, it would be company for both of you. If you want it, of course. I'm not suggesting you spend all your spare time together—I'm sure both of you will have other things to do, and Mary, as you know, has a mind of her own, but I know she'll be thrilled that you'll be about."

"What about you?" Dickon said.

"I shall have to divide my time," said Colin cheerfully. "Half the month down here, half up there."

"I'm not trying to get out of the business, you know."

"Good Lord, I never thought for a moment that you were."

"I'll carry on as before, as far as possible."

"Of course."

"Even come down here from time to time. But I'll base myself up there from now on, if you don't mind. I thought we might set up a branch office, if you agree."

"You and Mary."

"Well, I—"

"An excellent idea. Just what we need. A lot of our business comes from the north, after all, and with you two right there, it can only be an advantage for us."

Colin's expression showed nothing except concern for his wife and for his friend. Either he was the most generous-spirited of men, or a complete innocent, Dickon decided. Did he really think it was a good idea to push together two people who until recently had been conducting a love affair, who were bound together by the strongest of ties? Or did he not care what passions proximity might rekindle between them?

Looking at his friend, Dickon felt a worm of doubt creep into his mind. It wasn't natural. It didn't make sense. There was something else, there had to be. But Colin's gaze was clear, his fine features unworried.

In truth, Colin *was* worried. Of the three of them, he was the least trammeled by conventions. He came from a class which, while not aristocratic, nonetheless shared many aristocratic traits, among them the unacknowledged assumption that its members were free to live by their own rules. Colin was well aware that Mary and Dickon had been sleeping together until—for reasons he did not feel it necessary to explore—they had stopped. It seemed more than likely that they might do so again; if it contributed to their happiness, then it contributed to his own. Especially given the circumstances in which he himself operated. A love affair between Dickon and Mary was, he had decided, a love affair between all of them. For him, the *three*ness of them was one of the essential factors in their interrelationship. Which did not, and could not, stop him from suffering occasional pangs of enviousness. What he could not decide was whom he envied more: Dickon or Mary.

So it was decided, and by the time August came, Dickon had found and purchased a cottage three miles from Thwaite, and installed himself in it. By then, an efficient manager for the London office—Lewis Phillips—had been hired, Mary and Colin had been married for more than two months, and Craven & Sowerby, Landscape Artists, was flourishing mightily.

Dickon, settled in with his animals, his books and pieces of furniture, visits from his mother, a local girl found by his sister Martha to clean and cook for him, was far from unhappy. The knowledge that Mary was close at hand filled him with exhilaration. Instead of being downcast by her inaccessibility, he was uplifted by it. He had been brought up according to a rigid code: he had learned early that things were either right or wrong, good or bad, black or white. Now he surveyed the future and saw it composed of an infinite number of grays.

19

There were patterns, if she chose to look for them. Years ago she had come here, she had grown and gone away, and now she was back again. And whatever she called herself—Lennox, Sambourne, Craven—she remained the same Mary, with the same terror of being found wanting and, consequently, being disliked and rejected. Colin and Dickon, her uncle Craven, loved her. Would they continue to do so were they to penetrate her disguise and find the true Mary cowering beneath? At all costs, she must prevent them from recognizing what she really was. She could not rid herself of the notion that it was only a matter of time before they repudiated her, as her parents, who must have had some reason for not loving her, had done.

Dickon was waiting for her downstairs. Nonetheless, she lingered for a few moments on the window seat. Clouds floated loosely above the line of the moors. From here, the sky was wide enough for an observer to chart their subtle transformations as they moved from one side of the immense vista to the other. From here they seemed as white and solid as sheep; only by careful scrutiny was it possible to see that during their progress across the sky they were in a constant state of redefinition.

Dickon, whistling over the plans laid out on the billiard table, heard her step and turned as she entered the room. As always, his heart lifted at the sight of her.

"You've finished," she said.

"Had to stay up all night to get them done. I hope it's what you wanted."

She bent to study the drawings. "It's beautiful," she

said after a moment. "More beautiful than I could have hoped."

"It'll be a show piece, once we've built it," agreed Dickon.

"It's not that the one you and Colin built when you first started isn't lovely, just that I wanted something that the three of us could share. Something bigger and better than anything we've ever done before."

"It's that, all right. I reckon one of these days, folks'll travel miles to see it."

"But it's for us, Dickon. Not for anyone else. You do understand, don't you?"

" 'Course I do," soothed Dickon. Mary often was agitated these days, and he was pretty sure he knew why. He rolled up the plans. "Best to take these over for Mr. Nichols to look at first, before we start. As an architect, he'll understand better than I can about things like stresses and load-bearers and so on. We'll need an engineer, too, to sort out the boilers and piping."

"It's an entire garden under glass. A whole world."

"Big as the Crystal Palace."

Mary held his gaze. "The shape . . . you do see, don't you?"

"What I see," he said slowly, "is that . . ." Although no two women could have been more unalike, she nonetheless reminded him of his mother; it had not taken him more than a moment to recognize why.

"What?" she challenged. "What do you see?" She leaned one hip against the table. In her skirt of chocolate-brown serge and long cardigan, she possessed an almost forbidding elegance. Since her return to Misselthwaite, she had lost the nervy look which had settled on her before she went to France with Colin. She had grown plumper, sleeker. The shadows beneath her eyes had gone.

"Nothing," he said. Mother-of-pearl buttons marched from the red leather belt about her waist up to the high collar of her blouse, imprisoning her inside the tucked cream linen. Distancing her. This morning, with the moors brilliant in the sunshine, and birds singing, it seemed incredible that in the springtime his hands had held her breasts, his mouth had kissed her soft forbidden nipples, for the uninhibited then of his memory was still as real to him as the buttoned-up now. As so often when he was with her, desire moved him. For two pins he would have taken her into his arms, even though she was the wife of his closest friend. He smiled slightly. "Nothing at all."

She saw into his turbulent mind, recognized the desires which moved him. As they did her. Faintly, the blood moved up her face. Slates could not be wiped clean; the past remained. She cleared her throat. She wanted so much to explain to him, but she could not. "You do see that it's a clover-leaf shape, don't you?"

"A trefoil," he said. "Rather like the palm house at Chatsworth."

"Oh." She was crestfallen. "And I thought I was being so original. Anyway, we could have different arrangements of plants in each of the crescents, perhaps even different temperature zones, if your engineer can manage it. And I want a circular pool in the middle, which all three would share, so that there can be water-loving species as well."

"It'll be grand."

"It'll be magnificent. I want it to be big enough in scale that when you walk through it, you won't be able to see what's around the next bend. It'll be mysterious, exciting, like a jungle or a tropical rainforest." Mary clasped her hands. "Oh, I wish we could have birds in there too, parrots and cockatoos flying about among the branches. And butterflies."

"Like the Garden of Eden."

"Just like." She frowned at him. "Though, as I remember, there was a serpent in that particular garden."

"Aye, so there was."

She laid a hand on the plans spread across the green baize, facing him defiantly. "So do you see one in this Paradise?"

"Mebbe. Mebbe not."

"Enigmatic as always, Dickon."

He smiled at her again. "When's it due, Mary?"

Her eyes grew large. "What did you say?"

"You heard me."

She should have known she could not hide it from him. He had always been too much in tune with nature's rhythms, too much in tune with her. "How did you guess? I didn't know it showed."

He stepped closer and put his hands on her waist. Just so had his mother's body felt as the new bairns grew inside her, waiting to be added to the tumbling crowd in the cottage where he had grown up. "I thought at first you were just happy to be back at Misselthwaite. Remember how you grew so round and sweet when we brought the secret garden back to life—and you with it? But now I see it's more than that."

"Yes."

"Didn't you tell me once that you would never have another child?"

"I did. But however hard you try, these things aren't always within your control." She was close enough to smell the wind in his clothes. His hair was the color of a fox's brush. She loved him. Behind his head she could see the edge of the moors through the open windows, brilliant with gorse and broom. A thrush was singing. And a robin. "Dickon, I—"

"Is that why you went to France with him? Why you married him?" he asked, his voice suddenly harsh.

She was taken aback by his change of tone. "I don't know what you mean."

"I'll make it simpler. Did you marry Colin in order that your child should inherit the Manor?"

She said nothing, simply looked at him with her eyes full of sadness.

"Or did you want to make sure that it had a father who was a gentleman and not just some peasant off the moors?" Hurt and anger bubbled in him as though he were a cauldron of soup on a stove.

"You're talking nonsense, Dickon." She tried to release herself but he held her fast.

"Am I?" he said quietly. He let go of her waist and grabbed her arms, squeezing them hard against her ribs. "Whose bairn is it?" he said. "Mine or his?"

"I refuse to answer such a ridiculous question."

"Ah, Mary, Mary. You've no right to keep the truth from me. I stood by and let you go, because I could see how much more fitting it was that you and Colin should wed. But you ought to be plain with me. I love you: I deserve no less."

The years they must share stretched ahead of them like a spread patchwork quilt. In Mary's head, the great Palm House soared, its thousand panes of glass glittering under the sun, its exotic vegetation luxuriant in the damp heat. Orchids bloomed, huge moths hung like lanterns among the broad green leaves, jungle creatures stirred in the undergrowth. She said coldly: "Who else's child would it be but my husband's?"

"Naturally, you want the best for it," he said, as though she had not spoken. "Misselthwaite, no less. I can understand that. Just tell me the truth."

Again she did not answer.

His love for her rooted him there, so that he could not move away. But as he looked at her upturned face, at the frown between her heavy brows, he could feel a subtle alteration in its character. He had thought her perfect in all the ways that mattered; he accepted now her fallibility and found that it made no difference. He could not feel anger at her betrayal, not even sadness. And there would be time enough for the truth later. Whatever she did or said, he was not going to leave her. She needed protecting, and years ago, for better or for worse, he had taken on responsibility for the task.

"I will always be here," he said. "Even if I go away, I will come back. Remember that." He brought her close and kissed her forehead. "I'll always be here."

I will cum bak. He had done so once already. Mary tried to laugh and shivered instead. "I wish you didn't make it sound so much like a curse."

"When is the bairn to be born?"

"I'm about three months along."

His mouth thinned as he made the calculations. He let her go and turned back to the plans. "This glasshouse, now. We'll have to work fast if it's to be ready by the time the boy gets here."

"Which boy?"

"The one you're carrying."

"You sound very sure."

"You'll see. I'll ride over to visit Mr. Nichols this afternoon. The sooner we get started, the better. By the way, does Colin know that he's to be a father?"

"Not yet."

"Reckon he'll be right pleased."

"Reckon he will."

"When does he return?"

"In about two weeks."

It was nearer three. When he came, he brought with him friends from his university days: Freddie Avery, James Arbuthnot, Bertie Leggatt. In various ways, all three had already made a mark on the literary scene. Bertie had had two books of poetry published and achieved something of a *succès d'estime;* Arbuthnot had founded, and now edited, a little magazine which, despite the odds, had managed to stay precariously afloat for nearly eighteen months. Avery, now a junior don at his old college, also wrote poetry, and contributed polished little articles on the contemporary world of letters to anyone willing to publish them.

Mary had met them all at different times over the years. They were a witty brittle trio who always made her feel as though they inhabited an enchanted kingdom to which she was too inferior ever to be offered the key.

While the housemaid showed them to the sleeping quarters, Colin followed Mary to her rooms. "You look well," he said. "Positively blooming, in fact."

"It's the Yorkshire air."

"You don't mind Freddie and the others too much, do you?"

"You're free to invite whomsoever you please," she said. "It's your house."

"Our house. Our home." He sat down heavily in the brocade chair beside the fireplace and rested his forehead in his hand. "God, I think I'm a little squiffy. Bertie insisted we stop for lunch and I hate to think how many bottles we got through."

She sat down opposite him and looked at him affectionately. "How long will they be staying?"

"Only a week or so." He looked at her from beneath heavy eyelids. "Say you don't mind them too much."

"I can't pretend they're my favorite people. Or at least, Freddie isn't."

"Freddie." Colin grimaced. "He's a bit shrieky, I agree."

"But I expect I'll manage to tolerate them. As long as they don't seduce the maids."

"Darling Mary, it's not the maids they'll be after but the grooms."

There was silence. Colin groaned inwardly. Why hadn't he kept his mouth shut. He did not drink heavily all the time, but when he did he found he had little or no control over himself. Occasionally, the need to unburden himself was so strong that it could scarcely be contained; that was when he drank, for alcohol provided a ready-made excuse to give voice to things which later, when they came back to haunt him, he could recant. He resisted now the impulse to fling himself at her feet, bury his head in her lap, tell her everything.

Mary finally spoke, her voice scarcely audible. "You mean, they are homosexualists?"

"That's one way to describe them. A more polite way than most would use, I assure you."

"I never really understand why they are friends of yours."

It was a question he had more than once asked himself. "I suppose because I find them witty, amusing, clever. They're enthusiasts, like myself. They share many of my interests. They're as far removed from the people around here as—as Hottentots. How many more reasons do you want?"

"I doubt if Yorkshire society is as sophisticated in these matters as London or Oxford," Mary said coolly. "Besides, isn't it . . . what they do . . . a criminal offense? I hope you will point this out to them."

"I already have, on the way up here. Are you shocked, Mistress Mary?"

"I don't know. I think so. And puzzled, too." She reached across the space between them to lay a hand on his knee. "Colin, I must tell you something."

His heart sank. She was going to confess that she and Dickon had resumed their affair. And then he would have to produce an appropriate reaction. But what should it be? Since their marriage, he and she seemed to have reverted, however temporarily, to their former sibling state. If that was what she wished, he was content that it should remain so, especially since, these days, she was often out of sorts. He wanted no trouble. He recognized that with Mary as his wife he was, in so far as he could be, happy. "What is it?"

"I'm—we're . . . going to have a child."

"A child?" That sobered him. "We are? But . . . when? How?"

She laughed. "Colin dear, surely you must have some idea of how these things happen."

Yes, he thought. But not to me. Not ordinary decent things. On the other hand, against the odds, here he was, a married man. Why not a father, too? "Mary, my dear. I'm—I'm just . . . what can I say? I'm overwhelmed. I'm thrilled beyond words." He tugged at the bell-pull. "We must drink champagne. To—what do you call it: wet the baby's head?"

"I think that's done after it's born, not before."

"We shall do both," he said grandly.

Mary sat on the arm of his chair. "Are you really pleased?"

"I should say I am. And my father will be even more so."

When champagne had been brought and opened, he held the bottle over the glasses. "The Venetian goblets, Mary. Absolutely priceless. I've never used them before but I can't think of a more fitting occasion, can you?" He poured the champagne and raised the thin gold-rimmed glass.

"To you, my dearest wife."

Mary kissed his cheek. "One more to add to your list," she said. "Colin Craven, Father."

"This is a day I did not think to see. I wonder whether it will be girl or boy."

"Dickon says a boy."

"He knows, does he? You told him before you told me?"

"He guessed. He asked me. I couldn't deny it."

"Was he pleased?"

"I don't know. Probably." Mary set her glass down carefully. "I should prefer it, I think, if you didn't tell your friends. If they are . . . what you say they are, then they will not be particularly interested in the news. So let's keep it to ourselves for a while, yes?"

"Whatever you say." Colin was secretly relieved. He could imagine all too easily Bertie's shrill laughter, Freddie's mocking congratulations—"My dear, how too brilliantly virile of you"—the raised eyebrows and sly innuendoes. On his own, he could handle their teasing but Mary must not be subjected to any of that. They were not a spiteful group, by any means. It was simply that given the circumstances, there were only two ways open to the Berties and Jamies of this world: hiding, as Jamie successfully did, or flaunting, like the other two. And flaunting imposed certain attitudes, certain mannerisms. Bertie and Freddie had taken the braver course.

"Gentlemen, I'm sure you will excuse me," Mary said, rising from the piano stool. She had been playing to them for the past half hour, while they lay back and smoked their cigars.

"Mrs. Craven, surely you don't intend to leave us so soon." Arbuthnot leaped to his feet, followed by the others.

"I'm afraid so. It's been a long day."

Leggatt and Avery joined in the protests but she simply smiled at them and left. As Colin had said, they were amusing and clever, as well as charming, and she had enjoyed their company more than she could have imagined. James she positively liked, and Bertie was tolerable, though she doubted she could ever be at ease with Freddie. But for all their courtesy, she expected they would be happier without a woman present. She had not given much thought previously to men of their kind, assuming that the circles they moved in were unlikely to overlap her own. It was a surprise to find that they were not leering perverts or even mannered aesthetes. They seemed perfectly ordinary, no different from any of Colin's other friends. Of the three, Freddie Avery most easily fitted the accepted stereotype. She could not imagine what they did together. Colin might know, but she could not envisage herself ever asking for such information.

She could not sleep. This second pregnancy was much more uncomfortable than the first, and she often found herself pacing about in the small hours, hoping to ease the ache in the small of her back. Leaning from her open windows, she could see light spilling from the drawing room on to the terrace, but though the long windows had been opened, she heard no voices. Perhaps they were in the cellars, bringing up more wine. Certainly all four of them had drunk steadily during the evening, both at dinner and afterwards.

Through the trees came the distant sound of high-pitched laughter. Where were they? She listened again, and realized that they were down by the lake. They must have decided on a midnight swim. How many times she and Colin had done the same. By day, the water was the color of tea; by night, it acquired the rich caressing texture of black satin. She remembered how it covered her body like cool honey, how the ripples slid past her white limbs like fish. She remembered the delicious excitement of apprehension as they struck out for the center, never quite sure if there was, as Roach the gardener claimed, a monster lurking in the deeps, who would rise to the surface on moonlit nights in a burst of silver foam and devour whatever it found.

The young men called to each other beyond the trees. It was years since she had swum at night but now that the notion had come into her head, she could think of nothing more conducive to sleep than a dip in the cool water. Would they object if she joined them? Or perhaps she could head for the far side of the lake and slip in unnoticed. She changed into a bathing costume she had last worn before her marriage to Barney; though snug on her swelling figure, it was wearable. In sandals and a bathrobe, she went downstairs and on to the terrace. The moon sitting in one corner of the sky was so bright that she had no difficulty in following the path between the black tree shadows. As she approached she could hear Colin and his friends still splashing and calling to each other, but when she reached the lake and pushed through the screen of rhododendrons, there seemed at first no sign of them. Listening, she heard the murmur of voices, a burst of laughter and then, as she was about to step out from among the bushes and walk further around to where the bank crumbled into a tiny beach, she heard feet running along the path and Colin's voice breathless and excited. Instinctively, she moved back, out of sight.

"Get off, you filthy pervert." He was laughing. "Leave me alone."

A figure raced past her hiding place, pursued by an-

other. "Darling." It was Freddie. "You know what a
degenerate beast I am."

"Who better? But not here, at my home."

"Why not?"

"My wife . . ."

"Anyway, how could I leave you alone? Even if you
really wanted me to."

"We shouldn't," Colin groaned. "Oh God, why did I
drink so much at dinner?"

"Ah, my dear . . ."

Almost in front of Mary, the two men embraced. Both
were entirely naked, bone-white in the moonlight except
for the black bisected triangle at the groin. Freddie's
hand fondled Colin's body, just as she herself had done
a few weeks before in Paris. Surely Colin would not
permit such intimacies from a man. But then Colin was
responding, seizing Freddie's head between his hands,
kissing him. She blinked. Surely she must be mistaken
in what she saw. But now the two of them were falling
to the soft ground beneath the trees, murmuring to each
other, their hands urgent, their bodies both, plainly, ram-
pant. She shrank deeper into the leaves, biting down on
her lower lip to stop herself from making some revealing
sound. It could not be. Colin, a . . . She could not bring
herself even to think the word. Colin, one of them?

She squeezed her eyes shut, pressed her palms over
her ears in an attempt to block out the sounds they were
making. Oh God, she thought. I should have realized
that this is what Colin is; why else would he have such
friends? Opening her eyes a fraction, she saw them almost at her feet, the two bodies joined now, fitted together; she heard the unmistakable sounds of passion,
of climax. She heard words which she could not have
imagined one man saying to another. It would have been
terrible enough to have stumbled across her husband
with a woman; it was a torture of the worst kind to find
him making love to a man, to be powerless to get away
from a scene which she found truly revolting. She
wanted to break cover and run, but was too fearful of
the consequences. Colin would know at once who it was
and that she had witnessed something she should not
have done. Her marriage, her coming child, Misselthwaite: there was far too much at stake.

She thought of Dickon, so good, so gentle, so disregarded. She remembered his disgust at the incident in the nightclub when he had almost overturned a table into the laps of men such as as Bertie and Freddie. And Colin. She thought of Colin making love to her in Paris and murmuring Dickon's name. Had the two of them ever . . . ? But she refused to believe such a thing. Oh God, how long would they go on? For when she lifted her hands gingerly from her ears, she heard Freddie's voice again and Colin answering and understood that they had resumed their lovemaking. She was trapped here until such time as they finished. With tears pouring down her face, she could only grit her teeth, keep her eyes closed and her fingers in her ears and wait, while the dark leaves stroked her face like beguiling fingers.

It seemed as though hours had passed before, when she listened, she heard them in the lake, laughing and shouting like carefree boys. She ran then, back to the house, up the stairs to her bedroom. She closed and locked the door and got into bed where she sat with her knees drawn up to her chin.

What did she feel? Did any of it change her attitude toward Colin? She remembered Dickon's mention of a romantic interest, and her own jealousy; it had never occurred to either of them that Colin's "interest" might be male. Would it make a difference to their marriage? She wanted to think not. But the images of those two moth-white bodies in the darkness would not leave her; the sounds they had made echoed inside her head. They had sounded as intimate, as tender, as a loving man and woman might. So how were they different? *Why* were they different? She wondered whether Colin could be happy in that difference and knew he was not. Had his marriage to her been an attempt to prove his own normality, or simply a means of hiding from the censure of the world?

Below, she heard the slamming of doors, and voices along the passage calling good night. It would be difficult to look at Colin with the old affection tomorrow. And she thought of his face as he lifted the goblet of champagne, the sense of relief she had glimpsed there somewhere behind the paternal pride. She, of course, could never allow him into her bed again. Not after this. Even though that side of their relationship had more or less ceased, any further physical contact between them was now completely out of the question. And yet, could she condemn him? Could he help what he was? Could she ever find the courage to broach the subject with him? The answer to all three questions was a resounding negative.

20

The baby, as Mary had predicted, arrived early. Luckily, the nursery had been prepared and a nurserymaid already employed for the birth was a difficult one and, once it was over, the parents in no fit state to initiate such arrangements. Dr. Craven, having supervised the birth, now stood grave-faced beside the bed, had already intimated that Mary's chances of survival were slim. "Hemorrhage," he said. "Critical loss of blood."

Looking down at the drained white face of his wife, Colin envisaged what was left of Mary's life being measured out in bright crimson drops and added to a slow tide of blood which bore her away from him.

"Don't die," he said, chafing the cold hands which lay on the coverlet. "Don't leave us again, Mary. *Please.*"

"I want him to be called Richard," Mary whispered. Her eyes turned toward Dickon who stood behind Colin, one hand on his friend's shoulder. "Richard," she repeated, with difficulty.

"Of course," Colin said. "Anything."

There were tears on Dickon's cheeks as he stared at Mary's bloodless face on the pillow. Surely the Fates would not take her away from them. Both men were distraught, though Dickon, more fatalistic, hid it better. He knew that both he and Colin would survive her loss, but it would be as maimed and wounded things, half-men damaged by the knowledge that they could never be made whole again. Colin had called him to Misselthwaite as soon as it became clear that Mary's labor was not going according to plan and the two of them had watched at her side for nearly thirty-six hours until the midwife informed them that the baby was finally about to be delivered.

The child was baptized immediately, for neither it nor its mother was expected to last the night, and Dickon stood as sole sponsor at the brief ceremony. The priest had ridden over from Thwaite with the necessities of his office, and the nursery became a hastily improvised chapel. It seemed that as soon as they reached safe harbor, they were blown out to sea again among the wild winds and the storm-tossed waves. The years of war had been the most terrible of Dickon's life but he had always known that if he could only survive them, Mary waited at the end. To lose her now would be doubly cruel for it would mean that the war had been endured in vain.

As the priest murmured the sacred words over the child's head, Dickon held the frail scrap close, cupping its skull in his big hand, watching for each faint breath, never sure that it might not be the last. He guessed that this was as much of fatherhood as he would know. There came a moment, as the priest packed away his paraphernalia, when the space between one breath and the next grew so long that he knew the child was dead.

Frantic, he blew air between the fragile blue lips but felt no answering lift of the brittle ribcage, no flutter from the lungs. "Live," he shouted, while the cleric stared. "Live!" He blew again, willing images of life into the darkening mind: wind on the moors, the blue of a robin's egg, the honey smell of gorse. "*Live!*" and this time, there was the faintest of movements. He thought of all the things which might never be: Richard running down the long paths of Misselthwaite, bowling his hoop, riding his dog-cart, fair curls blowing, sturdy limbs, rosy cheeks . . . and blew once more. The delicate eyelids flickered, the baby's mouth trembled. Dickon could hold back the tears no longer. If—if either child or mother were to die now . . .

"Don't ever leave us, Dickon," Colin said, his own eyes red with weeping. "We need you to be strong. *She* needs you."

Who will be strong for me? Dickon thought, with bitterness. If she dies, Colin will at least have the boy. I shall have no one.

*   *   *

But Mary did not die. To those attending her sick bed, it sometimes seemed touch and go but by the time spring came around again, by the time her son was three months old, she was strong enough to sit up and eventually to get out of bed and lie, carefully wrapped up, on the sofa in her room. She was still deathly pale, her face so sharpened by illness that it looked like a mask carved out of ivory, but it was possible to see the old Mary behind the rare smiles which occasionally lit up her face.

"Three months," Colin said to Dickon, the day she was finally allowed downstairs. "and I dare say you feel as I do, that I have aged five years in that time."

"Ten," Dickon said. "If not more."

"I'm not a believer," said Colin, "but I've made bargains with every deity I could think of, and some I swear I created myself, if only she would recover."

"The boy, too."

"Of course. But I can never forget that while there could always be more children, there could never be another Mary."

Dickon did not trust himself to make any reply.

When they joined Mary in the morning room, they found her with her son in her arms. "Isn't he the most perfect, the most ravishing thing you ever saw?" she said. "Isn't he, though?"

All through her pregnancy she had been terrified that she would experience the same lack of feeling as she had with Charlotte Alice. In the periods of awareness after Richard's birth, when she had been conscious of how close she was to death, she had told herself that she would rather die than endure again that inner numbness. When she was finally strong enough to hold her son, she was overwhelmed by the current of love which swept over her. It was as though she had been swallowed by, was drowning in a giant wave. Now she knew what Barney had felt for Charlotte, and for the first time was able to appreciate the grief he must have known when she died. If anything ever happened to Richard . . . but such thoughts were not to be entertained. She knew quite simply that she would kill before she let a single hair of his head be hurt.

"I want to see the Palm House," she said.

"So you shall, just as soon as you're able to go outside," Colin said.

"But I've been thinking. Remember when we took you out for the very first time to show you the secret garden? And Dickon pushed you in that funny old invalid chair?"

"Of course I do."

"I want you to take me out in that. It's probably still in the carriage house."

"If the mice and the woodworm have left any of it."

"Will you look?"

"But wouldn't it be better if we ordered a new one from London? Or had one made for you? I shouldn't think that old thing's in working condition after all this time, and if it goes at all it'll be pretty rickety."

Mary's dark eyes filled with the easy tears of weakness. "I want that one," she said, like a child.

"I'll look for you," Dickon said hastily. Neither he nor Colin could deny her anything. He sat down beside her and took her hand. "Don't fret, lass. If it's there, you shall have it."

"And you'll push me there yourself?"

"There, and to Timbuktu, if that's what you want."

"Dickon," she said softly, leaning against his breast. "You're so good to me."

He kissed the top of her head.

Colin's throat was tight. I'm good too, he wanted to say. Don't leave me out. He looked at the blonde head and the red, bent over the child between them, and saw that they made a perfect whole. Although Mary was *his* wife, *he* was the one who was surplus to requirements, *he* was the one not chosen. It had crossed his mind to wonder whether the child was his; he had decided that it did not matter whether it was or not. It was the result of their triangularity and would eventually be master of Misselthwaite. That seemed to him the most complete and satisfying of conclusions.

However, looking at the three before him, he was seized with a desire to burst the bubble of their completeness, to push them apart and destroy the harmony which so clearly existed between them.

"You're going to be amazed when we take you to the Great Palm House," he said quickly. "That's what we've decided to call it, to distinguish it from the other one we built. It's the most stupendous thing you ever did see. Not that it's properly established yet, of course, but there's new stock arriving every day. Just this morning we received some orchids which actually live on air, if you can believe that."

"And there's golden carp in the pool," said Dickon, "and a fountain you can turn on or off and bamboo already taken root. And Colin's going to submit an article about it to one of these architectural journals they have, complete with photographs."

"Are you? Clever Colin."

"It'll do no end of good for the business, I shouldn't wonder," Colin said.

"How is the company doing?" she said, as though recalling some distant memory. "I've been out of action for so long that I've quite forgotten about Craven & Sowerby."

"We've been going from strength to strength," Colin said. He did not add that both he and Dickon had been rushed off their feet, determined that Mary should not be left without one or other of them beside her at all times and consequently each doing the work of two men. Even with the capably efficient Lewis Phillips handling affairs at the London office, the past weeks had been something of a nightmare. "Our order books are full from now until Christmas and we've been getting an increasing number of enquiries from abroad," but she was no longer listening, concentrating instead on the baby. On her knee, he stirred and gurgled, his miniature fingers waving like the fronds of a sea anemone. Dickon put out a thumb and the child clung to it like a drowning man to a lifebelt. Again, Colin felt the heavy weight of jealousy lodged in his throat.

Never in a million years would he admit to Mary that his main attitude toward his son was one of indifference. He was ashamed of these feelings; he attributed them to some immaturity in himself, an inability to accept that Mary's loyalties would henceforth be divided. He wanted her approbation for the new schemes he had in mind: perhaps a branch in Paris, an associate company in the Far East to whom they could subcontract their orders for exotic plants, and a development of the idea Mary herself had come up with, of administering their own nurseries. But while she continued in this role of besotted mother, he could see it would be pointless talking to her. He consoled himself with the thought that once she was well and could see that the baby was perfectly healthy, she would be able to turn her mind to other things. Including himself.

The invalid carriage was found in more or less working order. A little oil here, a lick of paint there, the cushions quickly refurbished by the sewing woman, and Mary was ready for her first outing.

"I'm so excited," she exclaimed. "It'll be like discovering the secret garden all over again."

"It still needs a lot of work," warned Dickon. "And plenty of time."

"So did the garden. But Colin's parents had already planted that. This is different because we've started it from scratch ourselves."

"Aye." Dickon leaned on the handle of the carriage and sent it smoothly down the sanded paths toward the Great Palm House just as, years ago, he had pushed Colin.

"Do you suppose . . ." Mary said.

"What, lass?"

"Do you suppose that one day, years from now, Richard—or his son, perhaps—will have to restore the Great Palm House, just as we restored the garden?"

"Give the poor little mite a chance," said Colin. "He's barely born and already you have the estate neglected, and him grown and orphaned."

"Don't!" cried Mary. "I'm not like you, Colin. I don't expect to live forever and ever. But I certainly intend to dance at the wedding of my grandson. If not my great-grandson."

Over her head, Dickon and Colin exchanged glances. A month ago, no one would have given much for her chances of even seeing the snowdrops push up in the park woods.

The new Palm House had been erected about half a mile from the house. Finally, they rounded a corner, passed through an opening which had been cut into a thick yew hedge—and there it was. In the pale spring sun, the panes winked and gleamed between their supports of gleaming white cast iron, fronded and petaled as elaborately as the plants inside. There was scarcely a straight line in the entire shining edifice, just curves and domes and arches, looping away from them, an ocean of glass.

Mary said nothing, simply clasped her hands against her chest, breathing as though she had been running. "Oh," she said after a while. "Oh."

"Do you like it?" asked Colin.

"It's . . . it's like a wedding cake. A wedding cake made entirely of crystal. It's so beautiful that I don't know what to say."

"Is it how you hoped it would be?"

"More than. It's a dream come true." She twisted in her chair to look up at them. "But we can't keep all this beauty to ourselves. We must let other people see it."

"Prospective clients, do you mean?" said Colin.

"No. People. Ordinary people. We should hire a bus, invite everyone we know to come, all the people who worked on it, have a Grand Opening. What do you think, Colin? Dickon? Wouldn't that be a wonderful idea?"

"It's a grand idea, lass." It was such a pleasure to see Mary so alive again that both of the men would have agreed to almost any suggestion she made.

In fact, as Colin pointed out later, when Mary had been carried back to her bedroom and the baby was sleeping in his crib beside her, it would make sound economic sense, quite apart from anything else. "We could invite the gentlemen of the press: the gardening correspondents, the representatives of women's journals, that sort of thing. It would really put us on the map."

"I'd have said we were already as much on the map as we can cope with," Dickon said mildly. "Any more commissions and we'll be working twenty-four hours a day."

"The trouble with a small concern like ours is that there simply isn't room for expansion," said Colin.

"That's a bridge we can cross later. For now, the main thing is that Mary's well."

"Well, of course it is. But that doesn't mean we shouldn't be looking to the future." Colin felt the old

hunger as he crossed the room to hand his friend a glass
of whisky. He wondered what the reaction would be if
he said quite simply: Dickon, I'm in love with you. I
want you in exactly the same way as you want Mary.

Would Dickon run as fast as he could go? Would he
understand? Would he resort to fisticuffs? Would he tell
Mary? Hard though it might be, if there was one secret
Colin was determined to carry to the grave, it was his
longing for the other man. Thank God neither Mary nor
Dickon had the slightest inkling of his proclivities—nor
ever would, if he could help it. Especially now that he
was a married man, a father. He had broken off relations
with Freddie and Bertie; he had not seen James since all
three had visited Misselthwaite during the first months of
Mary's pregnancy. He now had his hostages to fortune
and he had no intention of jeopardizing them, even if it
meant abstinence for the rest of his life. But oh: if
Dickon only knew just how much Colin longed to touch
the tender place beneath his ear, to stroke the shiny skin
across his knuckles, to lean his cheek against the coarse
red hair which sprang from his chest . . .

He frequently told himself how lucky he was, how
things had turned out well for him. He hoped that as
the years rolled on, he would be able to maintain his
equanimity. It was not always easy. There was a boy
who had come to work on the glazing of the Great Palm
House for instance. And, traveling down to London on
the train last month, he had fallen into conversation with
an Italian tourist, a young banker from Rome, who had
set his pulses racing. But such encounters now lay behind
him. The future must not be jeopardized.

Later, Mary was to say that, more than anything else, it
was the Great Palm House which set her firmly on the
road to recovery. Not the doctor's pills and medicines.
Not even her son who, after a poor start, grew sturdier
and stronger with every passing week. Watching the
changes which every day brought, drawing up designs
for the plantings, ordering stock, choosing which shrubs
to set against which trees, which blooms would look best
against which backgrounds, she was too busy to be ill.
Day after day, as the spring stretched into summer and
even summer began to fade, she had the invalid carriage

wheeled down the paths and would lie there for hours, wrapped in her cashmere shawl, supervising the work of stocking and establishing the plants which would eventually fill the great glass shell. The estate carpenter had devised a table with folding legs and this was set up beside her, together with plans and books and horticultural catalogues. She had her luncheon brought out to her in a basket, and she often recalled the days when she and Colin and Dickon would roast eggs and potatoes and wolf the fresh-baked currant buns made for them by Dickon's mother.

"What's the female equivalent of a rajah?" Colin asked once.

"A rani. Why?"

"You used to accuse me of acting like a rajah but you're exactly the same. Waving your hand about imperiously and watching them all run to do your bidding. Ordering this and that to be done and not liking it when it's finished so it all has to be done over again."

"I'm sure the gardeners don't mind, though. They're as involved in it all as I am. In fact, they're always coming up with ideas of their own, many of which are much better than mine." She gazed about her in satisfaction. "Oh Colin, isn't it like a wonderland already? Those hanging baskets . . . and the way the palms throw patterns of light—did you know there are hundreds of different palms? . . . all those variegated leaves . . . and some of the specimen plants are simply . . . oh, I can't properly express it, but it brings tears to my eyes, sometimes, to see how wonderful it all is."

"What's wonderful," Colin said, "is seeing you get better."

"I *am* better, aren't I?"

"It's just like when we were children."

"The Magic, yes. And here's some more magic: tomorrow I intend to walk to the Great Palm House. On my own."

"Are you sure?"

"Completely. I know exactly how you must have felt when you finally got out of *your* wheeled chair and started to run about."

"It was such an odd way to spend the first ten years

of my life: confined to bed for no real reason at all," Colin said.

"Except for that nonexistent lump on your back."

"Someone should have told me years before you did that there wasn't the slightest sign of a lump. Frankly, it's a wonder that I've grown up relatively normal."

Mary did not answer. Whatever the cause, she knew only too well that Colin was not normal. Lying in her invalid chair, she had often wondered if there was some way she could help him, cure him. Although she had tried to discover more about the subject, there was very little to be found, and she certainly was not going to write to book shops or lending libraries for material about it. Confused images of scandal and green-dyed carnations, the Love That Dares Not Speak Its Name and a fashionable playwright dying in a lodging house in Boulogne, were about the limit of her knowledge. She wished she was less ignorant, that there was someone she could ask about it. Apart from Colin's cousin, Dr. Craven, she knew no medical men, and he was the very last person she would discuss such a thing with. As for Dickon: she knew instinctively that he would find the whole thing far too embarrassing. Besides, she would not wish to give away Colin's secret. But she worried, wondering if it were a disease which could be caught, and whether it could harm her son.

Colin was still reminiscing. "What I find even stranger, looking back, is that until I met Dickon, I had never seen another boy in my life. Isn't that incredible?" Nor would he ever forget the way he had come into his bedroom with a newborn lamb in his arms and a red fox cub trotting by his side. When he dreamed of Dickon the fox was always there.

". . . a whole mass of scented geraniums," Mary was saying. "And jasmine and stephanotis overhead. And some of the cattleya orchids have a most amazing smell. We could plant honeysuckle, too, even though it grows perfectly well outside. Think of the scents when the sun is high."

"I had a letter from the engineer this morning," Colin said. "He thinks that there's a real demand for a conservatory like this—though perhaps not on such an enormous scale—as people try to replace their former collections. He'd like to come on to our pay roll, if we'll have him."

"And will we?"

"He's done an excellent job here. I think he'd be an asset."

Mary seized his hand and held it against her cheek. "There's so much to be done."

"And I'm going to do it all."

Mary got up early the next morning. She was determined that she was strong enough to walk the half-mile to the Great Palm House but she did not want any witnesses about if she should prove not to be. At first her legs, unused to walking, felt unequal to the task of carrying her but after a while she found herself perfectly steady, as if she had never been ill. The morning was fresh and clear, the leaves beginning to turn, a faint smoky tang drifting in the breeze. The moors were still yellow with gorse; high above her head larks pierced the blue air. Despite her anxieties about Colin, she could not remember when she last felt so happy. She came through the yew hedge and stopped in order to take in the full glory of the Palm House. Improvement seemed unnecessary, but she wondered whether, at some later date, they should build a reflecting pool in front of it, to double the dramatic impact of those glittering curves.

Turning the handle, she pushed open the door and was at once assailed by the damp heat, the jungle warmth, the rich smell of earth and leaf and exotic bloom. She was quite determined that they should build a waterfall in one of the crescents, falling naturally between rocks to the pool, and surrounded by ferns of various kinds, all growing in a naturalistic setting. She felt like a child given an infinitely adaptable toy to play with: there were so many variations, so many possibilities. She pushed aside the hanging creepers and heard ahead of her the sound of a missel thrush. Briefly she wondered whether a bird had flown in the day before and been unable to escape. Then she realized who it must be.

When she reached him, she thought how tired Dickon looked. His cheeks were drawn and he had lost some of his usual burnish. As she regained her strength, she had come to realize just how much long-drawn anxiety both he and Colin had undergone as they waited for her recovery.

"How could you have got here so early?" she asked. "It's only just after sun-up."

"I seem to remember you asking me the very same question a long time ago," he said, pulling aside the overhanging leaves of a Kentia palm. "And the answer's the same as it was then. How could I have remained abed on such a morning? And how could I have stayed away and missed a chance to see you?"

"But you didn't know I'd be coming here so early."

"Didn't I?" Leaves danced and shuddered around his head; the morning sunlight fell like prison bars across the graveled paths of the Palm House.

"How could you?"

"Perhaps I guessed."

Alarm showed in her face. "We're too close," she said. "Are we never to be free from each other?"

"Not until the end."

"Why us, I wonder?" she said.

She moved toward him through the smoke of battle. He heard the distant crump of shell fire. Old voices. Dead voices. *Maggots, lads. Watch out for the bloody flies. On your feet, soldier, there's work to do. Yess, Tommy.* A hand touched his sleeve, the flesh gone, ivory bone, mud between the knuckles. *Why us, Corp? Why wasn't it you?* Arms waved, beckoning, pulling him down under the khaki mud.

"Dickon!" Jason's mane against his face. Warm sweet breath on his face, rattle of artillery fire, shrapnel shriek.

"Dickon! Come back."

Mary's hair was brushing his face. He lay on the sharp gravel, eyes closed, hearing her voice, hearing the call of the dead, and wondered which was reality, which illusion. Lethargy lay on him, millstone-heavy.

She thought him still unconscious. "Oh, my dearest," she murmured, stroking his cheek. "My poor darling."

Would she have spoken so unguardedly if she had known he heard? Cannon fire faded, smoke cleared, the dead grew mute. He stirred.

She moved away from him. When he opened his eyes she was sitting back on her heels, watching him. "It's worse than it used to be, isn't it?" she said quietly. "You've not fainted before."

"I'm usually in bed when it comes on me, or sitting down."

"Dickon." She was brisk. "You must see a doctor."

"There's no cure for what ails me," he said. Though he often thought that if only she could drop her guard and say out loud what he knew was true, if she could only admit that she loved him, then not only would he be mended, but she might also.

21

The biggest threat Richard Archibald Craven faced was not to his constitution but to his character. Petted, courted, adored, he stood in grave danger of turning into the most selfish spoiled little horror ever seen. The older Misselthwaite servants, remembering how Colin used to tyrannize and demand, were so delighted by his son that they indulged his slightest whim. From love this time, not from fear. Those whose service was shorter and had no such memories, nonetheless fell victim to Richard's undeniable charm. He could have been a monster. In fact, something sweet and steadfast in his nature, and the determined efforts of his mother, saw to it that he did not turn into the kind of despot both she and Colin had been allowed to become through neglect and carelessness.

He spent much of his time up on Missel moor. Dickon showed him where the otters frisked at dawn, where the badgers played with their young under the winter moons, showed him the tiny nests of field mice swinging from the juicy grasses. He learned to whistle like the robins, to call to the thrushes and converse with the blue-black crows. He could stand so still that pheasant and squirrel and rabbit took no more notice of him that they would have of a tree or a rock. By the time he was six, he could distinguish between a plover's egg and a skylark's, ride bareback on the shaggy moorland ponies, find the secret places where wild strawberries and whortleberries grew.

At the same time, he loved to walk around the Misselthwaite estate with Colin and Archie Craven. It grew to be a familiar sight, the three of them coming back at the end of the afternoon, heads bent, hands identically clasped behind their backs, and although Richard sometimes found it hard to keep up with the other two and was frequently forced into an extra hop and skip in order not to lag behind, he only occasionally resorted to taking Archie's hand and was far too proud to ask either of them to slow down. He was as conversant with the workings of the estate as his grandfather, and seemed quite happy to spend hours at a time in the estate manager's office. "You see, Mamma," he told Mary once, looking very grave as he repeated something Colin must have told him, "one day I shall be a man, and master of Misselthwaite, so I have to know everything there is to know about it."

"Quite right." said Mary. "And will you be a good master?"

"I hope so. I *think* so because, you know, I will see that the cottage roofs are kept mended and the people have food and I will pay for the doctor if they need him, and I will never forget how lucky I am to live in this big big house when others have to live all squashed up together in little cottages."

He liked to stroll about the Great Palm House with his mother while she taught him the names of the plants which flourished there, their leaves pressing against the glass, the flowers perfuming the air. Spiky phormiums, paddle-shaped asplenium, glossy spathiphyllum: he repeated the difficult names after her until he had got them off perfectly. He would bury his face in the geraniums which tumbled over the gravel paths, trace with a finger the veined leaves of maranta or cyclamen, stroke the wax-and-velvet clusters of the hoyas. He liked the fact that the Great Palm House was the same age as he was; he liked to hear about the invalid chair and the collapsible table, and how he himself had nearly died and been baptized with an eye dropper of holy water with Nanny's white enamel bowl doing duty as a font.

"I'm very special, aren't I, Mamma?" he asked one day.

"Of course you are. In all sorts of ways."

"I mean, because I very nearly died and then Dickon brought me to life again."

"That would make anyone special."

"Mrs. Medlock says it was a miracle."

"It was, my darling."

"Does it—does it mean that Dickon is God, Mamma, if he can work miracles?"

"Perhaps it does, my precious," Mary said. "But perhaps you weren't entirely dead, just a little bit."

"If he's not God, is Dickon an angel, then?"

"I think he probably is," said Mary, remembering that she too had once called Dickon an angel, and perhaps never ceased to think the title apt.

Best of all, Richard liked to walk in the secret garden and hear the whole story of Mistress Mary Quite Contrary and Ben Weatherstaff and Rajah Colin and Dickon the Animal Charmer. "I should like to play a pipe like that," he said. "I should like to be a musician, I think."

"And what instrument would you play, my little Paganini?" Mary asked, trying not to laugh, for he had a serious way about him sometimes which it would never have done to mock.

"I like the piano," said Richard who, at the age of six, had for the past two years been receiving instruction in the instrument from his mother. "But I prefer the woodwind. The oboe most of all. It's kind of sad and jolly both at the same time."

"Then we must see how you get on with the oboe."

"And when I am very good at it, I shall sit under a tree, just as Dickon did, and charm the foxes and squirrels and feed them from my hand."

"All at the same time, do you think?"

"You're teasing me again," Richard said. "Why do you always tease?"

And sweeping him up into her arms, kissing him so hard that he protested that she hurt him, Mary said: "Because I love you so."

Although she tried not to let it show, Mary's thoroughly impartial view was that never in the history of mankind had there been such a handsome, energetic, intelligent, loving child as Richard. He had a quality which drew everyone automatically to his side: was it his gusto for life, his love of other people, his absolute involvement with everything he came into contact with? His capacity for knowledge was immense: he absorbed information as plants absorb water. He learned to read early, progressing rapidly from children's tales to eclectic foraging among the shelves of the Misselthwaite library. He read voraciously, as though there were not enough time to pack in everything he wished to know. As soon as he was old enough, a series of short-term tutors were engaged, not to teach but to guide him.

"For," as the latest of them, a clever young man just down from Cambridge, pointed out, when Richard was nine years old, "such a passion for knowledge, such a sense of wonder at the world, should not be trammeled yet by the routine fact-cramming which we call education."

It accorded so exactly with Mary's own views that she began to pay rather more attention to Mr. Hawkins than she had to his predecessors. She soon realized that while, to the careless observer, his way with Richard seemed detached to the point of indifference, he was, in fact, on hand at all times with answers, suggestions, discussions, questions of his own for his young pupil to respond to, above all with enthusiasm. When his term of office was nearing its end, Mary asked him to come to the study.

"According to your professors, you have a brilliant career ahead of you, Mr. Hawkins," she said, looking down at his references spread before her on the desk.

Hawkins snorted. "Such accolades are often the prelude to abject failure."

"These references speak of a position at the Foreign Office, or in the Diplomatic Service . . ."

"Those are indeed the fields I should like to enter, but unfortunately, although I'm quite clever, my family is quite poor," said Hawkins, shrugging slightly. "And while many a social barrier has been demolished, money remains impregnable."

"What exactly do you mean?"

"Posts of the kind I'm after are generally taken up by those with the means to support themselves while they climb the consular ladder."

"Whereas you . . . ?" prompted Mary.

"Whereas I have a—I know it's one of the clichés of Victorian fiction but in my case it happens to be true—have a widowed mother and two sisters. My father, you see, was killed in the war, and though he left a reasonable sum, it won't be enough to keep my family while I wait for advancement."

"Where did your father serve?"

"He was killed at Gallipoli."

"I'm so sorry." Mary could feel for the unknown Mrs. Hawkins and her two daughters. She came at once to the point. "What would you say if I were to ask you to stay until such time as Richard went to school, on the understanding that when you left us, we should see to it that, in addition to your salary, you were provided with an annuity handsome enough to allow you the freedom to begin your diplomatic ascent?"

"That would depend on how soon it is deemed necessary for Richard to be sent off."

"Three years, Mr. Hawkins. Five at the very most."

He pursed his lips. He had a thin clever face which reminded Mary very much of Colin when he was at university. Silently, she willed him to accept her offer.

After a while, he gave a rueful grin. "I'm extremely fond of the little chap, but I don't think I would be fair to myself if I agreed to postpone my career for five years, Mrs. Craven."

"Three, then?" The thought of sending her darling off to school did not make Mary happy but she had long ago accepted it as an inevitability.

"Would you think me venal if I asked for a properly drawn-up document?"

"Not in the least."

"And since Richard does not need me at his side twenty-four hours a day, might I be permitted to pursue my own field of research which deals, as it happens, with the origins and conduct of the last war?"

"Very well. And what exactly are your own views on it, broadly speaking?" Mary had hitherto not conversed very much with the young man. He had been hired in London by Colin and, at his own insistence, took most of his meals with Richard, except when the child was allowed to join his parents for dinner. All she could remember on such occasions was the way the two men had argued on almost every subject. Colin had found it stimulating. Mary was ashamed to realize now that she was usually so wrapped up with the Great Palm House or the burgeoning nursery garden side of the business, responsibility for which seemed to have fallen on her, that she had scarcely listened to them.

As if he realized this, John Hawkins smiled slightly. "I think that your husband speaks from a basis of ignorance and social prejudice when he talks about the relative death and injury statistics of the men compared to those of the officers. I also think it was a war which we had no choice but to fight."

"The war to end all wars."

"If you believe that, Mrs. Craven . . ." He smiled again, more broadly this time, and she saw that when he lost his angular boyish look, he would be an impressive man. She could picture him already, ambassador in a far-flung outpost of the Empire, standing on the steps of Government House beneath a waving Union Jack, ostrich plumes waving as he greeted royalty or quelled an imminent uprising.

"Will you stay?" she asked.

"For three years, yes."

Richard did not know of these negotiations but was delighted when Hawkins informed him that he'd decided to stay on for a while.

"Someone's got to see you right, Craven," Mary heard him say nonchalantly. "And I'm probably the best man for the job."

And Richard, having adopted his tutor's insouciant manner, merely responded: "I dare say you are, sir."

Craven & Sowerby, meanwhile, was growing ever more successful. No grand house was complete, it seemed, without its conservatory, its palm house, its winter garden; no conservatory was worthy of the name unless it had been designed and built by Craven & Sowerby. The company's services were required not just by the English but by citizens of all the European countries, even the Italians, though their homegrown architects and engineers already had a fine reputation in the field. Increasingly, customers in the United States, where fortunes were made daily on Wall Street, and millionaires were rapidly becoming more numerous than mice, were demanding elaborate greenhouses to complete their elaborate mansions. So much so that it had been deemed necessary to set up an office in New York, with its own staff and designers, but even so, only the palm houses personally supervised by either Mr. Craven or Mr. Sowerby were considered to be the real genuine one-hundred-percent McCoy.

Even the disaster of the Wall Street crash did not at first make a great deal of difference to their success. There was a certain amount of transatlantic retrenching; when the lease on the office expired it was not renewed, but as Colin pointed out, the company had been clever at diversifying and although they had lost a source of rich customers, they had by no means suffered a financial setback.

For some years the company had owned an *apartement* in Paris. Since Dickon absolutely declined to set foot on French soil, it was Colin who made most use of it. More and more so, it seemed to Mary. She wondered whether he used it for discreet liaisons with other men. The thought saddened her. Because of the possibility, she had never asked if she might visit him there, though she would have enjoyed a stay in the beautiful city, a wander along the *boulevards* and *quais,* a meal in one of the famous restaurants. Then one evening, when Colin was at the Manor, Richard said: "I should so much like to see this famous tower in Paris, Papa."

"Which tower is that?" Colin said abstractedly.

"The one built by Monsieur Gustave Eiffel. It is a marvel of the age, Papa. And I have been looking at some of the books in the library and reading about the Venus de Milo and that too is in Paris. Wouldn't it be a good idea if Mamma and I came to Paris with you next time you go?"

"It is such a capital idea that I cannot imagine why we have not thought of it before. What do you say, Mary? A second honeymoon?"

"I'd love it. The last time we were there . . ." Her voice faltered and died. Would Colin expect her to sleep with him? And if he did, would that make him less abnormal or more so?

"I bought this in Paris for your mamma," Colin said, picking up the shagreen box. "It was fearfully expensive, too. And there was a little cobbled square, I remember, where I asked her to marry me. It was very romantic, old fellow."

"I think I should like to ask a girl to marry me in Paris," Richard said solemnly. "I read in a book that Paris is the city of lovers."

"Quite right." Over his head, Colin winked at Mary, who found it difficult to smile back at him. They had not been lovers now for years: she often wondered if Colin thought it odd that husband and wife should live in such celibate conditions. Or did he imagine—her cheeks grew hot at the thought—that she had a lover? But why should she not? She was still young, still pretty. While she had often thought that she was perhaps less passionate than some of the women whose names and faces were regularly dragged through the newspapers— or was it that she considered some things more valuable than sexual intrigue?—she could not hide from herself the fact that were she to wake one night and find, say, Dickon, her erstwhile lover, in her bed, she would not be inclined to shriek for assistance but would turn to him as she had so often in the past, loving the feel of his hands on her, his mouth, his sturdy russet body close to hers.

"A lover is someone who loves someone else, isn't it?" Richard was saying.

"That's one way of putting it. But it doesn't really go far enough," Colin said.

"How far should it go, then?"

Colin looked down into the clear blue eyes lifted so trustingly to his. For a moment he was tempted to say more, to say everything, even though the child could not possibly comprehend. In the end, he said: "You'll understand better when you're a man."

"But you always tell me that when you were a boy, you hated it if people said that to you," Richard said.

"True enough. But when I was a boy, I didn't realize how right those people were."

"But, Papa—"

"Richard," Mary said. "You must not nag your poor father. Come over here and look at this picture with me." As Richard settled on a stool beside her, and Colin returned to his newspaper, she examined her husband. He did not look well. He coughed frequently; the collar of his shirt seemed several sizes too large for him. She was brushed with sudden alarm. Why had she not noticed before how pale he was? Although she teased him about his occasional bids for sympathy, when he would refer pathetically to his early years as an invalid, she reminded herself that there must have been some constitutional weakness in him, even though he had managed triumphantly to overcome it.

"Are you overdoing things, Colin?" she asked later, when he came to her room to wish her good night.

"The business is taking up much more of my time than it used to," he admitted.

"You're working too hard."

"I'm feeling a little tired, yes. There are storms on the horizon."

"What kind of storms?"

"Financial ones, mostly. I don't mean with the company. There's a lot of unrest in the country, my dear. Trade unionism is becoming a force to be reckoned with: you can hardly open a paper these days without reading about some new industrial disruption somewhere in the country."

"Does that worry you?"

"In one sense, of course it does, though we try to employ union men where we can. But as a symptom of the working man finally clamoring for his rights, no, it doesn't worry me at all. High time we had better industrial relations in this country. For us, the problem will be the coal industry; if the miners come out on strike, there's no question that it will directly affect our business. People use coal to heat their conservatories and glass houses. If there isn't any for a significant length of time . . ." He shrugged.

"Colin, shall we be in trouble? Shall we have to sell Misselthwaite?"

He laughed. "The way things are set up at the moment, we couldn't, even if we wanted or needed to. The only person who can change the conditions on which it's handed down from one heir to the next is the current owner. And that's my father—he's hardly likely to sell the Craven inheritance because of a possible financial hiccup in my business. Anyway, let's not talk about that."

"What, then?" Mary sensed that Colin wished to discuss something of significance.

"I've been thinking for some time that I ought to stand for Parliament—if they'll have me."

"What a splendid idea, Colin."

"I think I'd have something to contribute, especially coming from Yorkshire, which is mining country. I've discussed it with my father, and although he disapproves of many of my beliefs, I know he would be pleased. But I couldn't possibly contemplate such a step unless I had your wholehearted support." He looked at her nervously. "Darling Mary, what do you say?"

"I can't think of anyone who would do a better job."

"Really?"

"Absolutely. And I'd be completely behind you."

"It's only a thought for the future," Colin said. He smiled. "Oh Mary. Do you really think it would be a good thing?"

Mary was aware of a need for reassurance which was at odds with Colin's usual confidence. She put her arms around him. "The best I ever heard of," she said.

He kissed her forehead. "Good. Now, about Richard's suggestion with regard to visiting Paris: it's a perfectly marvelous idea and will provide me with a welcome few days away from my desk."

Mary frowned. "Dearest Colin, I would far rather that the company was declared bankrupt than that it should drive you to physical collapse." She held his hand between hers. "Can you imagine how any of us would feel if you were to be taken ill?"

"There's no question of such a thing."

"We don't need the money, after all."

"Exactly. Listen, Mary, why don't I take young Richard over to Paris with me next time I'm going? Show him the sights, that Eiffel Tower he's so keen on, some of the art collections—he's pretty fond of pictures, isn't he?"

"That's a wonderful suggestion."

"It would be nice if you came with us, of course, but it's occurred to me recently that I don't really see enough of the boy, and it might be good for the two of us to get to know each other better," Colin said, not meeting his wife's eyes.

He had never told Mary of his initial reaction to Richard's birth. He had been proud, of course. And delighted

that the Craven line—if indeed that is what it was—
would be continued, that there would be an heir to ad-
minister Misselthwaite when he himself was dead, but
he could not share her obvious devotion. Even Dickon
seemed to be more involved than he was. Though perhaps—the suspicion was always there—Dickon had reason. Yet Colin could remember only too clearly his own
early rejection by his father and had always been determined that Richard should not suffer as he had. He had
tried very hard to ensure that he did not, but as the boy
grew, so did the business, and inevitably he had seen
less of his family.

"No," Mary said quickly. "Much better that the two
of you go without me."

"Hurrah, that's settled then." Colin fidgeted for a moment with the cord of his dressing gown, then said:
"Mary, you *are* happy, aren't you? You don't regret getting married to me?"

"How can you possibly ask such a question?"

"It's just that sometimes, you seem . . . I don't
know . . . as if there were things you would like which
you can't have."

"What more could I want?"

Dickon, Colin thought. That's what you want. That's
what I want, too. And neither of us will ever be able to
say so.

As happened every year on the third Saturday in June,
the Summer Fête was held on the lawns behind the
Manor. A sporting duke who regularly traveled north
for the shooting, had been roped in to open the proceed-
ings which included everything from coconut shies to a
fancy-dress parade for the children, from a guess-the-
weight-of-the-marrow to stalls hawking white elephants,
homemade cakes and secondhand books. Richard had
been prancing around since dawn in his pirate costume,
striking attitudes with a toy sword and calling everyone
his hearties until they were thoroughly sick of it. Mr.
Hawkins had volunteered to tell fortunes in a small
striped tent. Colin had promised that there was to be a
surprise but refused to say what it was, despite Richard's pesterings.

"I shall be quite ill if you don't tell me," Richard

threatened, spoiling it by lifting up the black eyepatch which Mrs. Medlock had made for him. "I might even die—and then what would you say?"

"Does he remind you of anyone?" Colin said to Mary.

"Very much indeed," Mary said.

"Who?" demanded Richard. "Tell me who."

"An arrogant imperious little rajah-like person we all used to know," Colin said.

"I remember him," Dickon agreed. "Had a lump on his back, didn't he?"

"That's the fellow."

"A right nasty bit of work, he were, and no mistake."

But although Richard begged them to tell him who they meant, they would not, simply laughed and looked at each other with their usual affection.

Luckily Richard was spared and was thus able to stand at his mother's side in a cocked paper hat with a skull and crossbones painted on it, welcoming the visitors with the aplomb of a trueborn buccaneer. Mary knew she looked ridiculously besotted as he held out his hand and greeted everyone by name. He would make a good master of Misselthwaite when the time came: he had known these people since his earliest days and it was plain to see that they returned his obvious affection for them. The sporting duke not only gave a witty speech but also bought a homemade cake, saying there was nothing his wife liked more, and a thingamajig made of polished steel and ivory off the white elephant stall, insisting there'd been one just like it in the nursery when he was a boy though for the life of him he could not quite remember what it was used for. Even those inclined to spout left-wing sentiments in the pub on Saturday nights were impressed by his general air of being one of them.

Colin's surprise arrived at three o'clock, falling from the air like a large multicolored snowflake. It dropped toward them, quietly at first and then with a whoosh of escaping gas and the sound of wind-whipped ropes. A hot air balloon! It was manned by a small monkeylike person in tweed gaiters and a large cloth cap made of white cotton. The general opinion was that it was as good as fireworks, but there was a marked reluctance to come forward when the balloon's skipper asked who would be the first to go up with him.

Richard tugged at his mother's hand. "He'll be very disappointed if nobody goes up," he said anxiously.

"Will he?"

"He'll think we don't like it."

"But we do. Very much." Mary was riveted by the great dome dipping and swaying above their heads, anchored by scarlet ropes. Its gaudy outer skin, painted with stripes and and zigzags of brilliant color, stretched and wrinkled as though it were a living breathing thing panting to get away, to soar aloft, instead of being held down by three sweating farmworkers.

"But someone's got to—" Suddenly Richard had wrenched his hand from hers and was running over to the man standing alone in his wickerwork basket. Before she could do anything to stop him, he was being swung aboard, the farmhands had been given a signal, the crimson ropes were flung into the basket, the gas jets gushed and they were off, rising slowly and then with increasing speed as they reached the tops of the trees.

"What a lad," Dickon said admiringly behind her. "Just look at him up there."

Mary did so: could not have taken her eyes off him. Her mouth was open, her hands clasped to her breast. For the rest of her life she would remember the sight of the little face peering down at her over the rim of the basket, the piratical patch over one eye, the cocked hat perched on the fair hair as her son was carried away from her, up and away into the blue sky.

Come back, she wanted to scream, come back, but he was going from her, further and further, the balloon dwindling, fading, until she could see him no more, nothing of him left except a newspaper hat falling and tumbling through the air to land almost at her feet.

22

Stepping out of the train at Euston, Richard sniffed the air and wrinkled his nose. "It's very smoky in London, Mother."

"Not everywhere. There's a lot of steam here because of the train engines," said Mary.

"There's a painting rather like this in Paris." Richard stared up at the curved and vaulted roof where steam hung in insubstantial cushions. "By Claude Monet."

"Is there?" Mary looked around for Colin and saw him striding toward them. "Look: here's Father."

Colin swept Mary up in a hug and then turned to Richard.

"Bonjour, Papa," Richard said. He held out his hand. *"Comment ça va?"*

Colin looked at Mary. "Where's Richard, then? Where's our boy?"

"Don't be silly," said Richard. "I'm right here."

Colin did a melodramatic double take. "Oh, *there* you are. I'm sorry. I mistook you for a Frenchman who was passing by."

"Did you really, Papa?"

"Absolutely, I assure you."

"He's been working very hard on the language," said Mary.

"Do you think they'll take me for a Frenchman in Paris?"

Colin considered. "I don't know. What do you think, Mary?"

"Perhaps if we bought him a beret," Mary said.

"Or a baguette to stick under his arm."

"That would certainly do it."

"Papa."

"Yes?"

"I'm rather worried about something."

"What's that?"

"Whether I shall have to eat snails or not. Because, you know, I don't really think that I could manage to do it."

"Oh dear," said Colin. "That's about all they eat in Paris, snails."

"Except for frogs' legs," said Mary.

Richard's face fell. Then he said severely: "I think you're both teasing me, because I read in a book that French chefs are the best in all the world."

"Was this a book written by a French chef?" asked Colin.

Richard ignored him. "The reason I was asking about snails was because I didn't want them to think I was rude if I left them on the side of my plate."

"I expect they'll understand," said Mary.

They were to spend the night at Fitzroy Square. Colin and Richard would then take the train to Dover and cross to Boulogne by ferry, while Mary spent a few days in London before returning to Yorkshire.

After Richard was in bed, Colin and Mary sat in the drawing room, each with a glass of whisky. "I'm ashamed," Colin said, "that this trip will be the first I've taken with him."

"Why should you be?"

"I'm always so afraid that he will look back and see me in the same way as I see my own father."

"And what is that?"

"I love him, Mary. Of course I do. But I can never get over the memory of how he rejected me. I was ten before he came back to England and things began to be normal. Ten, Mary, a year older than our boy is now."

"There's no comparison between you and your father."

"I worry that I haven't done a good enough job as a parent."

"Colin. Dear Colin. You've been everything that Richard could possibly ask for. And will go on being."

Colin lit a cigarette. "I just hope I can keep up with him during our week in Paris. He's got every day crammed with the things we're to do, the food we're to try, the pictures we're going to see."

"He's been thinking of nothing else for weeks. Reading up on the galleries and the major sights, and studying French history with Mr. Hawkins."

"Such enthusiasm: I swear he already knows far more about the city than I do."

"Like father, like son," said Mary.

"How do you mean?"

"You were exactly the same when you were a boy," said Mary.

"Was I? But . . ." Colin got up and poured more whisky into his glass. Although it was years since he had even considered Richard's paternity, Mary's response was confusing.

He coughed awkwardly, then chuckled. "While we were waiting for the dinner bell, Richard treated me to a short dissertation on the art of *sfumato.*"

"What's that?"

"That's exactly what I said. Apparently, it's a technique used by Leonardo da Vinci when he painted the *Mona Lisa*—which, I can tell you now, we are scheduled to be standing in front of at eleven o'clock next Tuesday morning. Sharp."

They laughed together. "You'd better do some boning up yourself, if you are to cut any sort of a figure as a person of authority and learning," said Mary.

"He's already streets ahead of me. I shall content myself with the role of humble disciple, I think. I'll tell you what, though."

"What?"

"He may have got his zest and enthusiasm from . . . well, from me, but he's certainly inherited your bossy streak."

"I've told you before, I am *not* bossy."

"Perhaps I should have said domineering. Or arrogant. Or—"

"What a horrid man you are."

"Am I? Am I really, Mary?"

She smiled at him. "Of course not."

"Can you still charm animals, Dickon?" Richard said. He lay on his stomach in the soft grass of the secret

garden, reading a book, while Dickon sat with his back
against a cherry tree, glancing at a newspaper.

"I don't know."

"Why not?"

"I haven't tried, that's why. Not for years." Not since
that afternoon in France when unheard, unseen men
died screaming as they crashed toward the earth in
flames, while rabbits and herons, grass and water continued, in spite of everything, simply to be.

"But why *not*?" persisted Richard.

"Lost the wish, somehow."

"Why don't you try now? I'd very much like to see it."

"For one thing, I ha'n't got my pipe by me. And for
another, you're supposed to be concentrating on your
studying. Greek verbs or summat, isn't it?"

"Latin. I shan't be starting Greek until I go away to
school. But it's *much* more interesting to charm
animals."

"I only agreed to sit here with you because you promised me you'd be quiet. And so far, I've had a minute-
by-minute account of your holiday in France, and about
five hundred questions." Fondly, Dickon reached down
and ruffled Richard's hair. "What are you now, nine?"

"Ten on my next birthday."

"And never satisfied with one answer when ten of 'em
will do . . . you're going to be a regular encyclopedia by
the time you go off to school."

Richard rolled over on his back and squinted up between the branches of the cherry, waving his legs in the
air. "Dickon . . ."

"Aye?"

"Did *you* go away to school?"

"No."

"Then why should I have to?"

"Because your mother and—and Colin think it's best
for you. Besides, you'll get a far better education than I
ever did."

"I can't really see the point of education. If I don't
know something, I ask somebody and they tell me."

"Aye, and wear them out while you're asking."

"You're not really worn out, are you, Dickon?"

"I'll manage. But listen: where an education comes in
is, it helps you work out *what* it is you don't know. And

I'll tell thee straight, lad, if there's one thing you need when you go out into the world, it's a good education."

"But suppose I never go out into the world."

"You're going to be a monk, is it? A hermit, shut up in a cave?"

"No. But I might die. Then what would be the point? And if I *was* going to die and my whole life flashed before me, the way they say it does, I'd much rather remember that I could charm animals than that I could parse stuffy old Latin verbs."

"Would you, now?"

"Yes. Oh, Dickon . . ." Richard sat up and tugged at Dickon's hand. "Teach me to charm animals too, *please.*"

"Don't know that I can do it meself anymore."

"I'm certain you can if you want to."

"We'll see."

They were up on Scarston Fell. While Mary and Dickon paused for breath, fighting against the wind, Beggar suddenly spotted a rabbit and went racing down the slope after it, with Richard flinging himself along behind.

"Isn't he beautiful?" said Mary.

"He's that, all right." Dickon stared after the boy, chest-high in the bracken, his bright hair gleaming in the sunshine. Beyond him, the gray lines of dry-stone walls patterned the moors into fields. Huge clouds hung behind the line of the hills. Memory twisted like a thrown knife. Another boy, another day, rabbits jittery in the long grass, a fair boy shouting after them. Cornish Davey. Left to die with his country boy's face pillowed in the mud and a ragged song in his mouth.

"What is it?' Mary slipped her hand into Dickon's.

"It's nowt."

"The war again?"

"Mebbe."

"Oh, Dickon . . . after all this time."

"I told you it would never leave me."

"You did. But I hoped that you were wrong."

"It's just, our Richard reminds me of someone I used to know," Dickon said abruptly.

Richard came running back to them. "Did you see that? I almost overtook Beggar, I was going so fast." He took hold of their hands. "It was tremendous. Like flying. Why don't human beings have wings like birds?"

"You might just as well ask why birds don't have arms like human beings," said Mary.

"I wish *I* could fly." Richard gave a sigh. "Imagine being able to soar through the air." He remembered the hot air balloon he had flown in once, the way the earth had slipped away from him, the freedom he had felt as they sailed through the blue air.

"Here, lad," Dickon said. "I've summat for thee." He pulled out something wrapped in a spotted handkerchief.

"What is it?"

"See for yourself."

Richard pulled aside the cotton. "Oh," he said. "Look, Mamma, it's a real animal charmer's pipe. Just like Dickon's."

"It *is* mine, lad."

"Your very own?"

"Aye."

"Gosh." Richard blew a few notes. "*Thank* you. Did you know, by the way, that there used to be somone called Orpheus, who could charm animals just like Dickon can?"

"I've heard of him," said Mary.

"I bet Dickon was better at it than he was."

"Dickon's better at everything."

"Mother," Richard said. His voice was beginning to break and the word came out in two different registers.
"Yes?"

"Which do you love best, Dickon or my father?"

Mary reflected that although one of Richard's most attractive characteristics had always been his complete absorption in whatever subject was currently engaging his interest, it could sometimes be difficult to give him the exact information he required. "That's a hard question," she said.

"Why?"

"Because love isn't like that." She was conscious that almost any other woman, faced with such a question from her son, would answer that of course her husband was the man she loved best. "Because Dickon and Colin and I aren't like that."

"How do you mean?"

"We've been close friends for so long that it would be impossible for me to differentiate between them."

"Why didn't you marry Dickon?"

She was silent. How often she had asked herself the same question.

"I mean," Richard continued, "if you loved them the same, how could you choose one over the other?"

"It was very difficult . . ."

"Because, you see," Richard said, frowning, "there are so many people in the world that I was wondering whether, when I'm grown up, how I would ever be able to choose just one."

"You generally know these things by instinct." Mary wondered if she was getting herself into deep waters by this response.

"And was it instinct which made you choose both Dickon and my father?"

"I believe it was."

"Then you obviously love them both the same."

"Maybe I do."

The years of Mr. Hawkins' regime had come to an end. In the autumn, Richard would be going off to his public school—the same one as Colin and Archie before him had attended—a move which although she fully recognized its necessity, Mary anticipated with dread. Once Richard was gone, she would have lost her most dearly loved companion. Not just for the present, but for always; she was well aware that this near departure would only be a forerunner of that greater and more permanent break, when he finally left home to start his own life. He was still undecided on a future career, torn between the merits of becoming a vulcanologist, a hot air balloonist and a collector of orchids in their natural habitat. Listening to his plans, Mary was always reminded of Colin when he was a boy; she could not decide which of Richard's ideas she liked least.

"The thing is, Mother," he told her, "I shall eventually have to come back to Misselthwaite and take over, so I want to pack as much experience into my life before then as I possibly can."

"But volcanoes do seem so very dangerous."

"No more so than walking in the wrong part of London at the wrong time of day. Or crossing the road at Piccadilly Circus. Or riding to hounds. Or swimming in the lake. Accidents happen all the time: it's perfectly possible that I could be struck by lightning the next time I went out, or a tree could fall on me, or a mad bull escape from its—"

"Thank you, darling. I take your point." Nevertheless, Mary could not help being assailed by visions of her son toppling into a fiery crater or involved in a life-and-death dash down the side of some precipitous slope pursued by a red-hot river of boiling lava.

"On the other hand, think of discovering a specie of orchid which nobody had even seen before. They'd be bound to name it after me, you know."

"How proud we should be." If, that is, he got out of the jungle alive. Mary saw hordes of little brown men with blowpipes, she saw parted leaves and poisoned darts, the shrunken head of her precious son swinging from the roof of some pygmy chieftain's hut. As for hot air ballooning . . . but she told herself that no mother would really want her son's ambitions to be limited to being a bank clerk or something safe on the Stock Exchange.

When the time came, she and Dickon drove Richard to the railway station at York, Colin being detained in London, and handed him over to the master in whose charge he and other boys from the area would be traveling. He looked so small. How long ago seemed that balloon ride when he had been swept away from her into the sky. Now he was being swept away once more, this time out of childhood and toward maturity. She was bitterly aware that until this moment she had shared virtually every one of his experiences but now he would be going into places where she could not accompany him.

"Don't cry, Mother," Richard said, blinking his eyes rather hard. "I know it's jolly sad for all of us that I have to go away, but Mr. Hawkins says it has to be done and I must take it on the chin, like a man."

But you're not a man, Mary wanted to cry out. You're still a little boy. "I'm not crying," she managed, knowing that the other boys might in some way persecute him for having a mother who wept instead of looking stalwart and nonchalant, like other mothers on the platform.

Richard looked up at Dickon. "You will look after her, Dickon, while I'm away, won't you?" he said, gulpingly. "My father said she needs to be taken care of."

"Don't worry, lad," Dickon said, his voice unaccustomedly gruff. "She'll be in safe hands wi' me."

"I'm sure of it."

"And don't forget what I've told you about getting a good education."

"I won't, sir."

Dickon looked down at the lad. "Don't," he said. "Don't ever call me sir." He could feel Mary's hand clutching at his arm and knew how close she was to breaking down. He was not far off it himself.

Richard touched his mother's sleeve. "I shouldn't like you to think that I want to go away from you," he said carefully. "But, you know, it *will* be a bit of an adventure to meet other boys."

"Oh darling, have you been lonely, then?"

"No. Not at all. Not really. But Mr. Hawkins and my father have both told me that there are all sorts of jolly things to get up to at school. Like rugger, for instance, though I don't expect I shall be awfully good at that to begin with. And marbles. And tiddleywinks."

"What?"

"Mr. Hawkins says that at his school they played a lot of tiddleywinks, and he's been teaching me all sorts of wheezes. I might even end up as the tiddleywink champion of the school, he says."

"Do you think he might have been joking?"

"Absolutely not," said Richard. "He showed me a photograph."

"Well, I must say that takes a load off me mind," said Dickon. "Knowing that you'll be spending your spare time playing daft games. And here I was, worried you'd be wondering what to do with yourself once your lessons were over for the day."

He glanced over his shoulder at the group of boys gathered round the master in charge and bit his lip. Dickon knew that the longer they stayed, the more likely the boy was to start openly blubbing.

"Time to take your mother home," he said. "It's a

fair drive across the moors and the weather looked set to break when we were coming down."

"Right-ho." Richard was making a brave attempt at jauntiness. He hugged his mother, and Dickon too, then set off away from them up the long platform. He looked back once and they saw him square his shoulders as he approached the group of other boys.

"Come on, Mary. Best be away," Dickon said.

"It's such a stupid system," Mary burst out. "To send such a little boy away to live among strangers. Why do we do it?"

"Because that's the way of it." But Dickon too found it hard to contemplate their lad sleeping that night away from home, doing the rest of his growing up with people they did not know. He would come home at Christmas disconnected from them, unaffiliated, the affairs of school taking pride of place over the life he had led before he left.

In the car, Mary cried, staring down at the handkerchief she was twisting between her hands. "He's so small, just a child," she kept saying. "And I love him so. I can't *bear* it, Dickon. Truly I can't." And as she spoke, the wistful ghost of the little girl she had not been able to love came creeping into her heart.

"Course you can. You'll write him long letters and before you know it, it'll be half term and you can visit him, and in no time it'll be Christmas and we'll all be together again."

"We shall never be together again, I know that," Mary said sadly. "Not the way we were."

23

The winter of Richard's first year away at school, Archie Craven contracted influenza which rapidly developed into pneumonia. Although he recovered, illness had so severely weakened his constitution that, with Colin working much of the time in London, Mary found herself increasingly involved in the admininstration of the Misselthwaite estates, forced to scrutinize sheets of figures, consider financial forecasts, tax advantages, investment growth, capital gain.

Inevitably, as she took on more of Archie's social responsibilities, she found herself among people with a wider view on Europe than her own small circle in Yorkshire. The news from Germany was not encouraging. Although the country had managed, under its dynamic new Chancellor, to dig itself out of a deep recession, there were ugly stories of intimidation and civil unrest. Talk of rearmament and military expansion, coupled with the precarious balance of power in some of her neighbor states spelled, to her informants, only one thing.

"You mark my words, m'dear," said a retired senior civil servant who had taken over Archie Craven's role as chairman of the local housing committee. "War is waiting just over the horizon."

"Surely not."

"And sooner rather than later."

"But it's not even twenty years since the last one ended," Mary protested. "And that was supposed to be—"

"The war to end all wars?" the civil servant said with weary cynicism. "Nobody believed that at the time and if they did, it's not going to act as any deterrent to Germany's expansionist policies."

"But—my son," Mary said. Panic flooded her.

"What is he? Eight, ten?"

"Thirteen, nearly fourteen."

"I'm afraid that over the next few years you won't be the only mother worrying about her boy." The sympathetic expression on the man's face was enough to make plain to Mary that her worst nightmare might possibly come true. So much so that she found herself positively hoping that if war had to come then that it should come soon, before Richard was old enough to fight in it.

Talk of confrontation appeared increasingly on the front pages. Closely reasoned analyses in the editorial leaders of the newspapers made it all too clear that unless there was a complete reversal of German policies, war would begin again very soon in the European arena. Mary seriously contemplated taking Richard to the United States and starting a new life there where he could not be conscripted. She pored over the atlas in the library at the Manor, looking for a bolthole where Richard might be safe, wondering about South America, Australia, even India. The people who mattered most to her had come through the first war; she dared not hope that they would also survive a second. She was not really concerned about Colin and Dickon; it was Richard who would be vulnerable, Richard she would lose if the Fates decided that last time she had been lucky, and this time, it would be her turn to suffer bereavement.

Archibald Craven's death was peaceful, and not unexpected. For the past year or two, he had been visibly failing, his daily ride around the estate reducing gradually from three times a week to one and then sometimes not even that. When he finally took to his bed, Dr. Craven predicted that it would not be long until the end, and it was, in fact, just over a week before the nurse hired to care for him came running along the nighttime passages to knock at Colin's bedroom door. He was at the Manor having been summoned by his wife; at his insistence, Dickon was also there, sleeping in one of the spare rooms. They had decided not to disrupt Richard's schooling.

The three of them gathered about Mr. Craven's bed. "Don't weep for me," he said, his pale lips barely moving. Lightly he touched his son's bent head. "I've had almost everything . . . everything I could have asked for . . . you three . . . and young Richard."

"Oh, Father." Colin was in tears, his father's other hand grasped tightly in his own.

"And now . . . do you see . . . I'm going to join her." With an effort he smiled at them ". . . Lilias." And into the minds of all three flashed an image of the dead tree in the secret garden with the smother of dusky pink roses trained over it and the broken branch from which Colin's mother had fallen when she was still no more than a girl.

"Father!" Colin sobbed.

Archie Craven sighed and turned his head on the pillow for the last time. As the nurse leaned across the bed and gently closed his eyes, Colin was filled with a chilling loneliness. And panic. Misselthwaite was his now. The well-being of well over a hundred people depended on him: would he prove up to the job?

"He were right proud o' thee," Dickon said, as though reading Colin's thoughts. He put his hand firmly on his friend's shoulder. "Everyone knew it. He told my mam that you were everything he could ever have hoped for in a son."

And Mary, kneeling at Colin's side, echoed the words, though secretly she wondered what damage those first years of Colin's life had inflicted, and whether he—or she herself—would ever be free of the curse of being unloved. It was an experience they had shared and one which had always bound her and Colin together. It was not something which Dickon would ever truly understand because he had been loved from the moment he came into the world. It was also one of the reasons why she had never hesitated to demonstrate her love for Richard; too many children were discouraged from showing their affection, and too many parents seemed to think that there was something harmful in voicing even the most muted expressions of attachment.

After the funeral, Colin returned to London. Watching him being driven off down the vaulted avenue of trees

which led away from the Manor, she felt the familiar
rush of love for him, the usual regret that she would not
see him again for at least two weeks if not longer. They
might not enjoy a physical relationship, but they were
close and loving friends. The birth of Richard had not
changed their relationship though her unwanted glimpse
of Colin's activities had altered the way she viewed him.

That night, she sat in the small drawing room. The
windows were open, although the wind coming in off the
moor already had a pinch of winter chill about it. She
was tired, and disturbed by thoughts which, once she
had allowed them into her head, would not leave her.
She wanted Dickon. Had done for years. It was becoming harder and harder for her to work with him, to see
him so often, to watch him with her son, to know that
at the end of the day, he would go home to his house
and she would retire alone to her bedroom. When his
hand brushed across hers, she wanted to seize it and
crush it to her mouth; when he turned his blue gaze on
her she . . . She shook her head: such thoughts must not
be tolerated. Her reasons for marrying Colin had been
clear to her at the time, and good: she had no real regrets about what she had done. Quite apart from any
other consideration, she loved Colin. But for Dickon,
she had felt passion—and still did. Even before she had
met him, she had loved him. When she had asked him
if he liked her, he had answered without hesitation that
he did and though she was still a child, she had been
aware then that he always would. The wonder of that
moment had never left her; it lay at the heart of the
feeling between them. Now, she knew that however hard
she tried, she could not simply put him to one side of
her life. What worried her was his innate goodness. If
she went to him, if she explained honestly that she
needed him and the physical expression of the love
which they both knew existed between them, if she told
that although her life was good, rich and fulfilled, she
wanted more, what would his response be? He was a
man of principle. It was easy to imagine him spurning
her, to visualize the look of contempt in his eye. A married woman, another bored wife, not content with all she
had, wanting more, wanting everything.

He would never come to her, that much she knew. But suppose she were to go to him . . .

Perhaps he suffered as much as she did. Perhaps he did not speak because he feared to destroy the harmony which he imagined existed between her and Colin. He was far too modest to intrude. To presume. She foresaw years of loneliness and frustration. The situation they found themselves in was as close to hell as she ever wanted to come. If she had known how Colin was, would she have made a different decision? It was difficult to be sure. As it was, the three of them were condemned by mutual love, by good manners, by consideration for each other, to live out their lives each longing for something they could not have.

Tears spilled down her cheeks. She had no one to talk to about any of this. Her love for her son was no compensation when she also yearned for something—someone—else. Besides, Richard had grown, had gone away, had left her behind as he started on his new life. Could she not feel free now to find a fresh start for herself with Dickon?

The answer was negative. However hard it might seem, she must soldier on. She must keep the agreement she had made with herself when she spoke her wedding vows to Colin. She must suffer and be brave.

There was a movement at the open window. She looked up. Dickon stood there. "I'll wait no longer," he said. "Reckon I've waited long enough. Reckon my time's come."

"Reckon it has," she said quietly.

"I've fought with myself, God knows. I've told myself that you belong to Colin . . ."

"I belong to myself." And, she thought, to you.

". . . that I have no rights, that it's a sin to covet my friend's wife as I do, Mary, and always have done. But I can't keep away any longer."

"Dickon."

"Tell me to go, Mary, and I'll understand. I'll do as you say. But I've come because I believe you love me as much as I love you."

"More."

He came over to her. Took both her hands. Pulled

her up from the chair and into his arms. His mouth
brushed her lips. She closed her eyes.

"So what do you say?" he asked. "Am I to go or
to stay?"

For answer, she took him by the hand and led him up
the stairs, past statues and paintings, along the carpeted
corridors, between tapestried archways and into the
haven of her bed.

Archie's death brought about some changes. To Colin's
secret chagrin, he had left a letter for his son, explaining
that, while he admired and loved him, and applauded
his political ambition, in view of Colin's often expressed
sympathies with the socialist movement, he had deemed
it prudent to secure Misselthwaite for Richard and the
Cravens who would come after him, rather than risk the
possibility of it being turned toward some unsuitable
purpose, such as a home for retired trade unionists, or
a training center for socialist teachers.

Colin knew that there might come a time when this
move of his father's would prove something of a setback
to his plans. For the moment, he did not have time to
worry about it. His most immediate concern was the future of Craven & Sowerby. War was in the air and, in
light of this, he had already taken up a position he had
been offered at the Ministry of Information. Mary was
already fully occupied with the Misselthwaite Estate, and
Dickon did not want to have to replace Colin in Craven & Sowerby's London office. Reorganization was obviously necessary. The three of them sat one morning at
the big table which ran down the center of the Manor
library, together with Lewis Phillips and their accountant
from York, and listened to figures, looked at balance
sheets, discussed the best way to manage the future.

"Sell," Colin said.

"You'll not get the best price for it now," warned
the accountant.

"A year from now, we may be lucky if we can give it
away," said Colin. "With war coming, who's going to be
ordering new conservatories? Who's going to bother
with landscaping their grounds? The same factors will
operate as last time around. The price of coal will soar
even higher, the greenhouse gardeners will be sent off

to die for their country, as their fathers did before them, the big houses will become hospitals and billets, and no one will have time to spend collecting or caring for exotic plants."

"I've been looking at ways we can continue to operate at a reduced level," the accountant said. "Ride out the war years without too much capital loss."

"It'd be a sight easier to sell, I reckon," said Dickon.

"I agree," Mary said.

"Then let's sell. Who knows where we shall all be, this time twelvemonth. Or what we shall be doing."

"But if we sell, what will you do, Dickon?" Mary asked.

They turned to him. He said: "I was thinking I could mebbe take over the nursery garden side of the business. I'd like that, based up here, getting back to grubbing about in the soil, watching things grow. And if war it's to be, then we're going to need vegetables more than flowers. We could easily shift over when the time comes."

"I certainly can't carry on with it for much longer," Mary said. "What do you think, Colin?"

"I say it's a good idea," he said slowly. With the threat of imminent war looming over Europe like a vulture, poised to flap down and gorge itself on corpses, it would ease his mind enormously to know that Dickon was nearby to protect Mary and Richard. "In fact, it's an excellent one."

"You reckon?" said Dickon.

"I reckon," Colin said.

"That's that, then." Dickon's mouth turned up in a crooked grin; his whole body seemed to smile. Both Colin and Mary tried, a little sadly, to remember how long it was since they had last seen him look so happy.

Colin was causing Mary some concern. He had regularly suffered from bronchitic illnesses during the winter months; recently, he never seemed to be free of some respiratory complaint or other. Dr. Craven was now a frequent visitor to the Manor and more than once had informed his younger cousin that unless he slowed down, rested more, he was in danger of permanently undermining his health.

"I thought at first that it might be tuberculosis," he told Mary once, as she saw him to his car. "But we've had a report back on the samples I sent down to be analyzed and they say there is no trace of TB."

"Then what is it?"

"I don't know. His constitution was never of the strongest, and as a child, he had a bout of rheumatic fever which left him prey to any passing infection—but I thought he had overcome this. He played rugger for his school, did he not? And rowed at Oxford."

Colin Craven, Athlete, thought Mary sadly. "I believe he is working too hard," she said.

"Are there financial pressures?" Dr. Craven was always diffident about asking such questions. For some time, during his cousin's childhood, it was considered only a matter of time before he would himself become the heir to Misselthwaite and he was anxious that no one should consider that he still felt he had an interest. Not that there was any reason why they should, now that there was Richard.

"None at all, as far as I know. There was never any need for him to work, as you know, though Colin himself was always the first one to show scorn for those of his friends who had no occupation."

"What about his work?"

"He's doing too much, but that's his way. I've taken over most of the day-to-day business of running the estate, with the help of the estate manager." Mary did not speak of her own exhaustion: as well as the affairs of Misselthwaite to oversee, there was the Refugee Committee and the problem of billeting evacuees, if—or when—it came to that.

"I've prescribed a tonic," the doctor said. "I will also arrange a consultation with a Harley Street specialist. And meantime, if you can persuade him to take things a little easier, perhaps even to take a holiday in some warmer climate, it might prove beneficial."

"I can try." Mary did not expect Colin would agree to the plan. Nor did he.

"I'm much too busy for holidays," he said sharply, when she approached him.

"Surely the Ministry can manage without you for a while. Oh Colin, do say yes. I should so much like to take Richard to Greece to see the classical remains there. Since the two of you had that week in Paris, we've never been abroad together."

"How can you talk of classical remains at a time like this? Do you not realize, Mary, the situation in Europe? How close we are to declaring war?"

"If war really is inevitable—"

"It is."

"—then let's take the opportunity now."

"I'm sorry, Mary. There's far too much to do here." He coughed, clutching at his chest. "I hate the preparations for war, as you can imagine. I hate the propaganda that's already being churned out, and the jingoism which will be used to justify the thousands of pointless deaths, just as it did in the last war. But since it's inevitable, I want to be where I can do my bit to counter some of the more dangerous and time-serving misinformation that will be spread around the country."

"I can't understand how it's happened again," Mary said. "After all that talk of disarmament, how did Germany grow strong enough to declare war?"

"People will give you various reasons but my own feeling is that the Conservatives are more frightened of Russia than of Germany. What a bunch of hypocrites they are, allowing the dictators to be as aggressive as they pleased, despite the pleas of the Czechs, the republicans in Spain, even the Chinese nationalists. I tell you, Mary, it makes me ashamed to be English."

"What are you going to do about it, then?"

"I shall stand for Parliament. For years this country has been dragged down by its class system: I'm going to help to change that."

"Aren't we part of it?"

"Of course we are. That doesn't mean we have to accept it. And there are growing numbers of people who think as I do, men brought up in the same system as I was but who can see all too clearly how pernicious it is."

"I thought the standard of living was supposed to have risen much higher in the years since the last war. That we are all relatively prosperous now, compared with the way things were."

"We're two nations, Mary, and always have been. Remember that. One nation owns its own home, lives in decent conditions, runs a car, has reasonable health care, can provide its children with a proper education, has job security. The other has none of those things. Not yet, at least. But they will, if I can do anything about it."

"After the war is over."

"That's right."

War. The word hung between them, dangerous as a javelin. Colin wished he had not been so forthright with her, knowing that her thoughts would be entirely of Richard. They stared bleakly at one another, remembering the last war, such a short time ago. Now they had so much more to lose. Colin's initial indifference to his son had given way to a love almost as passionate as Mary's and, like her, he was terrified that Richard would become a casualty of another useless pointless war. If there was one thing he found it difficult to stomach, it was the possibility that he might lose his son for some-one else's expediencies, in particular, those propounded by the Conservative Government. The thought so profoundly depressed him that it had begun to erode his energy and confidence, so much so that dragging himself out of bed each day, let alone setting off for the office, was becoming increasingly difficult. And this damned respiratory problem did not help matters. He resolved that during the next school holidays, he would take Mary and Richard away for a few days by the sea. Scarborough, or Mablethorpe. Somewhere like that. The sea air might even help his breathing.

As the drums of war began to beat ever louder, Dickon grew more agitated. His nightmares returned. Once again, the living memories stalked him, catching him unawares. In his sleep, Richard and Cornish Davey became one and the same; he saw the bright head drowned in mud, and heard a cracked voice singing. For years he had managed to repress his guilt at not doing everything he could to save the young Cornishman; now, he could not help but torture himself with images of Richard dying on some other killing field, and no man lifting a hand to save him. He was haunted, too, by a fear of returning to the front lines. "I did my bit already," he said. "I'll not go again."

"No one would expect you to. Besides, who'd want

you?" Mary tried to tease him. "You're over *forty*. An old man."

"I could volunteer. But I won't. They can't expect it of me."

She could tell, from his words, that he was already wrestling with his strongly-instilled sense of duty. "But you have other responsibilities," she said gently.

"Which ones would those be? I've spent the time since the last show making money, turning myself into exactly the same kind of fat-bellied capitalist I used to despise so much."

"Fat-bellied? Such nonsense."

"Why shouldn't they want me to fight? I'm not doing an essential job. I've no wife."

There's me, she wanted to say. "But someone will be needed to produce food," she said. "That's what you'd be doing. No one will want to put you into uniform."

"Happen I could work at some desk job, if I had to."

"But you're—"

"I'll not leave England, though. T'wouldn't be fair. I'll not go back to the lines." His Yorkshire accent more marked, as it had been when he was a boy.

"They won't ask you to," she repeated.

"Back then, there was older men fighting alongside the farm boys, plenty who were the age I am now. Plenty of 'em. And what about our boy, our Richard?"

"Don't. I can't bear to think of it."

"Cannon fodder. Our beautiful boy. I'll tell thee straight, Mary, if summat 'appened to him, I'd—I don't know what I might not do."

All around her Mary felt the stir and flap of fear, as though a thousand invisible moths were trapped inside a cage. "Don't talk like that!" she shouted. "We've been through it once. I can't, I just can't face it all again."

Forgetting his own troubles, Dickon put his arms around her. "Don't you fret, Mary."

She shook him off. "How can I not, when you say such things?" Things which echoed much too closely her own frightened thoughts.

24

On September 1st 1939, Hitler's troops marched into Poland. Two days later, England officially declared war on Germany.

The summer had been one of the most beautiful Mary could remember, with weeks of breathless heat and intense blue skies. The Misselthwaite lake had receded; in the dales, the rivers and becks ran shallow. In the kitchen gardens, the raspberry canes were heavy with soft red fruit and the gooseberries were as sweet as plums. As autumn advanced, the orchard yielded a bumper harvest of fruit and on the moors, spindleberry and whortles glowed like jewels in the heather.

In the middle of the month, Mary saw Richard off again to school. Waving him goodbye, she remembered, as she always did, that first time, three years before, and how little he had seemed. Now, he was taller than she was, pushing toward manhood, the ties of dependence long since severed. She watched him being greeted by other boys who would be traveling back to school with him and shuddered at the gas masks—pig-snouted and goggle-eyed—they carried over their shoulders. Other reminders of war had already become commonplace. Barrage balloons floated above the rooftops, men hurried along the street with ARP helmets bobbing between their shoulder blades, there were queues outside butchers' shops. Food was growing scarcer; there was even talk of rationing being imposed.

The blackout was being enforced and the use of headlights was forbidden, so that she was forced to drive the last few miles across the moors in almost total darkness.

Vividly she remembered being ten years old and being driven across the same road for the first time, with Mrs. Medlock half-asleep beside her. The sound of the wind blowing through the heather had sounded like the sea. How unhappy she had been, though determined not to show it; she was just as miserable today, though for entirely different reasons.

She had little time to miss Richard. With Colin now working for the Ministry of Information in London, she was busier than she had ever been. Not only was there the estate to oversee, there were also the various committees on which she was required to sit: principally those involving the hospital and the welfare of the refugees from Europe, who had been arriving for several years before the official start of the war. Jobs had to be found for them, and places to live. Even at the best of times, it was discouraging work. The gaunt faces of the strangers for whom she found herself suddenly responsible haunted her; in their fearful eyes it was all too easy to see the reflections of what they had lost, what they had endured.

The evacuees from the big urban areas of England were also a constant problem, and she repeatedly found herself roped in to arbitrate between outraged hostesses and disgruntled townsfolk. There was right on both sides: the woman in Middleburn whose three children caught head lice from the two young brothers billeted on them, the homesick evacuee family from Manchester who found themselves, as the mother put it, "stuck in a field of bloody cabbages." On the whole, Mary tended to sympathize more with the families uprooted from the pound and throb of their close-knit back-street life and transplanted into alien territory. "It's not what we're used to . . ." both sides repeatedly told her, and indeed, she could see that it was not. Until now, she had not realized what a gulf lay between town and country, between middle and working class. It had never occurred to her before to wonder at a system which could produce such differing cultures. England, her country, her birthright, had become a meaningless concept once she became aware of the other Englands which coexisted alongside it, and bore no resemblance at all to the one she thought she knew. The men who marched away to war were fighting for an England quite different from her own.

Although hostilities had been declared, nothing much had happened. After a while, the evacuees began to drift back to their homes, to the fish-and-chip shops and cinemas and pubs on the corner; the Yorkshire families they left behind breathed a sigh of relief. Despite higher prices in the shops and an increase in income tax, life returned more or less to normal.

Mary, who had not seen Colin for two months, went down to spend a few days with him in London. He met her at Euston, and hugged her so tightly she could scarcely breathe.

"Oh, Mistress Mary," he said, rubbing his cheek against hers. "I've missed you so much."

"And I you." Under his clothes, his shoulders were frail. "But you look so tired, Colin."

"We're putting in all the hours we can. I know they're calling this the phoney war, because things are so quiet, but believe me, it's just the lull before the storm."

He took her to dine at the Ivy; they held hands and talked as though they had not met for years.

"At least we're entering this war better prepared than we did last time around," Colin said, as the waitress brought them coffee. "But only because most of us are working around the clock to get things organized before the rough stuff starts."

"Will it be bad?"

"Worse than you can possibly imagine."

"Oh God." Mary's thought fled to Richard.

"We've calculated that once it really begins, there'll be more than half a million civilians dead and a quarter of a million wounded—in the first two months alone. The war's going to be fought here at home this time, as well as at the Front."

"Quarter of a mill—here, in our own country?" The figures, so matter-of-factly told, were more chilling than any number of screaming headlines.

"The Treaty of Versailles . . ." Colin shook his head. "If they wanted to ensure another war within twenty years, they couldn't have found a better way. The terms were so humiliating for the Germans that it's no wonder they've reasserted themselves."

Mary squeezed his arm and tried to smile. "Can't we pretend for just a few hours that none of this is happening?" She dared not ask him how long he thought this war might last in case he told her. For the moment Richard was still safe, but in a couple of years, he would be old enough to die for his country.

They went to the National Gallery to hear one of the lunchtime concerts. Later, they sat in the drawing room at Fitzroy Square and listened to the exaggerated accents of William Joyce, "*Germany calling the British Isles, Germany calling . . .*" One evening they saw *Goodbye, Mr. Chips* at the cinema and Mary wept, thinking of her son.

At night, she and Colin slept together in the bedroom which had once belonged to his parents; they lay tightly curled together, glad for what they had. When it was time for Mary to return to Yorkshire, she stood in Colin's arms and did not even try to hold back the tears. "Don't cry," Colin whispered. "I'll be home soon. We'll have a good time together at Christmas. All of us."

It was the closest they came to mentioning Dickon.

That year, Richard brought a school friend back for the Christmas holidays, a boy from Austria whose Jewish family had sensed the coming holocaust and managed to send him to England just in advance of Hitler's invading armies. His father, a cellist with the Vienna State Orchestra, had been an outspoken opponent of Nazi policies; according to Richard, Carl himself was wizard on the viola. In answer to Mary's questions, Carl said he did not know where his parents were or what they were doing; as he spoke, a tic jumped under the pale skin at the corner of his mouth. The day before Christmas Eve, the two boys went out in woollen scarves and wellingtons and came back with armfuls of red-berried holly and long strands of ivy to decorate the hall and drawing room.

Later, Colin arrived. He had endured an exhausting day-long journey up from London, the train filled with troops, the heating not on, no means of obtaining any refreshments. He had been looking forward with an anticipation he did not attempt to define to seeing Dickon

again. They had not met since September; he wondered
how—if at all—his friend would have changed.

He was to spend Christmas with them and rode over
on Christmas Eve in time for dinner. They dined by
candlelight, the three adults and the two boys. Colin
could not help noticing the nervous way Dickon reacted
when spoken to, the way his hands trembled as he
reached for his glass, the lines which had deepened in
his outdoor face. For Carl's sake, they did not talk of
the war but Colin guessed that it was this which was
affecting Dickon so badly.

For his part, Dickon was taken aback by the signs of
ill health in Colin. He seemed painfully thin; Dickon
reminded himself that although he seemed to have
shaken off the problems of his childhood, he had nonetheless been a delicate boy. Living in London could not
be doing him much good; for his own part, Dickon knew
that if he had to leave the moors, the song of the larks,
the fresh air blowing down the dales, he would pine and
die. He'd tried it once, he'd given it a fair innings and
no one could have been more thankful to return.
Besides . . . he looked along the table toward Mary. She
needed him. She could not get along without him. The
thought filled him with a profound satisfaction. Once,
the fact that she was Colin's wife had seemed the worst
of the pains he had endured. They had matured, the
three of them, like the old roses in the secret garden,
which grew so entwined together that it was impossible
to see where one left off and the next began. And there
was the boy, too. The beautiful boy, made out of love,
a compensation.

Separately, Colin and Dickon thought that they had
never seen Mary look so beautiful. Despite the candlelight's softening, anxiety was sharp in her face; too often
her gaze leaped at Richard and away again. Nonetheless,
both men saw changes in her. The old stubborn Mary
was still there, but a more confident, more generous
woman was emerging from the awkward shell which had
for so long encased her. Mary had not told Colin of the
work she did locally, but while the table was cleared and
the dishes washed, Dickon did.

"Works like a beaver," he said, as the two men sat in

the study. "There's lots round here think she deserves a medal for all she does."

"Really?"

"Aye. Works every hour God gives. My sister Martha's always saying she'd never ha' believed it, not seeing what a sorry little miss she was when she first came to Misselthwaite."

"Knowing your sister Martha, I'm sure she attributes some of Mary's rehabilitation to you," said Colin. "You, and the secret garden."

"Happen she does. That's not to say she's right. And it's Mary herself, not anyone else, who's earned the respect and admiration of the folks hereabout."

"She was always good at getting things done, wasn't she? Remember how she took us two in hand when she first came back from India?"

"Aye." Over their cigars, the two men glowed at each other, proud.

"Mind you," Colin said, as Mary herself came into the room. "There are plenty of people who say it wasn't good organization but simple bossiness."

"Have you two been talking about me?" asked Mary.

"I believe your name figured in our conversation, yes."

"I wish you would get it into your head that I am not bossy, just efficient."

"Exactly what I said." Colin grinned at her. "Just because *some* people misinterpret it, doesn't mean *I* do."

"Nor me," said Dickon.

When the boys rejoined them, they gathered around the piano to sing Christmas carols. Richard played his oboe, Carl his viola. The servants gathered—Pitcher, very frail now, Mrs. Medlock with her arthritic hip, Norah, the young woman who cooked in exchange for a couple of rooms for herself and her baby, the fourteen-year-old school leaver who helped out. After winding up with *"O Come All Ye Faithful,"* they were about to disperse to the different parts of the house when Carl pulled the bow across his instrument in a long dark chord.

"On this night, in my country, people sing this," he said quietly, looking beyond them to the windows hidden behind thick blackout curtains. Slowly, he began to play

"Stille nacht, heilige nacht," and with breaking hearts, they listened as a lost boy with sad eyes played for the memory of those he might never see again. It seemed so bitter that men could kill when there was music to be made, gardens to tend, people to love. Dickon reached out to enfold Mary and Colin, Richard tucked himself against his mother, the servants linked arms and they began first to hum the beautiful tune and then quietly to sing along, silent night, holy night, while Carl's tears fell on to the burnished wood of the viola.

Clothes were rationed. The Guildhall and several fine Wren churches were badly damaged; incendiary bombs had started hundred of fires, the City was gutted. Rudolf Hess flew from Germany and landed in Scotland. Crete was attacked. Germany declared war on Russia. Time no longer flowed from one day to the next but stumbled by in bitter blocks, measured by events piled one on top of the next, bricks formed from the dust of hope, cemented with fear. As food supplies continued scarce, it gave Mary some solace to live as far as possible from their own resources, thereby leaving food for those less fortunate. She picked fruit, searched for duck eggs among the reeds by the lake, raised vegetables, fattened up a pig on scraps. Pitcher's grandson brought in pigeons and rabbits to be turned into pies; there were hens scratching about in the stable yard. Planes passed overhead in wedges, like wild geese when winter comes.

One Easter, Mary took both boys to London. Carl, by now, was almost a member of the family. They went to see John Gielgud play King Lear; afterward the actor stepped in front of the curtain to announce that though he had been warned that *Lear* would not work in wartime, the audiences had been marvelous. Walking to Fitzroy Square through the blackout, Mary could not help but wonder at the extraordinariness of ordinary things: theater-goers, lovers, women cooking for their families, babies being born, while far away, men murdered each other in the name of freedom.

Holland capitulated to the invading Germans. There was a day of national prayer. Belgium gave in, cutting off the British army, leaving them no escape except by coast. After Dunkirk, with Hitler only twenty miles or so away from southern England, with the whole country expecting imminent invasion, Mary looked into the possibility of sending Richard to Canada and discovered that exit visas were not being issued to boys over fourteen.

She telephoned Colin. "He's still at school," she protested.

"But he may be needed later on, do you see? It's only a matter of time before they bring in conscription. In fact, very soon he'll be able to sign up for himself. We won't be able to stop him, if that's what he wants to do."

She asked the question she had not dared to ask before. "How long, then, do they think it will go on?"

"At least three more years," Colin said.

"So Richard will be involved?"

"I'm afraid so."

She said: "What can I do, Colin? I'd do anything, anything at all, to save him."

"So would thousands, millions of mothers."

"Then why are we at war?"

He did not answer.

Although phone calls were supposed to be short and necessary, she said again: "What can I do?"

There was a pause. Then Colin said: "I had time yesterday to listen to a Haydn Quartet in the National Gallery. Such beautiful music."

"Colin—"

"And Dickon tells me the blackcurrants are thick this year. I expect Norah will be making jam, won't she?"

Mary put down the receiver.

Out on the moors, the wind stirred restlessly in the heather. She sat on a boulder and looked down to where the river ran flatly through the valley. Larks tumbled through the air above her but she did not hear them. Richard, she thought. My Richard. If only she could stop him, keep him a child, but she could not, he was growing older, growing nearer to war with every day that passed. He had written from school only that morning to say that they were making Molotov cocktails—*homemade bombs, Mother, bottles filled with petrol and a fuse at the top,*—for the Home Guard to use against the German invaders, when they arrived. She stared at the words, wanting to protest, wanting to ask the headmaster what kind of a way this was to bring up children.

Often she wondered what she would do, were anything to happen to Richard. Quite simply, her life would no longer be worth living. She buried her head in her hands.

"Don't fret, Mary. Don't cry." Dickon was standing behind her. "He'll be all right."

She leaned back against the strength of his body. "How did you . . . ?" But the question was superfluous: he always knew when she needed him.

"Listen to the birds sing," he said. "Look at the heather bells. See the way the sun glints on the rocks. These are things which last. Not war. Not cruelty. Not mud and death and . . . and . . ."

His voice shook. His hands trembled on her shoulders. She stood up, turned to hold him tightly against her chest.

"Don't," she said urgently.

"Not mud," he said, leaning toward her with closed eyes to rest his forehead lightly on her hair. He shuddered. *She walks in beauty* . . .

"It finished long ago, Dickon."

"No," he murmured, "it'll not be finished until hell freezes over." He heard again the sound of marching boots and hoofs slipping on wet cobblestones, smelled the acid stink of cordite, felt the old terrors. He had not told her the truth. They *did* last, mud and death and despair, as fresh in his memory as they had been twenty years ago, unfaded. "Mary," he said, out of blackness. He thought: *the last word a dying Tommy spoke.*

"What is it?" Mary heard him moan like an animal in pain. He was wounded. "What's happened?"

"My brother," he said. "Phil."

"What, Dickon?"

"We've just heard. He's been killed. During the last lot of air raids in London. He were trying to help some poor old biddy into the air raid shelters."

"Oh, Dickon. Your poor mother."

"I've just come from her house. What makes it worse, Phil's wife's expecting their first baby in three months' time."

Mary held him tighter. Would they never stop, the

circles of pain and bereavement? She had a vision of war following war, receding into the future, and mothers endlessly weeping for their sons.

Another Christmas. Snow falling. A tree brought in from the woods and decorated by the boys—some of the tarnished baubles dated back to Archie Craven's childhood. After lunch, listening to the King's broadcast on the wireless and the pathetic messages to parents from children who had been evacuated to the United States and Canada. Carl and Richard playing at a refugee concert in Middleburn, a scratch orchestra. News of the dead.

On New Year's Eve, Norah rang the passing bell, for Pitcher had died the previous spring, and they opened the windows on the terrace to listen. The night before, there had been another bombardment on London. The boys were full of jingoistic talk of joining up as soon as they left school at the end of the summer. As a European, Carl had decided to approach the Free Poles or de Gaulle's people; Richard wanted to get into the RAF. As they spoke of destroying the enemy, a cold wave of fear passed over Mary. Did they not realize what they were saying? Did they not understand that the enemy was made up of men and women, that all over Germany, families were sitting as they sat, mothers and sons together, fathers, uncles, grandparents? She raised her head from her sewing, wanting to scream at them to stop, and caught both Colin and Dickon staring at her with almost identical expressions. Dickon shook his head. Colin grimaced. She sighed. What could such young creatures know of the horrors of it all? To them it was no more than a game. What did death mean to those who were just embarking on life? She knew she could not change them; perhaps she should not wish to.

Before they boarded the train back to school, Richard tucked Mary's hand into his arm and walked her down the long platform. Away from the others, he said: "Don't be sad, Mother."

"I'm not," Mary lied.

"You are. You've convinced yourself that the minute I join up, I'm going to be killed."

"I—"

"I want you to be certain, Mother, that if I were, I should come back to Misselthwaite."

She tried to make it a joke. "As a ghost, you mean? We've already got several of those."

He was serious. "I mean it. I've been reading up on such things, the paranormal and so on. If you want to badly enough, you can return in spirit to places where you were happy. I'm sure of it. And besides, I wouldn't leave you on your own, Mother. I promise you."

Mary bit her lip. How like Dickon he sounded. *I will cum back.* It would be a sign of weakness to cry; her throat ached with the determination not to do so. There would be time enough for that when she was back at the Manor. But the years had gone so quickly. Her son was already a man.

Richard and Carl hitchhiked home from their last term at school in a transport lorry. Carl had won prizes for music and languages, Richard for mathematics and history. Both had places waiting for them at university; there had been no problem over Carl, with sponsorships from both Colin and an official at the embassy who had known his parents in peacetime.

But instead of going to university, both of them had decided to join up immediately, enrolling as fighter pilots. While they waited for their call-up papers to be processed, they helped with the harvest and learned to drive, just as Mary and Colin had done years before.

"You are so lucky, Richard," Carl said, as they leaned against a hay bale, eating the bread and cheese they had brought with them for lunch.

"Why?"

"All this." Carl waved at the fragrant hay, the hills behind, the line of trees which marked the edge of the field. "It is so . . . *English.*"

"What would you expect? That it would be Chinese?"

"You know what I mean. This is what we're going to be fighting for, me as well as you, even though it is not really my country." His face grew sad. In the years since he had first come to England, there had not been a single word from his parents; in his heart, he knew that there never would be.

"This is only one side of the place," Richard pointed

out. "You've heard my father on the subject too often to believe that it's all rural idylls and blue skies."

"Yes. Of course. But this—the moors, the people here, the streams in the grass—are as good a way to think of England as any other."

"As long as you don't think that's all there is to it."

Carl grimaced at him and took another bite of home-made bread. "I would much rather be making music than fighting," he said. "I hope that doesn't make me a coward."

"I'd much rather be flying than anything else. The fighting's just part of it."

"Are you not inspired by patriotism?"

"Not entirely, I must admit." Watching the butterfly which fluttered on his knee, its white wings folding and unfolding, Richard recalled again the balloon and how he had soared above the roofs of Misselthwaite and away.

"After the war is over, I shall become a professional musician," Carl said. Although he did not say so, he felt it would be as good a memorial to his parents as he could hope for. He had never thought to tell them that he had loved them; now, it was far too late.

"I don't know what I shall do. Father's dead set on going into Parliament, so perhaps I shall come back up here and run the estate for him. Become a simple farmer. I'll have to do it some time, so I might as well get started."

"No other ambitions?"

"I had plenty when I was younger. Now . . ." Richard shrugged. "This bloody old war certainly makes you think about the future a bit more seriously. I feel I can make just as much of a contribution simply seeing that things carry on as they ought. I'm not like my father, concerned to change things."

Carl laughed. "Remember that poem the headmaster read in chapel at Assembly? He's one of the movers and shakers, isn't he?"

"Remember the rest of it?"

"Yes, and I'm a music-maker."

"I must be one of the dreamers of dreams. I just want this sort of thing to go on forever."

"The same way Mr. Sowerby does."

"Exactly like him."

"No social conscience, then?"

"I don't know that that's exactly true. Perhaps not in the sense of changing things. I simply want to do the best I can for the people in my own little sphere. Father's determined to do the best for the entire country."

"Do you not admire him for that?"

"Of course. But it might be better to start small and gradually expand."

"No," said Carl. "I disagree. Better to have big ideals from the very beginning. Did you read the Beveridge Report?"

"Of course I did. And I agreed with everything it said. But it's a utopian concept: can it really translate into reality?"

"Why not?"

Richard pulled a hollow stem of hay from the ground and blew through it. "Do you really think that this'll be a brave new world, once the war's over?"

"I should like to think so, after all the sacrifices that have been made." Carl stared up at the sky; Richard knew he thought of his vanished parents.

"Dickon said that's what they thought after the last war. And look what happened: everything went back to the bad old ways."

"Not quite everything. And if your father gets into the House of Commons, the way he hopes to, and all the others like him, perhaps this time things will be different."

A pheasant scurried past them, clucking loudly, and both young men leaped to their feet to run after it. Carl got a hand to one of its elegant tail feathers, but Richard missed entirely, giving it a chance to fly top-heavily over the dry-stone walls and into the refuge of the neighboring field.

25

Norfolk, September 1943
   Dearest Mother,
   *I hope you are well. This is just a short note to tell
you that I've arrived here safely, and very uncomfortable it all looks, too. Thank God I went to a decent
school: I learned enough there about wooden mat-
tresses, cold-water showers, ghastly food etc, to be entirely at home here. Which is more than some of the
chaps are. The one in the bed next to me has never
been away from home before, has never been to London, never spent a night without his parents, even. Isn't
that strange? At night he snuffles into his pillow but to
preserve his dignity, I pretend I can't hear him. I can
remember my first night away from home all too
clearly, and how I blubbed then. I miss you all, of
course, but I'm afraid I'm not doing too much snuf-
fling myself. It's all so jolly exciting, and the sooner I
can get up into the air, the better pleased I'll be. Someone's got to teach Hitler a lesson and I'm more than
happy to volunteer if no one else will.
   I'll write again soon, and longer.
   Best Love . . .*

Reading this, Mary's first instinct was to crumple the
letter into a ball and throw it on to the fire. Despair
seized her. Fool! she wanted to shout. Don't you realize
what you're saying? He was eighteen, only a few months
out of school, and already he sounded like a veteran.
The folly of it all. The stupidity. How could the generals
and admirals responsible for the various services live
with the fact that while they were safely ensconced in

Whitehall, the bravest and best of the younger generation was doing the fighting for them? It ought to be the other way about. If anything happened to Richard . . . These days she thought more often about Charlotte Alice: the baby girl would now be a young woman, perhaps married, perhaps already a war widow with children to bring up on her own. Stooping, she was able to retrieve Richard's letter before it caught alight. Who knew? It might be the only one she ever received.

Suffolk, January 1944
Dear Father,
It was so good to see you briefly in London last week. As I told you then, I was looking forward to going up to university when this is over, but I must say that since then, I have been reconsidering. The difference between my school life, such a short time ago, and what I am doing now surprises even me. I have put away childish things, and all that—not that the Hundred Years War or Queen Elizabeth rallying the troops at Tilbury is childish, exactly, but you know what I mean.

They're quite a decent crowd down here. I even met a couple of chaps from school, a year or two older than I am, in the same squadron. Also a lot of chaps of a kind I've never known. Given your socialist principles, I do rather wonder why you sent me to your old school, where I would only meet people of my own sort. I'm discovering all sorts of things about our society of which I've not been aware until now, all sorts of unfairnesses and untenable assumptions. We haven't seen a lot of action yet, but any minute now, they keep telling us, and meantime we loaf around and indulge in rather silly games. Frankly, although I can't say this to Mother, everyone's nerves are a bit on edge, waiting like this for the balloon to go up (do you remember the day I floated off into the wild blue yonder and you thought I'd never come back? Such fun!) so I suppose the games are a way of letting off steam. In normal times, I can't imagine that I'd ever find myself crowded on to a table top along with forty-eight other chaps, hoping that when the fiftieth—or the fifty-first or fifty-second—climbs up, the table will break. The

*mess is all right, and there's a pretty decent pub down
the road, too. We've run into some rather nice girls,
too—even Mother would approve—but don't tell her,
please!*

Colin chuckled over this. He had known that Mary
would be fiercely jealous of any young woman who tried
to steal the affections of her precious boy, and it seemed
Richard knew it too. Thank God Richard was a normal
healthy young man, with the ordinary appetites.

Unlike himself. His appetites had never faded; he had
simply grown more adept at subduing them. When this
blasted war was over, he wanted to do what he had
always intended, and go into Parliament. It would be
impossible if there were the slightest breath of scandal
and he had schooled himself—with difficulty—into a
state of neutrality.

Only a month earlier, he had bumped into Freddie
Avery and been appalled at the sight of his former
friend. The fair curls had turned gray; the once-round
face was lined. A debauched cherub was the phrase
which had flown into Colin's mind. A cherub who had
sated himself on the bodies of too many young men; a
cherub with dead eyes and no illusions.

"I'm with military intelligence," Freddie said, drawing
out the vowels in his usual self-mocking way. "We've
commandeered some country seat in Bedfordshire or
somewhere equally bucolic. My dear, can you imagine?
I know nothing of the military except those lovely, lovely
uniforms, and even my mother would scarcely call me
intelligent." He made a ridiculous face.

Colin could not help laughing. "Your book on An-
drew Marvell got some splendid reviews," he said. "I
positively dined out on the fact that we'd been up at
Oxford together."

"Did you, darling?" Freddie's reptilian eyes roamed
Colin's face. "You're looking awfully Humpty Dumpty-
ish, you know."

"You surely can't mean overweight."

"More as if, however hard they tried, all the king's
horses and all the king's men couldn't put you together again."

"My boy's in the RAF," Colin said abruptly.

"I'm very sorry, my dear. It must be worrying."

"It is."

"Much better to be like me, entirely free of hostages to fortune. It only means tears in the end."

"I hope you're wrong," Colin said sombrely. "I don't know what my wife—what Mary would . . . if anything were to . . ."

Freddie took his arm. "Come and have a drink with me, darling. My club's just round the corner."

"I shouldn't."

"Frankly, if you don't mind my saying so, you look as if you haven't had any fun for a long long time."

"Do I?"

"And when I say fun, dear, I'm sure you know what I mean."

"I'm sure I don't." Colin tried to smile. "Anyway, those days are long behind me now. When I had fun, I mean."

"Oh?" Freddie raised one of his plucked eyebrows. "You can't honestly expect me to believe that, can you? Mr. Party Boy himself."

"Nonetheless, it's true." Colin was uncomfortable. There was something wild about Freddie; he had always been prepared to go one step further in outrageousness than anyone else, but now his flamboyance had a dangerous quality about it, as though, like the high walls of his college, he was edged in broken glass which could cut and damage.

"One quick whisky," Freddie said firmly, taking Colin's elbow. "I insist."

The one became two, and then a bottle. But despite Freddie's blandishments and the haze of whisky, Colin had enough sense of self-preservation to refuse to go on afterwards to dinner, or anything else. The club servants were eyeing them; Colin decided that in future, he must avoid being in the company of a man such as Freddie Avery.

Suffolk, May 1944
Dearest Mother,
Thank you so much for the butter and cream. I shared it round in the mess and you can't imagine how grateful everyone was to have such luxuries—and from

our own farms, too. The squadron's settling in to a busy routine here, flying escort duty most nights, but so far, no real sight of the Germans, except once in the distance, disappearing into cloud. I was sent out last week because a report came in of a U-boat caught in fishing-nets, but I didn't find anything. It was probably an extra-large mackerel. As a matter of fact, there are so many squadrons on the airfield, either coming in or taking off, that we're almost in more danger from our own chaps than from the enemy.

Please don't worry about me. I'm leading a charmed life, both on-duty and off. Last weekend we even went dancing. One of the flying officers still manages to run his old Rolls (!) and he drove a few of us over to the nearby US air-force base to hear Glenn Miller play. Quite an experience. The music was pretty tear-jerking, and I saw quite a lot of chaps wiping surreptitiously at their eyes when he played "Stardust" and "The White Cliffs of Dover" and, of course, "We'll Meet Again." (I imagine you've heard of these even in Yorkshire!)

Usually girls at dances won't have anything to do with us—they much prefer the Yanks because they're paid better than we are, and have access to all sorts of luxuries, like tinned fruit and silk stockings and scented soap. However, this time we must have been looking pretty good because we didn't do too badly. In fact I rather monopolized a very pretty American girl for most of the evening, so I felt there was a kind of wild justice in the fact that although they may steal our girls, we can also steal theirs.

Suffolk, July 1944
Dear Father,
Just wanted to say how nice it was to see you in Town last week and to repeat that I'm very proud of you for applying to be put on the list of prospective Labor candidates. I know that when you're adopted and elected, you'll be exactly the kind of public servant this country really needs.

Meanwhile, you're not looking all that well, as I may have mentioned more than once. Don't overdo it: I'm impatient to be able to swan about bragging about my old man, the MP.

We live hard and play hard here. Up most nights, across the Channel to the Dutch coast, trying to avoid the flak, back home exhausted at the end of the night. Sometimes we don't all make it. I wish I didn't find it all so exciting and, odd though it sounds, even beautiful up there with the moon high overhead and the flak bursting all round me like exploding stars and the velvety darkness below. Sometimes I feel half-drunk with it, and find myself wanting to shout bits of poetry at the top of my voice, or make love to a girl, or something.

I scored a direct hit the other night. We were coming back at dawn and met a group of Messerschmitt 109s. We were so close that we could see their leading pilot turning to bring his guns to bear before we were into a climbing turn which brought us into position above them. Someone let go a burst of fire at one of the planes which went into a half roll that brought him right into my sights and I turned the gun-button on and let him have it with all eight guns. Watched the thing burst into flames and spiral down into the sea: no time to eject. I thought I would be delighted at a job well done, at the fact that I was the one who survived the duel, but I'm not. In fact, I'm not really sure how I feel about it. Not sorry, of course: it's kill or be killed up there, but I can't help wondering what he thought about in those seconds before he crashed: his girl, his mother, the Führer? Or some small irrational thing like needing a shave. What would I think about, in similar circumstances? They're the enemy, I know, and if it hadn't been them, it would have been us, but even so, whatever the newspapers would have us believe, they can't all be baby-roasting, nun-raping monsters, can they?

Don't tell Mother, obviously, but we were hit on that op. Lost part of the wing, fire in one of the engines and a bullet hole through one window of the cockpit and out the other, just where my head ought to have been. Don't know where it was at the time—perhaps I temporarily lost it! The ground crew seemed to think we were damned lucky to make it back to base, given the state we were in.

The thing which amazes me most about the chaps who've been around for a while is their casual attitude to the whole business of flying. They treat their planes more like bicycles than killing machines, as if the whole thing—scrambling off, firing, bringing down, being brought down themselves—were just a huge schoolboy joke. Perhaps that's why they're so successful. Or perhaps after a while, that's the only way to survive—of the original squadron, there are only two left and I suppose if you stopped to think about that, you'd go to pieces.

August, Suffolk 1944
Dear Dickon
It was jolly decent of you to send the postal order and I assure you it was put to good use. I've met a really rather smashing girl, and I was able to impress her mightily with my (temporary) affluence.

We've completed several missions already—but I won't tell you about it because I know your feelings on the subject. When I'm off-duty, I "borrow" a bicycle and get out into the countryside. It's awfully pretty: very lush at this time of year, with wildflowers and different grasses in abundance. There are clouds of little butterflies which hover just above the meadows, and are the most beautiful powder-blue color, like the delphiniums you planted in the secret garden. I hope you won't laugh if I say that the aforementioned girl has eyes of precisely the same color. Remember that poem you were always quoting? She walks in beauty like the night/Of cloudless climes and starry skies;/And all that's best of dark and bright/Meet in her aspect and her eyes—it sums her up exactly.

But please don't run away with the idea that I've fallen in love or anything of that sort!

Amy Miller Monaghan sat hugging her knees to her chin. For a few hours, she could forget about the air-force base, the sound of airplanes taking off or coming in to land, the oil in the hangars, the odd smell—sweat and metal—in the Nissen hut which she shared with a dozen other female personnel. She'd cadged a ride into town with a bunch of boys all set to enjoy themselves for the afternoon in Cambridge, and now she waited for Richard to arrive. All around her, grasses grew as high as her chin, laced with cornflowers and poppies, buttercups and moonflowers. If she moved her head, she could see towers in the distance, and spires of ancient stone. At her feet, the river moved quietly. Back home, grass never smelled like this—the sun sucked the juices out of it before it got the chance—and rivers were not quiet. They roared and tumbled, or spread themselves miles wide, as though desperate to prove that of all rivers, they were the most riverly. She loved the quietness of England, the understatedness of it all. She loved the way nobody tried to impress. She rather thought she loved Richard Archibald Craven.

His hands. The way his yellow hair flopped into his eyes. His voice, which sent delicious shivers down her spine. And there was his cute accent, too. She wasn't exactly clued up on these things, but she guessed it was kind of upper class, because although he was quite young, even older men called him sir. And they'd been second in line in a taxi queue the other day, and the man in front had given way to Richard, although there was absolutely no need, and Richard had said so.

They'd been up to London a week ago, just for the day, and spent most of the time simply walking. Amy had marveled at the way the British refused to despair. Her impressions had been of a city bowed but not broken, of a people suffering but never submitting. Despite ruined churches, shattered buildings, the strain of living under seige, the English were clearly determined to keep their lives as normal as was possible in the circumstances.

Hand in hand, they had walked past the sandbagged machine-gun nest at the top of Downing Street and up to Trafalgar Square where a band was playing to the lunch-time crowd. In Oxford Street, the once-luxurious shops were boarded up; broken glass crunched under their shoes. John Lewis was a shell; signs outside a semi-boarded furriers read SHATTERED BUT NOT SHUT-TERED, BOMBED BUT NOT OUT! Above the jewelers at Oxford Circus, a sign exhorted the public to HIT BACK! And they were still selling flowers from barrows . . .

"I don't know how they have the courage to stay here," Amy said. "To carry on as if nothing out of the ordinary had happened."

"They're not going to let Hitler beat them into submission."

"I'm sure I would have got out."

"You probably wouldn't, you know. From what I've seen, the worse conditions are, the better people behave."

They turned eastward toward St Paul's Cathedral. There had been a lot of bomb damage here the night before, although the worst of the Blitz was now over. They passed a small shop where the owner was hammering up a board on which he had written BUSINESS AS USUAL, MR. HITLER, while his wife patiently swept glass into the gutter. In the next street, they came across a silent crowd which stood staring at a roped-off space filled with rubble. It appeared that a bomb had fallen on the left-hand row of houses during the night: three in the middle had been reduced to little more than a pile of bricks. Charred beams protruded into naked air from those still standing on either side. Fireplaces on the walls were intact; above one an undamaged gilt mirror still hung, not even crooked. From another wall, a team of footballers gazed impassively down, scarcely displaced by the blast. Men in boiler suits and tin hats with the letters H and R painted on them, worked to remove the rubble, flinging broken bricks and pieces of chimney-pot, planks and doors behind them as though they were hunting dogs going after a rabbit.

"There's a man and his wife down there, underneath that lot," someone explained in a whisper.

"It's Mr. and Mrs. Cooper," said another onlooker, speaking under his breath. "Silly buggers wouldn't go down to the shelter when they heard the Alert. Been telling them for weeks. Now look."

Someone shushed him. The street was so quiet that every now and then Amy could hear the shift of rubble and a scatter of debris. She realized that the absolute stillness was in order to give the digging men the chance to listen for the sound of survivors beneath the ruins: a faint call, a tap, a groan. She caught sight of a teddy bear with a blue ribbon around its neck lying half-hidden by brick dust, and realized there must have been children living in the houses. Torn curtains flapped at glassless windows. Every house in the street was damaged. A wicker laundry basket lay on its side, spilling socks and underwear. Overall hung a pall of dusty smoke and the smell of high explosive. One of the men in the crowd behind them had been blown out of his house and into the street by the explosion. A bedhead was uncovered by the men, and feathers flew from the remains of a pillow. Broken glass lay everywhere; smoke was still rising from the ruins.

Richard went up to the rope barrier and called across. "Want any help?"

One of the men raised a grimy face to him. "Better not, sir, thanks all the same."

"Sure?"

"Yes, sir. Besides, there's one still waiting to go off somewhere hereabouts."

"One what?" whispered Amy when Richard came back.

"Unexploded time bomb, I presume."

"But . . . it might go off at any time."

"I know."

"But they're working there without—"

"There are people trapped underneath," a woman next to them said. "They have to get them out."

"What happens if that bomb goes off?"

"Who knows?"

The simple bravery of the diggers overwhelmed her. One of them suddenly held up a hand and behind her, the crowd murmured like a river. "I can hear something," he said.

The silence was eerie. No traffic, no ringing of bicycle bells, no footsteps. A pigeon flew across the street from one roof to another, sunlight catching the pink feathers of its breast. With infinite care, the workers converged on one part of the rubble and began to work faster.

"Who is it, Jim?" one of the crowd called softly, and one of the Heavy Rescue men said, with tears running down his face: "Megan. It's Megan Cooper. And she's bloody singing."

A sigh swept the onlookers, a collective movement of

relief and thanks. "What's she singing?" someone asked, and the HRS man shook his head. "Can't tell."

"For all she's from Wales, Megan couldn't carry a tune to save her life," remarked the woman next to Amy.

"Hang on," the HRS man said, with a grin. "I think it's meant to be 'Don't Fence Me In.'" He looked over at Richard. "Like to say a few words, sir?"

And Richard had murmured the words of the doxology, while the crowd softly joined in.

It was strange, really. The minute you opened your mouth here, everyone knew who you were and where you came from. The rest of it, refinements like the old school tie nonsense and the blueness of your blood, came later. As soon as you spoke, you had defined yourself, for better or worse. She'd heard about the British class system, but experiencing it at first hand like that was something else. The way privilege was taken for granted. The assumption that because you had a title or two surnames linked by a hyphen, or the right accent, you were superior. She could not get over the way that HRS man had automatically turned to Richard, asked him to pray for them, although he was a total stranger and probably never been in the area before in his life.

She had two surnames herself, but they'd never entitled her to anything more than beans, except just very occasionally an extra big dollop of tutti frutti at the ice cream parlor downtown, and then only because Bobby Hooper behind the counter used to be sweet on her.

They'd argued about it on the way back from London. "Thank God I live in a democracy," she'd said, only half-joking.

Richard had got annoyed. "What kind of a democracy herds its native population into reservations?" he said. "What about the persecution of Negroes in the south? Some democracy, when most of them don't even have the right to vote. Or do you think skin color is a better way to discriminate against someone than accent?"

"Of course not. But—"

"But what?"

"The Negroes are different," she said.

"How?"

She'd floundered around a bit, but the truth was, she

hadn't been able to come up with much of an answer. Since she'd come over here, she'd begun to realize that the United States of America was very far from being the land of the free she had always been brought up to believe it.

Insects were chirping among the grasses. A gray-green grasshopper landed out of the air, quivered on her bare leg for a moment, took off again like a jumping jack. Two swans sailed arrogantly past, wings furled. There were shouts in the distance, the sound of boys playing football. Sudden tears caught at her throat. She knew that years from now, long after this bloody war was over, the sight of swans would bring back this particular summer moment, this anticipation, these intermingled emotions of joy and melancholy. So much had been lost and, at the same time, so much gained.

Richard, in particular. She was falling in love with him. She'd dated boys before, of course, she'd even been keen on one or two of them. But it had never ever been like this. Never this total submergence of self, this being taken over, so that she could only think of him, even on duty, even when casualties were brought in, when boys went missing. There was something depraved, she could not help feeling, about the way her delight in him illumined even the worst things with a bright glow. She did not want to indulge in such women's magazine sentiments, such easy romantic twaddle. For some time she'd fought against love. But when she saw him coming toward her, when he touched her, when he kissed her, she knew that every sloppy word she'd devoured back in her teens was true.

I'm trying to be sensible and adult about this, Richard had written to Dickon, *but it's difficult. If you could meet her, you'd see exactly what I mean. There's a kind of innocence about her, as if she hadn't quite grown up, yet at the same time, a wisdom which leaves me breathless. Is this just because she's American or because she's female? Is it something girls are born with? Am I talking about the Mystery of all Women? Or just the mystery of mine? I long to introduce you to her, so that you can judge for yourself.*

*   *   *

Amy got to her feet and brushed the stray seeds and burrs from her dress. Two o'clock, he'd said. I'll meet him at the station and then we'll take a punt up from the mill. You'll love him, he'd added, hugging her. He's one of my parents.

But not his father. Nor his uncle. Now, was that slightly weird or not? This Mr. Dickon Sowerby was not even his step-father. Amy knew about step-dads, she had one of those herself. But this guy wasn't any relation to him, though Richard said he was one of his parents. Three parents? It sounded kind of crazy, especially when Richard was so absolutely serious. She couldn't wait to meet this one, nor the other two, for that matter, though from what she had gathered, the mother might be a bit of an ordeal, not just because she doted on Richard—which was one thing they both shared—but also because, although Richard never said so, she was obviously a bit intimdating, the kind of Englishwoman who'd gone out and ruled the Empire with an umbrella in one hand and a dose of quinine in the other. The way Richard told it, Mary Craven sounded like a cross between Good Queen Bess and St Florence Nightingale, with a hefty dose of Hollywood-style glamor thrown in for good measure.

Round a bend in the river came the front end of a punt, and voices. She ran her fingers through her copper curls and tried to smile. Truth was, she felt as though this was some kind of entrance examination, though whether she passed or failed, it wouldn't make the slightest difference to how she felt about Richard. But it might make a difference to how he felt about her.

She thought of the knife-edge they all lived on at the base, the knife-edge Richard himself lived on. The planes scrambling out on moonlit nights or day-time raids, the young men jaunty in their flying boots and white scarves, the gut-churning tension until they came back. Along with everyone else, she had stood at dawn while the skies to the south-west grew brighter, watching as the first planes, no bigger than gnats, appeared on the horizon, listening as they drew closer, hardly daring to count them back in case there were fewer than were counted out. When that happened, the whole base was cast down, morale sunk to a gray-faced low; some of the younger ones—eighteen—and nineteen-year-olds—could not always keep back their tears.

The same thing, she was sure, happened at the British RAF bases. And one day, it might be Richard's plane which did not make it home. By falling in love with him, she was laying herself open to the possibility of a pain she might find she could not stand. If she admitted it, brought it out in the open, it would make it all the worse if the worst happened. So far, she'd pushed it down, tried to contain it, refused to tell Richard that she loved him, though he must know she did. But what she really wanted was to let go, to wallow in it, to embark on that screaming helter-skelter ride into—what?

"Amy!" There he was. God, he was so beautiful. So sleek and bright. No one could ever have handled a punt-pole with such grace and elegance. My boy, she thought, emotion choking her so that for a moment she could only wave, while her mouth trembled. My Richard.

He brought the punt into the bank and reached out a hand. "Darling," he said, "I want you to meet Dickon."

Darling, is it? Dickon said to himself. So that's the way the wind lies. He smiled at the girl Richard was helping into the punt. She's lovely, he thought. She's perfect for our boy. Just perfect. Those blue eyes, freckles across her nose, skin like the top skimmings off the milk pans in the dairy. There was something about her, too, which reminded him of Mary when she was a girl, a beguiling mixture of strength and vulnerability.

For her part, Amy saw a man with the autumnal coloring of a fox or a stag. Hair which reminded her of the fall colors in Vermont, a chestnut sleekness, round blue eyes, a smile the size of the Grand Canyon. Settling down next to him, she tried not to show any surprise. Because the really strange thing about this Dickon was how like Richard he looked, even though Richard was fair and this man shared her own auburn complexion. Dog owners were supposed to end up looking like their pets—or was it vice versa?—and she guessed that if you had three parents, all three might end up looking like you—or you like them, as the case might be.

"I'm so pleased to meet you," she said.

He caught her hand in both of his. "And I you."

His warmth was unusual: she had the fleeting sensa-

tion of being caught up by feathered wings and held
against a beating heart. His accent was not the same as
Richard's. More countrified: did that mean he was, in
the odd English manner, somehow inferior? Or simply
that he lived in a different part of the country? Richard
had told her about his home up on the Yorkshire
moors—(Misselthwaite Manor: it sounded straight out of
Edgar Allan Poe)—and sometimes, when he was especially excited, she could hear how his own voice altered,
the vowels lengthening, the language growing less
complex.

Hoping he was not staring too rudely, Dickon tried to
take in the girl's features. Mary would be sure to want
to know every detail, when he finally got back to Misselthwaite. He could see things in Amy's pale face which
he doubted Richard could, simply because Richard did
not yet need to see them. As well as beauty, there was
strength and confidence. And, which mattered most,
goodness. If Richard wanted to marry this girl—and he
rather suspected that he had been invited along today
in order to bestow some kind of blessing—then he,
Dickon, had no doubt that any little Richards which
came along would be brought up the right way. And
when you got down to it, Dickon told himself, it was
that which mattered in the end.

"Richard told me you were a stunner," he said. "He
were right."

"Why, thank you." Amy did not simper. If there was
one thing Dickon could not abide, it was a lass who
simpered.

"It's a right pleasure to be here," continued Dickon.
"And to meet you."

"For me too." A tic had started up under one of Dickon's eyes, and she could not help noticing the convulsive
movement of his hands, until he clasped one in the other
to hold them still.

"I hope Richard'll bring you up north and show you
our moors."

"Oh, so do I. He's told me such a lot, not just about
Yorkshire but about the house, too. The library and the
morning room—we don't have morning rooms back
home, you can bet—and the portrait of the little girl
with the parrot and the Great Palm House." Amy

leaned toward him confidentially. "Shall I tell you what Richard told me about you?"

"What were that?"

"He said lots of nice things, of course, but the one I remember most is that you can charm animals."

"Aye."

"Can you, then? Is it true?"

"Used to be."

"Played to them," Richard said from the end of the boat, "on a little wooden pipe." Behind him the green water stretched away between slanting willows. On either side, the fields spread flatly toward the sky. "My mother's told me about it hundreds of times."

"Sounds like Orpheus with his lute," said Amy.

"That's what he said years ago, didn't you, lad?"

"I did."

"Or Francis of Assisi," said Amy.

"The way my mother describes it," Richard said, "it was exactly like that."

"Did he tell you that he can charm creatures himself?" asked Dickon.

"No! Can you, Richard?"

"Not really."

"I gave him my pipe," said Dickon. "He used to play it, too."

"I did. But somehow the birds never listened to me. And instead of being charmed, any passing badgers ran as fast as they could in the opposite direction."

"Still got the pipe?"

"I most certainly have."

"One day, maybe I can come and visit your secret garden," Amy said. "And then perhaps Richard will play. I'm sure it would charm me, if not the animals." From Richard's accounts, Amy had imagined it often enough. The secret garden, the three children, roses tumbling everywhere, a robin nesting in the ivy, fox cubs and lambs and squirrels gambolling about or lying on the grass transfixed while a red-headed boy—this very person, in fact—played on his homemade flute. "I feel as though I'm meeting someone straight out of a story book," she said. "Richard's talked so much about you." She trailed her fingers in the river and sighed with pleasure. "Nothing like that ever happened back home."

"How do you like this country, Miss Monaghan?" Dickon asked.

"Please," she said. "Call me Amy."

"Amy, then."

"I like it wonderfully." Amy was surprised by the tremor which passed across Dickon's face as she said this. Perhaps he suffered from arthritis or something; her step-dad was the same. "So much so that I have to keep reminding myself that I'm not here for pleasure, I'm not here to enjoy myself. If there weren't a terrible war raging in Europe, I wouldn't be here at all."

"In that case, what would you be doing?"

"Nursing, I guess. That's what I trained for." Or married, she did not add. Back home, girls like her got married pretty young and settled into the lives their mothers had mapped out for them more or less the day they were born. She hadn't wanted any of that, hadn't even wanted to marry, not ever, though recently she'd rather changed her mind on that score. Or, rather, had not, not if she was sensible, not if she knew what was good for her. Maybe *after* the war, but not now, not while Richard was flying missions, every time edging nearer the statistics which they'd quoted her when she first arrived on the base. "Three weeks life expectancy, on average. A month, if they're lucky." Three weeks . . . And he'd been on ops for over twelve months. There was a enemy plane out there just looking for him, she knew that.

"What is it, lass?" Mr. Sowerby patted her knee. "What's up?"

Turning, she looked straight into his eyes and could tell that he knew exactly what she had been thinking, that he had thought it often enough himself. She bit down on the inside of her lower lip to stop herself from pouring out all her fears to him. Only last week Steve Schneider and Billy Coover hadn't come back. Billy the Kid, they called him because he was so young, only just out of high school. And he was never going to take up that football scholarship at Notre Dame now. Her chin was wobbling, but she didn't mind. Mr. Sowerby didn't look as if he minded either. The important thing was not to let Richard see.

"We'll stop soon and open our picnic, what do you say?" he was calling from the end of the punt. Water fell in an arc of drops as he stripped the pole. Above his head the sky was intensely blue; the river smelled earthy and cool; cows lowed in the fields.

Keep this, Amy, the girl urged herself. Put this day in the mental scrap-book because there might not ever be another one. Again she was aware that these special moments would always be pasted against the walls of her mind: the fair young Englishman in his white trousers, the man at her side with his wide unhappy smile and twitching hands, the river, the swans. And then a group of bombers droned heavily across the sky, heading south toward the English Channel, and she knew that this too, this disruption, would be part of the memory. They looked at each other, melancholy, then Amy beat at the water with the flat of her hand, raising bubbles and splashes, and laughed, and hoped that Richard would not hear the sadness behind the laughter though Dickon, she knew, would.

It's not fair . . . Dickon was thinking. These young things . . . our boy . . . Somewhere in the distant reaches of his brain, bony arms waved, skulls gleamed in the mud, ghostly voices called *Why us, Corp? Why not you?* but for once he was able to shut them out. Holding Richard in his arms as a tiny talcumed baby, he had thought that he could never again love as fiercely as he did then, but as the boy had grown, so had his love. He had told Mary that it would be impossible for him to carry on if anything happened to the lad, and it was true. She would have to manage without him, because if they took Richard, then he would have had enough, suffered enough, and he could no longer guarantee to protect her, not even his little wench. She had softened over the years, and he had always thought that if you were softer, in some strange way you were also stronger. Mary did not need him so much these days as she once had.

They tied up against a willow tree, and Richard lifted a basket from behind the sloping seat-back. He reached into it and brought out three glasses and handed them one each. Then he pulled out a bottle. "Look at this," he said reverently. "Dickon's brought us a bottle of the claret which was put down when I was born."

Which made it over twenty years old, Amy thought. "Should be delicious."

"When she heard I was going to see you, your mother insisted I bring some wine," Dickon said. He had not told Mary he was meeting Richard's girl; would she have been so eager to dispense the contents of the Misselthwaite cellars if she had known?

"Well, I've got oranges and Hershey bars from the PX," Amy said. "and I hope to goodness they're not as old as the wine."

"And *I*'ve brought egg sandwiches I got one of the boys in the cookhouse to make up for us," said Richard. "Guaranteed fresh this morning."

"Haven't had chocolate for a bit," said Dickon wistfully. "And as for oranges . . ."

"I hope that chocolate didn't cost you anything valuable," Richard said, pouring wine into Amy's glass.

"Like my honor, do you mean?" teased Amy. "No, I'm saving that for a special occasion." The look which passed between the two young people was hot enough, in Dickon's opinion, to have started a heath fire.

He coughed. "Norah sent down a roast fowl," he said. "She's sure you're wasting away, Richard, on RAF rations."

"Sounds like the whole family's joined in this picnic," Amy said, and caught Dickon's eye, and was aware that what she said was true, this was a group of people which was bound together more tightly than the cords of kindling wood which were delivered to their back door every fall. Would they let her be part of it, if Richard and she were to . . . ? But she was racing ahead, being previous, as her grandmother always used to say.

She did not want to rush things. This precious time of being in love would eventually change, she knew that. Either it would fizzle to nothing more than a remembered spark in the air, or else it would evolve into something steadier and deeper, if it were allowed to. She should cling on to the present, take it slowly, savor the seconds.

But the conditions of war inevitably added an urgency. The young men flying off into the unknown wanted to feel that they had left something imperishable behind them; the girls needed a token that the love they felt really had existed. For both, marriage, even if makeshift and hasty, was one way to second-guess Fate. Amy didn't want that. But despite her resolutions, she also knew that if Richard were to ask, she would accept him without a moment's hesitation, for a moment might be all they would have.

> *Suffolk, August, 1944*
> *Dear Dickon,*
> *What did you think? Isn't she wonderful? Isn't she everything a man could possibly dream of?*
> *I'm writing to ask you not to speak of her to my mother. I haven't asked Amy to marry me, but I shall soon, I think, and—if I'm lucky and she accepts me— I thought it might be rather nice if I could announce our engagement at the birthday party I know that Mother is planning for me—even though I've pointed out that I am no longer my own master, and if I can't get leave, I shan't make it. Besides, I should feel an awful chump if I ask Amy and she turns me down. So mum's the word for the moment, if you don't mind. I know I can rely on your discretion.*

> *Suffolk, September 1944*
> *Dearest Mother,*
> *I'm getting more used to the wide flat skies of East Anglia, though every time I look out of the window I wonder why someone hasn't painted in a few dales and added a moor or two. It's good being so close to Cambridge. Danforth, one of the fellows here, was reading history there until the war started and last week I went with him to call on his former tutor. We found the old boy sitting in the same paneled room where Danforth used to go for tutorials, drinking dry sherry and talking about the implications of the Corn Laws. I almost asked him if he knew there was a war on!*
> *We went square dancing at one of the American Red Cross Clubs in the evening: with all the do-si-doing and hi-yippee-yis, I felt as if I had stepped straight into a cowboy movie.*
> *I'll be due some leave soon though with things hotting up, you can never be certain and we never know when we might not be called on to step in for someone else at the last moment. If and when I get away from base, I'll take the first train up that I can, unless I try*

to hitchhike. There are so many bases up and down this coast that I could probably hop from one to another in the transport lorries without any difficulty at all and then just take a local train across to Thwaite. I'll let you know where I am somehow, even if I have to use a carrier pigeon. It seems such a long time since I last saw you, and I don't need to say how much I miss you and the Manor. Also, there is something rather important I want to tell you. It was splendid to see Dickon for the day a few weeks ago: I wish you could have come too. We went on the river and he took to punting as though he'd been born with a pole in his hand.

   Guess who I ran into in Piccadilly a couple of weeks ago—Carl! It was so good to see him again. He's well, and flying just like me, though he's based down in Hampshire. Didn't go to the Free Poles, in the end; joined the RAF instead. Said that after all those years at an English school, he was as British as the next man. He sent lots of love to you, and hopes to come and visit you one day soon.

   I imagine you are kept busy with the hospital, as well as all your committees. Don't get too tired, Mother. It won't do you—or any of us—any good if you exhaust yourself entirely. It'll be so good to come home again for a few days.

Mary wished she did not feel quite so apprehensive at reading this. What could Richard possibly want to tell her? She looked again at the word "we." Was he referring to his friends from the base? Or not? Was there a connection between the "we" and the important news he wished to impart? A woman. It had to be. Try as she might, she could not imagine her son and . . . A Woman. War, as she knew, could turn a boy into a man overnight, yet he still seemed to her to be much too young for that sort of thing. He was not, of course. How quickly the years had slipped away: before she had had time to relish him fully, he was leaving her for someone else. She told herself that she was far too sensible to want to be one of those smothering mothers who could not let their children go or, worse, the sort who tried to hang on to the affections of a son long after it was suitable.

Nonetheless, she was conscious of pique, of a childish sense that it wasn't fair. She was impatient for Dickon to return and tell her all about his afternoon on the river. He and Richard must have had such fun together. Richard might even have confided in him about this Woman of his. It would be good to have some warning before his leave; it would be good to know what to expect. If she had not been so busy, she would have gone down herself but there was so little time for anything these days, there was always so much to do. It was such a long time since he last came home.

Mary sighed. Why should she have leaped to the conclusion that Richard had a girlfriend? And if he had, wasn't that absolutely normal, at his age? She just wished that the last few years could have been slowed down. They would talk about it soon enough. Meanwhile, she would tell them in the kitchen to start saving butter and sugar so that he could have his favorite homemade cake when he came back. A duck could be killed, and she might even be able to beg some extra lamb cutlets from the butcher.

Amy. Darling. I know it's only an hour since we parted, but I wanted to say again how happy I am, and how I promise that I'll be the best husband the world has ever known and that you'll never have a moment to regret saying "yes." The future seems to me like a glorious golden sunrise: how I long for the war to be over and the two of us being together for the rest of our lives.

Darling Amy, I hope you're even a tenth as happy as I am. See you soon, soon, soon.

All my love, forever,

26

"You don't regret it, do you, darling?"

"What's to regret?"

"The wedding cake and white lace, I suppose. Champagne and a guard of honor and both our mothers crying their eyes out."

"Darling Richard, of course I regret all that. Particularly the bit about the mothers. Won't yours be upset at us doing it this way?"

"She'll be devastated, probably. But she'll understand."

"You hope."

"I *know*."

"Darling."

"Mmm?"

"If we didn't tell our families, we could start out fresh, couldn't we? When this is over, I mean."

Richard picked up Amy's hand and looked at the thin wedding band she wore with a small antique pearl set in gold. "We could. We shall. And you must have a proper engagement ring, for a start. There's a Craven sapphire which has been passed down for generations, and I'm not sure you aren't supposed to have a bracelet or brooch to go with it."

"We don't have too many traditions in my family," Amy said. "Not too many sapphires, either."

"Why didn't you tell me this before? I thought I was marrying into money."

"We're not poor, just not old." Amy squeezed her new husband's hand. "But what I meant, Richard, was that after the war, we could have another wedding, couldn't we, a proper one this time, with all the trimmings?"

"Do we get another honeymoon as well?"

"That could be arranged, I guess."

"Will you still love me as much as you do today?"

"More, Richard. Much much more." Yet as she spoke, apprehension filled Amy's chest, immovable as setting concrete.

"Then when this is over, why don't we arrange to get married every month?"

"Every week."

"Every *day,* my sweet darling wife."

From their hotel window they could see the spires of Canterbury Cathedral. Silver barrage balloons hung above the Close; bomb damage was plentiful. They had forty-eight hours before Richard had to report to Manston, and spent forty-seven of them in their room. Amy had brought along what she called their K-rations: two bottles of champagne, chocolate bars, some processed American cheese, a couple of bread rolls, some butter, four hard-boiled eggs and four oranges. One of the girls in her hut had lent her a silk nightdress and matching negligee, another had given her some scented bath crystals sent from home. There had not been time to put together a trousseau, even if she had wanted to, nor even to buy a new outfit. She had worn a pink rosebud in her buttonhole as they were married by special licence before a registrar, and felt no doubts at all as he finally pronounced them man and wife and wished them well.

When it was time to leave Canterbury, they drove toward Manston in the car which Richard had been able to borrow from a friend, along with the necessary petrol. Away from the coast, there were few signs of war as they maundered along the lanes, reluctant to reach their destination. Crops were greening toward harvest time, there were rabbits in the hedges, seagulls swooped and screamed above the fields. Richard was to drop Amy at the station at Ramsgate so that she could get back to Cambridgeshire by train. Her heart turned over as she kissed him goodbye. He looked so young, so expectant and ready.

Neither of them had spoken of the uncertain future;

the possibility that there might not be one was too terrible to contemplate. She had already applied to be moved nearer to him and they hoped to see each other again the following month.

"Amy." He reached up and handed her something wrapped in a checked handkerchief. "I want you to have this."

"What is it?" She felt the wrapped object with her fingers.

"Dickon's pipe."

"What, the one he charmed animals with?"

"That's right."

"But . . ." She stared down into his eyes. "Why are you . . ."

"Just in case," he said.

"Just in case . . ." The phrase seemed hideous with omen. "No. I don't want it."

"Please, darling."

"But if anything were to—if you didn't . . ."

"I should like to know you had it." His face was pleading. "That you'll take care of it for me."

How young he was. She leaned from the window and stroked his face. "My husband," she said. She could hardly believe she was a married woman.

"Amy. I don't know how to say all the—"

She touched his mouth. "Don't try. There's nothing to say."

"Or everything."

"But we've already said that, my darling."

"And will go on doing so for the rest of our lives, Amy, my love, my sweetheart, my wife."

"Yes."

Reaching up, he kissed her again. Then, as the train finally gathered up enough head of steam to lurch from the station, he ran along beside the train. "Wish me luck as you wave me goodbye," he called, and she waved once more at the tall fair-haired figure, knowing that the two of them were already brushed by the inexorability of fate.

Kent, October 1944
Darling Mother,
I've been posted down here, which means I'll have to postpone coming up to Misselthwaite until further

*notice. I'm sorry about this, but things are hotting up:
I love you, Mother.*
Your loving son,

Kent, October 1944
Dear Father,
*You probably know that there's a big show coming
up very soon. Whatever happens, and at the risk of
sounding soppy, I want you to know how good it's all
been, and how grateful I am for everything you've
done and been.*
Your loving son,

Kent October 1944
Dear Dickon,
*In case you never realized, this is just to say how
happy I've always been, how lucky I've always felt
myself to be, to have three of you instead of the normal
two. I know I don't need to say how much I love you,
but I'll say it anyway. Be good to my girl, Dickon, if
I'm not around.*
With thanks and love from your son,

*Darling Amy: I miss you so. I look forward more
than I can say to next weekend. Don't let's do anything
special, just book a room in that pub by the river and
spend the evening together. A bottle of wine and our
love for each other should be enough entertainment.*
*Always remember how much I adore you, how im-
patiently I long for our life together to begin.*
See you soon.

Colin was at his desk at the Ministry when his secretary
came in. "Sir Percy wants to see you," she said, while
he wrote a final amendment to the news release which
was scheduled to appear in the papers the following
morning.

From her tone, he knew at once that this was no office
matter. Carefully he blotted the words he had just
added, carefully he removed the cap from the end of his
fountain pen and fitted it over the gold nib. He looked
over her head at the door through which she had just
come.

"Thank you, Peggy," he said distantly. He knew that if he caught her eye, he would see in her face confirmation of his worst fears. Richard. It had to be something to do with Richard. He had lived with the fear that it might for so long, that any other eventuality did not occur to him.

"I'll tell him that you're—"

"Thank you," he said again, as he rose heavily to his feet, his mind already running through the arrangements he would have to make if it should prove necessary for him to travel up to the north.

"I'm sorry, Mr. Craven," she said.

Slowly, he walked the official corridors of brown and cream, the paint patched and peeling now after so many years without refurbishment. His feet moved across the brown linoleum as though weighted down with lead. He knocked at his superior's door and went in before Sir Percy could answer.

"Ah. Craven." The department head was the kind of overfed, heavy-jowled man Colin had always loathed, a paradigm of the social divisons which made it impossible for the ordinary working man to communicate with those who so heedlessly ran his life. Yet even as he thought this, he had to concede that Sir Percy had worked tirelessly since taking over this particular department of the Ministry, that he was always approachable, that the people who worked under him admired, even loved him.

"You wanted to see me," he said.

"That is hardly the word I would have used," Sir Percy said. He got up and came round his desk. "I'd give anything in the world not to have to see you at this particular moment, with this particular piece of news."

"Is it about my son?"

"I'm afraid so." Sir Percy put an arm across Colin's shoulders and then gripped his hand.

"What happened?"

"His plane was shot down over the Channel, I'm sorry to say."

"Any chance of . . . ?"

"I . . . I really don't think so, unfortunately."

"You're sure?"

"He was . . ." Sir Percy coughed. He knew something

of what Colin was going through; he had lost a nephew at Dunkirk and would never forget the anguish of his sister as she waited for news, the gradual dying of hope, the eventual sinking into an almost irrecoverable state of despair. Although in some ways, it was worse for the women than the men. "They believe he was dead before his plane even hit the water."

"I see."

"It's a damnable business all around."

"Yes."

"You'll need time off . . . your wife . . . up to Yorkshire . . . we'll manage without you . . . long as it takes . . ."

Dimly aware of his superior's words, Colin clung to the image of Dickon. Comfort me in this, he thought, as you have in so many other crises. Comfort me, Dickon, not by any overt action but by the security you have always offered.

Never had he missed so much as he did now the mother whose arms he had never felt, against whose breast he had never been held.

Mary was working in the secret garden when she heard the old gate swing open and the resident robin begin to chatter. That meant Dickon. Pushing back her straw hat with her wrist, she squinted into the sunlight as he walked toward her through tendrils of late-blooming honeysuckle and clematis.

It was not until he was close that she saw his eyes.

One hand at her throat, she reached for the back of the ornate wrought-iron seat beside her, the trowel falling from her hand. Richard. Something had happened. She tried to speak but her mouth was too dry to form the words.

"Mary," Dickon said. Through the mist of tears which obscured his vision she seemed to him as she had been years ago, a little girl coming through a gate into the wood, imperious and sorrowful, a child who, like the dead rose trees in the garden, needed pruning in order that she might bloom. "Colin telephoned me."

"My son," she said. Richard was dead—she could see it in his face.

He nodded heavily. "Our boy." He put his arm

around her and she leaned against his breast. Neither spoke because there was no need for words. They had journeyed together to this point and both knew that beyond it lay only disintegration. She watched as a bumble bee landed drowsily beside Dickon's shoe and staggered off between the grass stems. Mayflies jitterbugged beside the lilacs. Far away, a lawnmower hummed like a giant cricket and even further off, came the sigh of the wind on the moors, like the movement of a vast ocean.

After a while, Dickon said: "Colin should be here soon. I've told them that we'd be waiting for him here."

Like a starving rat, pain thrust between Mary's ribs and gnawed at her heart. She dared not look beyond this present moment, to the unimaginable bleakness of a future without Richard. "We must wait for him, then." At least they would be together, the three of them.

"Yes."

That was how Colin, stumbling across the grass in his City shoes, found them, side by side, she lying against his shoulder, as she had done years ago when Richard was new-born. "Dickon," he said. "Mary."

He sat down on Mary's other side. She was already hunched and shriveled with loss. His own body was gripped by a grief so intense that all other feeling had gone. Even so simple an action as taking Mary's cold fingers in his required such concentration that he could not complete it.

"This seemed the best place to wait for you," Dickon said.

"Where else?"

Again there was silence. The robin in the ivy scolded for a moment then flew down to perch on the curved back of the seat, its bright black eye unguarded.

In the weighted quiet, Mary could hear the heartbeats of the men on either side of her. Dickon's was deep and slow, like a funeral drum; Colin's fluttered, quicker, fainter, a pennant blowing.

"Our lad," said Dickon heavily.

"Our Richard."

"He asked us to be good to his girl."

"We must be so, then."

The voices came to Mary as though through water, through glass, words, syllables fogged and distorted. She

thought: I am drowning, I am encased. Dimly she heard
them speaking, the sound barely audible: ". . . over the
Channel . . . last flight . . . no time to eject . . . lost . . ."

She thought: was it cold, my darling, up in the bright
air? As you dropped toward the waves, did you think of
us, of home? Did you think of me? Or were you already
on that far shore? She felt the salt sea fill her mouth,
her eyes. She saw him, firm-bodied as a dolphin, plunge
into the water, saw his fair hair spread around his beautiful face as he rushed toward oblivion in a halo of bubbling light.

Their arms were strong around her but she knew their
hearts were as cold as hers. Grief swelled and billowed
somewhere out of her sight like thunderheads massing
on the horizon; all too soon this bright numbness would
dissolve and she would be plunged into the huge darkness of her pain.

It's over, Dickon thought. My hope, my faith, my future.
All perished, along with him. Our brave boy. Bony hands
waved, muddy voices called him: *It's your turn now,
Corp . . . your turn . . .* He did not try to shut them out.
This, for him, was the end. Mary and Colin still had each
other, and in any case, Colin's horizons had always been
wide. He had nothing else. When he was young, the world
had burned before him like a candle-flame; now there was
left only a melt of dirty tallow, a fire extinguished.

I can't help her. Colin felt the shaking begin in the
body he held so close. She has always been what I
wanted—but never *all* that I wanted. And I cannot give
her the help she'll need. Nobody can. Richard was too
much of a miracle to last. How I loved him. He shot
across our lives as though he were a comet and I think
I always knew that one day he would finally sink below
the dark horizon, leaving behind nothing but a flurry of
sparks. I shall try to make her see that we must be glad
for what we had of him, for it was so much more than
we could have hoped for.

Eventually, he found the strength to pull Mary's small
pinched face on to his shoulder and felt Dickon's strong
fingers lace themselves in his.

Touch any part of me and I shall shatter like glass. Push
me and I will splinter like a bottle falling from a shelf.

Nothing inside me but emptiness. People pain me. I languish. I will not die of this grief. I shall survive it—if I want to.

Memories. Like a photograph album I turn the pages of my mind and see him again, small, growing, grown. Memories. The beauty of him. Partial. Of course I was partial. He was my beloved son and he was, he *was* beautiful. He is carried from me in dreams. A speck against the sky. I scream after him, come back, come back to me, but then I wake and know that he will never come back, I wake and wish that I could sleep on forever, for this time there will be no pirate hat dropping toward me, twisting in the air currents, only the speck which falls like a feather, a bird, an apple, to land beside me in a scream of burning wreckage and twisted metal.

I groan, unable to bear my agony. The sound is pulled out of me as a needle pulls thread. I cannot be brave, but why should I be? What virtue lies in pretending there is nothing wrong, nothing broken? Colin. Poor Colin. So many hopes and dreams. A long line ended. And where is Dickon? Why does he not come? With Dickon here I can pretend that the years have stopped, have not even started. For the first time in our lives we are separated, grieving each one of us alone, not able to share this although we have shared so much else.

Ah, my boy.

Our boy.

Stiff with anguish, her pain only partially dulled by the sedative prescribed by Dr. Craven, Mary retained little more than impressions of the memorial service for Richard which was held in the Misselthwaite chapel. Mildew and damp stone. Whispers. The sound of women weeping. "Now the Day is Ended." A basket of white orchids from the Great Palm House, their perfume sad as tears between the pillars. Colin's voice breaking as he read from Ecclesiastes.

Dickon did not attend. Mary was too involved in managing her own grief to wonder why, and Colin simply assumed that he could not bear to come, that perhaps he was on the moors instead, attempting to walk off his pain in the environment where he was happiest. The mourners were invited back to the Manor but few came;

most of them had known Richard since his early childhood and felt his loss almost as keenly as his parents did.

Mary was at her desk the following afternoon, replying
to letters of condolence, when Norah came into the
room. "There's a young lady to see you, Miss Mary,"
she said.

"Tell her I am not at home."

"She says she thinks you would want to see her."

"She thinks wrong."

"Miss Mary . . ."

"Norah, I cannot see anyone, I *will* not."

"Please see me." The voice was soft, and transatlantic.

Mary turned in astonishment. A young woman stood
at the door, pale-faced and hollow-eyed. A black beret
sat on top of copper curls the color of new-minted far-
things. Mary stared discourteously at her. What effron-
tery the newcomer had, breaking into their privacy like
this. Perhaps, she thought scornfully, no more could be
expected of someone brought up overseas with a different code of behavior. "I don't know what you want,"
she began. "But—"

"Please, Mrs. Craven."

Mary frowned. Looking more closely, she realized that
she had briefly glimpsed the same girl the day before,
in the chapel, sitting at the back, staring straight ahead,
dry-eyed. "Have they not told you that this is a house
of mourning?" she asked haughtily.

The young woman wrapped her arms around her
body. "So is this."

"What is it you want?"

"I'm Richard's wife, Mrs. Craven."

"Wife?" Carefully, Mary capped her fountain pen and
laid it on the desk in front of her. "His *wife*?"

"We were married five days before he—before . . ."

"Without telling us? That's impossible. He would
never, never have . . ."

"We had forty-eight hours, Mrs. Craven. There
wasn't time."

"I don't believe you, I'm afraid. Richard would not
have kept such a thing from us."

"We weren't trying to keep anything from you. It was

simply that we had so little—so little time." There were
tears in the girl's eyes. "Ask Dickon. Mr. Sowerby."

"What does Mr. Sowerby have to do with all this?"

"Just that I met him—we spent the afternoon with
him on the river. He can tell you that we—Richard and
I—that we loved each other. And when they posted him
away to Kent, we decided to get married."

"Richard would have told me," Mary said stubbornly.

"There wasn't time." If Mary had been less the
woman she had known she would be, and kinder, Amy
might have explained how, on the evening before they
married, Richard had tried to telephone his mother and
been unable to get through. Because of Mary's hostility,
she remained silent.

"Why should I believe your story?" Mary demanded.

"My story?"

"This preposterous fairytale you have come out with,
regarding my son and yourself."

"Because . . ." The girl fell silent as she looked around
the room . . . She was painfully thin, as though she were
recovering from an illness. Shadows like smudges of violet ink lay above her cheekbones. Her gaze fell on the
portrait of Lady Caroline Leighton with the green parrot
on her finger, and her face softened for a moment, as if
she had recognized a friend. Then she said: "Oh, what's
the use? I only came because he made me promise I
would if anything . . . happened."

Her eyes, Mary decided, were almost exactly the color
of the smoky-blue delphiniums which the three of them
had planted in the secret garden so long ago. For some
reason, she thought of the lamb which Dickon used to
feed from a bottle, and the way it had nuzzled its tight-
curled head into the soft folds of Colin's dressing-gown,
seeking comfort. "There's no earthly reason why I
should believe you."

"None at all," agreed the girl. "And maybe I wouldn't
believe me either, if I were in your shoes."

"I presume you can support your claim."

The girl gasped as though she had been slapped across
the face. Her mouth twisted with scorn. "Show you my
'lines,' do you mean? Ah no. I wouldn't demean either
of us."

"In that case, Norah, would you be good enough to—"

The young woman moved her head disbelievingly from side to side. "Boy, you really are a piece of work, aren't you? And to think that Richard adored you. But, Mrs. Craven, don't think you have exclusive rights in him. Don't think you're the only one who mourns him, nor the only one whose world has been devastated. He had a whole life which had nothing to do with you, and I was part of that."

Perhaps because she suspected that the girl might be genuine, that even if they were not actually married, Richard and she had been in love—*I rather monopolized a very pretty American girl*—Mary found it all the more difficult to accept what she said. She did not want to share with a stranger the little that remained of her son; there was no room here for someone else's memories. Nonetheless, if the girl had traveled all the way up here . . . phrases like *got her hooks into him, on to a good thing, after whatever she can get,* stepped into her mind and would not leave, hideous vulgar phrases overheard in queues, on the Underground, whispered by daunting women with headscarves round their hair. "Can I offer you a cup of tea before you go back?" she said.

The girl gave a grimace. "I always guessed that the two of us would loathe each other at first sight. No thanks, Mrs. Craven, I won't stay for tea. But please remember, later, that I tried. That I did what Richard asked me to do." She threw her head back. Her chin began to tremble. "And let's hope you can feel that you did the same."

With that, she turned and left the room, pushing past Norah, her high heels clicking along the stone-flagged passage as she ran toward the hall.

"Just a minute." *He asked us to be good to his girl* . . . Mary pushed back her chair. "Norah!" she called. But it was too late. Hurrying to the French windows, fumbling with the blackout curtains and then the clasp, she saw the girl rush through the front door and down the steps to climb into an army jeep which had been parked in the drive, and though she rapped sharply on the glass as she tried to get the windows open—*there is something rather important I want to tell you*—by the time she had done so the jeep had turned on the gravel in front of the house and was heading rapidly away down the long arched avenue.

"Come back," she said, although they could not hear her. "Oh God. Please come back."

When the last sound of the jeep's engine had faded, she went inside and closed the windows again. The girl had worn rings, a wedding band, a single pearl. Richard, married? But surely he would have—wouldn't he? Wouldn't he have told his mother? *There is something rather important* . . . But even if he had not, how could she have been so cold, so abominably cruel to the girl who might very well be, who claimed she, indeed probably was, his wife?

She had said that she had met Dickon. Mary called once again for Norah and when the housekeeper did not respond, went in search of her. "Norah, can you send one of the gardener's boys with a message to Mr. Dickon for me? Tell him I need to see him most urgently."

Norah avoided her glance and Mary knew that she had heard the exchange and condemned her for it. As indeed she was fast condemning herself. "I'll send that new lad over on his bicycle," she said. "Messages is about all he's good for and even then you can't be sure he won't get it wrong. I'd go myself, Miss Mary, if my legs weren't so bad." Norah had suffered from rickets as a child and still had occasional problems with her lower limbs.

"But since they are," Mary snapped, "it is pointless of you to suggest it."

This time Norah did look at her and her mouth tightened. "I'll send the boy." She turned away.

"Tell him it's extremely urgent." For Mary had realized that if she was to find the young woman she needed at least to know her name.

They came to her that evening, pale-faced, avoiding her eyes. Norah and the boy, and behind them, old Mrs. Medlock, who did little these days beyond grumble and help out with the sewing, and the girl who gave a hand in the kitchen.

Sensing something which would test her to the limits

and beyond, Mary deliberately took a cigarette from the shagreen box and lit it before she asked them what they wanted.

"It's Mr. Dickon," said the housekeeper.

"What about him?"

"Go on, Arthur," Norah pushed the boy forward. "Tell Miss Mary."

The lad stood twisting his cap in his grubby hands and biting his lip. "Me uncle," he said.

"He's Mr. Dickon's nephew," explained Mrs. Medlock. "Son to Susan Sowerby's youngest. Go *on*, Arthur."

"Me uncle," Arthur said again. "They found him . . ." He turned away, while Mrs. Medlock tutted impatiently.

Mary's hand was trembling so violently that she could no longer hold her cigarette. Carefully she set it down. "Tell me, child," she said as gently as she could.

In the end, it became a composite tale. The boy had not found Dickon at home and, having been threatened with the direst of consequences if he failed to deliver his message, had gone round to the comfortable home Dickon had purchased for Susan Sowerby some years ago. She too had been trying to raise him for several days, surprised at his failure to keep in touch, particularly in view of recent events, for normally he visited her every day and if he were to be absent, informed her of his whereabouts. Eventually they had found one of his brothers who had then gone around to the different farms where Dickon supervised the growing and dispatching of fresh farm produce, and discovered that no one had heard from him for a week, not since the day, Norah added, they'd heard about Master Richard. Together, Susan Sowerby and the boy had returned to Dickon's house and, peering through the windows of the kitchen, seen several envelopes on the kitchen table. At that point, they had enlisted the help of the village policeman and he had climbed in through an upper window to discover Dickon's body lying on a bed, with his dog at his side.

"Taken something," Mrs. Medlock said. "Some kind of poison, they thought, something he used for the—"

"It doesn't matter what it was." Mary was determined not to break down in front of the servants.

"Dog wouldn't budge," Arthur said. "Wouldn't let them touch his master. Growled something fierce when they—"

"That's enough," Norah said. "The mistress doesn't want to hear about such things."

The mistress wants to die herself, Mary thought. With Richard gone and now my Dickon, what else is left for me? She caught the eye of the girl who helped out in the kitchen—Milly, was it? Polly? Something like that— and looked away, searching with fingers which seemed to belong to someone else for a fresh cigarette.

Polly had not seen Mary up near before. At the refugee concerts, at the Christmas parties for the Misselthwaite staff, opening the annual summer fête, she had not realized how old Mary was for from a distance she still looked little more than a girl. And right pretty too. No wonder she and Mr. Dickon were supposed to be . . . and brave, as well. Look at her, with her heart nigh broken, and she as haughty as a queen, as if a body couldn't see that underneath she was hurting right bad.

Boldly, she stepped forward and laid her hand on Mary's shoulders. "Don't tha fret," she said softly.

For a moment, Mary's face crumpled. How many times had Dickon said the same thing to her? And now he never would again. She pulled back her shoulders and gave the girl her most arrogant look. "Thank you," she said. "That will be all."

"Come along, girl," said Norah.

"Right away," Polly said. Eeh, she were grand, Miss Mary were. Spunky. She weren't going to let them see her cry, never mind that anybody with eyes in her head could see that cry was all she wanted to do. She were that near crying herself, too. Mr. Dickon were the nicest man she knew, bar her own dad, and him being dead were about the worst thing'd ever happened to her. Still, Susan Sowerby had told her mam that he'd never been the same since they brought him home from the Great War, that he were right moithered when this one started, so mebbe, in a way, he were at peace now, the way he'd not been for many a long year, or so they said.

Arthur was fumbling in the pocket of his breeches. He brought out a letter. "Me gran said to give thee this, Miss Mary."

"Susan Sowerby," Mrs. Medlock explained, in case Mary had not made the connection.

"Thank you." Mary could barely articulate the words. The writing on the envelope was Dickon's. Cold seized her and she began to shiver violently. Her teeth chattered together, her hands drummed against the leather top of her desk. She heard Norah say something about shock, felt a rug wrapped around her shoulders, saw tears jerk from her eyes and fall on to her lap. "Dickon." The name came from her in a formless howl. "Dickon! *Dickon*!"

Dimly Mary was aware of Norah picking up the telephone and asking the operator to find Dr. Craven and send him over to the Manor at once.

The child, Polly, had taken one of her agitated hands and was holding it tightly. Again she said: "Don't tha fret," and Mary wanted to explain that she must not, to forbid it, for these were Dickon's words, and she truly could not bear life without him, and then she was spinning in a nauseated circle, drowning in the gold-edged blackness which was advancing like an army across her mind. Something smashed against her forehead as she fell forward and then there was nothing.

27

My dearest Mary,

I often think about the secret garden. If it had not existed, would we three have traveled different paths? Would we have been less close & therefore more free? I remember how the clematis & the honeysuckle had twined themselves around those old rose bushes, & how we suffered when we realized that we could only separate them by pulling one of them out by the roots, & thus killing it.

Losing Richard because the world has once again gone to war has brought home to me the futility of life. So I choose death. Why can't men live like the creatures up on the moors, or grow quietly, like plants & trees? Why must they always be killing? No one will ever know how much I suffered during the years of the Great War. With Richard gone, I can suffer no more.

Don't think badly of me, Mary, my thorny rose, my missel thrush. I know he was my son. So did he.

Your always loving Dickon.

While Mary had been recovering from the breakdown brought on by overwork and grief, success had been achieved, and England was busy coming to terms with its pyrrhic victory over the enemy. The painful irony of Richard's death in the last few months of the war, with the Germans routed, the Allies pushing forward on every front, peace already in the air, only made it the more tragic. As she slowly recovered, she read stories of airmen who had been lost, only to reappear weeks or even months later, having baled out, or lost their memories. But she knew this had not happened in Richard's case. Too many people had seen his Spitfire hit the waves; the squadron leader had testified that he had been caught in enemy gunfire and was probably dead by the time the engine caught fire and the plane crashed into the sea.

Struggling back into awareness, she had understood too, that Dickon was gone for good. This time he would not come back. Looking back, she could see how his hold on life was already weakening in the last years of the war, particularly after the ugly news of the atrocities committed against the Jewish and ethnic populations of Europe began to be disseminated. He had never been able to come to terms with man's constant inhumanity to man. He had never understood the dark gods which other men worshipped or that the simple goodness with which he himself was imbued was not shared by everyone.

She came at last to realize that his death was only a logical extension of his life. In the end, the fact that he had died before seeing the pictures of the concentration camps or knowing of the atomic bombs dropped on Hiroshima and Nagasaki, was something to be thankful for.

With Mary, Colin always felt obliged to maintain a spurious aspect of resignation knowing that if he did not, the two of them might fatally fragment into singularity. Dickon had always been the pivot on which their tripleness depended. Without him, they were reduced to a relationship which would require far more effort from both of them if it were to endure.

Back in London, he was able for a while to give in to the black dog of despair which had seized him in its fierce jaws. Because of his recent bereavement, his superiors were sympathetic when his attendance grew erratic, or when he appeared at his desk looking less than immaculate. It was hard to say in what his occasional dishevelment lay: a patch missed while shaving, a tie which did not quite agree with his suit, a general air of having forgotten to look in the mirror before leaving the house, but his colleagues were agreed that his loss had wrought a fundamental change in his attitude. He wondered what they would think if they knew that his suffering was as much for the loss of a friend to whom he had never been able to speak of love, as it was for his son.

It was impossible to sleep. Night after night he would lie in his darkened bedroom in Fitzroy Square, murmuring his friend's name like a charm.

"Dickon. Dickon," and he would remember how, as a boy confined to his bed, the name had conjured up a multiplicity of promises. Sunlight, green leaves, freedom, roses. A world where squirrels pranced and foxes stayed in their tracks to listen to a boy with a pipe. Dickon's world. A world he himself could embrace if he only believed strongly enough in magic.

He had had no notion then, that the enchanted thickets of childhood would give way all too soon to maturity's dark forests.

Sometimes, soaked in misery, he found himself sitting on the edge of his bed in his shirtsleeves, still half-dressed hours after he had begun to push the first stud into his collar. What had happened to the moments in between? Increasingly, there were long gaps of time which he could not account for. Once he had found himself sitting on top of an omnibus as it pulled into the terminus at Brixton, without any idea of why he had boarded the vehicle in the first place, or why, having done so, he was still there at the end of the line. Little by little, his mind seemed to have shut down. Occasionally, studying the tremor in his hands, he wondered if he were suffering from a terminal disease. Even though he had cut down drastically on the amount of alcohol he consumed, he was still unable to account for the missing hours in his timetable. Where had he been, for instance, the time he returned to Fitzroy Square at two o'clock in the morning with no recollection of anything since leaving the office at six the evening before? Who had he been with? What had he been doing? Enquiries among his friends yielded no answers; searching his pockets he would sometimes come across torn theater-ticket stubs or restaurant bills, but even these failed to trigger memory. Three or four times, he had been greeted by total strangers, who appeared to have some degree of familiarity with him. What frightened him was that on at least two occasions, those strangers had been handsome young men of a type he recognized only too well.

What perhaps struck him most forcibly during the wakeful hours of the night was the possibility that if he had taken more time to talk to Dickon, his friend might still be alive. Looking back, he could clearly recall the signs of Dickon's increasing disturbance as the war progressed, and his own unacknowledged reluctance to take time from his preoccupations to try to help.

Regret was futile. There was nothing he could now do to bring Dickon back. Instead, he made a conscious decision to devote himself to a cause which would have been dear to Dickon's heart. When he was finally adopted by his local constituency party to stand against the Conservative candidate at the next elections, he made a promise to himself that, if elected, he would take on as his particular mission, the fight for the rights of all the men who spent their lives burrowing underground for a pittance, as Dickon's father had done.

It would be a small reparation.

Mr. Churchill, a man for the war but not for the peace, was voted out of office. A Labor Government was returned in a landslide victory, and along with it Colin Craven, returned to Parliament with a majority of nearly twenty thousand votes over the former Conservative incumbent. The mood of the country was for change. It was felt, or so he told Mary in something of a return to the old enthusiastic Colin of his youth, that it was Conservative business policies which had helped Hitler rise to power in the first place, and business interests which had kept the war going, that it was time the inequalities of the social system were finally destroyed for all time.

"Time for a change," he said, over and over again, striding up and down the drawing room, beating a clenched fist into the palm of his other hand while he talked of social injustice, of the Tory stranglehold on the country, of out-dated practices holding the country back. Sometimes he said: "Richard always said that after the war, things would have to change," or "Richard told me that his generation would never vote the Tories back into power," and she realized that the American girl who had come to see her was right: there was a whole side of Richard's life of which she knew nothing.

"Do you realize that before the war, nearly half the population of the British Isles was inadequately nourished?" Colin demanded fiercely. "We'll do something about that now we have power. And there must be free medical care for all, a comprehensive national health service to ensure that every citizen has access to medical treatment. Not just from doctors, but from dentists and opticians as well. The state of the nation's health is appalling."

"I've observed that, just from my experiences in finding homes for all those refugees," Mary said.

"And housing, too," Colin said, his mind racing ahead to the English utopia he would help to create. "Every family has the right to its own home, in a decent environment. Sweep away the slums and at a stroke, you sweep away one of the root causes of ill-health."

"It'll take more than that, I'm afraid. Who's going to pay for all this? Won't it cripple the nation? Especially while we're trying to pull things round after the war?"

"That's defeatist talk."

"Not at all. I'm simply being sensible. Running the country's a bit like running a house, only on a larger scale, and God knows I've had plenty of experience doing that."

"You've got to start somewhere," Colin said. "Already we're seeing a fairer system. Whether rich or poor, everyone's entitled to the same basic rations."

"Except that the rich are able to afford to buy extra on the black market."

"Only for the moment. And already we can see the results of sharing out what supplies are available. Mothers are better fed, which means babies are born healthier; children are less prone to disease. What we need to do now is build on that, and social planning is the answer. This time round, it'll be government policy that'll put roofs over the nation's head, not private enterprise, which only lines the pockets of the already rich."

Mary longed to be as committed as he was. Most of the time, however, she listened while he declaimed, but she did not hear. Only one idea penetrated the fog which filled her mind, only one interest held her. She had to find the girl who had said she was Richard's wife.

How bitterly she regretted her rudeness and—yes—

her cruelty. If the girl had indeed been married to Richard then she was already a widow, and mourning. Her own conduct had been inexcusable, even given the fact of her bereavement. She had not told Colin of the girl's visit; when she first emerged from the mists of illness, he had been busy electioneering and subsequently she had decided that she could not bear to have him think badly of her, as he most certainly would if he heard of the way she had treated that distressed young creature. Finding her, welcoming her, had become the impetus which drove Mary back into strength and health. This was not the only regret she felt. Lying at first in bed and then on the sofa in the morning room, she had plenty of time to revisit the past. So many times with Dickon, she had wanted to say *I love you* but the words would not come. It was as though she had been issued with a vocabularial ragbag, in which the words existed but only as separate entities, scraps of sound: *I* or *you* or *love*. Why had it been so difficult for her to fish them out of her heart and sew them together to form a sentence? She had so often envied the emotional ease to which those who could declare their love were entitled, to which she was not.

It was too late for Dickon, but the girl—Richard's wife—was still retrievable. As she grew stronger, she brushed aside the thoughts of *if only*. She stopped asking herself what might have happened if she had behaved differently and set herself to the task of discovering the girl's whereabouts.

She had thought it would be easy. It was not. By the time she was in a position to set the search in train, most of the American service personnel had departed for home, leaving behind them only the debris of their peaceful occupation of Britain: coat hangers, prophylactics, ammunition, toilet articles, sweaters, food, babies. Having decided to take on trust the girl's claim that she and Richard were married, Mary nonetheless did not even have a name to give the few authorities she was able to contact. Coppery curls and powder-blue eyes was not enough information to go on and she gradually became aware that Richard and his bride must have kept the marriage secret from her superiors as well as his, for no one had heard of a girl who had married an Englishman called Craven.

There had to be records somewhere, in some registry office but she had no idea which one the young couple might have chosen. The Cambridgeshire ones would have seemed the logical place, but her enquiries proved fruitless. She sent letters to the registrars around Manston, Richard's last posting, but from those who had even bothered to reply, she received only negative answers.

So where else would they have gone? The task of contacting all the offices possible and waiting while they went through their records and wrote back to her could take years. It ought to have been a simple task, but she discovered that during the war years there had been so much disruption of the normal routines, such difficulties in communication, so many registry offices destroyed by bombing or fire damage that many vital records were never dispatched to Somerset House. Daily she cursed herself for sending the young woman packing instead of being kind, instead of listening to what she had to impart. When she thought of what Richard would have said if he had been alive, she felt the deepest contempt for herself.

He had said once that were he to be killed, he was sure he would return to Misselthwaite, if he wanted to badly enough, and sitting in the Great Palm House as strength returned to her, she sometimes almost caught a glimpse of him, among the tangles of creeper or walking toward her between the bending palm leaves. She had never been a fanciful woman, but occasionally she was sure he brushed past her, and wondered then where he was going, whom he hastened to see.

His wife? If only she had a name for the young American woman. Questioned closely, Norah could only repeat that she had not given any name, simply asked to see Mrs. Craven. There had been a driver who waited for her in the jeep; a female, she thought, wearing an American service uniform, though she could not say which one. Colin, when the subject of Richard arose, denied any knowledge of the names of his friends. It was possible that Richard might have confided in his friend Carl, but in the confusion of war's aftermath, no one seemed able to give her any concrete information of his whereabouts. She had contacted the Red Cross but they had no knowledge of him, making it plain that their hands were full with other more important matters than the tracking down of a single individual. When she got in touch with those of his former schoolmates that she could remember, it was to find that of those who had survived the war, none had found it possible to maintain contact because of the demands of their wartime service.

One day, a young flight-lieutenant came to visit her. He told her his name was Johnnie Danforth and that he had known Richard at the East Anglian base, that they had been good chums. But when Mary asked if there had been any particular girls, he shook his head.

"Everyone was on the move, Mrs. Craven. Dickie—"

"Dickie?"

"Richard, I should say. We called him Dickie. He went out a couple of times with a WAAC called Ruth something, from Torquay, I believe, but I heard that she'd married a Yankee soldier and gone back to Minnesota or somewhere with him."

"Didn't he know some American girls?" Mary asked, not wanting her desperation to show, not wanting his pity.

"Gosh, there were so many of them. I saw him once in Cambridge with a rather peachy redhead but I don't know who she was and it never occurred to me to ask. And we went dancing from time to time, but I can't say I saw him with anyone in particular." He lifted his hand to smooth his brilliantined hair and she saw that three of the fingers were missing.

"Do you know the names of any of his other friends at the base who might know more?"

"To tell you the honest truth, I'm just about the only one left out of our little group. We all got our wings at the same time, and now they're—they're all . . ." He gulped a little and looked down at his wounded hand. When he had composed himself, he added: "Which isn't to say that Dickie didn't talk to someone else, but I think I'd have been among the first he'd have confided in. Are you looking for a special girl, Mrs. Craven?"

"I think so." Mary did not say that if Richard had chosen her she must have been very special indeed.

"Trouble was, it was very much the eat-drink-and-be-merry-for-tomorrow-we-die mentality among us pilots. We knew our chances were pretty rotten so we tried to pack as much into our free time as we could. There were plenty of girls, if you don't mind my mentioning it, and we were delighted to avail ourselves of any opportunities which came our way. Wouldn't do it now, of course. Sober citizen and all that sort of thing."

"This redhead . . ."

"I only saw her once, to be honest. Though now I think about it, there might well have been someone special, because I remember we started teasing him about the way he used to sneak off to Cambridge without the rest of us."

"If you're right, and it was a girl in Cambridge, she must have been based locally."

"But what as? Service personnel? Red Cross? A volunteer? Or maybe over here with a family connected with the war effort in some capacity. There was a huge amount of administration involved in bringing the Yanks—you did say this was an American girl, didn't you?—over here and maintaining them." Again he smoothed back his hair.

"Oh . . ." She bit her lip.

Danforth rose to his feet. "I hope you didn't mind me coming, Mrs. Craven. I feel dreadfully . . . well, guilty, I suppose, at being the only one of the fellows to come through. I wanted to visit their families, just to say how sorry I am, how jolly difficult it is to—to come to terms with the fact that I'm—that none of the others—" He was gulping again, folding his lips together under his moustache to stop himself from breaking down.

"I'm so grateful you did," Mary said. "It's a comfort to know that my son had friends like you."

"I just wish I could help you about this girl. If I hear anything or remember something that might be useful, I'll be certain to let you know."

*   *   *

John Hawkins also came to see her. "I couldn't go away
without telling you in person how devastated I was by
the news about young Richard," he said.

"You're leaving England?"

He nodded. "Posted to the Embassy in Washington."
He wore well-cut tweeds and highly polished handmade
brogues; the wild Byronic hair was tamed. The old enthusiasm was still there, but it was overlaid now with a
seasoned polish.

"Then your dream of a diplomatic career has come
true."

He seized her hands. "Don't think I'm not aware of
how much I owe to you and Mr. Craven," he said. "I
think so often of the years I spent here with you all. It's
such a pitiful waste, isn't it? Richard killed before he
had a chance to start his life properly. And whatever
path he chose, I know he would have been a success—
he was such a gifted chap."

Mary could only look at him and, in silence, agree.

"I bumped into your husband recently, and he kindly
invited me to dine at his Club last week," Hawkins said.
"He told me you'd not been well, that there had been
other tragedies here."

"You refer to Mr. Sowerby's death, no doubt."

"Indeed. He was one of the finest gentlemen I ever
knew."

"He was the finest man most people will ever know."
Mary came to a decision. "Mr. Hawkins, you say you
will be based in Washington."

"Yes."

"The fact is—" She hesitated, thinking how best to
put it. "Immediately after Richard's death, a young
woman came to see me. An American. She said she was
Richard's wife. I'm afraid that I did not behave as well
as I might, and the result was that she went away again
before I could secure even her name, let alone information about where she came from or what she planned
to do."

"You mean you showed her the door?" Hawkins saw
no need for diplomacy here. He could just imagine how
Mary, inwardly raging, had behaved at her imperious
worst.

Mary could not meet his eyes. "In a word, yes," she

said humbly. "I'm not going to begin to try and make excuses for myself."

"But now you wish to establish contact?"

"Exactly. Except that it seems almost impossible to do so. I've made various enquiries, but without any result. And the more time goes by, the less chance there seems of finding her. Dickon had met her and knew who she was, but—"

She broke off.

"I understand." Hawkins brought out a small notebook. "Give me what details you have—"

"I have none."

"—and I will see if anything can be done, though I think it will be difficult, if not impossible."

"Apart from the fact that she must be called Craven, I know nothing about her," Mary said, distressed. "I treated her abominably and I cannot blame her for not contacting me again. I would like to wish her well, that's all, to assure myself that she is not in need. I would like to—to share my memories of my son with her, and hear hers." And perhaps even invite her to stay, Mary thought. Show her the house where Richard grew up, the pictures and books that he loved, the secret garden, the Great Palm House, take her up on the moors, and swimming in the lake. Share him with her. "Now that Richard is dead, Misselthwaite will eventually pass to my husband's cousin, or his sons. I would like her to have seen Richard's home before it belongs to someone else."

"I'm afraid that there were a great many hasty wartime marriages, Mrs. Craven. It's quite possible that this young woman has remarried by now, which would make finding her even more problematic."

"Do you think so?" Mary thought back to that distraught young face. "Somehow, I hadn't imagined that she—" What she wanted to say was that the girl so briefly met had not struck her as someone who would lightly forget the vows she had taken, whatever the circumstances in which they were made. But she was young, pretty: in the normal course of events it was obvious that she would eventually remarry. What chance would there be of finding her then, once she assumed a new husband's name?

"And we must not forget that America is a vast country. Frankly, I can't hold out a great deal of hope, considering how little we have to go on." Hawkins rose to go. "I can only repeat that I will do whatever I can."

"Do you want a divorce, Colin?"

"A divo—? My dear Mary, what are you talking about?"

"I don't seem to be much of a political wife to you. If we parted, you could find someone younger and cleverer to help you in the constituency. Someone who would forward your career."

Colin put down the newspaper and carefully unhooked his gold-rimmed glasses from behind his ears. "Quite apart from the fact that I would infinitely rather give up my career than my wife, a divorce is hardly likely to improve my reputation. Besides, I often think that you're my greatest asset."

"But I ought to be more at your side. And you've been so alone in the past year or so. I feel I've become something of a liability."

"You're not trying to tell me in a subtle way that you want to pack it in, are you?"

"No. Never. Now that Dickon's gone, it seems more important than ever that we're together."

"Do you know," said Colin, taking her hand and turning the three-stranded gold ring on her finger. "It may sound fanciful, but I'm not sure that he has gone."

"You can feel him too?"

"Not so much in London, but yes, often, up at Misselthwaite."

They smiled gently at each other, two sad people. They had shared such a lot—but there were things Colin could never have told Mary. One of them was a fact which shamed him immeasurably but which nevertheless he knew to be true: losing his son in the war was a vote winner in a country still trying to emerge from the shadows of conflict. It more than counterbalanced the fact that although he was a Labor member, he was also the owner of a vast country house, and had always lived a life of privilege. Despite them, he had known from the moment this war had become inevitable, that it would result in social changes which would ensure a more equitable society and a better life for all. Without telling Mary, he had explored the possibility of breaking the trust which Archie Craven had set up, but it had so far proved impossible. There had been suggestions of hypocrisy cast at him from both sides of the House. Although he was by no means the only Labor member possessed of wealth and privilege, he was nonetheless afraid that his continued ownership of Misselthwaite Manor might prove to be something of a disadvantage. People found it difficult to believe that it was possible for a man of his background to be a Labor politican simply from personal conviction, from a belief in the fundamental dignity of all human beings. But Richard would always, now, be a guarantee of his good faith, his commitment, his belief in old-fashioned family values. With a son, no one was likely to peer behind the façade and accuse him of unnatural practices.

"I'll come down to London whenever you need a parliamentary wife," Mary said. "I'll do everything I can to help."

"Darling," said Colin. "You know how people in the constituency adore you."

"Do they?" Mary could never quite believe that anyone found her lovable. The only love she had known about which she had felt absolutely safe, was in her relationship with her son.

"So my agent up there tells me. And he also says that you're proving to be a terrific speaker. Compelling, was the word he used."

"I hate doing it. But I feel that for your sake I can't refuse when I'm asked."

"We'll see you standing for election yourself, one of these days."

Mary laughed. "I very much doubt that."

One Christmas, Mary and Colin received an invitation to attend a concert by the London Chamber Players which was being given in the nave of York Minster. On the back was written:

Please please try to come. If you are not there, I will telephone you and make arrangements to visit. Yours, Carl.

Parliamentary business kept Colin in London, so Mary drove alone across the moors through the early darkness of a winter afternoon. Snow had began to fall in random flurries; the dales were bleak and cold. She sat toward the back, wrapped in furs to keep out the chill of stone floors, listening as the intricate music of a Beethoven string quartet soared rapturously toward the vaulted roof. The young man on the viola must be Carl, yet Mary scarcely recognized him. There were hollows under his cheekbones and deep shadows beneath his eyes. Beneath one ear, she thought she could detect an ugly raised scar.

Outside, darkness fell and candles were lit around the vast stone spaces. The concert came to an end and as people applauded, the viola player stood up. "We are all Austrians," he said. "We have chosen to live in your country because of the tolerance and friendship we have found here. But occasionally we remind ourselves of our homeland. And so for you, and for us, we would like to play a carol which is always sung at this time of year in our country." He stared out into the candlelit darkness and Mary knew he spoke to her. Then, drawing his bow across the strings of his viola, he began to play "Silent Night," his friends softly joining in, the audience gradually taking up the tune and then rising spontaneously to their feet to join in the triumphant final verse, "Christ the Savior is born."

Mary's eyes were wet as she pushed her way forward to speak to Carl. He embraced her as if he would never let her go. "Oh, Mrs. Craven," he said. "I've thought of you so often in the past few years."

"Why didn't you come to see me?" asked Mary. "You know how welcome you would have been."

"It wasn't that easy," Carl said. "I was captured and made a prisoner of war. And when it was all over, I was not well . . . it was difficult for me to come." Looking down at her, he said: "How are they all—Richard and Mr. Craven? And Mr. Sowerby?"

Reluctantly she explained. His face paled at the news of Richard's death. "I thought it was bad enough in the PoW camp," he said. He touched the ragged scar on his neck. "But at least I survived."

"Richard told me you had met in Piccadilly once," Mary said.

"More than once," said Carl. "Until I was forced down and captured, we met regularly."

Once again Mary realized that her son had a life in which she had no part at all, that there were people who knew him in ways she would never do. "Did you know that he married?" she asked, though it was obvious that Carl could not, if he was imprisoned in Germany.

He shook his head. "I didn't. But I'm sure she is a nice girl," he said. "And a comfort to you and Mr. Craven."

Unable for the moment to speak, she simply stared at him while tears welled in her eyes again.

"What?" he said. "She was not also killed, was she?"

"I don't think so."

"Then what happened to her?"

She swallowed. "I don't know. I can only presume that she went back to her own country—she wasn't English. And I can't find her because I don't even know her name."

"But that is so sad. How could such a thing occur?"

"I can't talk about it. I had hoped that you might have known her name but obviously he met her after you were taken prisoner." Mary put a hand on his sleeve. "And you, Carl. Did you ever . . . did you find your parents?"

"No."

"My dear, I'm so sorry."

He turned aside and began to replace his viola in its case. "I think about them every day," he said. "It is why I must make music, in order to drown out the ugliness of war."

Carl, in a way, was her last hope. Letters arrived from Hawkins every now and then, and in each one, he explained that the confusions of war had made it almost as impossible to find someone without a certain amount of information about them as it was to find those who, for various reasons, did not wish to be found.

One day, he wrote, *there will no doubt be machines which can collate information at the speed of light and store it until it's needed. Dear Mrs. Craven, if only you had even the smallest clue to give me, how much easier it would be to be helpful to you.*

But she had, and continued to have, nothing.

28

Amy Monaghan Craven was not deliberately hiding herself. It had never occurred to her that anyone might be looking for her, least of all Richard's frightful mother. Two months after his death, she discovered that she was pregnant and as soon as she could, returned home to Elm Ridge, the little mid-western town where she had grown up and where her parents and many of her relations still lived.

The child was a boy; she called him simply Dickon. It was not only the loving diminutive of Richard, it was a way of commemorating Richard's other "parent," the kindly agitated man who had sat beside her on the punt cushions and tried so hard to stop his hands from shaking. Often she remembered that day on the river, the handsome young man who had won her heart, the fields full of unchecked flowers, the blue sky over all. Oranges would never again taste so sharply sweet, so orange, nor chocolate ever be more rich. Every day she wept for the loss of happy days she would now never know.

She got herself a job, working at the local hospital, and at the same time enrolled as a student nurse, hoping to get the qualifications she would need if she was to raise Dickon in the style he deserved. At the back of her mind was always the fear that if she did not, he would later be able to accuse her of denying him his birthright. But even with the devoted help of her parents, it was difficult for her to manage on her own. She was not worried about her son growing up without a father: there were enough relatives in Elm Ridge to cushion him from a loss he was still much too young to appreciate. Much worse was her own loneliness, and her inability to share with her parents the experiences she had known in England; she missed Richard more than she could ever say.

"You'll get married again, honey," her mother soothed one afternoon, finding Amy crying at the kitchen table with a letter from the bank in front of her. "Someone will take care of you soon enough. You'll see."

"Oh, Mom." Although the words were kindly meant Amy could not keep the exasperation out of her voice. "I want to be able to look after Dickon by myself, not be a parasite on some man."

"Like I have, is that what you mean?"

"Of course it's not. But you belong to a different generation, when marriage was the only thing girls wanted out of life. Things have changed now, especially after the war. I'm an independent woman—or I would be, if I could just somehow work out how to make ends meet."

"You know your dad and I are more than happy to do anything we can. Dickon is our grandson, after all, and you know we wouldn't deprive him of a single thing if it's in our power to give it to him."

"I know that, Mom. And I'm just so grateful. But it's not quite what I want." Amy sighed. She just had to accept that her mother did not understand what she meant.

At a birthday party for one of her cousins, she ran into Bobby Hooper. He was freshly back from the war, and one of few young men from Elm Ridge who had any knowledge of England. They talked enthusiastically, exchanging nostalgic memories of places they had both visited.

"Piccadilly Circus, the Gaiety Theater, Hyde Park," enthused Bobby. "Stratford. Say, were you ever in Stratford? Or Oxford? Now there's a place I'd really like to go back to some day."

"What about Cambridge?" Amy was surprised at the way she could say the word almost without a twinge. Was she forgetting so soon?

"Cambridge? I never made it up there," Bobby said. "Guess that'll have to wait until I go back."

"You seem very certain that you will."

"You bet. I'm not saying the US of A isn't the greatest country in the world, because it is, but those Europeans could sure teach us a thing or two about guts and perseverance."

When the party was coming to an end, he walked her home through the quiet tree-lined streets and asked if they could meet again. "Soon," he added.

"Sure." She smiled at him. Why not spend an evening with Bobby Hooper, forget for a while the stresses of the life she had come home to? It did not matter that he was not Richard. No one was, nor did she expect that anyone could ever take his place.

Having got back his old job at the corn and feed plant on the edge of town, Bobby energetically set about wooing Amy. His persistence finally wore her down; she regretfully hid somewhere deep inside her the knowledge that she would never love again the way she had loved Richard and accepted his addresses. When Dickon was three years old, she and Bobby were married.

She often thought of Richard's mother. As the years passed, Misselthwaite Manor became, in her imagination, more and more like something out of a gothic novel. She saw ravens flapping heavily from broken windows, bats swooping among fantastical turrets, cobwebs, giant rats. In retrospect, Mary herself grew ever more grotesque, her features evilly twisted as she squatted at the heart of the house and wove her poison spells. After talking it over with Bobby, Amy decided not to let the Cravens know that they had a grandson. This decision was due less to a wish to deny them their rights than fear of what might happen if Richard's parents were to learn of Dickon's existence. What archaic English law might they not be able to invoke to see that he was snatched from her and taken back to live in that terrible fortress of a house? What moral rights might they not assert over her adored son?

Richard himself remained enshrined for her in the glow of a summer afternoon, surrounded by sunshine. Occasionally the sight of a swan drifting, the scent of peeled oranges, would bring the past back to her with the vivid feel of acid on the skin. She did not regret marrying him; she did not consider that it had been one

of those brief wartime flings. Had he not gone down
with his plane, they would be husband and wife still,
happy together. They would, of course, be living in a
fashion quite different from the comfortable and familiar
one she enjoyed in her home town, where little had
changed here since her early childhood. Instead of quiet
streets and white clapboard houses, people she had
known all her life, a simplicity of outlook and occupation, she would have had tradition and a certain grandeur, the wild moors on the one hand and the
cosmopolitan thrum of London on the other. Theaters,
concerts, sophistication: none of those were much in evidence in Elm Ridge, nor did she regret them—or not
often. A wholesome and undramatic upbringing was
what she most desired for her son; there was more
chance of that in Elm Ridge than in England. On the
other hand, she often worried that he was missing out
on the kind of intellectual rigor which had been so ap-
parent in Richard and his friends. Once or twice, she
even toyed with the idea of sending Dickon to his father's old school, but the mere idea of sending him away
to live among strangers was too horrific to contemplate
for more than the briefest second.

"It might be OK for the British but it sure as hell
doesn't do for us," she told Bobby once.

"All the same, all that private education does seem to
turn out a real fine breed of men," said Bobby. "Some
of the guys I met over there were heroes, no two ways
about it."

"The war's over now: we don't need heroes."

"You're right, I guess." Bobby was happy to concur.
He was a large placid man, who could never get over
the fact that Amy had agreed to marry him. And the
kid was pretty fine too. He considered he'd been lucky
to have ended up with them both.

Nonetheless, Amy did not forget Dickon's birthright,
and never ceased to have qualms about the fact that she
was depriving him of it. She spoke often of his father,
realizing as the years went by how painfully little of him
she had possessed. She wove stories about the secret
garden, which she had never seen but which Richard
had described to her so many times. She spoke often of
the other Dickon, her son's namesake, the man who

spoke to robins, the man who could make friends with squirrels and foxes.

Two years after she and Bobby were married, Amy gave birth to twin girls. Prior to the birth, she and Bobby had discussed at length how they would explain to Dickon that he would no longer have the right to his parents' undivided attention.

"He's bound to be jealous," Amy said.

"We sure as hell don't want to put his cute little nose out of joint," agreed Bobby. "If he was a girl, we could give him a doll so he'd have a baby of his own, but he's not."

"I read somewhere about a child who stabbed the new baby with a pair of scissors," fretted Amy.

"Come on, honey. He's not that kind of kid. We'll think of something."

When Bobby brought Dickon to the hospital to see her, Amy had the ideal solution. "I've got three presents for you, sweetheart," she said.

"What are they?" Dickon gazed inquisitively into the nearest of the two cribs beside his mother's bed.

"First, there's these two little sisters. Aren't they the cutest things you ever saw?"

Dickon nodded doubtfully. He didn't know much about babies but he already sensed that they were bad news, as far as his privileged position in the family was concerned.

"They're a bit little," he said.

"That's because they're brand new."

"Was I ever that small?"

"Sure were."

"What are their names?"

"Sally," said Bobby. "And Sophie. What do you think?"

Dickon thought about it and then nodded. "Sally and Sofa: that's OK. Will they make a lot of noise?"

"Probably," Bobby said. "That's what babies are for." He gazed fondly at his daughters. Twins. Jeez, who'd ever have thought it?

"Grampa says babies wear diapers instead of Buster Browns."

"That's right."

"Grampa says diapers are nasty." Dickon twisted his legs round the bedpost. "Will I have to change them, do you think?"

"We'll leave that to their daddy," Amy said, laughing. "Now, come here, Dickon. I have another present for you." She handed him something wrapped in a checked handkerchief. "Know what that is?"

Dickon unwrapped it. "A pipe?"

"But not just any pipe. It's an animal charmer's pipe."

"A *real* one?"

"As real as they come," said Amy. "And guess what? It used to belong to the other Dickon."

"The one in England?"

"That's right."

Both of the twins began to wail and raising the pipe to his mouth, Dickon blew a few notes. Like magic the wailing ceased.

"Hey," Bobby said. "Someone ought to market those: they'd make a fortune."

"Did I charm those babies?" asked Dickon, fascinated.

"I think you did."

"Mommy."

"Yes, Dickon."

"Am I English?"

"Half English, yes, you are."

"Will I go to live in England when I'm grown up?"

"Maybe—if you wanted to."

"Would I live in a castle?"

Amy kissed Sally and Sophie and told them to go play outside in the yard. Then she said: "Why are you asking about England?"

"We were doing history in school," Dickon said. "About how the United States freed themselves from the English, and threw tea into the harbor, and how the English are all mean to the poor people."

"Is that really the way Miss Wilson put it?" Amy had not suspected unassuming Miss Wilson of republican tendencies before.

"Sort of."

"And did she say that English people all live in castles?"

"Except for the poor ones."

"Sounds to me much more like the sort of thing an eight-year-old kid might say," said Amy. "Particularly an eight-year-old kid called Nancy Myers." Nancy Myers, the daughter of Bobby's boss at the plant, had a strong personality and a fertile imagination.

"Yes," Dickon conceded, "but she swore on a stack of Bibles that it was true."

"This stack of Bibles was sitting around in the school yard, was it?"

"No, but if there had been one, she said she would have sworn on it." He put his head on one side, looking, for an instant, so disconcertingly like Richard that Amy clutched at the edge of the kitchen counter. "But is it true? Would I live in a castle if I went to England?"

Amy sighed. Increasingly, as the twins grew up, she had begun to see the unfairness of what she was doing by keeping the fact of Dickon's existence from his English family. Mary Craven might be an old witch, but she still had the right to see her grandson growing up, didn't she? And even if she and her husband tried to take Dickon away, Amy, less emotionally fragile now, with the twins to add to her security, knew that they would never be allowed to. Thinking back, she recalled Misselthwaite Manor's stone chimneys twisting against the sky, latticed windows, the long terrace in front, the impressive drive from the park gates to the front of the house. There had been deer under the trees, ancient roofs, a studded front door which would not have been out of place in a palace. "Yes," she said reluctantly. "I guess in a way, you would."

"Honest injun?"

"Yes."

"Gosh," Dickon said, his blue eyes growing round. "Would it be my castle? My very own?"

"Yes."

"Mom, can we go to England?"

"I think we'll have to."

"When? Soon?"

"Maybe."

"What does my English grandma look like?" Dickon asked one night, as Amy was supervising his bathtime.

Would you believe ten foot tall with vampire teeth and eyes that shoot flames? she wanted to ask. "I don't really know," she answered, showering soap out of his rusty-red hair. "I only saw her once." And that was one time too many.

"Does she live in a castle?"

"You've been talking to that Nancy Myers again."

"But does she, Mom, does she?" He wriggled as she put a towel over his head and began to rub his hair dry.

"Kind of."

"Is she young and beautiful, with lovely yellow hair like a princess?"

More like the kind of ugly old woman who'd eat a little boy like you for breakfast . . . "Grandmas aren't very often young and beautiful, Dickon. But I think yours has—*had*—yellow hair. Like your English daddy did."

"Why's mine ginger, then?"

"Because you take after me, that's why."

"Can we go to England, Mom? I'd really like to see my grandma."

"We'll see."

They moved to a bigger house, on the edge of town. It backed on to forest where a stream ran, where the rushing water had carved out a swimming hole. Dickon spent hours exploring the untamed country, watching the wild life which abounded, keeping a note of the birds and animals he observed, the differing habitats in which one plant would flourish but not another.

Musically precocious, he had long ago taught himself to play the magic pipe but it never again had the soothing effect on his sisters that it had when he saw them for the first time, indeed, rather the opposite. Nor, although he spent hours sitting under the dogwood in the yard, did it seem to make much impression on the chipmunks and mocking birds which appeared from time to time.

"Maybe it only works with English animals," Amy said.

"And English twins?"

"That's right."

"Mom, I *really* want to go to England."

"You will, son, I promise. One of these days."

"Do my English grandparents live in London?"

"They have a house there, yes. But most of the time I think they live in the north, among the moors." With a queer twist of pain, Amy heard Richard's voice again: *You'll love it up there, my darling. The wind wuthering, and the curlews calling. It's so wide, so open. It makes you feel that the world goes on forever. One day I'll show it all to you.* One day—but the day had never come and all she had now was promises which could never be fulfilled.

"What are moors?"

"Hills. Grassy hills, with heather growing on them, and streams running through them, and stones pushing through the ground. And huge wide skies above."

"I really would like to go there."

"You will, darling. I promise."

The situation was becoming impossible. "I shall have to take him over to England," she said to Bobby. "I just don't feel right about it anymore. Mr. and Mrs. Craven ought to have a chance to meet him, just as he should have the opportunity to meet them."

"Whatever you say, honey. We could save up and make it a family vacation: the girls would love it. When do you want to go? Next summer?"

So soon? The prospect was too raw. "I don't *want* to go. I just think I *should.*"

"But when?"

"Some day. Soon."

"How can a garden be secret, Mom?"

"I don't really know. I guess if you hid it behind walls or hedges or—"

"But that's not really secret. Someone would know it was there."

"Perhaps if everyone who knew had forgotten about it, or gone away, it would be secret. Especially if there was only one door into it, and the key had been lost, and no one visited it for years and years."

"How could you forget about a garden?"

"If you lived in a big enough place, with lots of other gardens, you might." Amy remembered the two miles which lay between the entrance to Misselthwaite Manor and the circular turn before the front door. How many gardens might not lie concealed among the trees in a place like that? "I bet a garden could go missing if you owned a lot of land."

"Like people do in England?"

"*Some* people."

"Like my English grandparents?"

"Maybe."

In the early fifties, the corn and feed plant was swallowed up by a large international corporation which had decided that the undeveloped land to the west of Elm Ridge was ideal for expansion of their existing factories. Opinion in the town was divided. Some said that the influx of money which the scheme would bring could only help the town toward increased prosperity—and the Lord knew they could all do with that. Others declared that their gentle way of life would vanish forever and what did they want with city folk, anyhows? As always, the prosperity factor won. More money brought with it many advantages: bigger shops, a better hospital, more funding for cultural projects. The school was voted new premises, the choral society's numbers doubled; touring companies and musical groups which used to pass by on their way to bigger metropolises now stopped.

One of these was a touring group from England, the London Chamber Players, and Amy took Dickon along to hear them perform. The local music society organized a covered-dish supper to honor the musicians after their performance, which was rapturously received, and Amy, as one of the designated hostesses for the evening, found herself chatting to them.

"We're from England, but not English," the first violin told her.

"We met at the Royal Academy of Music, when the war was over," explained the cellist, "and discovered that each of us had been sent as a child to England, in order to escape the Nazis."

"Is that why you got together?" asked Amy.

"It seemed the ideal combination for a string quartet," smiled the second violin. "Two of us, a cellist and a viola. What more could you want?"

"Did you . . . did you fight for the Allies during the war?"

"Of course. And our hero, here—" the second violin slapped the viola player on the back, "—even spent a couple of years as a prisoner of the Germans."

She nodded. "That must have been . . . interesting."

The viola player smiled. "That's one way you could put it." He touched the red scar on his neck. "At least they allowed us to make music, when they weren't punishing us."

Amy, watching the melancholy expression which drifted across his face, moved the conversation to other topics, afraid of stirring up too many bad memories. For the same reason, she did not tell them that she had once been married to an English fighter pilot. She wondered where Dickon had got to, and was rather glad he was not at her side, knowing that he would have bombarded them with questions about England.

Bobby was swiftly promoted within the new company. By the time Dickon was eleven, Bobby had risen to an executive position, and increasingly found himself liaising with the firm's overseas interests, traveling extensively, though mainly within the Australasian orbit. But a couple of weeks before Dickon's twelfth birthday, he came home in great excitement.

"How'd you like to go back to Europe?" he asked, kissing Amy. "Not just to visit, but to live?"

"How long for?"

"A couple of years at least, maybe more if things go well. They want me to head up the European side of the business."

"Where in Europe would you be based?" Amy thought of Paris, where Richard had promised her a proper honeymoon when the war was over. She thought of the Impressionists, of the Opéra and the Louvre, the Eiffel Tower. Paris would be wonderful.

"England," Bobby said.

"Ah." She was reluctant. England was Richard. England was the sound of bombers in the early dawn, air-raid sirens and uniforms, Piccadilly Circus and King's College Chapel. England was Gracie Fields singing

"Wish Me Luck As You Wave Me Goodbye," and the blackout.

England was rations and blue birds over the white cliffs of Dover.

England was being in love.

"More specifically, London," Bobby continued. "I know how much you want to go back, honey."

"Not *want*," she said.

"Besides, Dickon's growing up. Don't you think it's time he got to meet his grandparents? Seems kind of unfair after all this time not at least to give him the chance."

"I'm so afraid," Amy said. "You didn't meet that woman."

"Baby, we've been married quite a while now, and in that time I've heard so much about her that sometimes I almost think I know her better than I know *your* mom. But she can't really be the monster you've made her out to be."

Amy laughed. "You're right. I've let her become a demon. But if we went to London, would you let me get kind of pensive every now and then?"

"Sure I would. I'd feel the same if we went to Paris."

"I thought it was a signorina in Rome that you fell for, not a mademoiselle in Paris."

"Maybe I forgot to mention her." Bobby put his arms round his wife. "None of them was a patch on you, though. So shall I call back the boss and say we'll go, or not?"

"Yes," Amy said. "We'll go." All these years, she had refused to face up to her duty and now the fates had finally caught up with her, taken the choice out of her hands. She wished she did not find the prospect of living in England so daunting.

So terrifying.

29

Colin was dying.

Death had imprinted itself on his face, peered from his eyes, lurked in the deepening shadows beneath his jaw. Death took people by surprise, drawing them toward him over the spaces which lay between them, making them suddenly aware that Colin Craven was, after all, mortal. Across the House of Commons lobbies, or London drawing-rooms, or bleak conference chambers, they came to wish him well or simply to touch his arm and smile into the thin face. Flesh had dropped from his long frame; the color which the illness had added to his cheeks was spurious. Listening to him cough in other rooms made Mary's own chest ache. Lying awake in her big four-poster bed, she shuddered with anticipated loneliness.

She had hired a new manager for Misselthwaite, handing over to him much of the responsibility for the day-to-day running of the estate, while she herself spent most of her time in London, in order to be at Colin's side. Though it was what she wanted, she nonetheless chafed at the noise and the traffic after the peace of the moors.

"You should have been my father's child," Colin said one evening, as they dined at the Ivy. "You love it up there far more than I do."

"And would you then have been *my* father's son?" Sadly, she reflected that they might both then have been better loved.

"That would have been rather splendid. Remember the boy rajah, covered in emeralds and rubies? How I longed to be stuck all over with diamonds, like him. How I would have glittered."

"You were just like him, too. Such an arrogant little boy."

"While you, my beloved Mary, were the world's most imperious little girl."

"Made for each other, wouldn't you say?" Mary pressed Colin's thin white fingers. His wedding ring was so loose that it was in danger of flying off each time he waved his hands about.

"Suited right down to the ground."

Did he know that his illness was slowly killing him? It might have been easier for both of them if they could have discussed it. She would like to have reassured him that she loved him, that she would be there beside him to the last breath. But since he never spoke of it, neither did she, though wondering whether he remained in ignorance of his true condition or because he was being brave for her sake, as she was for his.

"They offered me a post in the cabinet," Colin said abruptly. "Spokesman for Health. I know we're only in opposition at the moment, but it was quite an honor."

"Did you accept it?"

"No. Not in view of the way things are."

"What do you . . ." Was this to be his acknowledgement at last that he was unwell?

"I've thought about it a lot. Ministerial office is all very well for the Attlees and the Bevans and so on. But there's always going to be a place for the lone voice, speaking with commitment, with only the interests of his constituents to worry about. Not that I'm implying that our top men aren't committed, but I've seen too often how the actual business of politics has a way of taking over."

"And I imagine there's always a degree of compromise."

"If the whole cumbersome machinery is to be kept going, then compromise is the only way. But I don't want that." Colin placed his knife and fork tidily together, although he had barely touched the food on his plate. "The funny thing is, that recently I've begun to think less about Dickon and much more about his father."

"But we hardly knew Mr. Sowerby."

"Exactly. And why was that?"

"He was very shy."

"And also he worked appallingly long hours. Up before dawn, home after dark. No wonder we didn't see much of him."

"I remember running into him in Middleburn once," said Mary. "He'd just come off his shift, and I hardly recognized him. His eyes . . . his face was black with coal dust and his eyes looked almost raw."

"Do you know how many of the pits still don't have showers for the men? Which means they have to put their everyday clothes back on after they've finished their shift. Can you imagine the effort it is for the wives to keep things even halfway clean? Yet something as simple as installing showers could make such a difference to their lives. That's why I turned down a ministerial post. I'm afraid that I'll forget about the little things—which aren't really little at all—if I accepted." He remembered lying up on the moors with Dickon, talking about little things, simple things, and the way they could revolutionize even the hardest of lives.

"I think you've made the right decision," said Mary. "An admirable decision."

Colin wanted to walk back to Fitzroy Square but Mary insisted on taking a cab. A sharp little wind darted between the buildings; she could smell snow in the air. One more heavy cold, and Colin might not recover. He needed to get away from the soot-laden atmosphere of London and the sudden freezing fogs which left black deposits on clothes and hair and did untold damage to lungs already ravaged by disease. She had tried many times to persuade him to return to Misselthwaite but he refused, saying he was needed in London, that there was too much legislation being passed for him to take time off, that the Whips would never allow it.

All she could do was ensure that he was properly cared for. The basement of the house in Fitzroy Square had been converted into a self-contained flat and Polly now lived there, keeping an eye on things when Mary had to go back to Yorkshire.

"I do me best, Miss Mary," she said, "but Mr. Craven doesn't eat enough to keep body and soul together."

"I know," said Mary, distressed. "You'll have to be firm."

"Easier said than done. I can't force the food down him, after all. And I can't dress him, neither. He goes out in this weather sometimes without his warm underclothes and it fair makes me shiver to think of it."

"He's got other things on his mind."

"I know that. Good things, like watching after folk who're too worn out to do it for themselves. But I tell him, I say, 'Mr. Craven, if you don't take more care, there won't be anyone looking out for us poor folk because you'll be dead and in your grave.' "

"What does he say to that?" Mary wished she dared be so forthright.

"Gets very hoity-toity. 'Thank you, Polly, that'll be all,' he says, but I say, 'Oh no, it won't, Mr. Craven. You owe it to us,' I say, 'to take care of yourself. What good's it going to do us,' I say, 'if you're lying six feet under?' Doesn't like it at all, I can tell you."

"You must just do the best you can. We all must."

"Bar keeping his room warm and a hot water bottle in his bed at night, there's little enough I can do for him," Polly said. She clasped her hands together and held them against her chest. "He's not well, is he?"

"No, Polly. He's not at all well."

"Reckon he'd do better if he were up at the Manor. There's air up there you can breathe, not this nasty dirty stuff they have down here. When I look at the state of my collars . . ."

"I know."

"Mebbe we could kidnap him. Bundle him up in a blanket and drive him up north and not listen, however much he howls about it."

"He'd just take the next train down here again."

The two women met each other's eyes and read the same message. Colin Craven was dying.

"You'll have to come down, Miss Mary. He's collapsed." Polly's voice was calm, but Mary could hear the panic underneath her broad north-country vowels.

"What happened?"

"Collapsed on the floor of the House, they said. He were brought home in a cab and I called the doctor at once."

"What did he say?"

Silence.

"What did he say, Polly?"

Mary could hear Polly break into sobs.

"Said that with his chest in such a state, it's a wonder he's—he's not been six feet under years ago."

"Did he say that to my husband?"

"Yes. And Mr. Craven said it weren't no business of his, that all he needed were a couple of days in bed and he'd be right as rain. But for all his brave talk, Miss Mary, he's so weak he—he can't even sit himself up against the pillows. And as for getting out of bed . . ."

"I'll drive down tonight."

"Best be quick," Polly said.

They took him back to Yorkshire. Mary had brought Arthur, Dickon's nephew, with her, and between them, he and Polly carried Colin out to the car, despite his feeble protests.

This is the end, Mary thought. It's over now. She drove the long miles as carefully as she could, so as not to jar the suffering man lying on the back seat, wincing each time she heard him cough.

"You're all right, Mr. Colin," Arthur said from time to time. "You're all right, sir," but all three of them knew he lied.

There were daffodils out in the London gardens; the window-boxes were already bright. Spring was less advanced in the north, the wind still icy, the moors sallow with dead grass. Despite Norah's best efforts, the Manor had a wintry feel about it. Along the passages, the tapestries stirred like lake water, windows rattled in their casements, fireplaces belched smoke as the wind surged through the chimneys.

Colin's bedroom was warm, the shutters closed against the gales outside. They got him upstairs: after the journey he was too weak even to pretend to walk unaided.

Above the hearth his mother's portrait smiled as they laid him tenderly between the sheets.

"I've made broth," said Norah quietly. "Good beef to give him strength. I doubt he'll take much else."

"Not yet," Mary said. "But we can hope."

"If only the spring would come . . ."

"It will, Norah. It always does." But how bleak will my spring be this year? Mary wondered. She thought of other springs. She thought of that first spring, and hopeful bulbs poking through the debris of winter.

"Tell me . . . about the young . . . rajah," Colin said, his chest heaving with the effort of speaking.

Once again she described the boy on his elephant, the chanting crowds, the heat and the dust as the procession passed, while jewels glinted in the sun. She spoke of the jugglers and the beggars, the snake charmers in their ragged loin cloths, the—but Colin held up his hand.

"He never did that."

"Who didn't?"

"Dickon. Never charmed any cobras."

But he charmed us, she thought. Enthralled us both, kept us under his spell all our lives. "Perhaps that's because there aren't a lot of cobras in north Yorkshire."

"No. I bet it was . . . he was afraid his pipe . . . wouldn't work on cobras."

"Oh, Colin."

"Sing me that . . . that song in Hindu," Colin murmured. "I should like that."

She leaned against the bed and stroked his hand, singing the little chanting song her *ayah* used to sing.

After a while, his black lashes closed but when she gently tried to withdraw, he held her hand tight. "I always . . . always wanted to go there," he said.

"To India?"

"To see the boy . . . stuck all over with rubies . . . and diamonds. To see elephants. And cobras."

She bit her lip to prevent herself from crying out. Circles, wheels, events orbiting back to the point where they started. Just so had it begun, the two of them, here in this room, here, with a sick boy, and a girl seated on a footstool beside his bed.

* * *

Her days took on a pattern centered on the sick room. In the morning, early, she discussed the estate with the manager, talked of fences blown down, trees which must be felled, roofs which needed mending, sowing which must be done. After that she went to Colin's room, taking her meals with him even if he appeared to sleep, always there in case he needed her, or called her name. Almost daily she saw him grow less, the bones standing out on his face, his eyes sinking deeper into their sockets.

"I should like to go to the secret garden," he said once, drowsily.

"I'll take you there," she said. "I promise."

"Dickon's there . . . waiting. I know he is."

"Darling Colin." She turned away in case he opened his eyes and saw the anguish on her face. How long it had been since she had last visited the secret garden. Not since Dickon brought her the news of Richard's death. Not since the three of them had last been together. Though it was much too cold, she prayed every day that winter might let up long enough for them to wheel Colin there in the invalid chair, as she and Dickon had wheeled him so long ago.

"I'm afraid there's very little I can do for him," young Dr. Alan Craven said, one afternoon, as she walked with him toward the entrance hall . . . "Even with the very best attention, it would be impossible to halt the disease. He's left it unattended for far too long."

"He always had so much to do."

"The people around here are well aware of that. The most popular Member in living memory, they tell me in my surgery. Always puts them before himself, unlike some who've held the seat."

"Can you give me a prognosis?"

He looked down at the ends of his scarf and tucked them unnecessarily tightly inside the collar of his coat. "Not good," he said eventually.

"How long has he got, Alan?"

Again, the doctor hesitated.

"How long?"

"Weeks, rather than months. In fact . . ."

"Yes?"

"Days, rather than weeks."

"We must talk about the future some time," Mary said, as he opened the big front door. The wind rushed in, setting up a soft tinkle among the glass facets of the big chandelier. The bare branches of the trees moved restlessly; beyond them, gray clouds moved across a sullen sky, occasionally allowing gleams of cold sunshine to lie palely on the moors.

"The future?"

"You did know that since your father died, you're the heir, didn't you?"

"Well, yes, I suppose I did. But it never occurred to me that . . . I mean, I can't imagine the Manor without you in it. I certainly wouldn't want to . . ."

"I know, Alan. But once Colin goes, the place will be yours. I wouldn't want to stay on. You ought to know that. You'll need to make preparations."

He nodded. "If you don't mind my saying so, Mrs. Craven, you're not looking all that well yourself."

"It's only because I'm spending so much time in the sick room."

"Nonetheless, it might not be a bad idea for you to come and see me when you can find the time. Meanwhile, if there's anything more I can do . . ."

"You can pray for a warm day."

Two days later, pulling back her curtains, Mary saw that the warm day had arrived. Everything was still. Up on the moors, the yellow grasses shone like gold; magpies glistened on the gravel below and even as she watched them strutting, a robin flew on to her windowsill and gazed at her through the glass, putting its head on one side in a way which made her catch her breath.

If ever there was a day to take Colin to the garden, this was it. She dressed hurriedly and ran downstairs. "Norah," she said. "Tell Arthur to bring the invalid chair to the front."

"Aye. He's been working on that old thing for days, ever since you told him it might be needed. Polishing and shining and touching up. It fair looks a treat."

"Good. And when he's brought it round, ask him to

come and see me. Be quick, Norah. We haven't much time."

By the time Colin had been dressed in warm clothing and carried downstairs, the sun was high overhead. "Eeh," said Norah. "It's more like spring than winter." She was right.

"It's graidely," said Colin, as between them they got him down the front steps and settled him in the chair. "I've seen a lot of afternoons . . . but I never seed one as graidely . . . as this 'ere."

"That's what Dickon said, the first time . . ."

"I know. Sometimes, Mary . . . I think I've forgotten . . . and then it comes back . . . all of it." He took hold of her hand. "All of it."

Arthur pushed the chair while Mary walked beside it. When they reached the gate, Arthur held aside the trailing ivy, and Mary pushed the chair through and into the garden. Before she could step through, she heard Arthur's quiet voice.

"I had a bit of a go, Miss Mary. Pruned the roses, like, and cleared the bulbs a bit. It's been a right long time since anyone took care o' the place."

"Thank you, Arthur. Thank you so much."

"I thought Mr. Colin mightn't want to see it left to run wild, like."

"You were quite right. And very thoughtful."

She could not help remembering Colin's first sight of the garden. "I'm going to live forever and ever and ever," he had cried. And on that first wonderful afternoon, it had seemed perfectly possible that he might.

"Look!" Colin said. "Bulbs coming up . . . snowdrops and . . . and narcissi . . . and . . ."

"Daffydowndillies," Mary said. "That's what Dickon used to call them."

"He's here, isn't he, Mary?"

"Yes, my darling. He is."

"Close by."

"Very close." And Richard too. Surely she saw Richard there, against the wall, smiling at them, his hair the color of daffodils in the sunshine.

"I loved Dickon," Colin said.

"We both did."

"And you." The words whispered through his lips like the shadow of a sigh.

"Colin." She took a deep breath and turned, meaning to say at last what she had never said, meaning to say how she loved him, but it was too late. His eyes were closed, the black lashes heavy on the ivory of his skin. His mouth was curved in a smile.

30

Returning to England after so many years, Amy none-theless half-expected to find London as she had left it, the streets full of uniforms from a dozen different coun-tries, broken glass underfoot, bombed out buildings, peo-ple still queueing for the most basic necessities of life. Instead, she found a busy optimistic city, restored and invigorated by the Festival of Britain, looking forward to the future. If there were cracks, they were well-papered over.

It took time to settle into the luxurious Chelsea flat provided for them by the company, to find schools for the children, to familiarize herself with her new life.

The twins took enthusiastically to London life, little princesses among their school contemporaries by virtue both of their American accents and their twindom.

Dickon, too, was contented enough at first. But sooner or later, Amy knew, the questions would start again, and this time, she would not be able to fob him off. His grandparents lived only a few hours away: both he and they had rights which could no longer be ignored. She spent much of the time alone for Bobby was caught up in his new job and was constantly traveling abroad, meeting with his European counterparts, attempting to engender new business.

She could not stop thinking of Mary Craven. In retro-spect, her own behavior seemed increasingly shabby: from the vantage point of maturity, she could see that any woman might have been fazed by a complete stranger showing up out of the blue on the day after her son's funeral and announcing that she was the new daughter-in-law. Hell, she might have done it herself.

Maybe.

As it was, she herself had been so blind with grief that she hadn't given Richard's mother much of a chance. And there was another question which she needed to answer: would she have rushed off like that if she had realized she was already carrying Richard's child? It was impossible to say. Either way, she accepted that it was unfair to keep Dickon from his grandparents any longer. Unfair for all three of them. It was a task she would have to undertake; she merely waited for the right moment.

Dickon did not like living in the city. He was used to space, to green things about him, to wild country, to woods where he could cycle with his friends, and pools where he could swim. He missed the wide spaces; he missed the garden where the mocking-birds flew.

"It's all so bare here," he complained. "So cramped and dirty. There's nothing green anywhere."

"You're exaggerating."

"I want to meet my grandparents, Mother. I want to see the secret garden."

"I want doesn't get."

"Very well. I would *like* to see the secret garden. And if you won't take me to meet my grandparents, I'm going to go and see them on my own."

Amy took him to Hyde Park and the Zoo, to Kew Gardens, in an attempt to feed his appetite for trees and grass. They took buses out to the countryside. They went by train down to Canterbury and she told him that she and his father had spent their brief married life there. He had always been proud of Richard. "Was he a hero, like Dad's always saying the English were?"

"I guess he was," Amy said.

"He gave his life for his country. That's real heroic."

"Yes, it is."

"His mother and father must be real lonely without him."

"You're right, son. We'll go visit them."

"When?"

"Very, very soon."

"Next time school's out?"

"Yes. I'll make arrangements for the girls, and then we'll go."

"Do you promise?"

"I promise, Dickon."

They visited Oxford, and Cambridge. They went on the river and both Bobby and Dickon tried their hands at punting, with very little success.

All the time, Amy knew that a longer, more difficult journey lay ahead.

There came a time when she was not able to postpone it any further. Bobby had gone to Italy for business meetings. Dickon's school term was almost over and there would be almost a month of Easter holidays. And then, reading the newspaper one morning, she read an obituary for Colin Craven, the Labor MP, who had died a few days earlier.

Guilt overwhelmed her. What would Dickon say? They had been here only a few weeks, but she should have made it a priority to travel up to Misselthwaite Manor. And now it was too late for him to meet his grandfather. She wondered if her son would ever forgive her.

As soon as school finished, three weeks later, she arranged for a baby-sitter to stay with the twins and set off to drive with Dickon up to Yorkshire.

If Colin Craven was dead, that meant Mary was alone. But much more than that, it meant that Dickon must—surely—be the heir to Misselthwaite. The castle he had dreamed of all his childhood was his. If he wanted it. Apprehension filled her. Would he want to stay behind when they finally went back to Elm Ridge?

She did not tell her son where they were going: she did not know what to say. But he guessed.

"We're going to see my grandmother, aren't we?"

"Yes."

"Do you think she'll like me?"

"She'd be an idiot if she didn't." Glancing at him, Amy wondered if Mary would recognise the Craven in her grandson. Those sky-blue eyes and rusty coloring, the turned up nose, that wonderful sweet-tempered smile of his: would they be familiar? Would she now accept that Amy had spoken the truth, all those years before, when she said that she and Richard were married. Or had she done so, long ago?

They stopped overnight in York. Setting off early the next morning, they took off over the moors. Beside her, Dickon said: "Mother, do you believe in reincarnation?"

"I'd like to. There's something nice about thinking you'll come back in the next life to all the places you loved in this one. Why do you ask?"

"It's just that this place seems so familiar. I feel as if I've been here before, as if I was coming home."

"Perhaps you are, in a way."

"Is this the moors?"

"I guess so."

"Can we stop for a moment?"

Amy pulled up beside the grassy edge, and switched off the engine. It was a marvellous spring day, the sky the color of a robin's egg, and everything shining as though it had been varnished. Dickon got out and ran across the sheep-nibbled turf to where a stream tumbled between overhanging grasses. All around them was the sound of larks singing, and the wind sighing in the heather.

"Isn't this wonderful?" Dickon called. He leaped on to a boulder and spread his arms. "There's so much air to breathe." He laughed aloud, as a rabbit jittered between the clumps of heather. "Oh, Mother, thank you so much for bringing me here. I want to run for miles, and shout and sing."

A bird appeared out of nowhere, a little flare of red-breasted bird with a twig in its beak. It landed close to Dickon's shoe. From where Amy stood, it looked like a robin, but they were birds which usually stayed close to human habitation, weren't they? Why would there be one this far out on the wild moors? Dickon gave a low whistling call, and the robin looked up at him enquiringly. For a moment the two stared at each other, then the robin flew up and was gone.

"Just listen," Dickon said. "The world is full of birds all whistling and piping and calling to each other. And everything's turning green and uncurling. Smell the air, it's beautiful." He stood on tiptoe as though he wanted to take off himself, soar into the sky like a lark.

Amy was afraid, suddenly. Where had he learned to

call to a robin? She had never heard him do it before. Her son was twelve years old and she was looking at a stranger.

There were tears in her throat. "Dickon," she cried suddenly. "Come back to me. Come back."

But the wind was strong, and he did not seem to hear her.

The nearer they got to Misselthwaite, the more agitated she felt. It was going to be bad enough to confront Mary Craven, the dragon lady herself. But how would Dickon take the news about his grandfather's death? Would he reproach her for keeping it secret? She kept an eye out for signposts but saw nothing which indicated where they were. Last time she was here, a friend from the base had driven them in a borrowed jeep; she herself had been devastated by the death of her new husband and had taken no notice at all of their surroundings.

"Where are we going?" Dickon said.

"A place called Misselthwaite." Amy stared down at the Ordnance Survey map she had purchased in London; navigation was not her strong point. "I wish I could make sense of this darn thing."

"Keep on this road for another ten miles," Dickon said.

She looked up sharply. For a moment, he had almost sounded like one of the natives from whom she had enquired the way. "How do you know that?"

"I saw a sign."

"I didn't. Where was it?"

"Back up the road."

She started up again. After ten miles, they reached walls and a half-ruined gate lodge. A pair of tall iron gates stood open to the road.

"Turn in here," Dickon said.

"Why?"

"You said we were going to Misselthwaite Manor, didn't you?"

Amy stared at her son. "That's not what I said."

"Well, we are, aren't we?"

"How do you know that?"

"I'm not entirely sure," he said. He turned his sky-blue gaze on her and for a second she saw a ghost in his face, a sad man whose hands would not be still. Obediently, she turned in between the park gates. The long drive she remembered stretched ahead of them, beneath arching trees. Dickon scarcely spoke as they came to fenced meadow land and trees protected by wire netting from the ravages of deer. Once, he said: "Look, there's a fox."

She saw it, running parallel with them, close to the ground, leaping the tussocks, glancing at them occasionally. Almost as if it were escorting them.

"And squirrels," Dickon said. "See them, Mother, in the branches?"

The drive meandered between the meadows until they saw chimneys ahead and a roof, and finally the whole house. It was at least as big as she remembered it, the chimneys still twisting, the lattice windows gleaming in the sunshine. Amy grimaced. Was Mary watching their approach, peering from some half-shuttered window, waiting to snatch Dickon away? She pulled up in front of the big door.

"Well, we're here," she said. Her hands were shaking and she gripped the steering wheel, wishing she were miles away.

Dickon got out of the car and confidently mounted the steps. She saw him lift the great bronze knocker and let it fall, saw the door open and the house receive her son.

There was an inevitability about it which she scarcely found strange. Ever since they had stopped on the moor, she had felt as though the two of them had entered a different dimension. Or fallen down a giant rabbit-hole. Or broken into someone else's dream. How otherwise to explain the way Dickon had talked to the robin, or the fact that he had seemed to know exactly how to get here? Or his entering the house without so much as a backward glance at her.

Afterward, she had no clear idea how long she sat in the car. It seemed like hours before she plucked up the courage to get out herself, to cross the gravel and in her turn, lift the knocker. When the door opened, she stepped inside and was greeted by a plump competent-looking woman in a flowered overall.

"You'll be young Dickon's mam," she said.

"That's right."

"Well, I'm Norah, the housekeeper here. Why don't you step down to the kitchen with me, my dear, and I'll mash you some tea."

"Um . . ." Amy looked around. "My son . . . ?"

"Don't you bother 'bout him."

"But do you know—what did he—we've come because—"

"I sent him off to see Mistress Mary. That's why he came, isn't it?"

"Yes, but—"

"She's down in the secret garden," Norah said.

"Will he know the way?"

"I reckon he will," Norah said. "And she'll be right pleased to see him, I can tell you. Especially when she's so sad and poorly."

"Poorly?" echoed Amy, following the woman down a long passage. "What's wrong with her?"

"Poor soul. Doctor's told her unless she picks up, she'll not last that long herself."

"That's awful." Like a pricked balloon, Amy's fear of Mary evaporated. The monster of her imagination metamorphosed into a pale invalid, with scarcely the strength to lift a bloodless hand to her fevered brow.

"There's folks as say he's got an interest in her going, but I don't believe that. I've known young Alan since he were a wee bairn and it's my belief he wouldn't want a draughty old place like this, no how."

"He's the—um—the heir, is he?"

"Aye. Seeing as Mr. Richard died, Misselthwaite'll be young Alan's when Mistress Mary's gone; his dad were first cousin to Mr. Craven years ago, and this one's next in line. Unless we was to find that after all, Mr. Richard had a bairn to pass it on to."

"I see." Events were moving away from Amy. She felt as though she had been picked up in the jaws of a large puppy and was being shaken from side to side without the slightest chance of preventing it. She sank down into a creaking wickerwork chair which stood beside a glowing range. It might be spring-like outside, but here, in this house of stone and inadequate central heating, it was distinctly chilly.

Norah changed the subject. Or was she merely car-

rying it on further, as far as it needed to go. "I know
Mistress Mary better'n any Dr. Cravens do, and I say if
she makes her mind up to it, she'll last these twenty
years or more. If she wants to, that is."

"And what do you think would make her want to?"

"She needs something to live for, that's all. With
Dickon gone, and now Mr. Craven, she's got no interest
in living," Norah said.

And my son is ready-made to provide one, thought
Amy. Well, invalid or no invalid, heirs or no heirs, she's
not having him. A man passed the window, fair-haired
and smiling; for a moment she would have sworn it was
Richard. "Who was that?" she said.

"Who was what, my dear?"

"The man who just went by, outside."

"Must have been a bird."

"No, it was—" Amy pressed her lips together.

"When we've had our tea, we'll go down and find
the others," Norah said comfortably. "Best leave them
together for the moment, though. So they can get
acquainted."

"You know who we are, then?"

"Knew as soon as I set eyes on Master Dickon. The
spit and image of his grandpa, he is."

MARY

Has time stood still, or merely turned full circle? This is where it started, here, in the secret garden. And this is where, in so many ways, it ended. A whole lifetime has happened and yet the garden looks as if it never began. The unkempt standard roses, the swinging tendrils of ramblers, the fuzz of new growth pushing up through unswept leaves and springing from gray stems: it is exactly as I first saw it. The urns are moss-covered; the flower beds neglected. Weeds have flourished. But the bulbs have multiplied: there are thousands of them now, snowdrops and narcissi, scyllas and grape hyacinths, and, at the wilder edges, the bluebells have run riot in the long grass.

We had such plans, such plans.

It has taken me longer than I expected to walk here and although I hate to confess to weakness, I am breathless, exhausted. But at least I have escaped Norah's concern for a while. She knows better than to disturb me once I am behind these walls. I remember how coming here as a child was like being shut out of the world. Or into a dream.

Strangely, as I look about at the uncared-for garden, I feel not despair but hope. It is a perfect spring day, the sky a fragile blue, the hesitant sun offering a promise of warmth to come. The emergent leaves are of a green so exquisite that it tugs at the heart. And there is blossom everywhere. I wish Colin had lived to see it.

What have I to hope for now, except an end to all this? The girl I looked for—Richard's girl—was never found. I was never able to ask for her forgiveness. As the darkness closes over me, that will be one of my chief regrets. There are others, of course. Given the way I was shaped, there could not fail to be.

Before I came out this morning, I stared at myself in the glass, trying to see myself as a stranger might. Forbidding is the word for me now. Imperious. I daresay I have not changed very much since I first came here as a sour little girl. We were both used to getting our own way, Colin and I, yet I can honestly say that in our marriage each always thought first of the other.

Ah, Colin. How I miss him. His enthusiasms, his desire to do everything, be everything. At least he was able to achieve his ambition of serving the people before he was finally struck downn. On his feet, rising to answer a query which had arisen from the white paper on local housing which he had just presented to the House. One moment in full flood; the next, lying among the green leather seats and the order papers. Carried home to die. Even though I had been bracing myself some time before his death occurred, it was nonetheless a shock. But how glad I am that it was such a gentle passing, that it took place here, with all of us around him.

I feel them with me now. Dickon and Colin and their son.

I miss Colin every single day: I have learned more about him since he died than I knew while he lived for I have his diaries and read them without any feeling of trespass. For the most part, he was a happy man, despite his illnesses, despite his proclivities, for after such a childhood as he experienced, everything which followed was better than that which had gone before. From the diaries, I know how much he loved me. And Dickon. And how much he wished to keep from us both his . . . tendencies.

I wish I believed in an afterlife: I should like to think of the two of them wrangling gently over some piece of celestial landscaping. They were always the best of friends. Odd that I, who was the most dependent of the three, should be the one left alone.

I am possessed by anticipation—but why? Can it really be the prospect of death which pleases me? I light a cigarette and watch the smoke rise palely to disperse among the blossoms. The sun is stronger now and it is almost warm in this sheltered place. The ivy on the walls